OUR SONG

Anna Carey is an Irish Book Award-winning novelist, journalist, editor and scriptwriter who spent her teens and twenties playing in bands.

She is the author of seven acclaimed novels for young adults. Her debut novel *The Real Rebecca* won the Senior Children's Book of the Year prize at the 2011 Irish Book Awards and *The Boldness of Betty* was shortlisted for the same award in 2020. Her drama podcast *The Famine Monologues* was released by RTÉ in 2021 and her play *The Making of Mollie* was staged in 2024 at the Ark Children's Cultural Centre in Dublin.

Our Song is her first book for adults.

She is married to her former bandmate Patrick Freyne and lives in Dublin.

Find Anna on social media @urchinette

OUR SONG

ANNA CAREY

HACHETTE
BOOKS
IRELAND

First published in Ireland in 2025 by HACHETTE BOOKS IRELAND

1

Cataloguing in Publication Data is available from the British Library

ISBN 9781399742382

Typeset in Sabon LT Std by Bookends Publishing Services, Dublin
Printed and bound in Great Britain by Clays Ltd, Elcograf S.p.A

Hachette Books Ireland policy is to use papers that are natural, renewable
and recyclable products and made from wood grown in sustainable
forests. The logging and manufacturing processes are expected to
conform to the environmental regulations of the country of origin.

Hachette Books Ireland
8 Castlecourt Centre
Castleknock
Dublin 15, Ireland

A division of Hachette UK Ltd
Carmelite House, 50 Victoria Embankment, London EC4Y 0DZ

www.hachettebooksireland.ie

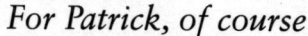

For Patrick, of course

Tad? Tah? Tag? How to pronounce Tadhg Hennessy's name

Vulture.com, 7 November 2008

Not since Saoirse Ronan was nominated for an Oscar at this year's Academy Awards has a name from the Emerald Isle caused so much confusion. Tadhg Hennessy's heartfelt love songs and sweet but spiky guitar pop have made him an international star, yet some of his biggest fans still aren't quite sure how to pronounce his first name. So we've decided to ask an actual Irish person how to deal with such an unreasonable amount of consonants.

'It's really easy,' claims Emma Hanlon, a New York-based photographer who was born and grew up in Dublin. 'It's basically the word 'tiger' without the er. Just the first syllable with a hard g at the end.' Simple enough. 'Of course,' Hanlon continues, 'the t at the start is soft, like a mix between a th and a d, so it's not exactly the same as a t in English ...' Oh no. She's lost us again.

'Fine, then,' sighs Hanlon. 'Just think of the tiger thing.'

See? That wasn't so hard, was it?

Prologue

This is what I want.

Not right now, obviously, I think, as I look around the function room of the hotel where my mother's retirement party is in full swing. But eventually. Some day. I want to be able to look back at my life with this sort of happiness. I can see myself in thirty years, laughing with my future husband and children and my friends and family, popping open a bottle of champagne, celebrating a career I loved and a life well lived, looking forward to future adventures. It's the best sort of dream – lovely, yet achievable.

Although hopefully my celebrations will take place somewhere a bit more glamorous than a hotel in the north Dublin suburb of Drumcondra, where my fiancé (it still feels so weird to call him that) Dave is currently singing my praises to my extended family.

'You know Laura used to be in a band?' he says proudly.

'Is that true, Laura?' My aunt Mary can't hide her surprise as she turns to me.

'Oh, it's true,' I say. 'But it was a long time ago. In college.'

'I'm sure I mentioned it at the time, Mary,' says my mam.

I roll my eyes and smile at Dave, who winks back at me.

'And you didn't keep it up?' says my uncle Gerry. 'The music?'

'Oh no.' I take a sip of wine. 'The band split up when we left college.'

'Before my time,' says Dave in mock sadness. He notices my mother's wine glass is empty and refills it.

'Thank you, David,' says Mam fondly. She turns to me. 'I always thought you'd find another band, Laurie. You were so devoted to your music.'

Well, she's changed her tune from the days of 'Shouldn't you be studying for your finals, Laura?'. But I'm not going to mention that now.

No, I am. 'In fairness, Mam, at the time you were delighted I was more focused on my first proper job than faffing around on the guitar.'

'Speaking of proper jobs,' says my dad, clearly keen not to revive those old arguments, 'Laura's ad agency just got bought by Zenith, the big consultancy company! She's going to get a promotion.'

'Visions isn't *my* agency!' I protest. 'I just work there. And I might *not* get a promotion.'

My mother ignores this. 'You know that funny TV ad about the ethical pensions?' she says. 'The animated one?'

The aunts and uncles all know it. It's on all the time. Not exactly the sort of fame you dream of, perhaps, but my friend Aoife and I did win an award for it.

'Well, Laura wrote that!' says Mam. Everyone is suitably impressed.

'You're doing very well for yourself, Laura,' says an aunt.

'Ah, thanks, I'm doing all right,' I say. 'Now, shouldn't the food have been brought out already—?'

'But you never thought of doing the music professionally?' says Gerry.

I shake my head. 'Oh God, no.'

This is a lie, of course. I thought about it a lot, once upon a time.

Dave laughs at the very idea. 'Being in a college band is like playing five-a-side football, Gerry,' he says. 'You do it for fun, but you know you're never going to play for Real Madrid.'

I feel myself bristle at this, just a tiny bit. Which is stupid, because he's right, I know he's right. But …

Then an unexpected voice behind me says, 'Laura's band was really good, *David.*'

'Oh yeah, I'm sure they were!' says Dave hastily. 'I didn't mean—'

'They were *seriously* good,' says my younger sister Annie, pulling out a chair next to me and sitting down. She lives in London but she's come home for the weekend to celebrate Mam's retirement.

'How do you know?' says Dad. 'You were still in school back then!'

'Laura sneaked me into one of their gigs,' says Annie. 'I thought they'd be terrible.'

'Wow, thanks,' I say.

Annie turns back to Dave. 'But you should have seen Laura on stage. She was incredible.'

'I'm sure she was!' says Dave. 'I only meant that loads of people are in bands in college and they don't make a career out of it. It wasn't an insult!'

And Annie says, 'Well, Laura's bandmate has made a pretty good career out of it.'

Oh shit.

I try to subtly give her a 'please change the subject' look but it's too late because Dave is saying, 'What do you mean?'

'She was in a band with Tadhg Hennessy,' says Annie. Her eyes widen in gleeful disbelief. 'Oh my God, didn't you know?'

I never knew what a stunned silence felt like until this moment. Everyone at the table – and some of my mother's friends who are standing nearby – are staring at me. I think at least one mouth has literally dropped open.

'What?' says Dave.

'Tadhg *Hennessy*?' says Dad. 'Who sings 'Winter Without You'?'

'Your cousin Cass saw him play the 3Arena!' says an aunt.

'Annie, don't be ridiculous!' says Mam. 'Laura wasn't in a band with Tadhg Hennessy!'

'Yes, she was!' says Annie. 'Tell them, Laura.'

The only other people who know I was in a band with Tadhg Hennessy in college are my friends who were around at the time. I've never told anyone since.

But maybe it was ridiculous to think I could keep it a secret forever.

'It *is* true,' I say reluctantly. I meet Dave's eye and he raises his eyebrows in exaggerated shock, which I hope means he's not too freaked by this revelation. 'But it wasn't a big deal.'

Well, that's another lie.

'What was he like?' says Mary. 'He seemed very nice on the *Late Late Show*.'

'Was he always that good at singing?' says Gerry.

'He was the best-looking man I've ever seen in real life,' says Annie unhelpfully.

To my relief, I can see waiters bearing down on us with large platters of triangular sandwiches.

'He was just my bandmate,' I say.

And there's one more lie.

I'm heading to the loo when I bump into Annie coming the other way.

I glare at her. 'Thanks very much for that announcement earlier.'

'I'm sorry!' says Annie. She doesn't look that sorry. 'How was I to know you'd never told your *fiancé* about Tadhg?'

'I never told him because the band was a million years ago!' I say. 'I can't remember the last time I picked up my guitar. I don't even know where my electric one is.'

'It's in the wardrobe of your old room with Mam's bags and winter coats,' says Annie.

'Well, there you go. The fact that I didn't know this shows what a serious musician I am these days.'

'Dave should fully appreciate how cool you used to be,' says Annie. 'A very long time ago. Obviously you're old and boring now.'

'Obviously,' I say.

But old and boring Laura isn't doing too badly, I think, as Dave and I bid farewell to the assembled gathering a few hours later and start walking home, hand in hand, to our flat in Glasnevin.

'I can't believe you're even more of a rock star than I thought you were,' says Dave.

'I should have told you I was in a band with Tadhg before now,' I say.

'Why didn't you?' says Dave.

He doesn't sound angry. He very rarely gets annoyed about stuff. It's one of the things I love about him.

'I've never really told anyone,' I say. 'I suppose … I suppose it felt like boasting.'

'If I'd been in a band with Tadhg Hennessy,' says Dave, 'I'd be boasting about it all the time. I don't suppose this means you could get us VIP tickets to his Malahide Castle gig?'

I force a laugh. 'I haven't seen him since the band split up in 2003, so no, I don't think so.'

'Fair enough,' says Dave. We cross the bridge over the Tolka and he says, 'I hope your mum had a good day.'

'She's had a great day,' I say. 'She got to show off her perfect future son-in-law.'

'Happy to be of service,' he says. 'I wish I could say my mum's birthday next week will be as fun.'

'It'll be great!' I lie.

'It won't,' says Dave. 'But I love you for saying that. And I apologise in advance for whatever offensive things she's going to say about you being from the northside.'

I laugh. 'Oh, I know I'm your bit of rough.'

'You bet you are,' says Dave with a grin, and kisses me. 'So! Do you fancy going to that food-festival thing tomorrow?'

'Are you not going to visit Joe?' I say.

Dave's oldest friend just finished his first round of chemotherapy.

'Ah no,' says Dave. 'I don't want to bother him.'

I sigh. Not this again.

'Dave!' I say. 'You haven't seen him in ages. You know he wants visitors, he said so.'

'I don't think he meant it,' says Dave. 'He's still feeling shit.'

'He did mean it!' I say. 'Come on, you need to show up for your friends at times like this.'

'But I'm no good at that sort of thing!' protests Dave. 'I'd be no use. Seriously, Laura, me sitting in Joe's house looking miserable isn't going to help him.'

He looks genuinely upset so I say, 'Okay, okay. But at least give him a ring.'

'I will,' says Dave.

It's a mild evening, and as we head down Drumcondra Road we pass a couple pushing a buggy with a tiny newborn baby in it.

Dave squeezes my hand. 'That'll be us in a year or two.'

I quickly reach out my other hand and brush my fingers against a tree at the edge of the pavement. 'Touch wood.'

His total confidence unsettles me, just a bit. We walk in silence for a moment and then I say, 'You haven't forgotten I've got that doctor's appointment next week?'

'Course not.' Dave looks down at me and smiles. 'Don't look so worried, love. It'll be grand.'

'But what if it isn't?' I say. I wish I could be as breezy as he is. Whether it's about health, or work, or the future in general, he always ignores the negative and focuses on the positive. 'What'll we do if it isn't?'

'But it will be!' says Dave. 'Seriously, Laura. There's no need to worry. It'll be fine. We'll be fine.'

And like a fool, I believe him.

Chapter One

2019

I'm clearing out my desk at Zenith when I find it.

Aoife, my friend and colleague – well, ex-colleague now – has just done a defiant sweep of the office kitchen for some cans of iced matcha tea and bars of allegedly healthy chocolate. That kitchen turned out to be the best thing about working here after the takeover. Maybe they thought if we had enough delicious treats we wouldn't notice Zenith didn't really care about running an ad agency at all. Which is presumably why, less than two years after I started there, Zenith are now 'restructuring' their communications department and letting almost all of us ad people go.

'God, I hate packing,' I mutter, recklessly chucking the award we won for the ethical-pensions ad into the box.

'What was that?' Aoife is trying to squash a large orange cushion into her box.

'Oh, nothing,' I say, as I dispose of a potted succulent. 'How did I accumulate so much shite in less than two years?'

'I think my notebooks have been breeding,' says Aoife. 'I definitely didn't buy this many.' She closes the lid of her box and sighs. 'There! The end of my Visions-slash-Zenith career.'

There's a lump in my throat. 'I can't believe we won't be working together anymore.'

Aoife and I started at Visions around the same time. We made it to senior creative level together. We're a great team. We *were* a great team.

'Ah, don't, you'll set me off.' Aoife's voice sounds choked up. 'We'll work together again. This is just a minor setback. Come on, pack the last of your notebooks and let's get out of here.'

I pick up the notebooks and that's when I see the card that had been lying underneath them.

There's a drawing of me on it, looking like something out of *Mad Men* in a chic sixties shift dress, my curly dark hair in an elegant updo, my fringe looking much neater than it does in real life.

And because I'm clearly a glutton for punishment, I put down the notebooks, open the card and read what's inside.

My lovely Laura,
You don't need me to wish you good luck in your new job because I know you're going to shine there like the total rock star you are. I love you so much and I'm so proud of you and I can't wait to marry you.
xxxxx Dave

It's been eight months now since Dave decided that actually, he didn't love me *that* much and he didn't want to marry me after all. It's been over seven months since I talked to him. And it's quite a few months since I've cried over him.

But when I read this card I have to close my eyes very, very tightly for a long moment to stop tears falling. Then I open my eyes, rip the card into as many pieces as I can and dump them all in the bin.

'What was that?' says Aoife.

'Nothing,' I say. 'I'm all done here.'

'Right.' Aoife puts her overflowing box down on the desk and throws an arm around my shoulders. 'Let's say goodbye and good riddance to this place and then take ourselves and these boxes down the pub.'

And it's then, at my very lowest moment, as we shuffle past our former colleagues, all desperately trying to avoid our eyes, that I hear those familiar opening chords coming from the radio in the fancy kitchen, followed by that voice, a little more gravelly than it was the first time I heard it but still, always and immediately, recognisable.

'The earth is cold and the world is still
The sun's not come back and it never will
I can't remember when the sky was new
But I remember that I love you
And I can't do
Winter without you …'

Exquisite timing, Tadhg Hennessy, as ever. The contrast between how our lives have turned out has never been starker.

Which might be why I can't help thinking of the first time I heard that voice.

And the first time I saw him.

Chapter Two

1999

'Who,' said Katie, 'is *that*?'

It was a miserable February afternoon and my best friend Katie and I were doing what we always did on Saturdays when we were seventeen. We'd got the bus into town from Drumcondra and wandered around the second-hand clothes shops of Temple Bar and the charity shops of George's Street, searching for kids' T-shirts from the seventies to wear with our Hobo combat skirts. Then we strolled on to Grafton Street, and that's where we saw *him*.

Or rather, them.

They looked about our age (we would later find out that they were, like us, in sixth year at secondary school). But they weren't spending their Saturday afternoon drifting about town. They were busking outside A-Wear, and they'd drawn quite a crowd. Of course, in 1999 buskers didn't use amps and microphones, so this was, by necessity, an acoustic set. But you couldn't miss them. Two of the band were playing guitar, and the other band member, a boy with a mop of black curls, was playing a single snare drum, sitting behind it on a camping stool. One of the guitarists was a girl with an intimidatingly perfect fringe and a glittery T-shirt worn under a fake fur coat, and the other guitar player, the one who was singing was … well, he was …

'Why don't we know any boys like that?' breathed Katie.

'Because we hardly know any boys at all,' I said, never taking my eyes off the buskers.

They were playing 'Femme Fatale' by the Velvet Underground, and the tall, lean frontman's husky delivery managed to convey the melancholy, bittersweet vibe of the original without sounding like a parody. His short hair was dark and wavy, and he was wearing a Jon Spencer Blues Explosion T-shirt, which showed he had excellent taste in music, and Clark Kent-style glasses, which only served to make him even more good-looking. This was definitely not true of me and my glasses – at least, that's what I firmly believed back then.

The band finished 'Femme Fatale' to a smattering of applause from the decent-sized crowd, and the frontman smiled in a slightly embarrassed way that made him look even better.

'Thanks a million,' he said. And then they launched into 'The Ship Song' by Nick Cave and the Bad Seeds, the most darkly romantic, swoony song imaginable. Even when played by three teenagers on a Dublin street full of busy shoppers in the middle of February.

'I think I'm in love,' I whispered to Katie, and I was only half joking.

'I'll fight you for him,' she whispered back.

We stared at the band, enraptured – although, let's be honest, we stared at *him* – until they finished the song. There was another round of applause; the crowd had grown bigger while they were playing and I wonder now if any of those applauding shoppers realised, years later, that they had seen Tadhg Hennessy – *Tadhg Hennessy!* – busking on Grafton Street when he was just a kid. Probably not.

I was both totally entranced and, I realised, wildly jealous. When I was fourteen I'd taught myself to play my dad's old acoustic guitar and ever since then I'd longed to start a band. I'd even started writing songs. The only problem was finding potential bandmates.

'Why amn't I in a band like that?' I whispered mournfully.

'Because you don't know any incredibly hot musical geniuses,' said Katie. 'Apart from me, obviously.'

'You play the clarinet,' I said. 'We can't start a band with one guitarist who can't sing and one clarinet player.'

'Clarinettist,' said Katie.

'The fact that we're having this conversation proves we're just not cool enough to be in a band like that,' I said. 'Why don't you learn the drums?'

'Why don't you learn to sing?' retorted Katie, which was fair enough. I'd long accepted that I couldn't sing, ever since

I was in fourth class and our teacher asked me, as politely as possible, to mime during the end of year concert in which we were performing songs from *Mary Poppins*. And I didn't care, not really. But it meant I knew I could never be a solo musician. I was always going to need someone else to sing the songs I wrote.

Eventually the band finished their set – the guitar case in front of them was full of pound coins and a fair few notes; they must have earned at least fifty quid – and Blues Explosion Boy addressed the crowd. 'Thanks a million, we're the Evil Twins and we'll be back here next week.'

Which meant, of course, that Katie and I would be there too.

And so we were. And the week after that. And the one after that. I started wearing my favourite band T-shirts and leaving my coat open in the pathetic hope of impressing Blues Explosion Boy with my taste in music, even though it was early March and freezing cold, so any potential coolness points I might possibly have earned would be cancelled out by the sound of my audibly chattering teeth.

At this stage, the Evil Twins had developed an actual fanbase. There were now several girls our age standing at the front of the crowd every week, gazing at Blues Explosion Boy with expressions of adoration on their faces; Katie and I told each other we would never be so blatantly obvious. We told our friends about the cute busking boy and they joined us in the crowd. It was kind of a joke to all of us – including me and Katie.

But behind the jokes there was something real for me. Not real love, not even seventeen-year-old me was deluded enough to think that. But real *joy*. That's the thing about a proper crush: it adds a pinch of glitter to everyday life. It wasn't like Blues Explosion Boy was all I thought about or all I talked about with my friends. We talked about books and films and music; we talked about our dreams of college and how much more exciting it would be than school; we complained about sudden skin breakouts and bad period pains (my periods were always heavy and painful, so that was mostly me); we had elaborate in-jokes that no one but us would ever find funny but which made us cry with laughter on a daily basis. And because we were girls who mostly fancied boys, fizzing with hormones while attending a single-sex school, well, whenever any of us actually found a boy she fancied, of course we sometimes talked about that too.

And fancying Blues Explosion Boy was *fun*. Even now, literally decades later, I can remember the sparkling thrill of having something to look forward to every Saturday, the pleasure of thinking about him during the rest of the week, blissfully imagining how our eyes would meet during his rendition of 'The Ship Song'; how I'd be walking away alone (both my friends and his band were mysteriously absent in this fantasy) when I'd hear him call 'Hey!'; how I'd turn around and realise that yes, he really was calling after me; how he'd run up to me, slightly awkward but clearly determined; how he'd tell me he'd noticed me in the crowd every week and how instead of being tongue-tied (which is what would definitely have happened if this extremely unlikely event had taken place in real life), I'd tell him how great the Evil Twins were and that I played the guitar too and he'd be really impressed, and we'd realise we loved all the same things and form an instant bond and then he'd ask if I wanted to go for a coffee and I'd say yes even though I don't like coffee, and it would all end, hours of intense conversation later, with him kissing me passionately at the number 16 bus stop on Westmoreland Street and the two of us living happily ever after.

But of course, when I finally talked to Blues Explosion Boy, it wasn't anything like that.

Easter was coming up, and Katie and I were heading to County Galway for the holidays with our friend Sarah. The three of us had been to the Gaeltacht three times before to improve our Irish-language skills, attending a pleasingly free-and-easy summer college in West Cork, where they weren't exactly sticklers for the whole 'speaking Irish all the time' thing. But now our Leaving Cert exams were approaching, and we were starting to wish we'd gone at least once to one of the stricter *coláistes*. Not too strict, obviously. Not the infamously dreadful one where they made you, like, march around an exercise yard and salute the flag every morning.

Then Sarah remembered that her elder brother had gone to a special Easter course for sixth-year students in a Connemara *coláiste* called Coláiste Laoise. It worked the same way as the usual summer Irish sessions – staying in the houses of local families, doing Irish classes in the morning and various activities in the afternoon, a céilí in the evening. No speaking English, ever. But there was also a proper music room with guitars and a drum kit, which sparked my interest. We'd be able to spend our afternoons playing music there. Maybe I'd actually be able to play in a band.

It was just two weeks. But it would be better than nothing.

Before we went to Coláiste Laoise, I finally got contact lenses. It took a lot of persuading before my parents agreed to give me my birthday present four months early. It wasn't as if I actually *needed* contact lenses. I could hardly tell them it was pure vanity, based on the hope that Blues Explosion Boy might be more drawn to someone who wasn't a fellow specs-wearer. I had never kissed anyone else who wore glasses before (full disclosure: I had only kissed two boys ever) and I was worried two pairs of specs might get in the way if my fantasies of bus-stop romance ever came true. It was safer to be glasses-free, just on the off chance we somehow ended up shifting over some guitar pedals in Music Maker one Saturday.

I didn't say any of this to my parents, of course, because I wasn't insane. I just thanked them for the early birthday present.

'Don't expect me to get you anything at all,' growled Annie. 'Ever.' She had just turned thirteen and was, I thought patronisingly, from my lofty position as a seventeen-year-old, 'going through a difficult stage'.

A week later, on a cold April afternoon, we were in the car park of Galway's main train station being herded onto one of several buses marked Coláiste Laoise. We didn't have time to get a good look at most of our fellow students before we were crammed into our seats, heading out of the city towards Connemara. We were, of course, meant to be talking solely in Irish at this point but, under pressure, every word of the language seemed to have vanished right out of our heads.

'I wonder what our house will be like,' I whispered to Katie in English, and a shiny-haired girl sitting in front of us turned and glowered through the gap in the seats and hissed, '*Gaeilge!*'

Eventually the bus stopped in a car park in front of a sprawling one-storey building, across the road from the wild Atlantic waves. As we stood, a little awkwardly, beside our bus, more students started getting off a vivid yellow bus a few metres away. I wasn't paying much attention to them but then Katie grabbed my arm.

'Ow! What's wrong?' I said. 'I mean, *cad atá ort?*'

'*Féach!*' she hissed. 'No, not over there! Look *there*!'

I followed her gaze. And I gasped.

'Oh my God!' I breathed.

'I can't believe it,' said Katie. 'I mean, *ní thuigim*. No, hang on, that's "I don't understand". What's "believe" again?'

I didn't answer. Because standing beside the yellow bus were none other than the Evil Twins' drummer and Blues Explosion Boy. His dark locks were tousled and he looked, if possible, more handsome than ever.

I genuinely thought I was hallucinating. It seemed impossible that he was there, with us, in this remote place. As we were all shepherded into the main building of the *coláiste*, I nudged Sarah.

'Sarah,' I whispered, nodding my head in the direction of the yellow bus. 'Is that …?'

If Sarah could see him, he was definitely there. She didn't fancy him enough to hallucinate him.

She glanced over and then grinned at me and raised her eyebrows.

He was real all right.

Chapter Three

2019

It's nine o'clock by the time I get home from the pub. I'm not exactly pissed – Aoife and I spent more time ranting about Zenith than swigging pints, and we made sure to get plenty of toasties 'for soakage'. But I'm not what you'd call entirely sober. Which is probably why, as I'm closing the front door behind me, the cardboard box that I've been precariously balancing on one hip falls to the ground.

'Lol?' Katie calls from the sitting room. She's the only person who stills calls me Lol. It was my nickname in school but, unsurprisingly, it faded from use once people started using LOL as an acronym. I like that Katie still calls me Lol, though. It makes me feel … I dunno. Known. 'Everything okay?'

'I'm fine!' I call back. 'Sorry. I just dropped my 'I've been fired' box.'

I leave it there and go into the sitting room, where Katie and her wife Jeanne are curled up on the couch.

'You weren't fired,' says Jeanne. 'You were just … restructured. Here, have some wine.'

'I shouldn't …' I say, but she's already pouring me a glass of Brouilly. 'Oh, all right then. Thanks.'

I take the glass and plonk myself down in a comfortable armchair. Katie and Jeanne's house is so nice. They're practically my only friends who own their own home. Last year I hoped me and Dave might be able to buy something soon … But I won't think about that now. I won't think about him at all. I won't even think about the fact that, as of today, I'm officially unemployed. I'll just remember how lucky I am to have friends who, without hesitation, offered me a room as soon as I told them that Dave and I had broken up. I feel tears come to my eyes. I love Katie. And I love Jeanne too. I'm lucky my best friend got together with someone so cool. And French. Her calm practicality perfectly balances Katie's energy. I look at them fondly, Katie with her bleached blonde bob and oversized sweatshirt with 'Meuf' emblazoned across the front, Jeanne snuggled next to her in a cobweb-grey cashmere cardigan, her braids tied up in a bun (it's such a French cliché but she really is more stylish than anyone else I know).

'Are you all right?' says Katie suspiciously. 'You look like you might be sick any minute. Don't throw up all over that chair.'

'How dare you!' I say. 'I was just thinking how great you both are. Though I'm not thinking that anymore.'

'Good to hear,' says Katie. 'Because if you had puked on

the chair I'd have made you spend your redundancy money on another one.'

'Ooh, my redundancy money!' I'm definitely a bit tipsy. 'That reminds me. The payment should have gone through today!'

'You're rich!' cries Katie.

'Well, not very rich,' I say. 'But slightly richer than I was this morning. Actually, I wonder how much it is after tax?' I reach for my phone and open the bank app. At least, that's what I meant to do. But a combination of several drinks and general distraction means I hit the Gmail icon instead.

And that's when I see it.

'Oh my God.' I drop the phone in my lap.

'What?' says Jeanne. 'Oh no, have you been scammed? Is all your money gone?'

I pick the phone up again and stare at the screen. No, I wasn't seeing things.

'It's not the bank,' I say. 'I got an email from Tadhg.'

'Tadhg who?' says Katie. Then it dawns on her. '*That* Tadhg?'

'That Tadhg,' I say, without taking my eyes off my phone.

'What's the subject line?' says Katie.

'"Our song",' I say.

'Maybe it's a promotional thing,' suggests Jeanne. 'Maybe that's the name of his new album.'

'Jeanne,' says Katie, 'do you really think Laura is signed up to Tadhg Hennessy's email list?' She looks at me. 'You're not, are you?'

'No!' I say.

'So why is he emailing you?' she says.

'I have no idea!' I stare at the unread email. The sender is listed as Tadhg Hennessy. Could it actually be him? And if it is, what do I want it to say? *Laura, I was young and stupid, you are the love of my life? Laura, I know it's been sixteen years since we saw each other but I still hate you for what happened that night? Laura, just a heads-up, my new album is all about how much I still hate you?* It could be anything.

Maybe I did just end up on his record company's mailing list.

'Read it!' says Katie impatiently.

Katie, Sarah and, at this stage, Jeanne are the only people I've ever talked to properly about Tadhg. They're the only people who know exactly what happened between us.

I take a deep breath. 'Fine.'

Then I scroll down and start reading aloud.

Hi Laura,

My name's Tara Kelleher and I'm writing to you on behalf of Tadhg Hennessy. We'd like to talk with you about a piece of music entitled 'our song', an unfinished composition you wrote together in the early '00s. We would like to meet with you to discuss how to proceed.

Tadhg is currently in Dublin, and ideally we would set up a meeting and resolve this as soon as possible. If this is amenable to you, please contact me at this email address or at the number below.

I hope to hear from you soon.

'And that's it.' I put down my phone and take a swig of wine. 'It's not even from him. Not directly.' I can't bring myself to admit how hurt that makes me feel.

'Tadhg probably hasn't written his own emails since 2010!' says Katie. 'I don't think this is the most important issue here.'

'The important issue,' says Jeanne, 'is that Tadhg Hennessy is interested in a song you co-wrote.'

'It's not that big a deal,' I say.

They look at me with identically sceptical expressions on their faces.

'I mean, I do *know* him!' I say. 'Or I did. It's not like getting praise from Beyoncé.'

'So what are you going to do?' says Katie.

'She's going to meet him,' says Jeanne. 'Aren't you?'

'I don't know,' I say. 'I mean, he can't even mail me himself.'

'What do you mean, you don't know?' Jeanne looks appalled. 'I mean, obviously I never met him, but from what you and Katie have told me he wasn't a total monster.'

'He wasn't,' I say. 'It's just … me and him. It ended *really* badly. We stopped speaking and that was it.'

I didn't see his face again until someone in work sent me the 'Winter Without You' video. The story of Tadhg Hennessy's meteoric rise is famous by now. 'Winter Without You' was his first single, released on his own no-budget indie label back in 2004. It got a smattering of plays on Phantom FM, but when YouTube took off a few years later, an artist friend of his made a video for it and that video went viral. A colleague at the agency where I was working at the time sent the link to our entire team with the subject line 'Best thing I've heard all year'. I remember how I felt after I clicked on the link and realised who I was looking at. I remember making myself sit through the entire thing and reading the ecstatic comments beneath it. I remember realising that Tadhg was now achieving what we'd once dreamed about doing together. My stomach churns at the memory, and it's not just the alcohol and toasties.

'But Lol,' says Katie gently, 'that was a *long* time ago.'

I look at her. She was there for all of it. It's easy to forget that now, because I made the big break with Tadhg all about me, but he and Katie had been proper friends. In that last year of college we'd been a little gang, the band and Katie.

'What are you saying?' I say.

'I'm saying – and remember I'm not totally sober – that this could be a good thing,' says Katie. 'Especially right now.'

'Really?' I roll my eyes. '"Hi Tadhg, I see you're a megastar now. How am I doing? Oh, I just got laid off from my copywriting job."'

'Everyone's been laid off at some stage,' says Katie. 'It's nothing to be ashamed of. And what I meant was, well, maybe this is fate.'

'Fate,' I say flatly.

'You lose your job and then, shazam, Tadhg asks you if you want to meet up and talk about a song you wrote together!' says Katie. 'How is that not a present from the universe?'

'First of all, we didn't write that song together, whatever he's claiming now,' I say. '*I* wrote it. He just sang it. And second of all, you're assuming I want to hang out with him.'

'Well, don't you?' says Jeanne.

Of course I do, even though I know he might not be the Tadhg I remember anymore. I don't say so, though. I take another gulp of wine instead.

'He must think the song is good, Lol,' says Katie.

'He probably just wants to make sure I didn't, like, record it on a Dictaphone or something back in 2003.' I feel a surge of righteous anger. 'God, I bet that's it. He wants to steal my song and he's making sure I can't sue him when he releases it on his next album. And I didn't record it so he'd win. He was the one who recorded our band practices, with his stupid minidisc recorder.'

'Or maybe,' says Katie, 'he wants to give you a proper songwriting credit.'

I get a flashback to sitting in a lecture theatre in college, imagining the credits of our first album. Maybe some girls imagined double-barrelling their names with the man of their dreams. The thought of changing my name when I got married has never crossed my mind. But I often found myself doodling 'All songs: Hennessy/McDermott' when I was meant to be taking lecture notes.

'Look,' says Jeanne. 'If you ignore this email, do you think you'll regret it in a year's time, when he has a new album out that could have had your song on it?'

'Maybe,' I admit.

'And you were really good friends with him once,' says Katie. 'Despite, you know, everything.'

'True,' I say. 'But he wasn't *that* great.'

There's a long silence as I ponder their words. Finally Katie breaks it.

'Well,' she says. 'He was really, really hot.'

'He still is,' says Jeanne. 'And I don't even fancy men.' So annoying that Tadhg's appeal transcends gender preferences.

'Fine, fine, I'll admit that he was hot. Is hot,' I say. 'Satisfied?'

'No!' says Katie. 'I *know* you want to do this. And more importantly, I think it'll lay some ghosts to rest. Give you closure about everything that happened back then. I think you should tell this Tara person you'll meet Tadhg for lunch.'

'Just to see if he's still hot in person,' says Jeanne.

'Exactly,' says Katie. 'Just don't reply now because I think you're a little bit pissed. As am I. Wait until tomorrow and then do it. If you still want to.'

I give in. 'Fine, fine, fine. I'll reply tomorrow. If I still want to.'

'Laura, this is a good thing!' says Jeanne. 'You have a special relationship with Tadhg Hennessy! That's pretty cool, no?'

I laugh. 'If you say so.' Jeanne hadn't been there. My relationship, if that's what I can even call it, with Tadhg Hennessy was definitely not cool.

Except, of course, for the moments when it really, really was.

Chapter Four

1999

By the time we were all bundled into the main hall of Coláiste Laoise for our official welcome by the staff, I had lost sight of Blues Explosion Boy. We were staying in a house called Tí Mhairéad, the closest house to the *coláiste*, and were soon brought there by one of the *múinteoirí* (we called all the staff *múinteoirs*, though they weren't all teachers), a friendly young woman called Áine. Katie grabbed both my arms as soon as we closed the door of our bedroom.

'Why is he here?!' she hissed. We had to keep our voices down so the *bean an tí* wouldn't hear us speaking English.

'It's a miracle,' I said reverently. And it really did feel like one.

We were the first group to arrive back at the *coláiste* for the céilí on that first night.

'Oh, look!' said Sarah. 'They have disco lights!' She said the last two words in English. It was all right to use the odd word of *Béarla* if it was clear you were genuinely *trying* to speak *as Gaeilge*. No one could possibly expect us to know the Irish for 'disco lights'. Then a gang of lads wearing rugby shirts turned up. Some of them started dancing in a piss-taking sort of way, swinging each other around. But one of them looked a little embarrassed by his friends' antics. He caught our eyes and shrugged.

Katie and I looked at each other and laughed.

'Poor creature,' said Katie in Irish. 'He's not ... terrible, isn't he not?'

I looked at her. 'Not terrible?'

'I don't know how to say' – she lowered her voice and switched to English – 'not bad-looking!'

I supposed he wasn't bad-looking, in a fair-haired sort of way. But I didn't have time to consider his charms because the room was filling up and there, coming through the door, wearing his actual Blues Explosion T-shirt (a sign, surely?) was Blues Explosion Boy and his pal. Then the music stopped and the voice of a *múinteoir* called Pól blared out through the speakers.

'Welcome to céilí number one! We're going to start with the Walls of Limerick. If you don't know it, don't worry, you'll learn quickly. You'll be dancing in twos, and we know if we wait for you to ask each other, we'll be here all night, so we're going to pair you up.'

Some students looked relieved, some terrified, as the staff started moving around the hall. Then Áine came up to our group and grabbed my and Katie's hands.

'Come on!' she said cheerfully. 'We'll get you dancing.'

To my horror, I realised she was leading us over towards the rugby-shirt boys. But she stopped in front of the fair-haired boy who had kept out of the shenanigans.

'You,' she said to him before turning to Katie, 'and you.'

She led me away. I looked back to see Katie and the 'not terrible' boy standing side by side, looking deeply uncomfortable.

And when I turned to follow Áine, Blues Explosion Boy was standing right in front of us. His eyes widened when he saw me.

'Okay,' said Áine. 'You two.'

Then she walked away, leaving me and Blues Explosion Boy staring at each other. Were we just going to stare at each other all night? Eventually he cleared his throat, gave me the slightly embarrassed smile I recognised from when the Evil Twins had to deal with hecklers and said, 'Hi. I'm, um, Tadhg.' *Is mise Tadhg.*

The first words he has ever said to me, I thought solemnly.

'I'm Laura,' I said. At most *coláistes* in those days, we had to use the Irish-language version of our names, if there was one. Those who already had Irish names, the Sorchas and Tadhgs and Caoilfhionns, were lucky because they didn't get called something that, in many cases, bore only the most spurious connection to the name their parents had given them. But happily for me, there wasn't really an Irish approximation of Laura, so I kept my usual name.

I wracked my brains frantically for something to say to Blues Explosion Boy that wouldn't make me sound stupid or insane. But the staff were now urging us to take our places for the dance. Me and Blues Explosion Boy, I mean Tadhg, found ourselves at one end of a long line of pairs, facing each other in groups of four.

'Take hands!' called Pól through the microphone.

Oh God.

Tadhg looked down at me. I had never realised quite how much taller than me he was. And then he took my hand.

His hand was warm but not hot or clammy; his grip was firm but not too tight.

It was perfect. It felt … right.

'All right?' he said. *Ceart go leor?* That slightly lopsided smile again. He made the Irish words sound like music.

I swallowed and nodded. He looked back at me as if he were making up his mind to say something.

'I think that I—' he began, but then noisy fiddles blasted out of the speaker and the dance began.

If you've never danced the Walls of Limerick before, it's pretty simple. You and your partner bounce towards the couple facing you, then back again, then you each dance over to the other side from where you started, twirl around and face the next couple. It's quite fun, actually, when you're not distracted by the fact that you're holding the hand of the boy you've lusted after from afar for months. I was pretty sure he recognised me, given that I'd been standing in front of him every week since February. But if that was the case, he knew that *I* recognised *him*. I had to acknowledge that or things were going to get even more awkward. And I wanted to do this in a clever way that would make him think I was incredibly cool and funny. But I feared that was beyond me in Irish. Even the basics felt beyond me. How did you say 'Oh, I think I recognise you'? The word for 'I think' was easy, that was *ceapaim*, but what was 'recognise' …?

We had reached the bit in the dance where we twirled each other around, and now his hand was on my waist, and mine was on his, and for a moment I couldn't think of anything else at all.

Now we were facing Katie and Rugby Shirt Boy, who both looked quite cheerful. To my great relief, Katie didn't give me any meaningful looks. She just grinned and said, 'Hi! Brían, this is my friend Laura!'

Brían smiled and said, 'Hi!' We danced towards each other and back again.

'I'm Tadhg,' said Tadhg, as it became clear I wasn't going to do any introductions, because I had apparently lost my manners as well as my mind. Then he and I were crossing over to face the next couple. I was running out of time. The dance was going to be over soon. I had to say something to him *now*. But how, in Irish? Wasn't there an Irish proverb that basically meant 'it takes one to know one' with the word for 'recognise' in it? Yes! There was! It literally meant 'a beetle recognises another beetle', but how did you say it in Irish? Come on, Laura, you did this in school, it's in there somewhere …

'*Aithníonn ciaróg ciaróg eile!*'

'Excuse me?' said Tadhg.

He was looking at me in confusion and I realised, to my utter gut-wrenching horror, that I had just said – no, shouted – those unhinged words out loud.

And that was my first conversation with Tadhg Hennessy.

Chapter Five

2019

When I wake up on Saturday morning, feeling almost but not quite hungover, and remember getting that email from Tadhg's employee the night before, I can't reach out and read it on my phone.

Ever since Dave and I broke up – that's how I describe it to other people, because it sounds better than 'ever since Dave dumped me', as if it might have been a mutual decision rather than something he did purely of his own volition, a horrific and initially utterly incomprehensible shock – anyway, ever since *that* happened, I've stopped having my phone in my bedroom at night.

Dave had been a bit distant for a while before that evening last year, but we'd had a stressful few months. It never crossed my mind for a second that he would end things. Until I came home from work one Friday and found him sitting on the couch with a small suitcase at his feet.

'Laura.' He cleared his throat.

'What's this?' I pointed at the suitcase and smiled. 'Oh wow, did you book that spa hotel again?'

I seriously thought he was going to whisk me off on a surprise weekend away. God, I was so stupid.

Dave looked really uncomfortable.

'Um, no,' he said. 'Laura, I don't … I can't …' He stared at his hands. 'We need to talk.'

'About what?' He was scaring me now. 'Are you all right?'

Dave stood up, walked to the window and then walked back to the sofa. I'd never seen him so agitated before. 'Okay. Okay, I have to just say it.' He took a deep breath. 'I don't think this is working.'

I stared at him. He wasn't making sense. 'What are you talking about? What's not working?'

He looked at the ceiling. At the floor. Anywhere except at me.

And eventually he said, 'Us.'

'*What?*'

He couldn't be saying what I thought he was saying. Could he?

'But … but we're getting married in three months!' I said.

Dave looked like he was on the verge of tears, but he didn't say anything.

And in that moment I could feel my life begin to fall apart.

The weeks after the break-up are still kind of a blur. I don't think I quite believed Dave was doing this to me, even when he went to stay with a friend for a few days and then came back to assure me he wasn't seeing anyone else and it was agreed – by which I mean Dave suggested it and I nodded mutely, because I had stopped crying and begging him to stay by then – that because he earned just about enough from his design job at a tech giant to cover the rent and I didn't, he would stay in our nice flat and I would move into Katie and Jeanne's spare room. So I left the home I had made with the man I thought I was going to marry, and I haven't talked to him since.

After I moved out I was determined that Dave would not see any signs of sadness or weakness in me ever again. From now on, he would think I was totally fine. Better than fine. He would think I was having the time of my fucking life. For some inexplicable reason, I decided that, as part of me showing Dave that I was doing brilliantly, I wouldn't unfollow him or block him on social media. Why would I need to? I was fine with seeing his life! I didn't care that most of our mutual friends turned out to be his friends and I now only saw them in the photos of nights out he posted on his Instagram stories. And if he was going out with a girl called Liz who had appeared in lots of those stories over the last six months, and I was pretty sure he was, then I was fine with that too!

But although I continued to follow him, I was afraid of accidentally liking a photo or story or, worse, leaving a soon-to-be-regretted comment during late-night or early-morning doomscrolling. So I started leaving my phone in the kitchen at night, and now I sleep much better as a result.

And so when I wake up, instead of rereading Tadhg's assistant's message, I get up, wrap myself in my dressing gown and reach under my bed. Then I pull out the dusty case containing my acoustic guitar from where it's been lying ever since I moved into this room eight months ago. I take the guitar out of its case, sit down on the bed and then – I do nothing. It's been so long since I've played the guitar, I can't even bring myself to touch the strings. But I think about playing it. And playing the song Tadhg wants to talk about.

We always called it 'our song' but that was just because I never got round to writing proper lyrics for it so it never got a proper name. It was my song, really. We both knew that, or at least I thought we did. My chords, my melody, my lyrics (such as they were). But I, or we, never finished it. We both knew it needed something else, something neither of us could quite capture back when we were twenty-one. A lead guitar line. A 'middle eight' – the bit of a song after the second chorus that has a different melody to the chorus and verses. We both suggested a few chords and guitar lines, but they never worked, somehow. So the song remained unfinished.

And now Tadhg wants us to finish it. Or at least he wants to make sure I don't cause a stink if he claims it, bangs a few extra chords into it and presents it as his own. Well, we'll see about that. He might be a megastar who can usually have whatever he wants, but this is *my* song. I'm struck by how protective I suddenly feel about it, about those chords I wrote in my bedroom when I was twenty-one, on a day when my emotions were too big to fit into any song lyrics. The idea of him claiming it, of it being praised or criticised as another Tadhg Hennessy song, maybe just an album track, its true authorship unknown to everyone … it feels like just another thing being taken away from me. And way too many things have been taken away from me over the last year.

God, I really am a bit hungover. I need some tea. That first pre-breakfast cup of the day is like a sacred ritual for me, and I'm very particular about the tea itself. Strong but lots of milk, and a tiny bit of sugar – I hate other people making tea for me because even when I say 'Just a quarter of a teaspoon!' they put in way too much. I put the guitar back in its case and go downstairs to put the kettle on. My phone is next to it on the kitchen counter, and while the kettle boils I read Tara Kelleher's mail again.

Tadhg is currently in Dublin, and ideally we would set up a meeting and resolve this as soon as possible. If this is amenable to you, please contact me at this email address or at the number below.

I'm not sure it is particularly amenable, but I do know that I'm going to contact Tara Kelleher. I think I knew it the minute I read the email.

When my tea is ready I sit down at the kitchen table and then, without quite realising what I'm doing, I pick up my phone again, open the browser and google the words 'Tadhg Hennessy'. I'm just about to click on 'News' when a cheery voice behind me cries, 'Morning!'

I drop my phone.

'Oh God, what are you up to?' Katie's platinum locks are sporting a serious case of bedhead and she's wearing a dressing gown and Ugg boots, but she still looks a lot more sprightly than I do this morning. 'You're not thinking of texting Dave, are you? Don't make me hide your phone again ...'

'No! God, the thought of that hasn't crossed my mind for—' I realise, with a jolt of surprise, that I haven't had to fight the urge to text Dave for weeks now. No, months. 'Ages.'

Katie's eyes narrow. 'So why do you look so shifty?'

I sigh and hold up the phone so she can see the screen. 'I was googling Tadhg.'

'Oh!' Katie sighs in relief. 'Grand. Google away. Yikes, imagine if we'd been able to google him back in the busking days. We'd have been terrifying.'

'I'm afraid I'm being terrifying now,' I say. 'Isn't this a bit creepy?'

'No!' says Katie. 'I mean, it would be if you were googling him every single day. But you just got an email from him!'

'I got an email from one of his minions.'

'With a message from him,' says Katie. 'So it's perfectly normal to check what he's up to at the moment. That's the good thing about him being famous, it's easy to find out.'

'You do know, don't you, that I don't keep tabs on him,' I say truthfully. 'I mean, if he does something majorly newsworthy, then of course I hear about it, but I don't make a habit of following his life.'

'Probably for the best.' Katie nods in agreement.

'What do you mean?' Oh God, please don't say he's done something really terrible …

Katie laughs and puts the kettle on. 'Nothing! I mean, nothing bad. I just meant it's healthy that you don't have, like, Google alerts set up for someone who broke your heart sixteen years ago.'

'Good, because I don't,' I say. 'Obviously. I don't even follow him on Instagram.'

I have, of course, checked his account more than once. But not very often. It just felt so weird to see someone I used to be so close to playing an arena to thousands of adoring fans.

'You're a model of restraint,' says Katie.

I open my phone's browser again, and click the 'News' tab.

Tad? Tah? Tag? How to pronounce Tadhg Hennessy's name

(This is an old Vulture story that gets updated and reissued every time Tadhg is in the news.)

Tadhg Hennessy's new love? Irish star pictured with mystery brunette in Paris

'Saint Tadhg' slams tax-avoiding celebs: rocker's rant causes a stir

Tadhg Hennessy confirms long-awaited new album

Tadhg Hennessy's artist ex: where is Amanda Sorohan now?

Tadhg Hennessy confirms split with human rights lawyer

'Mystery brunette, eh?' Katie glances at me, as if to make sure my heart won't smash into a thousand pieces at the thought of Tadhg with another woman.

'Katie, it's not 2003,' I say. 'I don't care if Tadhg has a new girlfriend.'

'I know, I know,' says Katie. 'Just checking. Let's click on it. This was only published last week.'

I do, and after a moment of surprised silence we both laugh out loud.

'Well, I hope to God that's not his new love because if so it really is a scandal,' says Katie.

'Wow, she hasn't changed a bit,' I say. 'They still look kind of alike.' I look at the photo of Tadhg and his sister Rosie. 'You'd think someone would have sussed they're related.'

We click on the other news stories. The story about 'Saint Tadhg' 'slamming' fellow celebs is less sensational than the headline suggests; it's on a big conservative newspaper's website that likes to present anyone who isn't borderline fascist as some sort of sanctimonious scold. Tadhg is a patron of an NGO called Ceol that supports young people from socially deprived and marginalised backgrounds in making music. At one of their recent fundraising events, he'd been asked why the organisation was important and had replied, 'Well, it shouldn't be necessary because the state should fund programmes like this to make sure all young people have access to music, but until they do, Ceol will do the work.' The journalist asked where the money for that would come from and Tadhg said, 'People like me should be paying a lot more tax than we already are. And we definitely shouldn't be moving our businesses abroad to dodge it.'

The story about the album is hardly a huge scoop – yes, Tadhg is working on a new album, but the last one came out less than two years ago so it's hardly a return from the wilderness.

The story about artist Amanda Sorohan is a reminder that she deserves better than to be described merely as 'Tadhg's artist ex'.

'She's not exactly pining after him, is she?' says Katie. 'She won a massive art prize last year. And she's married to someone else.'

'It's mad, isn't it?' I say, scanning the piece. 'They went out for six years and split up, what, four years ago? And she's done loads of cool things. But she's still being referred to as Tadhg's ex-girlfriend.'

I already knew about the human rights lawyer. Well, everyone did. Aideen Harrington. A beautiful, stylish thirty-five-year-old from Coolock who stood up to injustice all over the world. She and Tadhg had met at a protest two years earlier but had split up last year. Not that long before me and Dave.

'You know,' I say, 'now that I'm probably going to see Tadhg again, I almost wish more of his girlfriends were fellow megastars.'

'What do you mean?' Katie sips her tea.

'I mean, the likes of you and me can't compare ourselves to megastars,' I say, 'because we were never ever going to be megastars.'

'Speak for yourself,' says Katie.

'It's like they're another species or something,' I continue, ignoring her. 'But, like, being an artist or a lawyer isn't beyond the bounds of possibility for us. I could have been a lawyer.'

'No you couldn't,' says Katie firmly. 'Neither of us could. We didn't get the points to do Law. You have to get all As in your Leaving Cert.'

'Hmmm, good point,' I say.

I look down at the list of stories on my phone again and sigh.

'He's almost too good to be true. On paper anyway. Paying his taxes, dating age-appropriate lawyers, going to protests ...'

Katie gives me a look. 'Would you prefer he was a tax-dodging right-winger who shagged nineteen-year-old models?'

'No!' I say. 'Of course not. I just keep thinking how things have changed since we last saw each other. It would almost be easier to meet him now if I felt he was a stereotypical douchebag dickhead millionaire rock star. Then I wouldn't give a shit what he thought of me.'

'I can't imagine Tadhg really being a total dickhead,' says Katie. 'Stupid, yes. And thoughtless sometimes. But not a real prick.'

'Yeah, well,' I say, 'I wouldn't have been able to imagine Dave being a total dickhead either a year ago. But life can surprise you.'

'I know,' says Katie. And because she's my best friend, and she knows when I want to talk more about something and when I don't, she claps her hands together and says, 'So! Have you replied to your one's mail yet?'

'No,' I say. 'I'm going to wait until Monday morning. Business hours. To show this is all business to me. And that I'm not jumping as soon as he gets in touch.'

Katie nods in approval. 'Quite the power move.'

I laugh. 'I'll take my power moves where I can find them.'

I try not to think about Tadhg and Tara Kelleher and even the song for the rest of the weekend. On Saturday afternoon I visit my parents, who are clearly convinced my life has fallen apart at the seams now that I've been left by their beloved Dave ('Are you sure you can't patch things up, Laura?') and lost my job ('It's not too late to do the civil service exams, Laura!'). I never told them the details of my break-up with

Dave. I never told them why he decided to leave me. I knew it would upset them too much, and to be honest, I couldn't deal with their distress as well as my own. I'd been tempted to not tell them I'd been let go by Zenith, but the thought of the subsequent web of lies I'd have to weave was just too stressful. I know they mean well, of course they do, but their fussing makes me feel worse.

So now I have to listen to their helpful career advice ('You know, you can teach in private primary schools with just an arts degree! They don't care if you're properly qualified!'). It's so exhausting that I guiltily make my excuses and leave as soon as I reasonably can. But before I go, I get my electric guitar and amplifier out of the wardrobe in my old bedroom and then take them back to Katie's house.

If this were my own place I'd leave them in the sitting room, but I'm already conscious that, despite the fact that lots of my stuff is being stored in my parents' attic, my various belongings are already taking up more than enough space in Katie and Jeanne's home. I bring the guitar and amp straight up to my bedroom.

The next morning, I decide to clean the kitchen windows. Katie comes in when I'm trying to reach the top corners and says, 'You do realise you don't have to earn your keep here, don't you? This isn't a do-our-housework-for-your-room-and-board situation. Not that we're supplying your board. If anything, you're supplying board for us with all the groceries you keep buying. Wow, "board" is a weird word when you keep saying it out loud. Anyway, you don't have to earn it.'

'Yeah, I know,' I say.

'Do you, though?' she says. 'When I said you could stay here as long as you liked, I meant it.'

'I know that too,' I say, and I do. 'But I feel like …' What do I feel like? A charity case? An interloper? 'I dunno. A fifth wheel, for one.'

Katie scoffs. 'You're not a fifth wheel. Jeanne and I love having you here. You stop us squabbling over what colour to paint the stairs and what couch we can afford. Buying a house sends you mad, especially when you can't really afford it, so you're stopping us killing each other.'

'Okay,' I say.

'Plus, to be perfectly honest,' says Katie, 'the rent really helps. We're still paying off the credit union for these windows.'

'I could pay more,' I say, even though I'm not sure I can at the moment, given my employment situation. Katie and Jeanne are charging me way less than market rate.

'This is your home,' says Katie, 'for as long as you want it to be.'

Katie and I became friends before teenage girls routinely said 'I love you!' to their platonic female friends, and so it feels too contrived for us to say those words to each other, even now.

But this – this is love.

'Thanks, Kay,' I say.

'And besides,' she says with a grin, 'when Tadhg records your song and you've made millions from it, you can pay off my windows loan.'

Through supreme self-control, I manage to stop myself looking at any Tadhg-related content online for most of the weekend, but on Sunday evening I crack, open Instagram and type in @TadhgHennessyMusic.

Logic tells me he doesn't handle his own social media, but the vibe of the account really does feel like him. Or at least the him I remember from a long time ago. There are no self-conscious thirst traps of him gazing thoughtfully into the distance or smouldering into the camera. Some of the photos look like they were taken by professional photographers, but most of them don't.

'Our sensitive king!' says one comment, followed by several crown emojis.

He's not always that fucking sensitive, I think.

Chapter Six

2019

The next morning is my first day of freedom or unemployment, depending on how you want to look at it, but I don't have a lie-in. I wake up at seven thinking about how I'm going to reply to that stupid email. I don't have to say yes, I remind myself. I've survived without any contact with Tadhg for over a decade. I don't need to see him again.

But I know that if I don't say yes, the thought of what that meeting might have been like will drive me mad.

And so, while the kettle is still boiling, I start writing.

Dear Tara,
Thanks for your email.

Why am I thanking her? No, keep it brusque and professional. Polite but not too eager. Keep an air of mystery. Or at least unavailability. Oh God, why is this so hard?

Half an hour and two cups of tea later, I have this:

Dear Tara,

I can make time to meet Tadhg this week to discuss the song. Somewhere in the city centre on Wednesday or Thursday around lunchtime would be good for me. If you need to get in touch with me urgently you can contact me on the number below.

Yours,

Laura

Katie rushes into the room. 'Did I leave my runners in here?'

'Under the table,' I say. 'Can you take a look at this?'

Katie shoves her feet into her runners and takes my phone. 'Very good,' she says. 'Short and to the point.'

'I didn't want to say "I have no other obligations because I'm unemployed and desperate so I'm free all week and I'll travel anywhere",' I say.

'Yes, I got that,' says Katie. 'Now, I'm sorry but I'm late and I've got to teach some ungrateful brats about executions in the Civil War.'

But I don't hit send until Jeanne comes in, looking cool and collected as ever. I show her the email.

'But why Wednesday and Thursday?' she says. 'Do you have anything on today or tomorrow? Or Friday?'

'No,' I say. 'But I didn't want to seem too keen.'

'You're overthinking this, Laura,' she says. 'It is ridiculous. Just send the email.'

So I do.

An hour later, I'm alone in the house trying to distract myself by doing one of my favourite YouTube yoga videos. I'm breathing lots of love in and lots of love out when my phone rings. An unknown number.

This is it.

I answer the call. 'Hello?'

'Hello, is that Laura McDermott?' says an unfamiliar voice. Female, Cork accent.

'It is,' I say cautiously.

'This is Tara Kelleher,' says the stranger. 'I'm ringing on behalf of Tadhg Hennessy.'

'Oh,' I say, as nonchalantly as I can. Which I suspect is not that nonchalant. My voice sounds slightly higher than usual. 'Yes. You got my email?'

'Yes, thanks for getting back to me,' she says. 'Tadhg would like to invite you to lunch on Wednesday for a chat, if that still suits you.' She names a restaurant. 'Do you know it?'

Yes, Tara, of course I know it. It made the national news last year when it got a second Michelin star and the tasting menu costs three hundred quid. I hope that when she says Tadhg's inviting me to lunch it means he's paying for it.

But of course I don't say this. I say, 'I know it,' and hope this implies that I am a regular patron.

'Brilliant,' she says. 'So is one o'clock on Wednesday okay?'

It's famously hard to get a table in this place, but I suppose things are different for the likes of Tadhg Hennessy.

'Yes, it should be,' I say.

'Great,' she says. 'Thanks so much for this. I know Tadhg is really looking forward to seeing you.'

She sounds totally sincere, but I find this information hard to believe, given how Tadhg and I left things the last time we saw each other.

'No problem,' I say.

After I say goodbye to Tara and hang up, I try to go back to my downward-facing dog but my nerves are beyond yoga now. Why didn't I say I was free tomorrow? Or even today? Now I have to wait over forty-eight hours and it's not like I have a job to go to. How will I keep myself occupied? There's only so much yoga I can do.

But I get through those forty-eight hours. I email friendly acquaintances in other ad agencies, asking them if there's any freelance work going. I meet Aoife for coffee and manage to be genuinely happy for her when she tells me she's been offered maternity cover at a good agency. I go for walks and listen to podcasts. I ring Annie in London and she commiserates with me over our parents' annoyingness. I have silly conversations in various group chats, though I don't tell anyone about Tadhg getting in touch, not even my group with Katie, Sarah and our friend Aisling (it's just called The Birthday Party because we set it up to arrange Aisling's birthday drinks in the early, unimaginative days of WhatsApp). I feel a bit guilty not telling Annie, Sarah and Aisling, but I'm afraid any more fuss might make me panic even more about the meeting. Aisling doesn't even know about me and Tadhg – she didn't meet the rest of us until we'd left college and she and Katie started teaching at the same school.

Then, to my amazement, I get offered a job.

When my phone rings, my initial reaction is to wonder if it's Tara cancelling the meeting the next day.

But it's not Tara.

'Laura McDermott?' says an unfamiliar voice. 'This is Rachel O'Connor. I'm calling from the Leafe Agency. I heard you were one of Zenith's victims.'

'That's right.' I feel a tingle of excitement. Everyone in advertising in Dublin knows who Rachel O'Connor is.

'I've been looking at your previous work,' says Rachel. '*Very* impressive.'

'Oh!' I say. 'Thanks very much.'

'How would you feel,' she says, 'about joining us here for a few months? We need someone good to work on a couple of jobs we've got lined up.'

She tells me about the jobs. She tells me what I'd get paid. I close my eyes and mouth 'thank you' to the universe. My career isn't over after all.

'That sounds great,' I say.

'Brilliant!' says Rachel. 'We won't need you for another three weeks – does that suit you?'

'It absolutely does,' I say.

Katie and Jeanne are delighted by my news, but although the call has boosted my spirits and my confidence, I'm still a nervous wreck at the prospect of seeing Tadhg.

'I hate all my clothes,' I say.

'Well, I don't hate all your clothes and I have excellent taste,' says Katie. She's perched on my bed, surrounded by half the contents of my wardrobe, which I have spent the last hour trying on and then flinging away in disgust.

'I know I'm acting like this is a date or something ...'

'It is you who say it,' says Katie solemnly.

'But I ... Oh *God*, I know this is pathetic, but I really want to look my absolute best,' I say. 'So he doesn't have a reason to look at me and think, *Ah, God love her, the years have not been kind.*'

'First of all, they've been very kind, so kind that I'm starting to worry you've got a portrait in the attic like Dorian Gray,' says Katie. 'And second of all, *he will not think that!*'

'Well, I definitely won't look like the glitzy celebs he usually hangs out with,' I say. 'They all have designer wardrobes and, more importantly, stylists.'

Katie jumps off the bed, heads to the wardrobe and grabs a seventies day dress I got when I went to Paris last year. My last-ever holiday with Dave, though of course I didn't know it at the time. That doesn't seem so important now.

'Wear this,' she says. 'It's gorgeous, it's flattering and you can never, ever go wrong with vintage. It's literally priceless.'

'It cost thirty quid,' I say, 'in a kilo shop in the Marais where you pay by weight.'

'Tadhg won't know that!' says Katie. 'This dress is the sort of thing those celebrities send their stylists out to find. That's why it's beyond a mere financial price. Its value is that there is nothing else like it out in the world. You can always be confident in vintage, because what vintage says is simply that you have exquisite taste.'

Well, when she puts it like that …

'Wow, Katie,' I say. 'You should be a stylist or a life coach instead of a history teacher.'

'No way,' says Katie. 'I'd miss the long holidays.'

At one o'clock the next afternoon, I'm nervously pushing open the door of the restaurant. I'm wearing the Paris dress with black tights and stack-heeled ankle boots, and I spent an embarrassing amount of time on my make-up, trying to make myself look naturally radiant and fresh-faced. It's mercifully dim inside, the sort of low, warm light that screams 'luxury'. There are booths running down one wall, offering customers a modicum of privacy.

A haughty maître d' bars my path. 'Do you have a reservation?'

I draw myself up to my full height (five foot five, thanks to the heels). 'I'm meeting Tadhg Hennessy.'

His expression doesn't change. 'Oh yes? What's your name?'

I should have known it wouldn't be that straightforward. Otherwise any randomer who'd heard where a celeb was dining could roll up and claim they were joining them.

I sigh. 'Laura McDermott.'

The maître d' checks a list and then his expression does change. 'Ah. I beg your pardon. This way, please, madam.'

I follow him to the back of the restaurant, careful not to bump into a table in the elegant gloom.

And there, sitting in a booth, wearing a needlecord checked shirt, a navy blue cardigan and a pair of glasses that look like the ones he had in college, is Tadhg.

He's looking at his phone, thank God, so he doesn't see me until I'm practically at the table. I want to be cool, calm and sophisticated. I want to stride up there like classic Joan Collins on her way to buy up a rival's company. I want to just nod curtly, hold out my hand and say, 'Tadhg.'

Instead, as the maître d' discreetly melts into the background, I find myself raising my hand in a stupid half-wave and saying, 'Hey.'

He looks up at me, his face unreadable. And suddenly, for a second that feels like an eternity, I'm back there, I'm back then. I'm in a practice room in Connemara in 1999, I'm on a stage in 2002, I'm on a table in a flat off Camden Street in 2003, I'm at a bus stop on Westmoreland Street, I'm in all the times and all the places where Tadhg Hennessy and I locked eyes and couldn't look away from each other. Then he smiles that slightly awkward smile, straight out of 1999, and shakes his head and sort of laughs as if he can't quite believe what he's seeing.

'Wow, Lol,' he says. He looks down at the table for a brief moment, but when he looks up again the smile is a full-on beam. '*Fuck*, it's good to see you.'

And despite the fact that I'd planned to be haughty and aloof, despite the fact that I'm afraid he's trying to steal my song, despite everything that happened the last time we saw each other, despite all of this, something is happening to my face, I can't help it, and I realise that, despite all my better instincts, I'm smiling right back at him.

Oh, *shit*.

Chapter Seven

1999

In an ideal world I'd have given Tadhg some time to forget about my weirdness at the céilí before seeing him again. Like a week. Or maybe a month. But I had to go to the music room the next day. I couldn't miss the opportunity to possibly start a band. That didn't mean I wasn't nervous, though.

'I just have to go to the loo,' I said to Katie, as we made our way through the *coláiste* corridors. I needed a moment to compose myself.

'Stop dithering!' said Katie. 'We're already late.'

'I'll follow you on!' I said.

As I pushed open the door of the band room a few minutes later, it struck me that maybe Tadhg wouldn't be there and I'd been making a fuss over nothing, but he was there all right, already holding an electric guitar. There was no sign of his Evil Twin bandmate. Katie's new BFF, Brían, was sitting behind the drum kit, and Katie was standing by an impressive electric keyboard. Standing next to Tadhg was the shiny-haired girl who had glowered at me for speaking English on the bus the day before. Well, she needn't worry, it would be Irish-only in this room (apart from words like 'yeah' and 'okay', which even the sticklers couldn't object to).

'Laura!' cried Katie. 'You remember Tadhg and Brían from the céilí? And this is Caoimhe.'

'Hi,' I said.

'I'm just after telling Tadhg I think *maybe* we've seen his band on Grafton Street,' said Katie.

'Oh yeah,' I said. This was my chance to be a normal person. I turned to Tadhg and said, as casually as I could, 'I thought I recognised you.'

Tadhg said, 'I thought I recognised you too.'

Before I could say anything preposterous back to him, Caoimhe saved me from myself and said, 'We were just going to try working out a song. Do you play an instrument?'

'Um, guitar,' I said.

'Really?' said Tadhg. 'Cool.' He didn't say it in the disbelieving tone some boys used when they found out I played the guitar. He actually seemed impressed. 'We can both play guitar. There are two electrics. Do you want to play rhythm or lead, Laura?'

'I think I'll play rhythm,' I said, though I didn't really have to do too much thinking about it. If I was going to play the guitar in front of the boy of my dreams, I wanted to play in a way that gave me a chance to impress him. In my nervous state, I'd make a show of myself if I tried picking out any lead guitar lines.

'I'll play bass on the keyboard,' said Katie. Although Katie's main instrument was the not-so-rock-and-roll clarinet, she had done piano up to Grade One, so she was definitely up to the task of playing a simple bassline.

'What will you do?' I asked Caoimhe.

'I'll be singing,' she said. She looked uncertain, and I realised that, despite her head-girl vibe, she wasn't cocky. 'If no one minds.'

It was settled. I took down the other electric guitar from the wall and pulled the strap over my head. It was a battered Squier Stratocaster. I felt a little thrill of excitement as I grabbed a lead from a box and connected to it an amp. An electric guitar! I'd only ever had a go of one in a shop before.

'So … What song are we doing?' I said, after I'd tuned the guitar.

It turned out that while I was dithering in the loo, they had decided to figure out 'All Day and All of the Night' by the Kinks, a classic tight, loud pop song.

'We all know it,' said Tadhg, 'and the chords are easy.'

'Yeah, I can play it,' I said. I'd played it on my own in my room on my dad's old guitar plenty of times. And now I was going to play it with a band!

'I've already written new words for it in Irish,' said Caoimhe, holding up a piece of paper. 'They're not a translation. But the idea is the same.'

So the rehearsal began.

And we were *awful*.

I had to start the whole song off and I was so nervous I kept getting the rhythm wrong. But it wasn't just me. The drums were too loud. Then the keyboards were too quiet. Caoimhe's Irish lyrics might have looked good on paper, but they didn't always match the rhythm of the tune when she was actually singing them. Katie and Tadhg's backing vocals clashed. Tadhg tried to do the elaborate guitar solo from the original and it totally fell apart. It was an absolute mess. By the time we had staggered to the end of the song, I wanted to give up. I'd wanted to play with a band for so long, and now it turned out I was terrible at it. We were all terrible at it.

Except maybe we weren't. Because to my amazement, Tadhg said, 'Not too bad for a first try! Let's go again.'

So we did. And then we did it again. And again. And again. We played it for two hours. We only took breaks for the loo and to get water because it was hot and stuffy in that soundproofed practice room. And gradually, so gradually that for a while we weren't aware of it, we started to get better. Caoimhe tweaked her lyrics so they scanned better with the tune. Katie started hammering out a bassline and a top note on the piano that added an extra layer of percussion. I stopped overthinking and just let myself channel that gorgeous choppy garage riff. After a while, we stopped looking at our hands and the lyric sheet and started looking at each other instead, nodding our heads in time to the steady beat. It didn't matter that Tadhg was the boy I'd had a crush on for months because right now we were equals. We were part of a team. The five of us were in time now, we were in perfect sync, and when Tadhg finally played the solo perfectly, we all whooped and cheered. My right arm was aching, but I kept playing, slamming down each crunchy chord in perfect time with Brían's drums and Katie's bassline, and we were all joyfully singing our version of the final chorus and I didn't care that I couldn't sing, because now we weren't just a bunch of people who happened to play music. We were a band, playing as one, shouting together in pure joy and exhilaration.

'*An t-am, an t-am ar fad!*'

I smashed the last chord that finished the song and we all broke out into cheers and applause. Tadhg forgot we were meant to be speaking Irish and shouted, 'That was *brilliant*!' And Caoimhe was so flushed with happy excitement she forgot to give out to him.

It was my first time hanging out with Tadhg Hennessy.

It was my first time playing in a band.

And I knew, as if I'd been hit by a thunderbolt, that I wanted to keep doing both of these things for the rest of my life.

Chapter Eight

2019

Tadhg looks famous, and it freaks me out.

I don't mean he's, like, bedecked in gold. He doesn't look flashy. His vibe is understated and normal. But there's something about people who are seriously successful that differentiates them from us ordinary mortals. He has a sort of *glow*. And then there are his clothes. You can *tell* the plain navy cardigan is cashmere, and not the M&S washable kind. Those jeans are from some obscure eco-friendly Japanese label. The materials of his Clark Kent glasses speak of a wildly expensive optician, not Specsavers. His boots are rich, polished brown leather. He doesn't look like he still scours charity shops for what we used to call 'old dead men's suits'. He looks at home in this fancy restaurant. It feels a bit wrong.

And maybe it's the money, maybe it's clean living, maybe it's just good genes, but up close and personal, when he stands up to greet me, it's clear that the years have definitely been kind to him. His dark hair is still thick and wavy, cut short in the back and a little bit longer at the front, the way it always was. His skin is radiant, but with a few normal fine lines around his eyes. His face moves naturally. He doesn't have that slightly embalmed, tanned look of some male rock stars over thirty-five. His excellent cheekbones and strong nose are as satisfying to behold as they were twenty years ago. Even with the cashmere and the expensive jeans, he still looks like himself.

He looks very, very good.

I silently thank Katie for the vintage recommendation. Most of my regular new clothes would look tatty next to Tadhg's quiet luxury. And then I hate myself for caring so much about what he thinks of me.

We stand there by his table for a moment. He still looks pretty happy to see me, and for a moment I think he might be going to hug me and I'm not sure what I'd do if he did, but then he says, 'Sorry, where are my manners? Take a seat.'

I slide into the booth and realise that, while a booth with leather seats might be good for a celebrity's privacy, it's quite difficult to get in and out of with elegance and grace. I have to keep pulling my skirts from under me as I make my way along the padded leather.

'So …' I say. I'm about to say it's good to see him, because it is, despite everything it really is, but before I can say anything a smiling young woman with amazing hair and a dress I almost bought in Cos during the week but didn't because, well, I'm unemployed and also six inches shorter than her, approaches and says, 'Hi! You must be Laura. I'm Tara.'

'Hi,' I say, accepting her handshake before she sits down next to Tadhg. 'Nice to meet you.' A part of me is glad someone's here to buffer any potential awkwardness between me and Tadhg. Another, shamefully bigger, part of me is disappointed that he and I can't just talk on our own.

'You too! Have you had a look at the menu yet?'

A server miraculously appears at her side and presents us with menus.

I feel slightly faint as I read the prices. Tadhg orders first, a starter and a main. So this is going to be a proper long lunch. He orders sparkling water for the table then says, 'Sorry, do you want wine, Lol? I'm driving so I'll give it a miss.'

Though not a boozy one, which is probably for the best.

'No, thanks.' I need to keep a clear head.

Once we've ordered, silence descends on the table. I think of the days when Tadhg and I couldn't stop talking to each other and feel a sharp twinge of sadness. Tadhg looks as awkward as I feel. Thankfully, Tara breaks the silence.

'So, Laura,' she says breezily. 'I suppose you're wondering why we contacted you out of the blue.'

'You said it's about my song.' My voice sounds firm and controlled, to my own surprise, because I feel anything but.

'Your and *Tadhg's* song.' Tara's voice is still bright but now it's steely.

'Well, we played it together when we were in the band,' I say, 'but I wrote it.'

I don't look at Tadhg as I say it.

'Ms McDermott—' says Tara.

Oh, it's Ms McDermott now, is it?

'I wrote the chords,' I say. 'And I wrote the melody. And the words.'

'Do you have any proof of that?' says Tara.

I knew that's what all this was about. I fucking *knew* it. But I feel like I've been kicked in the stomach, all the same.

'Tara,' says Tadhg. 'Do you mind if I talk to Laura alone, just for a minute?'

'Sure,' says Tara.

She slips out of the booth and takes a seat at the bar. I look over and see her fiddling with her phone, but she keeps glancing over at us. Probably worried I'm going to leap over the table and attack Tadhg for trying to steal my song. Well, she needn't worry – if I wanted to attack him I'd have to wriggle out of this banquette first and that would take about ten minutes so he'd have plenty of time to make his escape.

'I'm sorry about that,' says Tadhg. He takes off his glasses and rubs his eyes. 'Tara's brilliant at her job and she's really sound, but as far as she's concerned this is just another business meeting. I'm not sure she gets how … well, how close we were.'

Oh. I didn't realise I needed to hear him acknowledge this. But it turns out I did.

'Well,' I say faintly. 'That was a long time ago.'

'Yeah,' he says. There's a moment of silence, but somehow it's not as awkward now. Tadhg clears his throat. 'The reason

I wanted to see you is because a few weeks ago I found myself playing that song and remembering how good it was. I want to finally finish it with you. Together. As co-writers.'

I don't say anything. I did not expect this.

'It's a really good song,' he says.

'I know.'

'And it'll be better if it's finished,' he says earnestly. 'I think we could make something great out of this, Lol. We were so good together.'

My eyes meet his and my breath stops.

'We were good together sometimes.' I take a sip of water.

'We were good together a *lot* of the time,' he says. The banquette suddenly seems small. I could reach my hand across the table to touch his, if I wanted to. If I dared. I can still remember what it felt like to hold those hands.

I pull myself together. I should tell him that he's thinking of another Laura. I should tell him that until this week I hadn't played my guitar in almost a year. I should tell him that the Laura he knew – the Laura who didn't write ads for pensions, the Laura who wrote songs and made people stare at her in awe when she played them on stage – doesn't exist anymore.

I should tell him all this. I know I should.

But when was I ever totally honest with Tadhg?

I say, 'How exactly do you want to do this?'

Tadhg looks relieved, as if he half-expected me to walk out before he could make his case. Then the waiter arrives with our starters.

'Let's talk about it in a minute,' he says, waving at Tara to join us.

The food is delicious. Between mouthfuls, Tadhg says, 'So, are you still working in advertising?'

'How did you know I worked in advertising?' I try not to sound as taken aback as I feel, but his expression suggests I've failed.

'Um, through Brian,' he says. 'Sorry, is it weird that I know? I just asked how you were doing and he told me.'

Brian, aka Brían, is an academic now and lives in Bristol. I knew he and Tadhg had stayed in touch. Tadhg couldn't make Brian's wedding five years ago because he was playing some massive gig in Japan. I remember how I felt when I realised I wasn't going to see him there. A mixture of huge relief and massive disappointment.

'No, of course it's not weird,' I say. It *does* feel a bit weird, but neither Tadhg nor Brian has done anything wrong or inappropriate. 'And yes, I am. Working in advertising, I mean. I'm freelance, but I'm starting a new job soon.'

'So does that mean you're free right now?' says Tara.

'Maybe,' I say warily.

'Good,' she says. 'So you should be able to spend some time in Tadhg's studio working on the song.'

I bristle at the assumption that I can afford to spend my time faffing around a millionaire's musical playroom.

'Well, it depends,' I say. 'As I said, I'm self-employed. I can't just ... not work or stop looking for work.'

'Oh God, I'm sorry.' Tadhg looks embarrassed. 'I should have made it clear. You'd be paid for your time.'

'You'd be working from ten to five, at top session-musician day rates,' says Tara. And she names a sum that is well over twice as much as I was planning to charge per day for doing a freelance stint in an ad agency. 'More if you end up working late.'

I stifle a gasp. This is a *lot* of money.

'Where's the studio?' I bet it's out in Wicklow or Meath or something. And it'll take me an hour and a half to get there every day. Oh well, now I've heard the day rate I'd be willing to take three buses to earn it.

'Fairview,' says Tadhg.

I think I'm hearing things. 'What do you mean, Fairview?'

'Come on, Lol, you know what Fairview is. The northside suburb. You know Marino Crescent?'

Of course I know Marino Crescent. It's the only Georgian crescent in Dublin, a beautiful curved row of tall eighteenth century houses situated two miles from the city centre, facing a little park that used to be the owners' private garden but is now open to all.

But more relevant to me is the fact that it's fifteen minutes' walk from Katie and Jeanne's house.

'You have a studio in Marino Crescent?' I think I must be goggling at him.

'Well, and a house. I live there.'

'I'm sorry, *what*?'

How the hell did I not know that? I've been buying vegetables at the little grocer's across the road from the Crescent for the last eight months! But I suppose Tadhg isn't exactly popping into the local shops. I picture the Crescent and realise that one house isn't quite like the others. While the rest of the front gardens are bordered by low painted iron railings or hedges, one house has erected an elegant 'green wall' full of plants, as well as a high wooden gate. There are lots of cameras too. As if whoever lived there really cared about their privacy and security and didn't want to give callers easy access to the front door. And actually, you do sometimes see quite a lot of teenagers hanging around in the little park in front of the houses. I always thought they were kids from the school down the road. But now I come to think of it, lots of them had that indefinable style (and, in many cases, the golden tans) that suggested they were from America or continental Europe rather than a community school in rainy north Dublin.

'Is it the house with the plant wall?' I say suddenly.

'Yeah.' Tadhg looks surprised. 'How do you know it?'

'I live down the road,' I say. 'Just off Philipsburgh Avenue.'

'You do not,' he says, laughing in disbelief.

I can't help laughing back. 'I do. I'm in Fresh Market practically every day. God, I can't believe you live in such an ordinary area.'

'Well, I did grow up down the road in Clontarf,' he says, as if I'd forgotten.

'Yeah, I know! But I assumed you'd live in Killiney or Dalkey or somewhere equally posh now.'

Tadhg shrugs. 'Sure what would I do out in Dalkey?'

'Hang around with Bono? I don't know what they do over there!'

'Well, exactly,' says Tadhg. 'Neither do I. Northside for life!'

We're grinning at each other now.

A memory hits me. 'Do you remember whatshername who went out with Brian? Caroline? She told us you couldn't walk around the northside without getting mugged.'

Tadhg laughs. 'She was convinced it was like *Mad Max* once you crossed the Liffey.'

'She said we were "so brave" living there!' I say.

'She's probably running an investment bank now,' says Tadhg.

'No way,' I say. 'She did History of Art. I bet her parents bought her a little gallery or a lifestyle boutique or something.'

And then I remember that these days Tadhg could buy someone a little gallery or lifestyle boutique if he wanted. I pull myself together. Tadhg and I aren't the same anymore. And I can't be won over by a little trip down memory lane.

The main courses arrive, and as I'm eating the most exquisite thing I've ever put in my mouth, Tara says, 'So, Laura. If you do agree to join Tadhg in the studio, you'll have to sign a few things.'

Oh, here we go.

I sigh. 'I'm sorry, Tara.' Although I'm not sorry at all. 'I'm not signing away the rights to my song.'

'I didn't mean that.' Tara's tone is more soothing now. 'No one's trying to take any rights. It's a standard contract for session musicians. And, well, there'll be an NDA.'

'*What?*' I feel my cheeks grow hot. 'Do you think I'd ... I dunno, sell stories about Tadhg to the press?'

'Tara, Laura doesn't have to sign an NDA,' says Tadhg firmly. 'If she wanted to sell any stories about me – and I don't think you ever would, Lol, don't look at me like that – she could have done it years ago. It's fine.'

I'm aware that he could be just playing the good cop to Tara's bad cop, but I feel slightly consoled.

'Sorry, Laura.' Tara's tone is still brisk. 'It's just a formality.'

'Not needed in this case,' says Tadhg.

'So, about the schedule,' says Tara. 'Tadhg has a small window of free time this month, so if you're free too, how about the next few weeks? Could you come in then?'

'I haven't said I'll do it yet,' I say.

'But if you do?'

Things seem to be happening very quickly. Maybe I should pretend I'm incredibly busy next week, keep them waiting, give me time to think.

But I'm not busy next week. I'm not going to be starting at Leafe for a while. And it hits me that if I accept Tadhg's offer I could pay Katie a *lot* more rent with the money. I could actually give her and Jeanne something in return for all their kindness to me over the last eight months. I really could pay off a chunk of their window loan. I might even be able to pay the rental deposit on a place of my own.

'If I say yes, next week would be okay, if I move stuff around,' I say, 'what exact time frame are we talking about?'

'Two weeks in the studio, if it's working well,' says Tadhg. 'Then I have to go to Nashville for a while.'

I'm still cagey. 'And if it's not working well?'

'If, at any time, you feel it's really not working then we call it a day,' says Tadhg. 'But you'll still be paid for the whole fortnight.'

Oh shit, this really is too good to turn down. I'd be playing music again for two whole weeks. And what's more, I'd be getting paid to do it. I just have to make sure that I'm not going to be bamboozled by money and helping Katie and conveniently located studios. I have to make sure I don't let Tadhg or his bad cop take away the best song I ever wrote. I have to remember this is just for a fortnight – and then back to normality. But I can do that. I can hold firm.

Can't I?

I take a deep breath.

'Okay,' I say. 'I'll do it.'

'Excellent,' says Tara cheerily.

'Thanks a million, Lol.' Tadhg's smile is warm as he raises a glass of sparkling water in a toast. 'You won't regret it.'

I really, really hope he's right.

Chapter Nine

1999

The thing about me and Tadhg is that, from that very first practice until it all fell apart four years later, and despite everything that happened, things were never really awkward between us.

I can't explain it easily. I fancied him madly, but somehow, after that first session in the band room, we just *clicked* together. I felt ... safe with him. Comfortable. And yes, sometimes I would look at his forearms as he skilfully played the guitar or at his profile, the line of his jaw taut with concentration, as he worked out a solo line, and I'd be hit by a wave of pure lust so strong that I sometimes found myself biting gently on my knuckle. But combined with that strong attraction there was an easiness, one that I had never, ever felt with a boy before.

At first, maybe it was all the happy hormones triggered by playing together that made us so comfortable with each other. When, on the afternoon of our first practice, a bell rang to signal that it was time for the students to head back to our various houses for tea, we all agreed we'd be spending our afternoons in the band room for the rest of the fortnight. When we left the *coláiste*, Katie was deep in conversation with Brían and Caoimhe, and I found myself walking out with Tadhg, chatting as if we'd been friends for years. And even through the stiltedness of talking in Irish, we just … got on. He told me he and his curly-haired friend Ciarán went to a state school in Raheny (so he wasn't a posh southsider).

'Ciarán didn't really want to be in the Evil Twins but his brother has a drum kit so we … How do you say 'pressganged' in Irish?'

He asked where me and Katie were from, and when I said Drumcondra he grinned down at me and said, 'I knew it. *Aithníonn* northsider northsider *eile*!' and instead of dying with shame I laughed because it was clear he wasn't being mean and instead had made me feel like we already had a little in-joke. He asked me how I learned to play the guitar, and we bonded over how much we each wanted an electric guitar of our own. I told him about being patronised by men and boys when I went into guitar shops, and he sympathised and said his bandmate Susie experienced the same thing. 'They always think I'm the one who wants to play the bass and she's just my girlfriend.'

'Is she your girlfriend?' I said, trying to sound nonchalant.

To my huge relief, he laughed and said, 'God, no! We live on the same road. She's like my sister.'

It wasn't like my fantasies of instant connection in Dublin city centre. It was better. It was funnier. We were bandmates now. We were friends.

He and Brían were staying in the same house, and we kept talking until we reached the turn-off that led to it. After I bid him farewell I guiltily turned around to find Katie was still deep in conversation with Brían. She didn't seem to care that I had accidentally been monopolising Tadhg and I felt a wave of relief. When the boys left we caught each other's eyes and I said, 'Well!'

'I did not see this coming,' said Katie in English.

'Are we in a band with Blues Explosion Boy?' I said.

'And do I fancy one of those rugby boys?' said Katie.

'Well,' I said. 'You did say he was "not terrible".'

From that day on, I was dreading the end of the course, and time seemed to speed up as the fortnight went on. We spent every afternoon in the band room figuring out and perfecting different cover songs. I'd always been a bit lazy in school, but I never minded working hard in that band room. Now that I understood we needed to practise each song for ages in order to sound good, being in a band was everything I'd hoped it would be. I spent so many hours playing the guitar, the fingertips on my left hand developed blisters, which turned into tiny, smooth calluses.

Eight days into the course we went on an outing to a beach.

Tadhg sat next to Caoimhe on the bus, across the aisle from me and Katie, and when I caught the way she looked at him I felt a surge of jealousy so strong I felt sick. How had I not realised she liked him before?

I couldn't see how he was looking at her.

When we got to the beach, the sun was out. People started paddling, including Caoimhe and her school friends, shrieking at the chill of the Atlantic. The sea was too cold for me, so I left my own friends ankle-deep in the water and sat on a rock gazing out towards America, away from the crowd, and tried not to think about Tadhg and Caoimhe. It was peaceful up there. And surprisingly warm for April.

A shadow fell over me. I looked up, shielding my eyes from the sun's warm glare.

'Hey,' said Tadhg. 'Can I sit here?'

'You can.' I scooched over so he could sit next to me on the warm rock.

'There's no one nearby.' Tadhg lowered his voice. 'Do you think we could …?'

I looked up at him. He pushed back a lock of dark hair and looked left and right before turning back to face me. My mouth felt very dry. I mean, I definitely thought we could, but here? We weren't *that* far away from the rest of the group!

'Speak English?' whispered Tadhg, in English.

'Oh!' I said. 'Um …'

'I mean, I do actually like speaking Irish. I just thought,' Tadhg continued in English, 'it'd be cool to talk without having to wonder if we actually know how to say what we want to say. Do you know what I mean? Shit, I think I might have *forgotten* how to speak English.'

I swallowed. 'Same,' I said, in English.

'Okay, great,' said Tadhg. 'Actually I didn't just come over for chats *as Béarla*, I came to tell you Áine just asked if we'd like to play a few songs on the last night.'

I stared at him. 'Seriously?'

'Yeah! Like a mini-gig.'

'Wow,' I said. I felt I should take better advantage of this English-speaking interlude and say something witty and clever, but this gig news had thrown me.

'So what do you think? It'd be cool to finish things up with a proper show.'

'It would but ... I've never played in front of an audience before.' My stomach churned a bit at the thought. It was one thing fantasising about playing on stage. It was another to actually do it.

'You'll be grand!' said Tadhg. 'You're a brilliant guitarist. You're better than me.'

'No, I'm not,' I said honestly. I couldn't play a fancy solo if I tried.

'You really are,' said Tadhg. 'You don't just strum basic chords like some annoying lad at a party, you find interesting ways to play them. And you always look so ...'

He stopped.

'So what?' I said.

'You look confident,' he said eventually. 'When you're playing. You make it look like it's not a big deal to play as well as you do. It's very cool.'

I tried to play things down so he wouldn't know that these words had made a light go on inside my chest. I laughed. 'That's proof that I should go into acting, not music. I don't feel very confident.'

'Well, you should,' said Tadhg.

There was something in the air between us, just for a moment, but I didn't know what to do with it so I said, 'What about you? You're not exactly unconfident yourself.'

'See, this is why it's good to have a little English-break,' said Tadhg. 'I wouldn't know how to say confident in Irish, let alone unconfident. Though is that even a word in English? Anyway, I'm not that confident – it's just that busking is so terrifying that after you've done it once, no other gig can ever scare you.'

'Really?'

'Oh, yeah! The first time you open your mouth and start singing in the street, it feels so incredibly wrong. Every part of your brain is going "Shut up!". But you get used to it. I'm going to miss doing it. And not just because we get decent money now.'

'Your band's not splitting up, is it?' I sat up a bit straighter.

'Well, kind of,' he said. 'We have to spend our Saturdays studying until the Leaving exams. Then Susie's going to visit her grandparents in Korea for the summer. And I think Ciarán will refuse to keep going anyway. Which is fair enough – he never wanted to be in a band.'

He turned to look at me and I was suddenly very conscious of how close he was. 'But you know,' he said, 'once the exams are over, we should keep this Coláiste Laoise band going. I mean, we all live in Dublin ...' Then I heard someone calling our names and realised that everyone was heading back to the bus.

'Back to Irish then.' Tadhg jumped down from the rock. He reached up his left hand to help me down.

'Guitarist's fingers,' he said in English as I landed on the sand. He hadn't let go of my hand. His thumb moved over my fingers, the shiny invisible calluses on the tips. It felt as intimate as a kiss.

'What?'

'Your fingertips. You can tell you play the guitar.'

And, astonished at my own daring, I moved my thumb over his fingertips, felt the same calluses there. 'You too.'

'Tadhg! Laura! Come on!' Áine was looking over at us, tapping her watch.

I let go of him as if I'd been burned and we hurried over to the bus.

But I could still feel the touch of his hand on mine.

Chapter Ten

2019

The Birthday Party

You: So ... guess who I met for lunch today?

Katie: Heads-up, I already know because I live with her, so let us please skip this guessing-game tomfoolery because I don't trust myself not to blurt it out.

You: Okay fine. I don't trust you not to blurt it out either.

You: I met Tadhg.

Aisling: What Tadhg?

Sarah: OMG TADHG Tadhg?!!!!! Hennessy?

Aisling: I'm sorry what? You know Tadhg Hennessy?????

You: Yup. We were in a band together in college.

Aisling: 🫠

Aisling: WHY DID NONE OF YOU EVER TELL ME LAURA WAS IN A BAND WITH TADHG HENNESSY?

Sarah: They had a big fight! And then we were forbidden to mention his name ever again!

You: He contacted me out of the blue and now I'm going to his house next week to work on some music.

Sarah: WHAT?! This is insane.

You: You're telling me!

Aisling: How? Why? When?

You: It's a long story ...

Sarah: Please get a photo with him. I need to prove to Ellie that I haven't been lying about knowing him back in the day. Why did we never take cameras on nights out back then?

You: There will be no photos! They almost made me sign a fucking NDA.

Sarah: WTF?

You: If you're free to meet at the weekend I'll tell you all about it!

Sarah: Hell yes. Friday 8pm at the usual place if we can get a table?

Aisling: I'll have to see if Kev can look after Síofra. But if so then definitely yes!

I roll my eyes when I read this but I don't say anything in the chat. It's not my place to tell Aisling what I think about her husband's approach to childcare, which is basically that he goes out with his mates whenever he likes without checking with her in advance, but on the rare occasions that she wants to see her friends in the evening she has to ask him to look after his own daughter. Like he's doing Aisling a favour. And then he gets all helpless and acts like he doesn't know how to change a nappy and rings Aisling when she's in the middle of dinner asking where the wet wipes are. I've always got on really well with Kev, but I've seen a new side of him since he and Aisling became parents two years ago. It's like she's married to someone from the fifties.

Not that I would say any of this to Aisling. She seems happy, and I am very aware it's none of my business. I have said it to Katie, though, more than once. But not Sarah. Three of us talking about Aisling's marriage would feel really bitchy. Besides, Sarah could say, with justification, that Katie and I don't know what parenthood is like. I don't think she *would* say it, but she could.

Sarah's daughter Ellie is twelve now and a huge Tadhg fan. Sarah got pregnant with her when she was only twenty-four, very much not planned. Sarah seriously considered going over to England for an abortion, as Katie had done a year earlier. But she and her boyfriend Rob decided that they were (just about) able to have a baby, albeit about ten years earlier than they had intended. Back then, no one we knew had kids, so it was pretty lonely for Sarah. But over the last couple of years, it feels like almost everyone has had a baby. Everyone except me, obviously.

You never really notice the path society sets out for you until you step off it. One minute I was doing the same acceptable middle-class thirty-something things as most of my friends. I had a long-term relationship and a permanent job. I was about to get married. I was about to have kids.

And now … I'm not.

But I'm about to do something else.

On Friday, Katie and I are the first to arrive at our favourite Korean restaurant, and I'm relieved to have a little breathing room. Despite the fact that our lives are all quite different now, our gang still gets on as well as ever. Whenever we're together we always quickly fall into the easy shorthand of old friendship, full of jokes and confidences. But since Dave and I split up I've been conscious of a sense of … difference, I suppose. For years we were all in serious relationships, and while both Aisling and Sarah had kids, Katie and I didn't, so I wasn't the odd one out. But since last year I've been the only single one. And not just the single one, the tragically dumped one. The one living in her friend's spare room. The one who no longer says 'we' when talking about future plans. Sometimes I feel that the others are avoiding talking about things they're doing with their partners because they don't want me to feel left out, which of course makes me feel even more left out. I'm aware that this feeling is probably in my head, but I can't help it. I can't bear the thought of them feeling sorry for me. Poor dumped, lonely Laura.

But would anyone feel sorry for someone who was going into a studio to work with a rock star? Hmmm. They would not.

Over delicious dak galbi and bibimbap, I give Aisling a very edited version of my history with Tadhg and tell her and Sarah about Tara and Tadhg and the studio. They make suitable noises of amused amazement and then Sarah says, 'Do you trust him?'

'I dunno.' I take a sip of water. 'I mean, after talking to him I don't seriously think he's got an evil scheme to steal my song from me. He hasn't changed that much.'

'Well, that's good,' says Aisling.

'But … do I think he might be keeping his hands clean and his conscience clear while his team play hardball and try to give me a flat fee for the full rights to the song I wrote so he can make a fortune with it and leave me with pennies? Um, maybe. I mean, perhaps you don't get to be as successful as him without being a *bit* ruthless.'

'Wow, it really is bizarre, isn't it?' Katie shakes her head. 'All this fuss and secrecy about someone we once saw dance to Five's 'Everybody Get Up' in a glorified school hall in Connemara.'

'I doubt he thinks you're stupid enough to sell your rights. And he does want to get you involved,' Aisling points out. 'If he wanted to steal an ancient song, he could just steal it.'

'He might,' says Sarah 'just really, really want to see you again.' She looks innocently up at the ceiling as I glower at her. I would rather die than admit it out loud, but that thought has crossed my mind.

Later we move to the bar part of the restaurant, and after we order pints, Aisling and Katie go out to the smoking area, where they will each smoke one cigarette from a packet Katie has been taking on nights out for literally months. This always happens when we meet up. Both officially gave up years ago, but every so often they smoke just one, 'just to prove we don't need to!'. I'm pretty sure any addiction expert would argue against this, but I've given up.

After they leave, Sarah says, 'Are you still okay to come to Ellie's birthday party next month?'

'Of course!' I say. 'Why do you ask?'

'After everything with Dave,' says Sarah, 'I wasn't sure you'd want to do, you know, happy family stuff.'

I smile at her. 'It's very good of you to ask. But I'm grand. Seriously.' And I mean it. I nudge her with my arm. 'What if I ask Tadhg to film a birthday message for Ellie as a surprise?'

'That would make her year!' says Sarah. And then she's quiet for a moment.

'Everything okay?' I say.

She takes a deep breath. 'I'm sorry, I wasn't sure I should tell you this tonight but ...'

Words like that never mean something good is coming. I brace myself.

'Dave is seeing someone,' says Sarah.

I thought I'd known this already. I'd guessed anyway. The girl in his Insta stories. But somehow hearing it confirmed hurts more than I thought it would.

'Is her name Liz?' I say.

'Um, yeah.' Sarah looks surprised, then sighs. 'Oh, Laura, I thought you'd have seen sense and blocked him on Insta by now.'

'How do you know?' I pause. 'How *long* have you known?'

'Just since last night!' says Sarah. 'Rob bumped into them in town. He was out with his old school friends, and Dave and this woman were at the next table.'

'Oh.' I have a ridiculous urge to go out and smoke one of Katie's cigarettes. 'Did they look ... Is it serious?'

'I honestly don't know,' says Sarah. 'Rob couldn't exactly ask them. I'm so sorry, Laura. I hate being the bringer of shit news.'

I stare down at the table. Dave has a new girlfriend. Instead of Dave and Laura, it's Dave and Liz. Maybe he just has a thing for women whose names begin with *L*.

'Well, I suppose it's been over eight months.' I can't believe I'm almost defending him.

'If he had any sense, he'd still be mourning letting you slip through his fingers.'

'It's better for me that I slipped,' I say, and I really do believe that, but when Sarah goes to the loo, I unfollow Dave on Instagram. I don't want to see his happy new life anymore. And I don't give a shit if he knows that or not.

Because I know – I really do know – that I'm better off without him.

But still, but still, but still. I don't want to see how much better off he is without me.

When Katie and Aisling return, we all bundle into a taxi and head to Katie's house because, as Sarah declares every five minutes of the journey, 'There are preparations to be made!'. Like choosing an outfit for my first day with Tadhg. I don't want to wear polyester vintage frocks in a hot, stuffy studio every day for two weeks, so I'd better set an attainable style standard early on. I want something casual but also cool. With my friends' help, I eventually decide on a pair of high-waisted wide-legged jeans and a cotton patterned button-up shirt I bought in the Parisian kilo shop where I got the excellent dress I wore to Tadhg's lunch.

'You'll look like a thirties bohemian crossed with an American housewife in a seventies film,' says Aisling approvingly.

'My two biggest fashion inspirations,' I say honestly.

'Tadhg will be very impressed,' says Sarah.

'Maybe my incredible style will distract him from how rusty my guitar playing is now,' I say.

'Well,' says Katie. 'There's something you can do about that ...'

A few minutes later, the three of them are bellowing out 'Wicked Game' while I play along on guitar. I'm a little awkward at first, but my hands quickly remember what to do.

I'm good at this. How did I forget how good I am at this?

We move on to 'Jolene', and soon a wine-fuelled singing session is in full swing.

'Play one of your band's old songs!' cries Aisling, after we open a second bottle.

I shake my head. 'I can't. Tadhg was the singer.'

'Oh my God, I can't believe you're on, like, first-name terms with Tadhg Hennessy.' Aisling pretends to swoon. 'But come on, you can sing them now, can't you?'

Katie and Sarah exchange glances.

'Lol doesn't sing in public,' says Katie.

'We don't count as the public!' protests Aisling.

'She didn't even sing in front of her band!' says Sarah.

'But how did you write songs?' Aisling looks confused.

'When I wrote the vocal melodies I'd sing them at home in my room where no one could hear me,' I say. 'Or I'd hum them in my head. And then I'd play the tunes for Tadhg on a keyboard at band practice so he could learn them.'

'So who wrote the words?' says Aisling.

'Both of us,' I say. 'But mostly him. The words always came later, after we'd come up with the melodies.'

'Well, who needs Tadhg,' says Katie, 'when you've got us? Come on Lol, play 'I Know Him So Well'.'

'All right,' I say. 'But I'm not singing it.'

I keep playing cover songs, and the others keep singing them, and I realise just how many songs are still inside me, songs I haven't played for so long. When Jeanne comes home, she joins the session, singing Françoise Hardy songs in her husky, sweet voice.

'I didn't know you could sing like that!' I say. 'Maybe you should be going round to Tadhg's studio instead of me.'

Jeanne shakes her head.

'Absolutely not!' she says. 'You're the only one he wants.'

Chapter Eleven

2019

I feel jittery with nerves when I set out on Monday morning, carrying my Danelectro electric guitar in its padded case. I spent most of yesterday playing it. Tadhg was always saying what a good guitarist I was, and I want to make sure I'll live up to his memories. It takes me barely fifteen minutes to get to his house in Marino Crescent. The boundary of his property is too beautifully designed to look like a fortress, but that's almost what it feels like. The green walls separating his front garden from those on either side are at least ten feet high, as are the huge wooden gates facing the footpath. A smaller gate is embedded in the left-hand gate for pedestrian access. There's an intercom at the gatepost next to it; I press the button.

'Yes?' says a female voice. Maybe all our meetings will be attended by his staff. Maybe I'll never find out what it's like to be alone with Tadhg again.

'Hi. It's Laura. Um, McDermott.' I glance up and notice a security camera pointing at me.

With a buzz and a click, the smaller gate's lock releases, and I head through it and into a perfectly ordinary front garden. I'm not sure what I was expecting – not, like, topiary cut into the shapes of guitars or something. But I'm aware of a faint surprise that it's all so, well, normal. A narrow gravel drive and an electric car, which is plugged into a charging station. A paved path leading to the front door. Lots of plants. It's very nice, but it could be anybody's. You'd never know a music superstar lived here.

The front door (painted a very nice and doubtless expensive teal) opens and, to my relief, Tadhg is standing there, wearing an olive-green T-shirt with a navy shirt over it and what are possibly the same jeans he was wearing last week. I'm not sure what I would have done if I'd been greeted by a butler or something.

'Hey!' His smile is warm, genuine. I try to gauge the vibe. Are we just … going to keep pretending nothing bad happened sixteen years ago? Pretending we're just old pals who, because circumstances led them in different directions, haven't seen each other for over a decade and have now bumped into each other again?

But now I've decided to do this time in the studio, I need to make the best of it. If he wants to pretend, then I'll pretend too.

'Hello, neighbour,' I say.

'Come in!' He stands aside and I walk into the hall. The ceilings are high, the walls a lovely peacock blue covered in framed artwork, the floors beautifully polished parquet. The Danelectro case nearly bashes into a table.

'Brilliant, you brought your guitar,' says Tadhg. 'You found the place okay, then?'

'Well, I do only live down the road.'

'Of course, you said.' We stand there in the hall for an awkward moment. 'Um, do you want a cup of tea?'

'Sure.' Suddenly I have a flashback to 2003, our practice space in Brian's parents' garage in Stillorgan. Tadhg making endless cups of tea because he needed caffeine to keep going but he didn't like coffee. Same as me.

'The kitchen's back here,' says Tadhg. I follow him to the rear of the house, into an airy room with tall windows, eau de nil cabinets and a big table with the weekend papers still scattered across it. The table is a beautiful mid-century design rather than bog-standard Ikea, and there's a framed poster on the wall for an achingly cool indie film; I remember Tadhg wrote a song for the soundtrack that was nominated for an Oscar. Through the windows I can see a garden with what looks like a stable building at the end of it. I take a seat at the table as Tadhg fills the kettle and takes some mugs out of a cabinet. There's no sign of the person who answered the buzzer. An embarrassingly painful thought strikes me: just because the tabloids haven't reported that he has a new girlfriend doesn't mean he's still single. He's always been good at keeping his private life private.

'So it's just you living here?' As I say it, I realise it sounds like I'm fishing, and I suppose I am.

'Yeah.' He pops tea bags into the mugs. My shoulders relax a little.

Tadhg turns to face me and leans back against the kitchen counter as the kettle starts to steam. 'It's a bit big for one person,' he says. 'I'm kind of rattling around in it.'

I fight the urge to roll my eyes. Am I seriously meant to feel sorry for him, living in his big four-storey townhouse while I'm lodging in Katie's spare room?

'Well, there's a housing crisis going on, you should take in lodgers.' Then I catch the look on his face. 'Jesus, I was joking! I'm not trying to guilt-trip you.' Although maybe I kind of was.

Neither of us says anything for a moment.

Tadhg runs a hand through his already messy hair. 'God, Lol, this is really weird.'

At least he's acknowledging it.

'Yeah,' I say. 'It's strange for me too.'

'I don't just mean us … talking again.' He turns back to the counter and pours water into the mugs. They're good mugs, seventies-style ochre-coloured earthenware.

'What *do* you mean?' He's taking milk out of the fridge now. I want to jump up and say I'll make my tea myself, to make sure it's just right, but I also want – I need – to hear what he has to say.

'I mean it's weird you seeing me like this,' he says. 'In this big house. With this … this life.'

'You don't see any other old friends?' I'm genuinely shocked at the thought. I can't imagine the Tadhg I knew back in the day ditching people because he got rich and famous.

Tadhg comes over to the table with the mugs, and it's his turn to look shocked. 'Of course I see old friends! Ciarán was here last week.'

'Then I don't get it.'

He passes me the tea, and for a split second our fingers touch.

'Most of my old mates, I saw them all the way through … everything.' He sits opposite me at the table. 'It all happened gradually. They were there when 'Winter' took off. They were there when I started playing bigger venues. They were there for the whole Glastonbury thing. But it's different with you. The last time we saw each other I wasn't …' He trails off, looking squirmingly embarrassed.

'Really fucking famous,' I finish for him.

'Um, yeah.' He looks down at his mug.

I take a sip of the tea. It's perfect – just the right amount of milk and …

My eyes widen and meet his. He half-smiles.

'Just barely a quarter teaspoon of sugar, right?' he says. 'I don't know why you look so surprised. I made you enough cups of tea back in the day.'

I smile back. I can't help it. He is, I realise with a start, the only other person who has *ever* made my tea exactly the way I like it. Even Dave always put in too much sugar and not enough milk. 'I suppose fame hasn't changed you *that* much.'

He takes a sip from his own mug. 'Well, I still drink about ten cups of tea a day, so I suppose you're right.'

'I bet you always take a box of proper tea when you go abroad,' I say.

'Of course I do.'

'So do I,' I admit. 'Though I'm squeezing it into a Ryanair-approved carry-on bag, not taking it on a private jet.'

'Laura,' he says, 'I have *never* gone near a private jet.'

'I know,' I say, and then realise this shows I've read about his vocal opposition to celebs using private planes. 'I mean, I'd assume so.' To change the subject I say, 'So you have to travel a lot?'

'All the time.' He doesn't look excited about it, so I change the subject again and ask what I've been wondering since he said he lived alone.

'Who buzzed me in earlier? Over the intercom?'

'Tara,' says Tadhg.

'Oh, right. Does she work here every day?'

'Oh no, she's not in the building,' says Tadhg. 'She's in my office in town. I just asked her to monitor the door this morning in case I was playing music too loud out in the studio when you arrived and didn't hear the buzzer there. She can access it remotely.'

Tadhg doesn't even have to answer his own doorbell. It *is* weird seeing him in this life.

'So ... how is this all going to work?'

'How's what going to work?' Tadhg looks at me across the

table, his expression quizzical. His glasses are slightly crooked and he clearly hasn't shaved today.

'I mean this whole thing,' I say. 'Me coming here.'

'Oh! Right,' says Tadhg. God, this is kind of excruciating. Every time I think we're being normal, things get awkward again. 'Well, I thought we could start by just playing music together before we try working on the song. Warm ourselves back up.'

It makes sense. Diving straight in to 'our song' would be too disorientating. It could bring up arguments too, and right now I think I have to keep things peaceful.

'Sure,' I say.

'Cool.' And then he grins. A proper smile, no awkwardness at all. 'Want to see the studio?'

'Wow.'

From the outside, the studio looks like what it is – the well-kept former stables at the bottom of the garden. But inside …

'It's beautiful!' I stare around at the blonde wood, the beautiful grand piano, the drum kit, the mid-century chairs and couches, the rugs on the floor, the collection of beautiful guitars sitting in their stands. We're in the main recording studio, having gone through an airlock-esque little entrance room and another room containing the sound desk. There's a vocal booth on the other side of the main studio space. It's so, so much nicer than any professional studio I have ever been to for work, and it's basically just his home office. It's also bigger than my and Dave's entire flat.

'Well, today it's all yours.'

As Tadhg walks over to the row of instruments, I forget that he's a rock star and this is his own private studio. I feel like we're in a music practice room again. I unzip my guitar case and pull out my beloved Danelectro. It's an aqua-blue pastel dream of an instrument, a retro confection, with a lovely twangy sound and a hot-pink vinyl strap. I feel guilty for ignoring it for so long. As I pull the strap over my head then take a lead out of the pocket of the case and plug it into an amplifier, I realise Tadhg is looking at me. Or rather at my guitar.

'Is that the same …?'

'Yeah,' I say. 'It's my old guitar.'

I wish I could say I then put my foot up on the amp and launch into an amazing solo, but instead I say, 'Um, have you got a tuner?'

Tadhg passes me one, picks up a bass, and we spend a minute tuning the instruments, which at least avoids another potentially awkward silence. Now here we are, facing each other, instruments in our hands. In a practice room together for the first time in sixteen years.

'Want to play a song?' says Tadhg.

'Sure.' I swallow. Why is my mouth so dry? Why is there no tea left in this charmingly retro mug? 'What's a good warm-up song?'

'D'you know 'Everything is Free'?'

I nod. Tadhg starts playing the bassline of the melancholy but beautiful Gillian Welch song – since when has he been a bass player? Years, probably – and I launch into the chords, making them spikier and sharper than they are on the acoustic original.

Then Tadhg starts singing, his gravel-and-honey voice blending perfectly with the bittersweet lyrics. I'm picking notes as well as playing chords, catching Tadhg's eye to make sure I come in at just the right moment, and for a few minutes we fall back into our old easiness, our old mutual understanding. How have I not done this in so long? We're at the final chorus now, and Tadhg lets the last note linger. When it ends, we stare at each other in silence.

'When was the last time you played with other people?' he says.

'Oh wow, I'm not sure.' I flop into a chair and lean back, holding the Danelectro across my body like a shield. 'Ten years ago, maybe?'

After our band split up I tried to start other bands. After I got my first job, I briefly joined another friend's band. But none of them lasted long. We never clicked musically. We never even got far enough to play any gigs. They were never right.

Nothing was ever as good as being in a band with Tadhg.

'Haven't you missed it?' says Tadhg.

And I have. Oh God, I have.

Chapter Twelve

1999

We approached that mini-gig at Coláiste Laoise with the seriousness and dedication of Beyoncé preparing for a stadium tour. The mini-concert would take place before a 'disco', which was replacing the usual céilí on the last night of the course. We'd play three songs, the choice of which we deliberated over as if we were negotiating a peace treaty. Then we practised. And practised. And practised.

Throughout it all, I was always aware of Caoimhe and the way she glanced at Tadhg when she thought he wasn't looking. Had he ever held *her* hand a little too long? In the evenings I'd look at them whenever they danced together at the céilís, my heart twisting every time she made him laugh. I couldn't hate her, though. She still had head-girl energy but I liked her. We were friends now. How could I blame her for being in love with him too?

♪♪

On the last night, I was so full of adrenalin I kept bouncing on the balls of my feet to try and shake it off.

'Oh shit.' I grabbed Katie's arm. 'I don't think I can do it.'

'Certainly you can!' said Katie. 'It'll be fun!'

But all I could think of, once we were up on the stage, was that I was going to play my first-ever gig and I was terrified of messing it up. I looked at my bandmates. Caoimhe looked like she was going to be sick. Brían was taking deep breaths. Only Tadhg and Katie looked unconcerned.

Everything suddenly went very, very quiet.

Then I looked out at the packed hall, at all those expectant faces, and I felt something I hadn't expected to feel. The energy surging through my body no longer felt like anxiety.

It felt like power.

We were a *band*. And we were going to give them a proper show.

'*A haon, a dó, a haon, dó, trí!*' shouted Brían, and we were off.

At first, I thought my fears were going to be realised. Brían was drumming slightly too fast, which threw us all off. Caoimhe tried to speed up the first line and had trouble breathing at the right moment. I could see people in the front row exchange sympathetic looks. I could almost hear their thoughts: *Jaysus, after all that practising you'd think they'd be better than this.*

But something happens when a band plays together, even after just a few weeks. You learn to communicate without words, you learn to sync up by catching each other's eyes, by looking at each other's hands. And that's what we started doing.

Now the song was back on track, and the awareness of this, combined with the palpable relief of the audience that we weren't going to crash and burn embarrassingly before their eyes, filled us all with a fresh wave of confidence. Suddenly we weren't just playing – we were *performing*. And we were, perhaps to our own amazement, kind of good at it.

Without being conscious I was doing it, my whole body was moving with the music, not just my hands. I looked straight down at the audience with a confidence that would have been unimaginable two weeks earlier. Some of the boys I'd been hanging around with for the last fortnight were looking back up at me as if they'd never seen me before.

When we finished the first song there was a split second of silence and then a roar of applause so loud it felt like we really were headlining a stadium. By the time we got to our Kinks cover, *'An t-Am ar Fad'*, the audience was dancing and singing along to the chorus. From the opening chords on, I was locked into the riff. When the song built up towards Tadhg's big solo, I threw my head back and held the guitar low, and as I looked down at the crowd, I felt like a fucking goddess.

I was almost eighteen, playing my very first gig. I was sweating, under the hot lights and the exertion of playing, and I knew my unruly hair must look even wilder now but I didn't care.

I thought, *I want to feel this way forever.*

When it was over, the crowd roared their approval and we all felt high as kites. Caoimhe flung her arms around me with such enthusiasm I nearly fell off the low stage. I hugged her back, then she was hugging Tadhg, and I was embracing Katie, and then Tadhg jumped down from the stage and I found myself facing him. The stage was only about a foot or so high and for the first time our faces were at the same level. Up close, the greeny-brown colour of his eyes was even more beautiful.

Suddenly his hands were on my face, his face was close to mine. 'You were brilliant, Laura!' *Bhí tú go híontach, Laura!*

And then he kissed me.

I was almost but not quite sure, *never* quite sure, that he was aiming for my cheek.

But just for a second, his lips brushed mine.

Then he drew back, looking faintly surprised at what he had done. We both kind of laughed but my mind was racing. Was that meant to be a proper kiss? Like, a *kiss* kiss? Was that the start of something? Or was it the sort of spontaneous kiss you'd plant on the cheek of a little kid or an extremely platonic friend? I didn't know, I couldn't know, and there was no time to analyse it because I had to get off the stage and we had to make our way through the crowd of unashamedly surprised friends and well-wishers and take our instruments back to the music room.

Fuck it, I thought. *I don't care how cheesy it is. I don't even care if he says no. If there's a slow set tonight I'll ask him to dance with me. I'll find out if that kiss meant something real, whatever it takes.*

Two hours of goofy dancing to chart hits later, it was almost the end of the night and there still hadn't been a slow set. Maybe I was never destined to dance with Tadhg like that. Maybe I would have to wait until we were back in Dublin to find out what that almost-kiss meant.

Then the first notes of 'My Heart Will Go On' rang out and everyone groaned theatrically.

'Oh no, they're actually doing it,' said Sarah.

Then one of the rugby lads came over and asked her to dance and she seemed quite pleased and said yes. Brían, looking extremely nervous, asked Katie.

Now I had no excuse for not asking Tadhg. I took a deep breath. Right. Where was he?

Hang on, seriously, where was he?

I scanned the room – Brían and Katie were shifting now, good for them – but there was no sign of Tadhg. And with a lurch, I realised there was no sign of Caoimhe either.

A few boys asked me to dance – 'I didn't know you could play like that! That was so cool!' said one – but I said no. The song seemed to last forever, and after a few minutes I couldn't take standing there on my own trying to hide how upset I was starting to feel, so I headed out to the loo, inconveniently situated at the end of a long corridor. Maybe I was being ridiculous. Maybe I'd go to the girls' bathroom and find Caoimhe there. Maybe …

I was almost at the bathroom when I saw the door of the band room was ajar. There was no light on inside. I went over to shut it and saw that someone was in there.

Two someones.

Tadhg and Caoimhe were sitting on the bench that ran down one side of the room. Their heads were close together, close enough to kiss if they just moved an inch.

And his hand was clasped in hers.

They didn't look up. I didn't know if they'd seen me. I just backed away and then ran down the corridor. I stayed in the bathroom so long that when I eventually returned to the hall, the slow set was finishing up and the night was ending. Tadhg and Caoimhe were already there, Tadhg standing with Ciarán, Caoimhe with her school friends. I avoided both of them. Áine gave a speech about what a great group we'd been and how she wished us all the best in our Leaving Certs. Around me, girls were wiping tears away, which was a good thing because no one thought anything when I wiped away a few tears too. I forced myself to look at Caoimhe, but her back was to me now. Tadhg was standing behind me, but I refused to turn around and look at him. When we were filing out of the hall, he came over to me.

'There you are!' he said. 'We need to arrange our first Dublin band practice. You're all getting the train home tomorrow, aren't you?'

I didn't trust myself to speak, so I just nodded. It hurt my heart to look at him.

'Cool,' he said. 'Me too.'

Everyone was subdued the next morning when we gathered at the *coláiste* to get the buses to Galway. Now we would return to the full horror of Leaving Cert study, and exams, and then the torturous wait to see if and where we'd got into college. But while we were waiting, we could still have the band. If I could bear it.

Brían and the rugby lads were on our bus again, but Tadhg, Ciarán and Caoimhe and her friends were on *múinteoir* Pól's bus, so after we'd all stowed our luggage in the holds, we went over to say we'd see them at the station in Galway.

But when we arrived at the station in Galway there was no sign of Tadhg, or Ciarán or Caoimhe, or anyone who'd been on that bus.

'They're just running late,' said Katie. 'The train isn't going for twenty minutes.'

Then we saw Áine talking on her mobile, and when she had hung up she said, 'That was Pól. His bus broke down so they won't get here in time for our train.'

'But …' I said. The implications of this were dawning on me in slow horror. We hadn't exchanged phone numbers yet. We'd assumed we could do that during the long train journey. And now ...

'It's okay, they can make the next one,' Áine said cheerfully.

On the train, I asked around to see if anyone had got Caoimhe's or Tadhg's or Ciarán's contact details earlier, a feeling of rising panic spreading through me. But no one had.

Tadhg was gone. I had no phone number. No email address. And, pre-social media, I had no way of finding him.

I wouldn't see him again for nearly four years.

Chapter Thirteen

2019

No pressure, no emotional baggage. Cover versions turn out to be the perfect way to ease back into playing music with Tadhg. After about an hour, when we finish playing 'Random Rules', he raises his arms over his head and stretches, leaning over to one side. The hem of his olive-green T-shirt rises above the waistband of his jeans and I carefully avert my gaze.

'Wow, Lol,' he says. 'You're even better than I remembered.'

The neck of my guitar almost slips out of my hands. 'Sorry?'

'Oof, I've been hunched over the bass for too long,' he says, stretching over to the other side. 'You're an even better guitarist than I remembered.'

'Oh. Um, thanks.'

He's definitely a better musician now than he used to be. He should be, I suppose, seeing as he's been able to do nothing but play music for the last decade or so. Lucky him, I think, but I try to push those thoughts out too, because if I start feeling bitter about all this, well, it'll eat me alive.

'Do you think we can justify taking a tea break?' says Tadhg.

'Definitely.' My arms and fingers are aching, as is my back. Shit, I really am getting old. In the kitchen, I rinse out the mugs and Tadhg takes over tea-making duties.

'So,' says Tadhg, 'how do you feel that went?'

'Good?' And I suppose I mean it. 'I feel musically warmed up now.'

'Me too.' There's silence as he finishes making the tea. After he's handed me my mug, he says, a little awkwardly, 'Do you want to try any of our old stuff? Band stuff? If you remember the chords?'

I do remember the chords of most of our band's songs, but I don't want to admit it in front of him. 'Do *you* remember them?'

'Well, yeah,' he says. 'I mean, I did write them.'

I stare at him in disbelief. Is that how he remembers it? Seriously? 'Oh, *did* you?'

'Shit, that came out wrong,' he says. 'I meant I co-wrote them. With you.'

'Yeah,' I say. 'With me.'

'Sorry, Lol,' says Tadhg. 'I'm not trying to … Sorry.'

I know I should probably just accept his apology and move on but I can't let it go. 'You didn't write a single song for that band on your own.' I sound bitchier that I intended. 'Not *one*.'

'Okay, you've made your point!' There's a pause and he says, 'You know I'm actually capable of writing songs on my own, right?'

'I never said you weren't capable of writing songs on your own!'

'Didn't you?' he says.

There's a very uncomfortable silence.

I clear my throat and say, 'Okay, so you do remember all of the old songs.'

'Maybe not everything,' says Tadhg. He takes a deep breath. 'But, like, 'Tourniquet' and 'Midnight Feast'—'

A laugh escapes me despite myself. 'God, they were terrible song names, weren't they?'

He grins. 'Terrible's a bit harsh. But yeah …'

''Midnight Feast' is definitely a terrible name,' I say firmly. 'And I can say it because I wrote the terrible lyrics.'

'Okay then, yes, I'll admit it. It's absolutely godawful.'

'Says the man who called a hit single 'End of My Garden'.'

'Ouch!' says Tadhg. But he's laughing. 'Fair point.'

Okay. This is getting a bit more normal. It's good that we can take the piss out of each other again, right?

'Every time it came on the radio Katie and I used to say the title sounded like a hideous euphemism.' I put on a creepy old man voice. ''Would you like to see the end of my garden, little girl?''

This time his laugh sounds a tiny bit forced. I think I might have struck a nerve.

'Yeah,' he says. 'I definitely can't blame you for that.'

My cheeks flush as I realise what I've done. A joke about a bad song title is one thing, especially after I've just mocked my own efforts. But I've basically just told him that Katie and I, two people who used to be his friends, have been sniggering about his song together behind his back. It sounds way more cruel than I meant it to be, especially given how he and I left things back in 2003.

'It's still a good song,' I say. My cheerful tone sounds fake even to me.

'Ah well,' says Tadhg with a wry smile. 'Maybe not one of my best.'

The silence that follows feels actively painful. I'm worried he thinks I hate him. I'm worried he's regretting asking Tara to send that email. I'm worried this isn't going to work.

And I want this to work, I realise. I *really* want this to work. I want to make music again. I want things to be okay with Tadhg again. But so far I'm still aware of a distance between us. Every so often we forget things are weird, just for a few minutes, but then there'll be a moment that reminds me we've essentially been estranged for sixteen years. Fuck it, I have to do something about it or this whole working-together thing is going to be unbearable.

'Tadhg …' I say hesitantly. 'We're … we're cool, right?'

Tadhg's laugh definitely doesn't feel forced this time. 'Well, I think we've just established our lyric-writing skills leave a lot to be desired.'

'No, I mean … things between you and me. Are they cool? I know stuff … I mean …' I'm stumbling over my words, and a part of me wishes I'd never started speaking, but I can't stop now. 'I know it all ended badly between us back then. But can we decide to just, I dunno, have a fresh start? It was a long time ago, and I'm pretty sure we both did and said things we regret ...'

I pause. I'm coming worryingly close to talking about our last night together in 2003. And while I do regret a lot of things about that night, I really, really don't want to go into the details of it now with him. I don't want to think about how I felt that night. Or what I did.

I take a deep breath.

'Can we start again?' I say. 'Pretend we've just met? Or at least pretend we never fell out?'

Tadhg looks at me. Those hazel-green eyes, the eyes that must have gazed out from a million teenage fans' walls, from thousands of billboards and bus posters and album covers, are fixed on mine. I bite my lip nervously. But I don't look away.

He raises his mug with a smile and I feel my shoulders sag with relief.

'To new beginnings,' he says.

I clink my mug off his. 'New beginnings.'

If we haven't totally cleared the air – I'm not sure if that will ever be possible now – we've at least opened the windows and waved our hands around (figuratively speaking). And it's just enough to make a difference. When we head back to the studio, I feel a new lightness.

'What'll we try first?' says Tadhg. "Midnight Feast'?'

'If you can ignore the dreadful lyrics,' I say. 'Do you actually remember them?'

'Oh, I remember them all right,' says Tadhg with a grin.

I groan. 'I wish you didn't.'

'They were about … What was his name? Darren? No! Dan! That was it!'

I hide my face in my hands. 'Oh God, I can't believe I ever told you that.'

'Did he know?' Tadhg is highly amused now. 'Did you ever tell him?'

'That I wrote a song about him? No, absolutely not! Anyway, it was grand, he never came to any of our gigs so he never heard it. I wrote the lyrics, like, a year after we broke up.'

'Poor old Dan,' says Tadhg, though he doesn't look too sad as he pulls the bass strap over his head. 'This is for you, Dan, wherever you are!'

He starts playing the bassline that opened 'Midnight Feast'. I start playing the choppy chords. I haven't played this song for over a decade, but my hands still know exactly what to do. Across from me is Tadhg Hennessy, one of the most famous musicians in the Western world, singing words I wrote about a boy I went out with for a few months seventeen years ago. It's so surreal I almost start laughing. We mess up the chord changes a few times, and at one stage Tadhg stumbles a bit with the lyrics, but the old ease between me and him is back, and I find myself reminded of those first practices in Coláiste

Laoise. How simply fun it all was. How it literally felt like *playing*. How right I felt when I was playing an electric guitar. How can I have let this feeling slip out of my life for so long?

We finish the song with a crashing chord from me, and when we look at each other, I see my own expression of pure happiness reflected back.

'We've still got it!' says Tadhg.

'Well,' I say. 'As much as we ever did.'

'It's a good song!' Tadhg insists.

I think about it for a second.

'You know what,' I say, 'I think it actually is.'

'Apart from the lyrics,' he adds.

'Well, obviously.'

'Do you want to play it again?' he says.

I do. So we do.

At one we take a break for lunch, and Tadhg suggests we get sandwiches from a café on the seafront.

'I can go and get them,' I say. Surely Tadhg can't just stroll into local cafés without attracting attention.

'There's no need,' says Tadhg. 'They'll bike them down to us.'

'But that place doesn't do deliveries,' I point out.

'Yes they do,' says Tadhg. 'I order from them pretty much every week. All the cafés around here deliver.'

'I think,' I say dryly, 'they might only deliver to *you*.'

'Ah.' Tadhg looks down at his feet. 'Um, maybe.'

After lunch we run through all of the band's old songs, replaying the particularly rusty ones until they shine again. I can feel the songs coming to life in our hands. Which shouldn't be surprising because we wrote most of them together. And while some of them sound a bit generic – predictable chord sequences, melodies that don't really go anywhere – some of them really are good. Like, surprisingly good. We could do something with them, I think, and then I stop that train of thought before it can go any further. Tadhg doesn't want to get the old band back together over this fortnight. He just wants to finish one song. My song. And after that, I'll probably never see him again.

Playing our old songs is, I have to admit, really enjoyable, but after a while I'm aware that something's missing, and eventually I realise what it is. Which means I also know it's just missing for me, and not for him.

It's hope.

It's the hope that all this chemistry between us could mean something on top of the magic of making music. That hope was always there in the past, whenever we played together, despite everything that was going on in our lives. The hope that when we caught each other's eye it meant more than a musical connection. The hope that every joke, every confidence shared meant more than friendship. The hope that he felt the same way about me that I felt about him.

And after what happened that night I know for sure he didn't. He never did.

But that doesn't matter, I tell myself. The music is enough. It was always enough. The hope was just the glitter on top. And yes, I can register that he is still very attractive. Yes, when he rolls up the sleeves of his shirt, the sight of his forearms as he plays the guitar is, to a shocking degree, having the same effect on me as it did twenty years ago. I still fancy him. But that's just a basic, chemical response. I can't help it. It means nothing.

When it comes to Tadhg Hennessy, I have no expectations or hopes at all.

Chapter Fourteen

2002

When I was eighteen, I got my heart's desire for Christmas.

After years of hoping and sometimes begging, my parents gave me an electric guitar. And not just any electric guitar, a beautiful Danelectro, bought at a bargain price from my dad's friend's son. When I saw it under the Christmas tree, along with a miniature amplifier, I burst into tears of joy.

'Now, you'd better not let this distract you from your college work,' said my mam, when I'd stopped hugging her.

As it turned out, she needn't have worried. For three years, I didn't spend nearly as much time playing that guitar as I'd hoped.

For months after we left Coláiste Laoise, I yearned to see Tadhg again. I looked out for him on Grafton Street every time I went into town, but he was never busking there. He'd said he wanted to study music in university, and when Katie and I started at Trinity that autumn, me studying English and French and her studying history, I was convinced we would find him there. But we didn't. Dublin feels small sometimes, but it's also possible to go for a very long time without bumping into someone.

I settled in quickly at college. I made new friends. I developed an unspoken crush on a hot boy who sat near me in the library every day. I even briefly joined a classmate's band, the dreadfully named Fennel, a month after I got my Danelectro. That was when I discovered there's an alchemy to creating a good band. You need the right mix of people, and it's harder to find than you might think. But we did play one gig before I left the band, and that night I got proof of something I'd only suspected when I played that gig in Coláiste Laoise and saw how boys looked at me on stage: if you are a pleasantly average-looking person and you want to, if only briefly, know what it's like to be really, really hot, then just play a gig, act like you're confident and don't be totally terrible.

After I left the stage that night, more boys than I could count came up to tell me how good I'd been or just to give me their phone number, and I was so unused to this sort of thing I didn't know what to say to any of them. Then my library crush, who had shown no signs of being aware of my existence until that night, came up and asked if he could buy me a drink and, to cut a long story short, his name was Fiachra and we went out for the following nine months.

♪♪

Over the next few years I'd sometimes think of our band at Coláiste Laoise, and Tadhg, and how lucky I'd been to find, even briefly, a band that worked so well, and I'd wonder what might have happened, on many different levels, if that bus hadn't broken down. It almost became a joke between me and Katie – the boy who got away and the band that got away. Her romance with Brían, or Brian as we called him now, had fizzled out by the time we started college, but he was studying science in Trinity now and we'd stayed friends.

Then, in the spring of third year, Brian got a drum kit from his cousin, and I discovered Katie's classmate Joanna could play the bass, so the three of us started messing around in Brian's family's garage every week. Katie declined our offer to join the band because she was already working on *Trinity News*, the college paper. She'd also just got together with Tina, her first girlfriend, and between the paper and her love life she didn't have time for music.

The only problem with this new band was the fact none of us could sing. I wrote vocal parts for all the songs, but there was no one to sing them. And so, by the time I arrived back in college in the autumn of 2002 for the fourth and final year of my degree, I was in a band and also not in a band.

'I'm basically Schrödinger's guitarist,' I said to my friend Ruairí, who was studying philosophy and psychology and so would hopefully appreciate such highfalutin references.

'Do you know who you should talk to?' said Ruairí. He was one of life's fixers – he was involved in a bunch of college societies and was always organising things. 'My old friend Tim.'

'Um, why?' We were sitting on the big felt-covered blocks in the Arts Block that everyone inexplicably called the chocolate boxes.

'He's a really good musician,' said Ruairí. 'He's just moved back to Dublin to do the Music and Technology master's.'

I'd heard of this new postgrad degree in Trinity. It was very hard to get into, and the students worked with prestigious composers. But being an expert in experimental plinky-plonk music didn't mean he was right for an indie rock band.

'Can Tim actually sing?' I asked cautiously.

Ruairí laughed. 'He definitely can. He started a band when he was, like, sixteen.'

'Why didn't you introduce me to this genius last year? I needed a singer then.'

'I told you, he just moved back here,' said Ruairí. 'He's been doing a music degree down in Cork for the last three years. And his gorgeous Cork girlfriend dumped him just before he left, so he'll need some cheering up.' His face brightened. 'Why don't I text and ask him to meet us in the Buttery later?'

I shrugged. 'Sure.' It couldn't hurt.

It was the first Thursday of term, and the Buttery bar was busy enough when I arrived. Ruairí was there before me; he'd bagged a corner table and already had a pint in front of him. The mysterious Tim had yet to arrive, but Ruairí promised me he'd be there.

'I didn't tell him about you being here, though,' he said.

'What?' I stared at him.

'I didn't want him to think he was auditioning!' said Ruairí. 'I just asked if he wanted to have a drink. And said some of my friends *might* join us.'

'Well, I hope he's not too disappointed not to have a cosy tête-à-tête with you!' I said with a laugh. 'Right, I'm going to the bar.'

The bar was busy and I had to wait for ages to get served. While I waited, I texted Brian and Joanna and suggested we get together the next afternoon. If the mysterious Tim seemed promising, I could invite him along to meet them. I finally got my pint and fought my way through the crowd to our table.

'At last!' said Ruairí. 'Laura, meet Tim. Tim, meet Laura.'

Startled hazel eyes met mine. My pint slid from my fingers and smashed on the tiled floor, to the whoops of a gang of second years.

Because Ruairí's old friend Tim was, unmistakably, Tadhg.

'*Laura?*' he said.

'Hang on, you know each other? Brilliant!' said Ruairí. 'Let me get Tim a drink and generously replace that pint, Laura, while you get over the shock.'

He headed to the bar and I sank into a chair opposite Tadhg.

'I'm sorry, I had no idea ...' I said. 'Ruairí said his friend's name was Tim.'

'My name *is* Tim,' said Tadhg.

'What?' I said. 'No it isn't!'

'Well, I was called Tadhg in the Gaeltacht every summer,' said Tadhg. 'But usually I'm Tim. Hang on, did you really not know?'

'No!' Even though Katie had been called Cáit, and Brian had been Brían, somehow I had always just assumed that Tadhg was, well, always Tadhg. It never crossed my mind it could be an Irish version of another name. 'So you mean ... everyone calls you Tim? All the time?'

He laughed. I'd forgotten what a lovely laugh he had. 'Pretty much. I mean, it *is* my name.'

I shook my head. 'This is so weird. It's like finding out Ruairí is really called Roderick or something.'

'Well, you can still call me Tadhg if you like,' he said. 'It's a better name than Tim. Anyway.' He smiled at me across the battered black-painted table. 'It's really good to see you again.'

And I smiled back at him. 'You too.'

By the time the generous Ruairí got back with pints, Tadhg (I couldn't think of him as Tim yet) and I were catching up.

'I felt so bad when I realised we weren't going to see all of you on the train,' said Tadhg. 'I always hoped we'd bump into each other again.'

'Well, we finally have.' I couldn't stop smiling.

'So,' said Ruairí, sliding into the seat beside Tadhg, 'have you asked Tim yet?'

Tadhg looked intrigued. 'Asked me what?'

'So ...' Now I realised that I was asking Tadhg, *the* Tadhg, my ultimate teenage crush who'd played that dazzling guitar solo at our Coláiste Laoise gig, to be in my band, it felt like a bigger deal than when I was just asking Ruairí's random friend Tim. 'I'm in a band. With Brian – I mean Brían, from Laoise.'

'No way!' said Tadhg. 'And Cáit? Although isn't her name usually Katie?'

'It is Katie,' I confirmed. How did he know her name was Katie and I had no idea his real name was *Tim*? 'But she's not in the band.'

'So what do you need me for?'

I told him, and he immediately said, 'Okay, I'm in.'

'Seriously? You don't need to think about it?'

'Of course I don't!' said Tadhg. 'It feels like fate, doesn't it? If it wasn't for that bus breaking down, we'd have been in a band since 1999.'

'Good point,' I said. 'Okay, brilliant! I'll tell the others.'

Ruairí was absolutely delighted with himself.

'See, Laura?' he said, raising his pint in a toast. 'I told you Tim would be perfect for you!'

Chapter Fifteen

2019

'Tell me everything!'

Katie is waiting for me in the hall when I get home from Tadhg's place, bouncing up and down with excitement.

'Have you been standing here since you got in from work?' I say.

'Of course not, I'm not that unhinged,' she says. 'I was correcting essays in the front room and I saw you come up the path. So how was it? I was expecting lots of messages from you and I got nothing!'

'Let me put my guitar down first,' I say.

In the kitchen, Katie puts the kettle on. 'Don't worry, I'll let you make your own,' she says. 'So why didn't I get minute-by-minute updates all day?'

I laugh. 'I was with Tadhg pretty much the entire time! I couldn't keep taking out my phone.'

'You could have taken it to the loo,' says Katie. 'Anyway, come on! Tell me everything! Was it really weird? What's the house like? How was the whole day?'

'It was …' Awkward? Fun? Painful? Kind of magical? 'It was grand. Mostly. He hasn't changed as much as you might think.'

'Well, that's good to hear,' says Katie.

'I think he finds being famous kind of embarrassing,' I say.

'As well he might,' says Katie. 'Remember that *Vanity Fair* thing in that ruined castle?'

'I won't forget that in a hurry.' It had been a cover story full of cringeworthy Irish clichés. The *Vanity Fair* team had him posing on a bit of rampart, gazing off into the distance. He wasn't wearing a cloak fastened with a Celtic brooch, but he might as well have been.

'I hope you didn't mention that,' says Katie.

'No, I didn't!'

'And you didn't react to his music the way you usually do, did you?'

'Jesus, of course not!' I cry. 'I do have some manners!'

Because here's the thing about Tadhg's music: it drives me mad.

Not, by the way, because I'm still madly in love with its creator and find it too painful to hear his voice. But because every single time I hear one of his solo songs, ever since the first time I saw the 'Winter Without You' video, I want to change it. It's not that the songs are bad or anything. They're actually great. It's that I know exactly what I'd have added to them if we'd written them together. I want to adjust the melodies, I want to change the intros just a tiny bit, I want to tweak the middle eights. It's like a terrible, terrible itch I can't scratch.

'So,' says Katie, 'what did you do all day?'

I tell her almost everything. I don't tell her about my shameful pangs of lust. But I tell her everything else. Including the fact that towards the end of the day we ended up playing some of Tadhg's solo songs. It was me who suggested doing the latter, to Tadhg's mortification and Katie's amazement.

'Seriously?' she says. 'The songs you always say could be better?'

'Yeah,' I say. 'I think it was because I felt guilty about the 'End of My Garden' thing.'

'And how was it?'

'Good,' I say. 'I think. No, definitely good.'

'And you're sure there wasn't a hint of … you know. The old magic between you? Because seriously, I don't want you to risk being upset again …'

'There was absolutely no old magic!' I protest. And I mean it. The magic was in the hope. And that hope is long gone.

Katie insists on cooking dinner, and even though it's a Monday, Jeanne opens a bottle of wine 'to toast your musical adventure'. It started raining just after I got home and now the beautifully designed kitchen feels very cosy. I twirl more bucatini onto my fork.

'You know, this house is even nicer than Tadhg's fancy Georgian gaff,' I say.

'I know we can't just arrange to meet him in a local pub or anything,' says Katie. 'But do you think … Could we invite him over some evening? Would that be inappropriate?'

A week ago the idea of Tadhg Hennessy calling over to Katie and Jeanne's Edwardian terrace would have been laughable. Unthinkable. But now … maybe? Yes, I'd feel a bit odd asking him. But I think about how well he and Katie got on back in the day. I've always felt bad that my and Tadhg's bust-up torpedoed that friendship. I owe this to Katie.

'I don't think it'd be inappropriate,' I say.

'Of course not,' says Jeanne. 'There you go. Invite him!'

'But will it be weird for you?' Katie asks me.

'I mean, this whole thing is weird,' I say truthfully. 'But actually, maybe all of us hanging out together rather than it just being him and me alone in a studio would make it … slightly less weird.'

'Excellent,' says Katie cheerfully. 'Check if he's free on Saturday. I want to see him ASAP in case the two of you have another fight and I don't get another chance for twenty years.'

I throw her a look but I say, 'I'll ask. And thanks, both of you. For everything.'

'No need to say thanks.' Jeanne waves a hand dismissively. 'We're now living vicariously through you! It's like we're all having a little adventure.'

I laugh. 'Yeah, right.'

'Today you played music with Tadhg Hennessy,' says Jeanne. 'I spent the day trying to persuade a client that we couldn't put 'just a few centimetres' of her extension in her neighbour's garden.'

'And I had to talk about 1923 prisoners of war all day,' says Katie. 'You're adding some glamour to our lives! Ooh, were there paparazzi outside the house?'

'No,' I say. 'Though there were some fans hanging around the Crescent park.'

'*Attention*,' warns Jeanne. 'There are some crazy fans out there. They might think you're his new girlfriend.'

'I doubt it,' I say. 'I was wearing a parka.'

'What difference does that make?' says Katie.

'Rock stars' girlfriends don't wear parkas,' I say.

'Don't be ridiculous,' says Katie. 'Oh my God, did any of those kids take your photo? Or film you? Did you notice them waving their phones at you?'

'No! I mean, I don't think so …'

'How did we not think of this?' cries Katie. 'You could be all over the tabloids tomorrow! You could be his next mystery brunette!'

'Do you really think I could?' I take a gulp of wine.

Jeanne's face lights up. 'Maybe you should wear a disguise tomorrow. I have a wig you can borrow …'

'I am not going in disguise!' I say. 'It'll be grand.' I imagine a photo of me emerging from Tadhg's front garden appearing on a tabloid website. I imagine all of the media fuss that would almost certainly follow. I think of my old colleagues who avoided me when I was let go, and I think of Dave and his new girlfriend and all Dave's friends who I don't see anymore since he dumped me. I imagine them all seeing a perfectly recognisable picture of me under a headline like 'Tadhg Hennessy's new mystery woman'.

You know what, maybe I could live with that.

Chapter Sixteen

2019

When I reach the Crescent the next day, I keep an eye out for potential amateur paparazzi. Though they won't be able to see much of me, given that the weather is hideous and the hood is up on my parka. There is a large-ish bunch of young people hanging around the park in the drizzle, all looking over at Tadhg's house. Before I go through the gate, I look back and see all the fans watching me. It's unnerving, that feeling of being observed. I wonder, not for the first time, how Tadhg deals with it.

The front door is already open as I hurry up the steps.

'Come in! What a miserable day.' He's wearing a Pavement band T-shirt and jeans and a navy hoodie, and he hasn't shaved again today. He looks more like himself – or at least the Tadhg I remember – in his own house than he did in that fancy restaurant.

'You've got a little fan club out there in the Crescent,' I say.

'They didn't bother you, did they?' Tadhg looks concerned.

'No, not at all.' I pause. 'Do they ever bother people? Visitors, I mean?'

'Not usually,' says Tadhg. I follow him into the kitchen where the kettle is just boiling. He starts making the tea. 'They're generally pretty respectful. But you never know … Sorry, I really should have warned you before we started all this that there might be people out there.'

'It's fine, I kind of guessed there would be.' I sit at the kitchen table. 'Have any of them ever, well, done anything weird? Like tried to get in here? Oh my God, do you have bodyguards hidden around here somewhere?'

Tadhg hands me a cup of tea. 'Yes, there have been one or two weird moments but nothing too terrifying. A girl did try to get in here once but didn't succeed. And no, I don't, but a security company does monitor the cameras twenty-four hours a day.'

I sip my tea. Perfect. 'What do the neighbours think of all this?'

Tadhg groans. 'They're not exactly my biggest fans, I can tell you that much.'

I suppose I can't really blame them. It must be a massive pain in the arse having a megastar living next door. I don't say this to Tadhg, though. Instead I say, 'What do you want to do today? In the studio, I mean.'

'Well,' he says, 'I was thinking we could try *the* song. Our song. See if either of us has any fresh ideas for how to finish it.'

My heart sinks, just a little. I've been enjoying our new-found harmony. Trying to work on the song might add a sour note. We might find ourselves thinking about why we never got round to finishing it in the first place.

But that's what I'm here for, so I say, 'Sure! Will we take our tea out to the studio?'

I spend a little too long setting up, but all too soon we're both sitting there, our instruments in our laps. When we wrote songs for the band back in the day we'd sit facing each other like this. Except not exactly like this.

Tadhg says, 'Do you remember the chords?'

'Of course I do!' The *I wrote them* is silent but heavily implied.

'Sorry, I didn't want to presume …' he says. 'I mean, it's been a very long time …'

'Do you remember the words?'

'Yeah, of course.' Tadhg takes a deep breath. He's tense too.

'Well then,' I say. 'Let's play it.'

I start the chords that begin the song, and after a few bars Tadhg comes in, playing the bassline, and when he starts singing the melody in his beautiful honey-and-gravel voice, a wave of nostalgia hits me with such force that I almost gasp.

'Here we are
We've been talking through the night'

I try not to think about the last time we played this song together. I try and fail not to think about what happened next, everything we did, everything we said to each other. I wonder if he's thinking of it too. I wonder if he's forgotten all about it. Could you forget something like that? I certainly can't. I can't even look at him. My fingers almost stumble over the strings and I curse myself for getting distracted by stupid, painful memories. I need to stake my claim to this song and that means being actually able to play the bloody thing.

We play a verse and a chorus and another verse and then we finally catch each other's eyes. This is as far as the song ever got. We never wrote a middle eight. We never wrote a lead-guitar line. And the second verse never even had any lyrics, so Tadhg just repeated the first verse. In fact, the few lyrics I wrote for this song back in the day were just what we used to call 'placeholders', words that would do for now until I wrote proper ones; the chorus was something vague and silly and meaningless about how someone was going to be Tadhg's 'summer girl'. I wasn't good at writing lyrics that year. The only subject I wanted to write about was my feelings about Tadhg, and that was obviously out of the question. Besides, Tadhg was always better at writing lyrics than I was. I'd always given him that.

But still, even with the vague lyrics, the song works. What there is of it. Tadhg plays one loud chord and we stop.

'Was it just me,' he says, 'or did that sound pretty great?'

'It didn't sound terrible,' I say.

'Are you sure I can't persuade you to sing harmonies?' Back in the day, we'd enlisted Joanna to sing the harmony I wrote for the chorus.

I shake my head. 'Absolutely not.'

'You know the whole 'would you go back in time and shoot Hitler' thing?' says Tadhg. 'Well, first I'd go back in time and shoot that teacher who told you you couldn't sing before she had a chance to say it. Or I'd threaten her with a gun anyway.'

'You should have made me sign that NDA,' I say. 'I'm going straight to the tabloids. I can see the headlines now: 'Saint Tadhg's shocking gun threat!"

Tadhg laughs and then groans. 'God, those Saint Tadhg headlines. I do come across as a sanctimonious dickhead sometimes, don't I?'

'Meh, better a sanctimonious dickhead than just a dickhead. At least it shows you have principles,' I say, and immediately regret it because, while things are definitely better between us, I'm pretty sure we're not quite back to the point where we can do affectionate slagging. 'I'm joking! You're not sanctimonious! Or a dickhead,' I add hastily.

'Oh, I'm definitely a sanctimonious dickhead sometimes,' says Tadhg. 'But I try not to be.'

'You clearly believe in stuff,' I say. 'That's not a bad thing.' And I mean it.

'Eh, I suppose,' he says. 'But I'm not sure what difference I make to the world. Unlike Aideen. My ex. I think she thought I was a bit of a dilettante sometimes.'

I'd forgotten about her. The brilliant human rights lawyer who presumably got all As in her Leaving. 'Are you still ... How are things with her?'

He sighs. 'Ah, grand, I suppose. We're sort of still in contact. The odd text, that sort of thing.'

'Did it ...' I'm wary of overstepping boundaries. This is the first time we've talked about anything vaguely personal in our current lives. 'Did it all end badly?'

Tadhg shrugs. 'It just kind of ... fizzled out. We were both always so busy and travelling all the time. And then when things calmed down and we eventually did spend more time together, well ... I suppose we had less to say to each other than I thought we would.'

'I'm sorry,' I say. But I must confess that it does make me feel a bit, shamefully, happy to know that although I'm not a high-powered glamorous lawyer, Tadhg and I always had plenty to say to each other.

Then I remember Katie's invitation. 'Katie says hi, by the way.'

His face lights up. 'Tell her I say hi back. God, I'd love to see Katie again. How is she?'

'She's very good,' I say. 'She actually wondered if you'd like to come over on Saturday for dinner?' I'm struck by sudden nervousness. Maybe this is all a bit too much. No, it's definitely too much. This is only my second day here and I'm inviting him over to my home. Why didn't I tell Katie we should wait until next week? 'I'm staying with her at the moment and – obviously she'd understand if you'd find it too weird ...'

'Not at all!' Tadhg looks genuinely delighted. 'That'd be brilliant.'

'Cool,' I say. 'I'll tell her. And Katie's wife Jeanne will be there, of course. She's lovely. And French,' I add impressively.

'*Formidable*,' says Tadhg. 'How long have you been staying with them?'

'Since last summer. It's just temporary, though.'

'Oh yeah? How come?' Tadhg looks genuinely interested.

I take a deep breath. I might as well tell him. 'My ex-fiancé and I split up last year. So I had to move out of our apartment.'

'Ah,' says Tadhg. 'I'm sorry.' He pauses. 'Or should I say congratulations?'

I laugh despite myself. 'A bit of both? He broke up with me. But I …' The next words to come out of my mouth take me by surprise. 'I'm glad he did.'

And I realise I genuinely am.

We go back to playing our song, but once we've run through those two verses we hit a block again. We try various chords and melodies for a middle eight, but nothing we come up with is right.

I groan in frustration. 'Why isn't this working?'

'Let's take a tea break,' says Tadhg.

Once we're in the kitchen and the kettle is on, Tadhg leans back against the counter and says, 'D'you know what, I think we're putting too much pressure on ourselves.'

'Maybe,' I say. 'But finishing this song is literally why I'm here.'

'Yeah, I know,' says Tadhg. 'But why don't we approach it by, I dunno, a circuitous route?'

'What do you mean?'

'Okay,' says Tadhg. 'This song was our ... white whale. The song that kept getting away from us. Correct?'

'Correct.'

'So finishing it became a big deal. We both really did want to finish it, right?'

'Well, yeah.'

'But it's been years since we wrote music together,' Tadhg continues, 'so maybe starting again with the white whale isn't the best approach. Maybe we need to try writing something new from scratch. To get used to being songwriting partners again before we tackle *the* song.'

'It's been a while since I read *Moby Dick*,' I say, 'but I'm not sure the white-whale thing is holding up now.'

'Seriously, Lol, what do you think?'

Seriously, I think it's a good idea. But this is more than I signed up for. I agreed to spend two weeks finishing one particular song, not writing new ones. Now he wants to change the whole arrangement, just like that. I suppose when you're Tadhg Hennessy you can always change plans on a whim and expect people to go along with it.

But still ... call me Ishmael, because I really do want to finish our song. And if that means writing a few more songs first, then so be it.

'Okay,' I say. 'Let's give it a go.'

He hands me my cup of tea. 'Clean slate.'

'Clean slate,' I say.

If only.

Back in the studio, we're faced with the freedom and terror of the blank page.

'So what now?' I say.

'Do you have any rough things you've been working on?' says Tadhg.

The thing is, I actually do. After dinner last night, I got out my guitar and came up with a chord sequence without a melody, just a riff and a lead guitar line. But I remember my early suspicions, my fear that Tadhg wanted to find out if I had proof I wrote our song. I do trust him now. But I still want to have my own recordings of whatever we write today.

'I have what *could* turn into a song,' I say. I take out my phone. 'Want to mess around with it and I'll record it if we come up with anything good?'

And for the first time in sixteen years, we write a song together.

It's incredible how natural it feels. I play the riff, and after I run through it a few times, Tadhg starts singing over it, no words, just *da-da-da* sounds. After a while something happens and we look at each other and I know we're both thinking the same thing. This is it. He's come up with the perfect tune for these chords. We play through it again and I record it on my phone.

'Have you thought of chords for the chorus?' he says.

'Not yet,' I say.

He picks up his guitar. 'How about going into a D minor? And then …' He plays a series of chords that contrast perfectly with the chords of the verse.

'That's not bad,' I say. It's better than not bad. It's brilliant. In my head I'm humming a possible melody. 'You keep playing those chords and I'll pick out a tune on the piano and you can sing it.'

He rolls his eyes. 'Oh, come on, don't fuss around with the piano. Just sing the melody.'

'No,' I say.

'This is ridiculous,' he says. 'I've heard you sing before.'

'What? No you haven't!'

'Lol, you sing all the time without even realising it! Or at least you used to,' he adds.

'I don't!' I've sung the songs in my head, of course I have, and maybe I sometimes hummed very quietly at practices, but could I possibly have been singing out loud in front of other people? Loud enough for them to hear? Surely not.

'You used to sing at practices all the time,' he says. 'I never mentioned it because I thought you'd get self-conscious about it.'

'And I would have,' I say, 'because my voice is terrible.'

'No, it's not,' says Tadhg. 'Look, I'm not going to force you to sing now. Obviously. But I know you can.'

'No, I can't,' I say. This isn't annoying false modesty. It's just honesty. 'Not like you.'

I can only describe Tadhg's voice as a beautiful sound. Warm but not too smooth. A hint of rasp. Capable of shifting seamlessly, perfectly, from heartfelt to affectless. It's been distinctive ever since he was a teenager, and it's only become more powerful with age. My off-key croak sounds nothing like it.

'No, not like me,' he says, and I appreciate that he's not trying to flatter me with bullshit. 'But – and I know this sounds patronising, but I swear to God I don't mean it like that – it's good in another way. You can *deliver* a song.' My expression must be sceptical because he says, 'Okay, fine, go on, play the piano. But seriously, Lol, think about singing. I'm not talking about doing it on stage for an audience. Just in here. Just for me.'

Suddenly it doesn't sound so bad, singing just for him. Then I imagine how embarrassingly terrible it would actually sound. I open the piano lid and start playing.

An hour later, we have the bones of a song. It's a bit rackety, it still has no words, but it is, very definitely, a song.

'Let's run through the whole song one more time so I can record it, and then we can leave it for now,' I say. I go to pick up my phone from the table where I left it, and Tadhg says, 'No need, I'll record it.' He's holding up his phone.

'We can both record it,' I say.

Tadhg gives an exasperated sigh. 'Lol, you know I won't, like, do anything with the songs we write here without your full permission, don't you, whoever has them on their phone? And obviously if we ever record and release anything properly, you'll get a full credit for everything.'

'Well, I should hope so,' I say.

'Sorry.' Tadhg looks a little awkward. 'I just want you to know I'm not, like, trying to exploit you or anything.'

'Good,' I say. But my shoulders relax a little. It's good to hear him actually say those words. 'Because I wouldn't let you.'

'I'd expect nothing less,' says Tadhg. He shows me his phone, which reveals that it's not recording. 'Go on. You record this one.'

'You don't have your old minidisc recorder hidden in your pocket, do you?' I say.

Tadhg laughs. 'Just hit record, Lol.'

When we return to the studio after lunch, he plays me a chord sequence and melody he's been messing around with recently.

'I know it needs something more,' he says. 'Any suggestions?'

The song fragment is good – it's very good – but I feel that old itch to adjust it that I've always felt when listening to Tadhg's music. That urge to tweak things just a bit, a chord here, a melody there, make it even better, make it shine. That urge I felt in the band, the urge I still feel every time I hear one of his songs on the radio or in the soundtrack to a film.

'Play it again,' I say, and when he does I say, 'In the first line of the chorus, bring the tune up at the end instead of staying on that note. Like this.' And without thinking, I hum the revised melody.

'Laura McDermott,' says Tadhg, 'am I hearing things or did you actually just sing?'

'Oh, shut up,' I say. 'I was just humming.' But I'm smiling.

By late afternoon, Tadhg and I have written two whole songs. It's not all smooth sailing, of course – we clash sometimes, over whether a bassline works, over whether a guitar line should cut out during the verses, but we always find a solution that pleases both of us. It's work, it's serious, concentrated work, but God, it's so much *fun*.

'I've missed this, you know,' says Tadhg after I've played back the second song and we've agreed it's pretty much done apart from the lyrics. 'Us. Working together, I mean.'

There's a hesitancy in his voice that catches my heart.

'You've missed it? Really?' I say, as briskly as I can. 'With all your jet-setting about the place? I presumed you'd forgotten me years ago.'

'Come on, Lol,' he says. 'I was hardly going to forget about *you*.'

I smile back at him and I'm filled with such fondness for him it takes me by surprise. We were friends once. We were real friends. And maybe we can be friends again. Maybe we already are. Maybe we're …

A familiar old feeling pervades me, one I almost don't want to name.

Hope.

Tadhg's phone buzzes. He looks at it and says, 'Oh, bollocks.'

'What's wrong?'

'Nothing,' he says. 'I just didn't realise how late it was.'

'How late is it?' I say.

'Just after six.' He sighs. 'Sorry, Lol, I don't want to kick you out but we'd better call it a day. I've got to be somewhere at seven.'

'No worries,' I say. 'I should head too.' Though I don't have anywhere to be apart from Katie and Jeanne's house, and I'd have happily stayed playing music with Tadhg all evening if he'd asked me to. 'Where are you off to? If you don't mind me asking.'

And I find myself silently praying, with an intensity that shocks me, *Please, please, please don't let him say it's a date.*

'Just a dinner thing in town,' he says, which could be anything. A hot date. A business meeting. His mother's birthday.

Or a dinner with some other woman like me, a woman who used to be in love with him and is, I very much regret to inform myself, in danger of falling in love with him again.

Chapter Seventeen

2002

At four o'clock the day after my surprise reunion with Tadhg, the band – and Katie – were sitting in the café section of the Buttery. The Buttery occupied the lower ground floor of the eighteenth-century Dining Hall building, with a bright, busy café on one side and a cosy, windowless bar on the other. We had grabbed a table by the windows.

'I can't believe I'm going to meet your long-lost bandmate,' said Joanna. I loved Joanna. She dressed, as she said herself, like someone going to work in a bank, and people who judged others by their appearance – especially annoying boys – were always taken by surprise when they found out she was an awesome bass player.

'I can't believe you didn't know his real name was Tim,' said Brian.

'You only knew because you stayed in the same house in Laoise!' said Katie. She and Brian were still close. Though right now I was glad that, on my orders back in 1999, she had never told him about my teenage crush on Tadhg. 'Hey, there he is!'

I raised a hand in greeting and Katie waved wildly. Tadhg's face broke into a smile as he approached us.

'Fancy seeing you here!' said Katie, jumping up and giving him a hug. 'I hope you don't mind me joining your band meeting. I just wanted to say hi.'

'Course not,' said Tadhg. 'This is brilliant. Hey, Brían!'

'Alright, Tadhg?' They did some manly back-slapping.

'And this,' I said, 'is Joanna. Jo, this is Tadhg. Sorry, I mean Tim. Sorry, Tim.'

It felt very weird calling him Tim. I'd been thinking of him as Tadhg for three and a half years. Not that I'd been thinking of him *that* much.

Tadhg smiled at Joanna and I could see her take in just how attractive he was. 'Nice to meet you,' she said.

'Great to meet you too,' said Tadhg. 'And you know what, Tadhg's fine.'

'Are you sure?' I was dubious. 'Feel free to correct us any time we use it.'

'Nah, it's grand.' Tadhg pulled out a chair and sat down next to me. 'I always liked being Tadhg every summer. It's a bit more rock and roll than Tim.' He grinned. 'It can be my stage name.'

'Is your actual full name Timothy?' Katie's eyes sparkled with mischief. 'Please say it is.'

Tadhg groaned and took out his student card. There it was: Timothy Hennessy. Good Lord.

'I'm named after my great-uncle,' he said. 'He was a Jesuit priest.'

'You do have quite a priestly air about you,' said Katie. 'Father Timothy.'

'Okay, that's it,' said Tadhg. 'Definitely feel free to call me Tadhg.'

'I can't promise anything,' said Katie. 'You just look like a Timothy to me now.'

Tadhg shook his head in mock frustration and looked at Brian. 'Are you two still …?'

'Oh no,' said Katie.

'Katie fancies girls now,' said Brian cheerfully.

'Girls and boys,' said Katie airily. 'I'm not fussy. About gender, I mean,' she added. 'I'm pretty fussy about people.'

'You can't be that fussy,' said Jo. 'You went out with Brian.'

'Hey!' said Brian.

We told Tadhg about our practice space and it was decided that we'd have our first practice together on Saturday afternoon, just two days away.

'We have a few songs that still need vocal melodies,' said Joanna, 'if you want to try coming up with something.'

'I'll give it a shot,' said Tadhg. He leaned back in his seat. 'This is deadly, lads. I was in a band in Cork but obviously we had to split up when I moved back here. I'd been thinking I'd need to start a new band. But now I've found my old one. And you, Joanna.'

'What about the Evil Twins?' said Katie. She turned to Brian and Jo. 'That was his really old band.'

'We're on permanent hiatus,' said Tadhg.

'So there are no rivals for your attention,' said Katie. She kicked me under the table and I carefully ignored her. 'Musically, I mean.'

'Nope. I am totally available,' said Tadhg, and I had to look down and pretend I was searching for something in my bag in case my face gave me away.

Tadhg immediately fit right in our little gang, as if we all hadn't lost sight of each other for three and a half years. But after almost an hour Brian said, 'Oh shit, I've got a lecture at five.'

'Are you doing Ed Rafferty's Civil War tutorial?' Joanna said to Katie.

'Oh yeah.' Katie got to her feet and put her jacket on.

'Are you all going?' Tadhg looked at me. 'Do you have to go now too? Or can you stay a bit longer?'

'Um, no. I mean, no, I don't have to go straight away – my last lecture of the day was at two. So yeah, I can stay.'

'Cool,' said Tadhg. 'Same here.'

The others hurried off – Katie gave me a meaningful look as she went, but luckily Tadhg was telling Joanna how great it was to meet her and didn't spot it.

Then it was just me and him. Alone. For possibly the first time since we sat on that rock on a beach in Connemara.

'Do you want more tea?' said Tadhg.

♪♪

It seems bizarre and magical now, the fact that when I was in college I could just hang around with a friend for hours on end. It's easy to forget what student bars and cafés were like, how they were primarily there for hanging out rather than buying stuff, how everything was built around being able to sit around and chat and drink tea (and then, at a certain stage in the day, pints) and flirt and eat chips for as long as you liked.

We drank multiple cups of tea and talked about his time in Cork and my time in Trinity so far, about our college bands (he had been the lead singer and main songwriter of a band in Cork that had played support slots for some big local bands; I turned my time in Fennel into what I hoped was a funny story), about our summers working abroad (Paris and London for me, London and Boston for him). We had both just been in London for the summer, which struck each of us as remarkable.

'I can't believe we never bumped into each other,' said Tadhg, and I agreed, forgetting that since that Laoise fortnight we had spent two other summers living in Dublin, a much smaller city, and had never crossed paths at all.

Maybe, I thought after an hour had gone by, I should quit while I was ahead. Tadhg seemed very happy to be there too, but perhaps he was just being polite. Perhaps he was dying to get away from me and find his new musical-genius classmates. Perhaps he just wanted to go home.

But then he said, 'Do you want to get food while they're still serving?' So we went and got chips, and kept talking, and then he said, 'I don't suppose you want to get an actual drink?' So we went to the bar part of the Buttery and got pints and settled in to a corner table. And we talked, and talked, and talked.

We laughed a lot too. He told me about his older sister, Rosie, who like me had done French in college.

'She went on Erasmus to Lyon,' he said. 'And when she got home she claimed she'd basically forgotten how to speak English. It went on for ages. You'd ask her something basic like 'Where's the remote control?' and she'd pause and point at the couch and say, 'What's the English word for that again?''

I told him about Annie, who was now in sixth year in school and had mellowed a tiny bit since her spectacularly grumpy early teens.

'We actually get on quite well now,' I said. 'Which is a huge deal considering four years ago she chucked my favourite top in the bin after I dared mock her love of NSYNC. There was a lot of loud door slamming in those days. Anyway, she's a goth now so at least she's stopped playing NSYNC.'

We were on our second pint by then, which is probably why I said, 'Speaking of teenage years, what happened with you and Caoimhe?'

'Caoimhe?' said Tadhg. 'Which Caoimhe? Oh, Caoimhe from Laoise?'

'Yeah,' I said. 'Didn't you, like, get together on the last night?'

Tadhg looked confused and said, 'No! Why did you think that?'

I wished I hadn't mentioned Caoimhe, but now I had to tell him. 'I thought I saw you together in the practice room on the last night. I was on my way to the loo and the door was open,' I added hastily, lest he think I was spying on them creepily.

'Ah,' said Tadhg. '*That* night.' He paused and said, 'I suppose me telling you doesn't matter now.'

He didn't say anything more and I said, 'Go on.'

'Caoimhe told me she liked me,' said Tadhg. 'And I had to tell her I thought she was great but we should just stay friends. And she was embarrassed – though she had no reason to be, I was very flattered – and kind of upset and asked if we could just sit there until she was ready to go back in the hall, and of course that was fine with me. But nothing, like, happened between us.'

'Oh,' I said. 'Shit, sorry. I totally got the wrong end of the stick. So did you stay in touch?'

'Ah, no, we didn't,' said Tadhg. 'We met up once but it was kind of awkward. You know what it's like when a friend tells you something like that. I didn't want to hurt her, and I didn't want to lead her on or anything, so I think we both felt it was easier if we didn't see each other.'

I was suddenly very aware of two things. One was relief. Relief that he hadn't been into Caoimhe at all. Which meant there was a chance that post-gig kiss had been a real kiss after all. Which meant maybe there was a tiny chance he had liked me back then the way I liked him. Maybe there was a tiny chance he could like me that way now. Because I knew I still fancied him. A lot.

But I was also aware that I could never, *ever* reveal these feelings to him – not unless I was a hundred per cent sure he returned them. I didn't want to be the latest in a long line of female friends who revealed their love to an embarrassed Tadhg. The idea of him kindly telling me he didn't fancy me was too horrific. He might say he was flattered by Caoimhe fancying him, but that was just him being a gentleman. No one's immediate reaction to being told that a friend has unrequited feelings for them is 'Oh, what a lovely compliment!'. It's 'Oh God, this is really fucking awkward – why the hell did they have to say anything?'. I couldn't bear the thought of that. I couldn't bear him feeling sorry for me, and maybe feeling guilty about hurting me, and then resenting me for making him feel guilty, and then drifting away from me. And besides the general awfulness, that would destroy any chance of having him as a bandmate. And a friend. Today had reminded me how much I simply *liked* him. I couldn't mess that up. No, I would always behave in a strictly platonic fashion unless given very, very explicit indications otherwise.

I wanted to ask Tadhg if he was going out with anyone now, but I didn't trust myself to sound cool and disinterested when I said it.

But then he said, 'So, what about you? Are you seeing anyone at the moment?'

'No, not right now,' I said, as breezily as I could, as if I were temporarily between boyfriends and another one would doubtless come along in a minute.

'Same here,' he said, and my heart soared.

Then I glanced at Tadhg's watch and realised it was after ten o'clock. My heart wanted to stay here with Tadhg until they kicked us out, but my brain knew it was definitely time to quit while I was ahead, before I said anything I'd regret in the morning.

'I should probably go,' I said regretfully.

'Oh, really?' Was I imagining it, or did Tadhg sound genuinely disappointed? Just a little bit?

'Yeah, I've got a nine o'clock tutorial tomorrow,' I said. 'It should be a crime to arrange nine o'clock classes on a Friday.'

'Where's your bus stop?' said Tadhg, as we gathered our jackets and bags.

'Westmoreland Street,' I said.

'I'll walk you down there.'

'Ah, you don't have to,' I said, although I really wanted him to.

'It's no problem,' he said. 'It's basically on my way.'

So we walked out of the Buttery and across Front Square, the cobbles glistening with rain that must have fallen while we were cosily ensconced in the windowless pub, through Front Arch and out into College Green.

'You're not too cold, are you?' said Tadhg. I was wearing a denim jacket, which had been fine in the daytime when the early October sun was still mild but was proving itself to be inadequate now. 'You can borrow my hoodie, if you need it. My jacket's pretty warm.'

'If you're sure you won't be too cold ...'

'I won't be,' he said. 'I got this jacket in a Vincent de Paul shop down in Cork and it's way warmer than it looks.' He took it off – it was corduroy lined in silk, which explained the warmth – removed his hoodie and put it around my shoulders. I had to fight the undoubtedly creepy-looking urge to hold the fabric to my face and smell it.

'Better?' he said.

'Much,' I said. We crossed the road at the Bank of Ireland. 'My teeth were about to start chattering before I put this on.'

I wished my bus stop was further away but here it was. 'Well, this is me.'

'I'll wait for you till the bus comes,' he said.

'I mean, if you're sure it won't put you out ...'

'I'm grand,' said Tadhg. 'I'm not in a hurry.'

I would have been happy to wait there with him for hours. Though obviously I didn't say that either.

'Oh, before I forget,' he said, reaching into his jacket pocket and taking out a phone, 'can I give you my mobile number? I'm not going to risk losing you again.'

'Oh yeah, good idea,' I said, as casually as I could.

'Can you give me your phone?' he said. I handed over my aqua-blue Nokia. 'I'm going to put myself in as Tadhg. You don't know any other Tadhgs, do you?'

'I don't,' I say. 'Or Tims. Give me your phone.' He passed it to me and I opened the contacts. 'I'll put myself in as Laura Guitarist.'

'Just put Laura,' said Tadhg. 'You're the only Laura in my life.'

For a moment we stood there, smiling at each other. Was I completely deluded or was there something happening between us this evening? There was, wasn't there? Were we almost … flirting?

But Caoimhe had probably thought they were flirting too.

'Oh, there's my bus!' I saw the number 16 approach with a mixture of relief and disappointment. 'Here, quick, take your hoodie.'

'You'll need it for the walk home,' he said. The bus was pulling up now. 'You can give it back to me on Saturday. At the practice. Why don't we get the bus out there together? We could meet at Front Gate of college at twelve.'

'Oh! Yeah, sure.' The doors of the bus were opening. There was no time for a grand farewell. 'Well, see you then!'

When I took my seat upstairs, I did bury my face in the fabric of the hoodie. It smelled of washing powder and a fresh green scent that I guessed was his shower gel or deodorant, and under that was a pleasant, clean, slightly musky boy smell that I suppose was basically just … Tadhg.

The weather was even colder by the time I got off the bus and started walking the short distance home, but I felt warm and toasty inside. And it wasn't just because of the hoodie.

Chapter Eighteen

2019

'How was your dinner thing?'

I ask Tadhg this question as if I haven't been thinking about his mysterious 'dinner thing' since yesterday evening. Not all the time, obviously. But enough. A lot. Too much. I didn't mention it to Katie after I got home last night. I barely wanted to admit to myself how much it bothered me, so I was hardly eager to tell her. I just told her we'd written a couple of songs together and she said, 'Two songs in one day? Wow, it really is like old times. Apart from you pining after him, of course,' she added.

'Ha! Yeah, of course,' I said.

'There's no pining, is there?' she said suspiciously.

Bloody Katie, she knows me too well.

'No!' I said. 'Absolutely none. Don't worry, it's not like before.'

'Really?' said Katie.

'Really,' I said. 'This time, I know what I'm doing.'

But now, in Tadhg's kitchen, I'm not sure I do know what I'm doing. I'm not even sure I managed to sound all that casual when I asked him about the dinner. Maybe it's for the best if he tells me it was a hot date.

Tadhg sighs. 'It was just Hugo.'

So it wasn't a date. Unless Tadhg is into men as well as women now, in which case good for him, but not good for me, because although the thought of Tadhg with another man is pretty hot in theory, it would not be hot at all for me in reality; in reality I don't want him to be with anyone else of any gender …

Bloody hell, this is getting ridiculous.

'Um, who's Hugo?' I say.

'Hugo,' says Tadhg, and now his face is so grim I stop worrying that Hugo was Tadhg's date, 'thinks he's my manager.'

I'm embarrassed by how relieved I am to hear this.

'And isn't he?' I hand him a cup of tea. We're taking turns to handle tea duties now. I'm getting very familiar with his kitchen.

'Thanks.' Tadhg takes the cup. 'And no, he isn't, not if I can help it.'

'Then why …?' I ask gently.

Tadhg sighs. 'His dad, Jim, was my manager. He signed me after 'Winter Without You' broke through. He was brilliant. Really brilliant. He got me that Glastonbury slot. He's basically why I broke America. And he was really sound too. Just the perfect manager.'

'So what happened to him?' I say, though I can guess.

'He died a few months ago,' says Tadhg. 'Which was ... yeah. It was a shock. He just dropped dead of a heart attack.' He takes a long breath.

'I'm sorry,' I say.

He nods his acknowledgement. 'Anyway, he owned the management company and his son Hugo was working for him, managing a few other acts, but after he died Hugo inherited Jim's artists as well as the company.'

'Ah,' I say. 'And I take it you don't ... see eye to eye?'

'No, we do not,' says Tadhg. 'God love him, he's not the worst person in the world, but we just don't have the same outlook. I'd have trusted his dad with my life but ...' He trails off.

'You don't trust Hugo?'

Tadhg sighs. 'I suppose I don't, really. Not the way I trusted Jim. And Hugo knows I'm actively looking for new management. Which is why he decided to pop over from London to try and persuade me to stay. Hence the dinner last night.' He rolls his eyes. 'I almost forgot about it. He told me last week that he was coming over but I suppose I tried to push it out of my mind.'

'So how did it go?'

'Not great,' says Tadhg. 'He's obsessed with shaking things up – his words, not mine. He's into all that disruptor bollocks.'

'And how does he want you to do that?'

'Oh, he has many ideas.' Tadhg sits on the edge of the kitchen table, his long legs stretched out in front of him. 'There's a couple of producers he wants me to work with, one in Sweden and one in America. Max Ahlberg and Jack Johns. He thinks I should have some songwriting sessions with them.'

It is, I know, ridiculous of me to feel a twinge of jealousy at the thought of Tadhg working with professional producers, but I do.

'What do you think?' I say. 'Do you want to be, um, shaken up?'

To my surprise he says, 'Well, maybe.'

'Seriously?' I say.

'Just not by those guys,' says Tadhg. 'They're not terrible or anything but I don't want to write songs with them.' He picks up a pen from the table and twists it around in his hands. 'My stuff can be pretty poppy but not their sort of pop.' He mentions a few Grammy-winning acts Ahlberg and Johns have produced, and I see what he means. 'We wouldn't be a good match.'

'It doesn't sound like it,' I agree.

'But ... I've been doing a lot of thinking lately,' says Tadhg. 'Since Jim died. About what I want to do next musically.'

'And?' I say.

'Well, I do kind of feel that I'm in a rut.' He stops fiddling with the pen and looks at me. 'Or at least that I want to do something different. So I started thinking seriously about writing songs with other people.'

'Have you ... have you ever done that before?' I'm genuinely interested. I haven't paid enough attention to the details of his career to know who he's worked with. 'Professionally, I mean.'

'I've tried a few times,' he says. 'But it never worked. I've never been able to write songs with anyone else.' He pauses and then says, 'Apart from you.'

I don't know what to say to this. I'm flattered – more than flattered – that I'm the only person he's ever written with. But it all reminds me that this is all about Tadhg's job. His career. This reunion is primarily about work. Not our old friendship.

'In fact, that's what made me think of our song,' Tadhg continues. 'And after I started playing it again, I really, really wanted to finish it. That's why I asked Tara to mail you.'

'So what did you say to Hugo last night?' I ask.

'I told him I didn't want to write with Ahlberg and Johns,' says Tadhg. 'And that I was already in the middle of a songwriting session. With you.'

He's telling his manager – well, his sort-of manager – about me? This fortnight of workshopping really is serious. 'And does Hugo approve?'

'Well, he still wants me to work with Ahlberg and Johns,' says Tadhg. 'He thinks working with them will be good publicity, if nothing else. Show I'm going in a 'fresh new direction' – his words, not mine. But I told him I didn't need their direction and I was sticking with you. And that's that.' He clasps his hands at the back of his neck and looks up to the ceiling. 'I've got to sort out meetings with new managers. I've kind of been letting it slide.'

'Well, you did say Jim only died a few months ago,' I say. 'You can't rush into things.'

'I suppose,' says Tadhg.

'And you'll get out of that rut,' I say. 'You don't need any help to do that.'

'I think I do,' says Tadhg, with a wry smile. 'Sorry for banging on about this.'

'You haven't been,' I say. 'I know I haven't won any Grammys, but do you want to go to the studio and write some more songs with me?'

Tadhg laughs. 'There is nothing I'd like more.'

It's as if yesterday's work has ignited some fresh creative fire. Yesterday we were bringing each other fragments of songs we'd already written; today we're coming up with brand-new music. We write a whole new song there and then.

'I'd love to play that last one with a full band,' I say. 'No offence to your drumming, of course. But it would be great to …' I trail off and Tadhg grins.

'Play with a proper drummer? I agree. And actually,' he adds thoughtfully, 'we might be able to do something about that. I can see if my friend Sam's free to call in for a few hours this week. He only lives in Glasnevin. I'll give him a ring right now.'

And he actually does it. He takes his phone out of his pocket and makes the call. 'Hey, man, how are you? Good, thanks. Really good. Listen, how are you fixed this week? Do you have any spare time? No, I'm working on some songs in the studio with my friend Laura … Um, yeah, that's right. She is. Yeah.' Tadhg looks at me and whispers, 'Sorry, I'll be back in a sec,' and leaves the room, closing the kitchen door firmly behind him.

I can't help feeling slightly paranoid. What was this mysterious Sam asking about me?

Tadhg comes back a minute or two later.

'So,' he says, 'if it's okay with you, Sam will call over for a few hours this afternoon. What do you think?'

'I think we'll make a lot of noise,' I say. 'In a very good way.'

'Excellent,' says Tadhg.

We spend the rest of the morning working on all the new songs. We still don't have proper lyrics for them, but I tell myself they can come later. Writing lyrics feels weirdly intimate at the moment, and I don't know if either of us is ready for that. What would we write lyrics about? In the past, we never really wrote lyrics together. Because Tadhg was so good at it and I was so unwilling to write about what I was actually feeling, he became our primary lyricist by default. Which was probably for the best, given the lyrics I did write, like 'Midnight Feast'. I suppose we could divide the songs up between us now, but the only lyric subjects that spring to my mind are my complicated new feelings for Tadhg and the memories of my anger and hurt at Dave. And I don't feel like sharing any of that with Tadhg at the moment.

I'm also not exactly eager to listen to any potential lyrics about Tadhg's recent love life. Or current love life, if he has one. If he does, I don't want to find out about it by playing the guitar while he sings heartfelt words about it. I'd rather leave the songs wordless for now.

We're just finishing lunch when I think of Sarah's daughter Ellie. I feel a bit weird asking him, but then I think how happy it would make Ellie and I realise my embarrassment isn't as important as her getting a message from her hero.

'Um, can I ask a favour?' I say.

'Sure,' says Tadhg.

'You remember my friend Sarah? Well, her daughter Ellie's a big fan of yours and … oh God, this is a bit cringe, in fact it's extremely cringe, and I'm only asking because she's such a great kid. Would you mind doing a video message, just saying hi and wishing her happy birthday? It would make her so happy. She sang 'Another City' at her school show last year.'

'Of course, I'd be delighted,' says Tadhg. 'Her name's Ellie?'

'That's right.'

'Okay. Get filming.'

The video is very charming – Tadhg starts by wishing Ellie happy birthday and saying he's honoured she sang his song at her school show, then says he hopes making music makes her happy and that she keeps on doing it. He finishes by whispering, 'Oh yeah, and your mam and her friends are all extremely cool and you should listen to their wisdom at all times.'

I laugh and stop filming. 'That was perfect,' I say. 'Thanks.'

'My pleasure,' he says, and then the doorbell rings.

'Sam's early,' says Tadhg in surprise. 'That's not like him.' He gets up and goes out to the hall, where a screen linked to the security camera shows whoever's waiting at the gate. But instead of the buzzer that opens the gate, I hear Tadhg's voice saying, 'Oh, for fuck's sake.' I go out to the hall.

'What's up?' I say.

Tadhg points at the screen. 'I should have known Sam would never be early. It's Hugo.'

'Hugo the manager? You weren't expecting him, were you?'

'No, I was not,' says Tadhg. 'Shit, I suppose I can't leave him waiting there. Tara's not checking the door today.' He presses an icon on the screen and says, 'Hugo? Did we have an appointment I forgot about?'

'Tadhg! Hi!' The accent is south Dublin private school, the tone ingratiating. 'I just thought I'd pop round before I head back to London.'

'Okay,' says Tadhg. 'But you know I'm busy in the studio right now, don't you?'

'Of course, of course!' says Hugo. 'I just want to run something by you. It'll only take five minutes.'

'Fine,' says Tadhg. 'Come on in.' After he hits the buzzer and opens the front door, he turns to me and says, 'Sorry about this.'

'It's grand,' I say. 'I'll make myself scarce.'

'Would you mind staying just a minute?' says Tadhg. 'Hopefully seeing you will make him realise this fortnight with you is serious and he'll give up on the other lads. Ah, Hugo.'

A fair-haired, pink-cheeked man in his late twenties is climbing the steps and now stands in the doorway, clad in an expensive-looking wool coat over jeans and polished brogues.

'Tadhg!' he cries. He beams at me. 'And who do we have here?'

Tadhg steps closer to me. 'This is Laura. I told you about her last night. We're working together at the moment.'

'Of course!' says Hugo. 'Great to meet you, Laura. What did you say her surname was, Tadhg? Murphy?'

'McDermott,' I automatically correct him.

He sticks out a hand and I shake it. His grip is painfully firm. 'Hugo Delaney. And you're not a professional musician, are you, Laura McDermott?'

'No, I usually work in advertising.'

I'm not just some wannabe musician, Hugo! I have a proper career!

'Cool, cool,' says Hugo. 'Where do you work? I have a lot of pals in the business.'

'I'm freelance at the moment,' I say.

'But you must have worked at some agencies, right?' he says.

'Um, I was at Visions before Zenith took over.'

'Visions! Wow.' He literally looks me up and down, taking in my slightly messy hair – I am suddenly painfully aware my fringe is looking a bit wonky today – and scruffy runners. 'You worked there? Very cool.' He sounds insultingly surprised and then turns to Tadhg. 'So, what you said last night about your songwriting session gave me a great idea.'

'Okay.' Tadhg doesn't sound very enthusiastic. 'Let's go into the sitting room and you can tell me about it. But like I said, Hugo, we're in the middle of work at the moment. Sam Chu's coming over soon.'

'The little drummer boy?' Hugo pretends to drum a *parrup-a-pom-pom* beat. 'Brilliant.'

Tadhg turns to me. 'Can you wait for me out in the studio? This won't take long.'

'No worries,' I say.

'Thanks, Lol,' says Tadhg.

They go into the sitting room and close the door.

Out in the studio, I start messing around on my guitar and come up with a guitar riff that might be too pop for Tadhg but which is great fun to play. I'm playing it so loudly I don't hear the studio door open.

'Hello! *Hello?*'

The voice is loud, male and unfamiliar. I let out a little cry of shock and whirl around to see a stocky man about my age with black hair and a friendly expression standing in the studio.

'Shit, sorry, I didn't mean to startle you,' he says. 'I'm Sam.'

He holds up the cymbals case that he's carrying in his right hand.

'Oh!' I say. 'Of course. Sorry for screaming.'

'Sorry for giving you a fright.' He grins. 'Can we stop apologising now?'

I laugh. 'Sure. Where's Tadhg?'

'He's still in there with young Master Hugo.' He does a pretty good imitation of Hugo's accent when he says his name. 'He'll be here in a minute.'

'Cool,' I say. I feel a little self-conscious. This is the first time I've met one of Tadhg's friends from his post-me life, and I'm not sure what to say to him.

'Anyway,' says Sam, 'great to meet you at last!'

At last? 'I've actually only been here since Monday. Tadhg just asked me to do this last week.'

'I know,' says Sam. 'I just meant it's great to finally meet the famous Laura!'

I stare at him. 'The what?'

'I first heard about you when me and Tadhg started playing together back in, Jaysus, it must be 2007?' says Sam. 'It was just after I made the 'Winter' video.'

'You made that?'

'Yeah!' says Sam. 'I used to be a video artist. I mean, I suppose I still am, but I'm mostly a session drummer these days. Anyway! Tadhg wanted to start playing live with a full band, and I'd been the drummer in a band when I was in NCAD so I stepped in. And I've never stepped out.'

'Oh,' I say. 'But, um, what do you know about me?'

'Almost nothing!' says Sam cheerfully. 'Just that back when we started seriously playing music together, there were loads of times in the studio when Tadhg would play, like, a fragment of a song that sounded really good, and I'd ask to hear more of it so we could do something with it, and he'd say, 'No, that was a song I wrote with Laura.' And obviously I asked who Laura was and he said you were his old bandmate. Actually, for a long time I presumed you were his ex-girlfriend as well.'

I force a laugh and say, 'I definitely wasn't.'

'That's exactly what he said when I eventually I asked him,' says Sam. 'Anyway, I hadn't heard your name for years, and then today I got a call saying you're back working together! So I had to come and meet you. And my wife's picking our daughter up from school so I can stay as long as you like. What was that song you were playing when I came in? It was really good.'

'Just something I was messing about with,' I say. 'But I don't think it's right for Tadhg.'

'Well, it doesn't have to be right for Tadhg,' says Sam. 'It could be right for someone else.'

'What do you mean?' I say. 'I can't sing myself …'

'You could sell it to another artist,' says Sam. 'You know, I work with a lot of producers – I could put you in touch with people.'

'Seriously?' I say.

169

'Yeah, of course,' says Sam. 'If you're half as good a songwriter as Tadhg says you are, you could make a real go of it.'

I feel a tingle of excitement. Could I really do that? Could I actually be a professional songwriter?

The door of the studio opens and Tadhg walks in with a face like thunder.

'Are you okay?' I say.

He takes a deep breath. 'Yeah. It's fine. Just Hugo being Hugo.' He rubs his chin. He'd clearly shaved since I saw him yesterday evening but it looks like the stubble is growing back already. 'Anyway, he's gone now. Sorry to keep you waiting. You've met Sam?'

'I sure have!' I sound ridiculously chirpy.

'Great,' he says.

'Sure you're all right, bud?' says Sam. 'You look a bit rattled.'

'I'm grand,' says Tadhg. 'Sorry. It's just … ah, it's nothing. Just another reminder that I really need to get a new manager.'

'You'll find someone,' says Sam. 'Right! I'm going to get set up.'

While Sam arranges the drum kit to his liking, Tadhg says, 'I think I've got Hugo off my back about working with those other producers. So don't worry, he's not going to make a fuss about us working together anymore.'

'Oh,' I say. I hadn't known for certain that he *had* been making a fuss about us working together, but I guess now I do. 'Well, that's good. Isn't it?'

'Yeah. Yeah, it is. Sorry, Lol. Let's forget about him for now.' He picks up his bass. 'How are you doing there, Sam?'

Sam gives us a thumbs up. 'All good!'

His jovial vibe helps dispel the cloud cast over Tadhg by whatever Hugo said in the house. Tadhg smiles and says, 'All right. Lol, will we try playing this morning's one? And Sam, just come in when you feel like it.'

It only takes Sam a few bars before he's right in the song with us. I can see why Tadhg's been playing with him for all these years – he's a dream band member, staying connected to both of us rather than just doing his own thing. When we finish the song – Sam plays one last drum roll and somehow ends with a perfect tight bass drum beat just as I play the last chord, despite the fact that he's never heard the song before – I feel the same way I felt in that band room back in 1999. A joyful amazement that I've just been part of something that sounded that good.

'Not bad!' says Sam. 'Not bad at all!'

'Sam,' says Tadhg, 'you're a godsend.'

'Can we try another song?' says Sam.

'We can try *lots* of songs,' says Tadhg.

That's what we do.

And for the whole afternoon, Tadhg and I are in a band again.

Chapter Nineteen

2002

It was a miracle.

From the moment Tadhg stepped into that scruffy garage in Stillorgan, the four of us were a unit. He fit right in as if he'd been playing with us for years, and more than that, he made us complete. Beforehand, we'd been three friends playing music together. After Tadhg arrived, we were a band.

We'd always gone into town for drinks after band practices, and after Tadhg's first session with us, we took him to the Stag's Head and found a free table in the snug, right under the stuffed fox.

'So, um, did I pass the audition?' said Tadhg.

He had.

'Then I'm getting a round,' said Tadhg. 'What's everyone drinking?'

'You can't get the first round,' said Joanna. 'You're our guest.'

'No he's not,' I said. 'He's one of us now. Whether he likes it or not.'

I caught Tadhg's eye and we smiled at each other.

We'd arranged to meet Katie in the pub, and she arrived a few minutes after Tadhg had returned from the bar with the drinks.

'Hey!' she said. 'I hear they're deigning to allow you in the band. Which is more than they've done for me.'

'Oh, shut up,' I said good-naturedly. 'You chose the paper over us.'

'And I regret it every day,' said Katie in mock sadness.

'It's just as well, though,' said Brian affectionately. 'What with our torrid romantic history, Cáit.'

'Nothing worse than bandmates hooking up,' said Joanna, with the thousand-yard stare of someone who'd survived more than one messy band implosion in her time.

'Really, nothing?' I tried to keep my voice light. 'Not plague, war, famine?'

'*Nothing*,' said Joanna. 'Things get way too complicated.'

I could hardly start arguing in favour of bandmates hooking up in front of Tadhg so I said, 'Fair enough. We wouldn't want things to get complicated.'

'To keeping it pure and simple!' said Tadhg, raising his pint, and we all clinked our glasses together.

We got ham and cheese toasties for dinner and stayed in the snug for the rest of the night. Tadhg was squashed next to me in the corner, and at around half ten, when Jo, Brian and Katie were getting into an argument over whether *Buffy the Vampire Slayer* would ever get good again, he turned to me and said, 'Thanks for this.'

'Oh, there's no need to thank me,' I said.

'Nah, there is,' he said. 'Today's been brilliant.'

I smiled back at him. 'It has, hasn't it?

'I think,' said Tadhg, 'we could make a pretty good team.'

I couldn't look away from him.

'Yeah,' I said. 'I think we could too.'

'And obviously,' said Tadhg, 'the next step is fame and fortune and world domination.'

'Well, of course,' I said. 'It'll be all private jets and fur coats by Christmas. Bags first go on the jet.'

'Don't be ridiculous,' he said. 'We'll have a jet each.'

'Lol!' Katie was tapping me on the shoulder. 'Doesn't the *Buffy* musical episode make up for that awful episode in the fast-food place?'

'What?' I said. 'Um, yeah, I suppose so.'

Katie turned back to Brian. 'See? Lol agrees with me.'

Tadhg and I didn't talk alone again for the rest of the night.

But the hope began to grow.

I didn't only see Tadhg at band practices, of course. On the Monday after our first practice, he texted me to see if I wanted to go for lunch. I met him on the Arts Block ramp, and when I got there he was talking to a very pretty, tall blonde girl in a sheepskin-lined denim jacket.

'Hey!' he said when he saw me. 'Laura, this is Jess from my class. Jess, this is Laura.'

'Oh, your new bandmate!' Jess's smile was warm and friendly. 'Tim was just telling me about the band. It sounds great.'

It felt weird hearing her call him Tim.

'Oh, we've only had one practice so far,' I said, 'so I'm not sure how great we are!' I immediately wanted to kick myself for being self-deprecating. 'Um, so you're a music person too?'

'Yeah, but mostly experimental stuff, you know? A lot of hitting found objects with sticks and things like that.'

'Oh,' I said. 'Wow. Well, that sounds pretty cool.'

I suddenly felt like an ignoramus, even though Jess's manner hadn't been in any way patronising.

'Anyway!' she said. 'I'll let you go. Lovely to meet you, Laura. Bye, Tim!'

'See you later,' said Tadhg.

Jess waved and went into the Arts Block.

'She seems nice,' I said honestly.

'Yeah, she's great,' said Tadhg.

'Does everyone in your class call you Tim?' I said.

'Well, yeah,' he said.

'Would you prefer if I called you Tim?' I said.

He smiled and said, 'Absolutely not.'

'Really?'

'Really,' he said. 'I'll always be Tadhg in the glamorous world of rock and roll.'

'Okay then,' I said, smiling back at him. 'Tadhg it is.'

That was the beginning of what became our routine for the rest of the college year. Every Saturday I'd meet Tadhg outside college and we'd get the bus out to Stillorgan. From the start I loved those bus journeys, chatting about his course (he loved it but it was very intense), about my course (not very intense, in retrospect – I seemed to have endless time for just hanging around with my friends), about books and films and music and life in general. The journeys always felt too short.

When we got to the garage we'd practise the old songs and write new ones. Or rather, Tadhg and I wrote them. Sometimes we'd bring each other ideas, like little offerings – a chord sequence or a bassline from me, a melody or a riff from him – and create something new together. Sometimes we'd give each other songs that were almost complete. When I did that, he never added much to my songs, but whenever he brought me a song, he'd say, 'I know it needs something else, Laura. I just don't know what.'

But I always knew.

Afterwards we'd all go into town and get a drink in the Stag's or Doyle's, where we'd plan our future musical triumphs, more often than not joined by Katie.

♪♪

One night in November we were sitting in the Stag's and Katie said, 'At this stage I feel like an honorary member of the … you still don't have a band name, do you?'

We didn't.

'You should let me pick a name,' said Katie. 'I've got loads of band-name ideas. I've been thinking of imaginary band names since I was in school.'

'No way,' said Brian. 'I'm not trusting you to name our band.'

Katie looked at Joanna and Tadhg hopefully. 'Jo? Timothy?'

'Hmm, I'm not sure,' said Joanna.

'Maybe if you hadn't called me Timothy,' said Tadhg.

'Curses,' said Katie, shaking her fist.

'Anyway, there's no hurry with finding a name,' I said.

'Actually,' said Katie, 'maybe there is. I have news.'

She paused for dramatic effect and Tadhg said, 'Go on then, *Cáit*!'

'All right,' said Katie. 'You know Ruairí, right? Well, Tadhg and Laura do. I bumped into him on my way here. He's organising a gig for his friend's band, Sourpuss, the week before Christmas. And they've decided they need a second support act! So I said I'd ask you lot.'

We all looked at each other.

'We've got a month,' said Brian. 'We'll be good enough to play a gig by then, right?'

'Probably?' I said.

'I think we can do it,' said Joanna.

'Of course we can,' said Tadhg. 'Thanks, Katie.' He grinned at her. 'Maybe you should name the band after all.'

Katie rubbed her hands together in glee.

On a Wednesday evening in late November, I was crossing Front Square when I saw Tadhg with a group of his classmates. Including Jess. I'd met her a few times on nights out, and she was always lovely to me, but I couldn't help being weirdly intimidated by her. She was so tall and blonde and cool. Tadhg waved at me, said something to his friends and made his way over to me as they set off in the direction of the Arts Block.

'Hey!' he said.

'Hey yourself,' I said. 'Where are you off to?'

'I'm actually going home,' said Tadhg. 'I think I might need to eat some food that isn't chips.'

'Is that possible?' I said.

'I'm pretty sure there's something containing vegetables in my parents' fridge. What about you?'

'I was just about to go to the library to check if anyone was around to get dinner,' I said.

'Oh,' said Tadhg. 'Um, will I do? If you fancy going somewhere that serves veg, of course.'

I smiled up at him. 'I know just the place.'

Ten minutes later we were sitting on some battered armchairs in the wood-panelled basement of Gruel on Dame Street, a place where they served wine in tumblers and you could get a delicious dinner for a tenner. Over the last two months we'd had plenty of tête-à-tête lunches and cups of tea in college, talking and laughing and eating terrible Buttery food, but we'd never gone out alone in the evening before. We'd certainly never, like, gone out for dinner. It almost felt like … a date.

'This is brilliant,' said Tadhg, leaning back in his Naugahyde-covered armchair, a tumbler of red wine in one hand. 'I had no idea there was anywhere like this in Dublin.'

'I know!' I said. 'I can't afford to come here too often but I love it. And they do green things and everything.'

'Amazing,' said Tadhg. 'Maybe I won't die of scurvy after all.'

'You were never going to die of scurvy, Tadhg,' I said. 'There's vitamin C in chips.'

Later, when we were on our second glass of wine and eating vegetable tagine (Tadhg) and risotto (me), he said, 'So, listen, how are you feeling about this gig? You're definitely okay about playing it, right?'

'Definitely,' I said. And I really was. Nervous, sure, but also excited.

'And, like, we'll only be playing about six songs,' said Tadhg. 'We can finish with 'Midnight Feast'. It has all the words.' He softly sings the chorus. 'Couldn't make it work / no matter how you tried / It's a midnight feast / but I'm not satisfied.'

And because I'd had two glasses of wine, I unthinkingly said, 'I hope Dan's not in the audience to hear it.'

'Dan?' said Tadhg. 'Is that the guy you went out with last year?'

I groaned. 'Forget I said anything.'

'Is the song about him?'

'No! I mean, it doesn't matter!' I could feel myself blushing.

'I'm starting to think,' said Tadhg, 'that this whole midnight-feast thing isn't actually about food.'

I hid my face in my hands. 'Oh God!'

'Well, if Dan is listening in the audience,' said Tadhg, 'it'll serve him right for, um, not trying harder.'

'Shut up!' But I laughed, despite myself. 'So go on, who are your lyrics about? What about 'Anyone But You'?'

'Unlike you, Lol,' said Tadhg with a grin, 'I'm a gentleman. I'm saying nothing.'

He'd never called me Lol before.

'Well,' I said, 'I'm no gentleman.'

We'd finished our second glasses of wine. I couldn't really afford another one. (I couldn't technically afford this dinner.) I actually had an essay due on Friday. *I really should go home.*

But shit, I didn't want to. I really, really didn't want to. I wanted to stay with him. I wanted to hear him call me Lol again in that fond, familiar way.

Then for some reason I suddenly thought of Tadhg's cool classmate Jess. Would she tipsily urge Tadhg to stay out for one more drink that neither of them could afford on a Wednesday night, when both of them had early starts the next day? If she wanted to spend more time with him, would she be so blatant about it? Probably not.

So I sighed and said, 'We should probably head.'

'Really?' said Tadhg. He looked at his watch. 'Oh. Yeah. I suppose you're right. I have a psychoacoustics class first thing in the morning. You'd want to be awake for that.'

He didn't exactly seem like he was dying to leave, and for a moment I considered saying, *Fuck it, let's go to the Buttery and get a cheap drink.* But reason prevailed.

'Let's get the bill,' I said.

A few minutes later, we were walking past the Bank of Ireland on College Green.

'Thanks,' said Tadhg, 'for introducing me to that place. We should go there again.'

'Yeah,' I said. 'We should.'

We walked in companionable silence for a moment and then Tadhg said, 'Have I said how glad I am that we've found each other again?'

'Not in so many words,' I said.

'Well,' he said, 'I am.'

We reached my bus stop. And suddenly the atmosphere was different. Now there was something crackling between us, something that had always been there but was now charged with electricity.

'Yeah?' I said.

'Yeah,' said Tadhg. 'Very glad.' He took a step closer towards me.

For a moment I was *sure* he was going to kiss me. For a moment I thought I might even kiss him first.

Then a voice went, 'All right, lads?'

I turned around and Ruairí was strolling towards us, his hand raised in greeting.

'Ruairí!' said Tadhg, stepping back from me. 'Hey!'

'You on your way to the bus?' said Ruairí. 'I'll walk with you.'

'Um, yeah, sure,' said Tadhg. He turned to me. 'You'll be okay on your own, Lol?'

'Course I will,' I said brightly.

'Okay,' he said. 'I might see you before practice on Saturday.'

'Sure!' I said. 'See you soon.'

Perfect timing, Ruairí, I thought as they walked towards O'Connell Bridge. Thanks a bloody bunch. But the hope was growing blossoms now. *There'll be another moment like that, I thought. We'll have another chance soon.*

That's what I thought. That's really what I thought.

And then the gig happened.

Chapter Twenty

2019

I'm humming to myself when I let myself into the house after our session with Sam. One of Tadhg's melodies – now slightly tweaked by me – is stuck in my head.

'Lol?' Katie's voice calls me from the back of the house.

'It's me!' I say. I prop the Danelectro case up against the wall and unwind my scarf from around my neck.

'Were you *singing* just now?' says Katie from the kitchen.

'No!' I say. 'Why does everyone keep accusing me of singing? I was just humming!'

'Sounded like singing to me,' says Katie. 'And it didn't sound bad, to be honest. How did things go today?'

'Really good! Tadhg's friend came over to play drums and he was great. He's coming back tomorrow afternoon.' I stroll into the kitchen to see Katie standing at the fridge, unpacking groceries. 'Ooh, did you go to the posh supermarket?'

'I did. I'm going to have to get another loan from the credit union because I've spent all my money on cheese.'

'Can I have some?' I say.

'You can have some on Saturday, when His Highness comes over for dinner. How are things with him?'

'Good! I think. Want some tea?' I put the kettle on. When I turn around, Katie has closed the fridge door and is looking at me with concern.

'You like him again,' she says.

'Tadhg?' I take some mugs out of the press below the counter. 'Yeah, of course I like him. I mean, we're friends again. And I don't really think he wants to steal my song anymore. Come on, Kay, you know I'm not still angry with him.'

'I don't mean you like him as friends,' says Katie. 'I mean you *like* him, like him. I can tell by the way you're bouncing around the place. *And* singing!'

'*Like* him, like him? What are we, fifteen?' I put teabags into the mugs. 'And I wasn't singing.'

'You know what I mean! You fancy him! And don't talk shite about it being a chemical response or whatever. I mean you're into him! You have feelings for him.'

Ridiculously, I can feel myself starting to go red. 'I don't! I mean, not like before.'

'Are you sure?' says Katie. 'Stop messing around with those mugs and look at me.'

I sigh. 'Look, if I do – and I'm not saying I do – it really isn't like it was before. I'm not like I was before. And neither is he. We're sensible adults now.'

'I know,' says Katie. 'I just … Remember I asked you if you were pining for him again?'

'Yes, and I told you I wasn't,' I say.

'And I believed you. I hoped this whole thing would be really good for you. I hoped it would remind you how brilliant you are at music. But now … now I'm thinking working with him might be a mistake.'

'It's not a mistake!' I protest. 'I'm really enjoying it.'

'I know you are,' says Katie. 'Which is great. But please tell me it's because of the music and not just because of him.'

'It's not just because of him,' I say. Which is true.

'Good,' says Katie. 'Because you know you don't actually need Tadhg to play music, right? There are other options. Options that don't end up with you heartbroken again.'

'That isn't going to happen, Kay,' I say. 'Back in college I had … delusions. I mean, they turned out to be delusions. I thought he had feelings for me too. But he didn't. I accepted that a long, long time ago. So it's all fine.'

'Is it?' says Katie.

'I told you before,' I say. 'It's just for a fortnight and then I probably won't see him for ages. Seriously, you don't need to worry. I've got through what happened with me and Dave all right, haven't I? And that was a lot more serious than my … my unrequited college crush.'

Katie's worried look softens. 'Yeah, you have. Sorry, Lol. Maybe you and Dave is why I'm being a bit …'

'Ridiculous?'

'Overprotective,' says Katie. 'But you're right. You're a grown woman, and I trust you to look after yourself.'

'Thanks, Mam,' I say.

'Say that again,' says Katie, 'and I won't let you have any of the posh cheese.'

Later that evening, I'm in my room messing around on my acoustic when a text arrives from Sarah, with a voicenote attached.

Sarah: Sorry, I know it's not her birthday for weeks but she winkled it out of me!

The voicenote is from Ellie, and it's three minutes forty-eight seconds long, the majority of which is just Ellie screaming my name and then Tadhg's. 'Thankyouthankyouthankyou I am dead I am DEAD this is the greatest thing to ever happen. If you see him again can you ask him what Taylor Swift smells like? Okay, thank you love you bye. Oh, you don't have to get me a birthday present now. Unless you want to.'

I'm still laughing about it when I ring Sarah. 'So am I the best honorary auntie now?'

'You beat all the other aunties forever,' says Sarah. 'I'm so happy you've sorted things out with Tadhg.' She laughs. 'Remember what you were like when you arrived in New York that summer after your big bust-up? You'd cried so much on the plane I wanted to take you to the ER and get you put on a drip! I would have too, if we'd thought our travel insurance would cover it.'

'Ha, yeah,' I say, a bit too cheerfully. 'Don't worry, there's no chance of that now!'

But later, in bed, I realise it doesn't matter how much I tell my friends I've moved on, and it doesn't matter how often I remind myself that Tadhg and I are just friends. The illogical old hope that we could be more than friends keeps creeping in, no matter how much I remind myself of what happened the last time I had that hope, no matter how hard I try to crush it now.

But I really have to crush it if I want to keep making music with him, just for a while.

I just have to get through this fortnight.

That's what I tell myself when I set off for the studio the following morning. It's what I tell myself when Tadhg answers the door, wearing a dark-olive and navy checked shirt that brings out the green in his eyes. It's what I tell myself when he looks all happy to see me, and it's what I tell myself when, as he's making the first cups of tea of the day, he says, 'So ... I have a proposition for you.'

I try to look normal. 'Oh yeah?'

'Yeah,' he says. 'I'm playing this big gig in August. It's the only proper show I'm doing this year. You know the Moveable Feast festival?'

'Of course,' I say. Moveable Feast is one of the few 'boutique' festivals in the country that has actually kept its independent, distinct vibe. It takes place in a different beautiful location every year. The headline acts are always spectacularly good, especially for such a relatively low-capacity festival, and tickets always sell out within five seconds of going on sale. The calibre of the performers is so high that highlights are now televised and streamed all over the world.

'So I'm actually headlining Sunday night this year, and I know it's six months away but I was wondering …' Am I imagining it, or does he look a bit nervous? 'I was wondering if you'd like to play with me.'

I stare at him.

'On stage, I mean,' says Tadhg, when it's clear that I'm not going to say anything any time soon. 'At the gig.'

'I know what you mean,' I say. 'But … why?'

'Why?' says Tadhg. 'Well, first of all, you're one of the best guitarists I've ever played with. And second of all, Cara, who usually plays lead in the band, is moving home to New Zealand. So I'll be looking for a guitarist to do this show anyway. It wouldn't be a huge time commitment either. We'd just have to practise every week for a few months coming up to the festival.'

'But it's in front of thousands of people,' I say. 'And that's not counting people watching it online.'

'Yeah,' says Tadhg. 'But, you know, you've played gigs before. An audience is an audience.'

'Tadhg,' I say, 'I haven't played in front of anyone for, like, over a decade. And you may not remember this, but we weren't playing to massive crowds back then.'

'I know it's a big ask,' says Tadhg. 'And obviously you don't have to decide now. But will you think about it?'

'Of course I will,' I say.

Not only will I think about it, I know I will be thinking of nothing else for the next twenty-four hours, and possibly the next six months. Possibly the rest of my life, regardless of what I decide. Playing a gig. And not just any gig, a massive festival. I think of the thrill I got playing live back in the day. I imagine feeling that thrill again for the first time in sixteen years. I imagine having regular practice sessions with Tadhg and Sam. Being in a band again. Just for a while.

We decide to spend the day working on arranging the new songs we already have rather than starting new ones. It turns out that messing around with Tadhg's state-of-the-art sound desk is just what I need to stop myself overthinking his offer and what the future might hold.

'This software is amazing,' I marvel in the afternoon, as we listen to a gorgeous cello line stream out of the speakers. 'You'd never know that wasn't an actual cello.'

'Speaking of amazing software,' says Tadhg, 'I rang Tara yesterday and asked if she can arrange to have my old minidiscs digitised.'

'The ones you made of our old practices?' I'm stunned. 'You still have them?'

'Yeah, most of them,' says Tadhg. 'I don't have an actual minidisc player, but I do have the discs. They were in my old wardrobe in my parents' house – my mam found it when they were doing up my old room.'

'You mean your parents haven't preserved that room as a shrine to their only son?' I say.

'They have not,' says Tadhg. 'They've turned it into a spare-room-slash-office. Anyway, the box has been in my archive …'

'You have an *archive*?' I say. 'Did you bequeath your papers to the nation or something?'

'No!' says Tadhg. 'It's just a big filing cabinet in my office in town!'

'Sorry,' I say. 'I'll shut up now.'

Tadhg gives me a mock stern look that makes me feel quite peculiar and says, '*Anyway*. Tara just texted me and said she's found a place that can do it and she's couriered the discs over there. So she'll send you the files when they're done. It should just take a day or two.'

'Wow.' Our old practices. Our younger selves. Together. Am I actually ready, or able, to listen to that? To my stupid, hopeful younger self, especially my stupid, hopeful younger self interacting with Tadhg? I really don't know.

But ready or not, I know that I'm going to listen to it anyway.

♪♪

By the time I get home I feel a bit overwhelmed by, well, pretty much everything. I need to think about the whole playing-in-front-of-thousands-of-people thing. I need to think about what doing it could mean for the future.

It's not just about the excuse it would give me to spend more time with Tadhg. It's about whether this might actually be what I want to be doing – for myself. All the time.

For years now, I've never thought about playing music as anything other than something I did for a while in college. My career was – *is* – in advertising, and I've never questioned that it was the right fit. The sensible, grown-up fit. And – as a sensible grown-up – I've got that job lined up for when this fortnight with Tadhg is over, when I'll put down my guitar and focus on rebuilding my life.

But what if I want that life to look a little different now? Or very different? I think of Katie urging me to keep playing music. I think of Sam's suggestion that I could sell my songs to other people. What if it's possible to make a life playing music and writing songs after all? With or without Tadhg?

Jeanne and Katie are out tonight, and I'm glad, because I need some quiet time to myself to do all this thinking. But as I'm sitting down to dinner, ready to ponder all these serious issues over a bubbling mac and cheese, my mobile rings. Maybe it's Tadhg ringing to say Hugo has persuaded him to ditch me for that Swedish producer and he's very sorry but my services are no longer required …

But when I go out to the hall and pick up my phone from

where I'd dropped it on the table, the caller ID doesn't say Tadhg. It says someone I wasn't expecting.

And I'm so surprised I accidentally answer the call.

'Oh shit!' I fumble with the screen, trying to hang up again.

'Laura? Laura? Are you okay? Um, it's Dave.'

'I know,' I say. I lean back against the wall and close my eyes. I feel very weary all of a sudden. It's so weird, hearing his once-familiar voice after so long. But I can't hang up now. 'Your name came up.'

'Oh, right. I thought you might have …'

Deleted him from my contacts? Maybe I should have.

'Why are you calling, Dave?' I say. 'Did you finally find my passport? It's okay, I reported it lost months ago. I've got a new one.'

'No, it's not that,' he says.

'What is it then? I have to go in a minute,' I lie.

'I'm guessing you know about me and Liz,' he says.

'Yeah, I do,' I say warily. What is going on? Why on earth is he ringing me about this?

'Well.' He clears his throat. 'I thought I should tell you we're engaged.'

I'm shocked but, I'm pleasantly surprised to discover, I'm not particularly upset. I don't feel jealous or bitter. A bit hurt at how quickly I've been replaced as his fiancée, yes. I mean, I have my pride. But I realise I wouldn't trade places with her for anything on earth. Wow, I really wouldn't. I feel proud of myself! I genuinely have moved on.

'Oh,' I say. 'Congratulations. Okay, I'd better go.'

'No, wait!' he says. 'There's something else.'

And when he says that, I *know*. I don't know how, but I do. I know exactly what he's going to say. And this time I really, *really* don't want to hear it.

'Liz is pregnant,' says Dave. 'We're having a baby.'

A wave of nausea hits me. I grab onto the coat stand to stop myself sliding down the wall to the ground.

'I thought I should ring you and tell you directly,' he says.

I don't say anything.

'Laura? Are you still there?'

For a moment I physically *can't* say anything.

'Are you okay? Laura?'

'Why?' I say eventually.

'Um, sorry?' says Dave. 'Why what?'

'Why did you think you should tell me directly?'

'What do you mean?'

'Did you ring me because telling me over the phone would make *you* feel better? Because you think it's the brave thing, the *right* thing to do?'

'Well … it is, isn't it?'

'No, Dave!' I yell. 'No, it's not the right fucking thing to do! Next time you drop a little bombshell like this on someone, send them a text or write a fucking email so they don't have to pretend to be okay while they're talking to you!'

Then I hang up. And then I do slide down the wall and sit on the ground, and I stay there for a long time.

Chapter Twenty-One

2019

'Are you all right?'

Katie's brow is furrowed with concern as she looks at me across the kitchen table the next morning. I lean back in my chair and sigh.

'I'm fine,' I say.

'Are you sure?' she says. 'Because when we got in last night you were sitting on the floor of the hall with your head on your knees. That doesn't say fine to me.'

'I *am* fine,' I say. 'I mean, I will be.'

'I know you will be,' says Katie. 'But what about right now?' She bites her lip. 'I don't like leaving you alone …'

'You don't have to worry about me!' I protest. 'I'm not … I'm not going to do anything stupid.'

'I wasn't thinking that!' says Katie. 'I just … I don't like the thought of you being upset on your own today.'

'I won't be on my own,' I say. 'I'll be at Tadhg's.'

'But are you sure that's a good idea?' says Katie. 'Going over there, I mean.'

'Of course it is!' I say. 'What am I going to say? "Sorry, Tadhg, I can't come and work with you today, my ex-fiancé has impregnated another woman?"'

'Well,' says Katie, getting up from her chair, 'when you put it like that …'

'Look, you know I don't want to be with Dave anymore,' I say. 'You know I've accepted … all of it. But …' My voice starts to wobble a bit. 'But when he told me last night, it was just … I just …'

I can't say any more. But I don't have to. Because now Katie is beside me, and now her arms are around me, squeezing me tight. 'I know,' she says softly. 'I know, Lol. I know.'

When I woke up this morning, way too early, there was a moment of blissful peace before the memory of Dave's phone call last night hit me. I didn't want any aspect of his news to take me by surprise at some random moment in the future, so I lay in bed and forced myself to think about it all in great detail, as if really torturing myself now would somehow inoculate me against it causing pain later. Dave, the man I used to love, the man who used to love me, is going to have a baby. Dave will be a father. He'll have a new family. He's getting exactly what he wanted while I'm still mooning over a boy I fancied twenty years ago. He'll be thanking his lucky stars he dumped me when he did. I think about all this again now after Katie goes to work. I remember him pointing out that couple with the tiny baby and saying 'That'll be us in a year or two'.

It'll be him and Liz now.

Then I pull myself to my feet and go to the bathroom. If I do cry in the shower, well, no one hears it.

It's a mild, sunny day that actually feels like spring, and as I walk to Tadhg's house I try to be happy that winter is over, instead of wondering when exactly Dave's baby will arrive. How long did he wait to impregnate his amazingly fertile new fiancée? But he and his baby are none of my business, I tell myself. He's nothing to do with me now.

Sam meets me at the door, and when we go through to the studio, Tadhg is sitting in front of the giant computer screen at the sound desk, doing something mysterious with various tracks. He turns around when we enter.

'Morning!' he says. His face changes. 'Everything okay?'

'With what?' I say. 'With me? Of course! Why do you ask?'

'Sorry,' he says. 'You just look … I thought something was wrong.'

'I'm fine!' I say. 'I just slept badly last night.'

'Ah,' he says. 'That must be it.'

But he doesn't look totally convinced.

I do my best all morning not to appear too subdued. It helps that Tadhg asks if we're up for trying out a song he's been working on recently, so I don't have to present something of my own.

After lunch, Sam says, 'Right, pals, I'll love you and leave you. I've got to pick Etain up from school.'

He promises to come back next week and Tadhg walks him to the front door. As soon as they leave the kitchen I slump down in my seat. God, I'm tired. I'm tired of everything. I close my eyes and rub my temples, as if that can push out all the stupid painful thoughts.

'Are you *sure* you're okay?' says Tadhg.

My eyes snap open. 'I'm grand!' I say, too brightly.

'Sorry,' he says. 'You just seem a bit … down today. I shouldn't pry.'

Wow, I used to be better at hiding my feelings.

I sigh. 'No, you're not prying. I just … I got some news last night. About someone I used to know. Nothing terrible. It just threw me a bit, that's all. I'll be fine.'

'Ah,' says Tadhg. 'Do you want to talk about it?'

'No,' I say. 'But thanks for asking.'

'No problem.' He's silent for a moment and then says, 'Do you fancy taking a break and going for a walk? Just down to the seafront or something.'

The thought of some fresh air and spring sunshine does sound very appealing.

'I wouldn't mind,' I say, 'but can you, like, just go for a walk? Will you not be besieged by adoring fans?'

'We'll go out the back and I'll wear my contacts and a hat,' he says. 'And besides, we can take a route where we won't meet anyone.'

'We are talking about Clontarf seafront, right?' I say. 'The one where people go for runs and walk their dogs all day?'

Tadhg grins. 'You'll see. Trust me.'

I feel like a spy as Tadhg opens a door at the back of the studio that I'd barely noticed before and we emerge into the mews behind the Crescent. When he closes the door behind us, I see that it's built so skilfully into the outer wall of the studio that anyone passing would barely notice there was a door there at all.

'Come on,' he says, and we head down the mews, past a row of cottages.

'So this is your secret escape route?' I say. I gesture at the cottages. 'What do the locals think?'

'They're cool about it, mostly,' says Tadhg. 'People tend not to hang around here, which helps. Probably because the family in that house have a very loud dog whose bark is definitely worse than his bite. I don't think he even *has* a bite.'

But I noticed Tadhg still has to check for lurkers. Before we left the studio he looked at the stream from a security camera mounted on the external mews wall of the studio to ensure no one was hanging around outside.

We reach the end of the mews and turn right towards the

Howth Road. I glance up at him, the brim of his flat cap pulled low over his eyes.

'I like your hat,' I say.

He looks down at me, amused and sceptical. 'Really?'

'Really!' I protest. 'I've always thought more men should dress like farmers. Farmers and Victorian street urchins.'

He laughs. 'Well, that's good to hear because those are exactly the two looks I'm going for.'

'I thought they might be,' I say.

It's the first time we've walked anywhere together since college. It's easy to forget when we're sitting around the studio that he's six foot two, almost a foot taller than me. But now, as he shortens his long stride to match mine, the way he used to when we walked somewhere together back in the day, I'm very aware of it.

As we cross the road at the Presbyterian church, a woman crossing from the opposite side does a literal double-take.

'I think you've been spotted,' I say. 'Are you sure this is a good idea?'

'Pretty sure,' he says. But he pulls the hat down a little bit further.

'Can you actually see where you're going from under there?'

'Just about,' he says. We're on the narrow bit of pavement under the railway bridge now, and a man around our age is coming towards us. As he gets nearer I can see his eyes narrow as he peers at Tadhg.

'Hey,' he says. 'Are you Tadhg? Your man who does the winter song?'

And to my immense surprise, Tadhg says, in a truly terrible Yorkshire accent, 'No, but I get that all the time!'

'Oh, right,' says the stranger. 'Sorry, man.' And he walks on.

When we're out of earshot I grab Tadhg's arm and say, 'Oh my God, what was *that*?'

Tadhg looks sheepish. 'I know the accent could do with some work.'

'It definitely could!' I realise I'm still holding his arm and let go. 'Especially if you're always giving people that line.'

'I'm not!' he says. 'I mean, the public pay my wages. I always try to be friendly and polite and everything. I don't mind having a chat. But sometimes, if I'm distracted or busy or there's something I should be focusing on, then I just kind of fob them off as best I can. And this walk is meant to be for you. So I fobbed.'

'Oh,' I say. I'm touched by his concern. 'Well, thanks for doing a terrible accent then.'

'Don't mention it,' he says. 'Come on, let's cross here.'

We cross the road and walk onto the wide grass band that divides the main coast road from the pedestrian path that runs alongside the sea wall of Dublin Bay. I presume we're going to follow the main path, the one that runs parallel to the coast road. But Tadhg turns in the opposite direction, where the path curves around the bay and ends, after just a few hundred metres, in a tangle of brambles broken by a stone wall and some railings.

'This walk is going to be much shorter than I thought,' I say. 'This is a dead end.'

'You'll see!'

When we reach the stone wall, I realise that there's a gap in it. There's a boulder in front of the gap, so it isn't as evident from a distance, but you can walk around the boulder and pass through the gap. And there, behind the wall …

'How did I not know this was here?' I gasp.

In front of me winds a sandy, stony path. On the right of the path rises an embankment of thick brambles. On the left is a large patch of grass and some low trees, and behind them is the sea, sparkling in the early spring sunlight. The greenery blocks the noise of the busy nearby roads. It's like we're suddenly in the middle of the countryside.

'We used to drink cans down here when I was a teenager,' says Tadhg.

I look around this secret slice of seaside in the middle of the city and feel a little of my tension melt away.

The path is so narrow we have to walk in single file, with Tadhg leading the way.

'So,' he says, 'now our first week's almost over, how do you feel it went?'

I'm glad he can't see my face as I try to figure out what to say. My old instincts kick in. Don't be more into being with him than he is into being with you. Don't, for the love of God *don't*, give even a hint of how much hanging out with him again is starting to mean to you.

But I can be honest about the music. Because playing music with him again has been, well, magical.

I say, 'Um, good. I think. We've got a lot of work done. What about you? How do you feel it went?'

'Also good.'

Now I wish I could see *his* face.

'Very good, actually,' he adds. 'I'm really glad you agreed to do this.'

'Yeah,' I say to his navy wool-coated back. 'So am I.'

We climb up a narrow path with brambles and bushes on both sides, then the path widens, the embankment on the right is replaced by a playing field, and we're in a clearing. There are railings between us and the sea, and we lean on them and look out at the water. I take a deep breath of salty air, let it out and gaze across the bay to the distant horizon.

'Ever tempted to just take to the waves and sail off into the wide blue yonder?'

'Once or twice,' says Tadhg.

'You don't have a super yacht in the Med or anything, do you?'

Tadhg laughs. 'No, I don't! They're my idea of hell.'

'I wouldn't mind having a small boat,' I say. 'Like the ones they have at Clontarf boat club. Just to, you know, pootle about Dublin Bay.'

'That actually sounds pretty good,' says Tadhg. 'A little rowing boat with an outboard motor.'

'You could get a sailor hat,' I say. 'It'd be even better than your farmer's cap.'

'Aye aye, captain,' says Tadhg.

For a while we look out at the little boats bobbing in the distance in companionable silence.

'Next week,' says Tadhg, 'we should give our song another go. Now we've got used to working together again.' He turns and looks at me. 'What do you think?'

Well, we couldn't keep putting it off forever. And besides, I feel differently about it now than I did at the start of the week.

'Yeah, sure,' I say. 'That'd be good.'

When we get back to Tadhg's house, we play through the song we did this morning and I tweak one of his songs from yesterday. All of which keeps us busy for what's left of the day.

It's not until after he's told me how much he's looking forward to tomorrow's dinner and I've said goodbye and left the house and started walking home that I realise I haven't thought about Dave and his news once all afternoon.

Chapter Twenty-Two

2002

'I need to buy a suit.'

It was less than two weeks to our first gig and I was sitting in the library trying to read about deconstructionism when Tadhg sat down at the desk next to mine and made this declaration in a stage whisper.

'A suit?' I whispered back. 'Why?'

'For the gig!'

'I know you've got a grant,' I said. 'But I doubt it's going to cover a decent suit.'

'I'm going to try the charity shops on George's Street,' he said. 'Would you come with me? We've got nearly an hour before they close. I bet I can find a suit in an hour.'

I looked at the Jacques Derrida book on my desk. The thought of leaving it for Tadhg was more than tempting. 'What do you need me for to buy a suit?'

'To make sure I don't look like a total wanker in it,' he said.

'Oh well, in that case,' I said. And I put on my coat.

We had just left the library when we bumped into Ruairí.

'I was just going to email you two! Does your band have a name yet? I need it for the poster.'

Tadhg and I exchanged glances. The four of us (five when you included Katie, which we often did) had discussed potential band names ad nauseam in the pub over the last few weeks, but the conversations usually descended into joking. We still didn't have a serious contender.

'We're still finalising it,' I said.

'Well, you'd better do it fast,' said Ruairí. 'I want to print out the posters tomorrow.'

'We will!' I promised.

As soon as we were out of earshot Tadhg said, 'We really do need a band name.'

'Maybe we'll find some inspiration in Oxfam,' I said.

It was a few weeks now since our trip to Gruel, and there had been no opportunities for us to generate the sort of electric tension that had been there at my bus stop that night. We'd just seen each other in groups, apart from the odd hasty cup of tea between lectures. But that was okay, I thought. We both had a lot on. It was coming up to the end of term, and there were essays and assignments and stuff. Tadhg and I were in no hurry. We would get another moment. I certainly wasn't going to try and force anything.

'There's definitely *something* between you,' said Katie, who had endured a lot of these conversations with me already that term. ('I don't mind,' she assured me when I apologised for unloading all my angst on her. 'You had to deal with me and Tina breaking up in the summer. *And* we were all living together in London, so that was even worse for you. Now it's my turn.') 'Like, it's definitely not in your head. But, you know, there's one way you could know for sure …'

'No way,' I said firmly. 'I'm not making the first move. You heard him that night: "To keeping it pure and simple." If he doesn't feel the same way, everything's wrecked. The band. Our friendship. My dignity. Everything. I'm not going to risk it.'

I was very familiar with the George's Street charity shops. When we arrived in the first one, Tadhg went straight to the men's clothes and I had a look at the dresses. I might as well find something for myself to wear at the gig too. I immediately grabbed a floral maxi dress with short floaty sleeves, fitted at the bodice and sweeping down in an A-line. *I could probably play the guitar in this, right?*

'Hey, Lol,' called Tadhg. 'How about this one?'

I joined him to find him holding up a dark chocolate-brown suit with a slight flare in the trousers.

'I'm aware someone probably died in this,' he said. 'But I think it might fit?'

I glanced over at the two rickety changing booths in the corner.

'You try it on while I try on this dress,' I said. 'If you're in a suit the rest of us should probably dress up too.'

In the cramped, mirror-less booth I pulled the maxi dress over my head and tried not to think about the fact that, on the other side of the curtain, Tadhg was also taking most of his clothes off. I was doing up the zip, almost dislocating my arm in the process, when Tadhg said, 'You ready, Lol? Come out and tell me what you think.'

I quickly yanked the dress into place and pulled back the curtain.

Tadhg said, 'I'm worried it's a bit—' Then he caught sight of me and said, '*Wow*. Cool dress.'

For a few seconds, I was simply speechless. Even in the grim fluorescent light of a charity shop, he looked astonishing. The suit fitted him as if it had been tailored for him. He always looked good but now he looked … elegant. He looked dashing. And ridiculously cool.

I swallowed. 'Nice suit.'

Then I caught sight of myself in the mirror on the wall next to the changing cubicles and realised just how low-cut the dress actually was. Tadhg followed my gaze to the mirror and for a moment neither of us said anything. We stood side by side and looked at our reflection. We could have been an incredibly chic bohemian couple in the 1970s, throwing a dinner party in our conversation pit. In this context, my unruly dark hair looked like something out of a seventies *Vogue*, even under the terrible lighting. My navy-blue dress with its hot-pink and orange print perfectly complemented his rich chocolate suit. The cut of the dress, the way it swept down to the floor, somehow made me look tall and even elegant. It also, undeniably, made my boobs look incredible.

'Well, this will be the first album cover,' said Tadhg.

'I don't know if I can play the guitar in this dress.' I was about to add 'it's a bit tight', but I didn't want to draw attention to what I realised was the extremely flattering nature of the tight fit.

'You should buy it anyway,' said Tadhg.

Our eyes met in the mirror.

And then a phone started ringing in his changing cubicle, and whatever spell might have been conjured up was broken.

He disappeared behind the curtain and I heard him say, 'Hello? Hey! No, I'm charity-shop trawling with Laura. Yeah! I did find one. Ha! Pretty much. I'm going to pay for it now … Oh, okay. Um, yeah, I think so. But I have a band practice that afternoon and we do have the gig next week … Yeah, I'll let you know. Thanks for asking me. Cool. Okay, see you tomorrow.'

He emerged from the curtain. 'That was Jess.'

My stomach twisted a bit. His voice on the phone had sounded so … affectionate. So happy to hear from her. And she clearly already knew about his quest for suits.

'Anything up?' I said.

'Um, yeah. Her family are having a big party for her brother's eighteenth and she's asked me to go with her. She says she doesn't want to be stuck talking to teenagers or old relatives all night.'

'Oh, right!' I prayed my feelings didn't show on my face. 'Cool. So are you going?'

'Well, it's this Saturday.' He rubbed his chin, making a rasping noise. 'So if I go I won't be able to make the post-practice pub debrief.'

'Oh, that doesn't matter!' I said as breezily as I could. 'As long as you can make the practice.'

'Well, yeah, it's just that it's the last practice before the gig,' he said. 'Maybe I shouldn't run off straight away.'

The temptation to say 'Yeah, you're right, you shouldn't' was so, so strong. Jess was clearly asking him out. And for fuck's sake, he must know that. If you just want some company at a family party you ask one of your mates. You don't invite the hot man you've only known for two months to be your plus-one. But what was I going to say? 'No, you can't go to the party with that gorgeous girl who you clearly really like, you have to go to the pub with me?' What would *that* sound like? I thought of the fondness in his voice when he talked to her. Pathetic, that's what it would sound like.

So I said, 'Don't be silly, of course you should go!'

'Are you sure you don't mind?'

'Why would I mind?' I said, wrinkling my nose as if that was the most ridiculous suggestion I'd ever heard. 'Come on, we'd better change and buy these before the shop closes.'

'It's not definitely a date,' said Katie the next day.

'It's not *not* a date,' I said miserably. We were sitting in the Buttery eating unsatisfactory sandwiches. 'It's not just a little thing in her family house. It's in some fancy hotel in town.'

'Laura!' I looked up to see Ruairí approaching our table, a rolled-up tube of paper in one hand. With a sinking feeling I realised I'd completely forgotten to contact the others about deciding on a band name.

'Oh shite, Ru, I'm so sorry, something came up—' I began but Ruairí interrupted me.

'Look, when I didn't hear from you I had to finish the posters anyway.' He unrolled the tube and held up a poster.

'Oh my God!' I stared at him in horror as Katie let out a gleeful hoot of laughter.

At the top of the poster, over a diagram taken from an old sociology book about juvenile delinquency, were the names Sourpuss, then Shatner and then finally The Band Laura's In.

'You left me no choice!' said Ruairí. 'I don't know what the hell Tim's calling himself these days. And I couldn't remember your other bandmates' names.' He handed me the tube of posters. 'Can you put these up in the northside music shops?'

I nodded. When he'd gone Katie said, 'Well, at least you're asserting yourself in the band!'

I hit her with the roll of posters.

Luckily my bandmates were more amused than annoyed by my accidentally hogging the limelight.

'A lesson learned,' said Tadhg. 'We'll have to have a proper name by our next gig. And besides,' he added, 'you're clearly the star of the show, Lol.'

I smiled back at him, but the jokey compliment didn't land quite the same as it would have a few days earlier.

♪♫

On Saturday afternoon, roughly half an hour before we usually wrapped up our weekly practice, Tadhg untangled himself from his guitar strap.

'Sorry, all,' he said. 'But I'd better head now. I've got to get home, dump my guitar and change before I head back to town.'

'Ready for your hot date?' said Brian with a grin.

Tadhg laughed. 'It's family party, I wouldn't call it a hot date. Sorry I can't help with the tidying up.'

'Don't be ridiculous!' I said. 'You go and have a great time with Jess.'

If my smile didn't reach my eyes, I hoped he didn't notice.

But still, said a voice in my head, *he did say it* wasn't *a hot date*. And the hope continued to bloom.

I couldn't bring myself to contact him the next day, and he didn't contact me. Then on Monday I was crossing Front Square when I saw him walking towards me from the direction of the Áras an Phiarsaigh building, where he had most of his classes. He was with Jess. My stomach lurched. I had an urge to run back through Front Arch and hide. But it was too late, he'd seen me and waved, so I had to join them.

'Hi!' I said in my most cheerful voice. 'How was your party?'

Jess looked at Tadhg in amusement. 'It was great. Almost too great, to be honest. I think my family prefer Tim to me now.'

Tadhg laughed. 'I wouldn't go that far.'

'I would.' She turned to me, smiling. 'The sound system broke down and Tim managed to find a guitar in the hotel and entertained everyone until they fixed it.'

'Wow!' I said. 'Well done. That sounds fun!' Why did I always sound so blandly stupid when she was around? 'Anyway, I'd better run, I've got a lecture in ten minutes.'

'I saw your gig posters, by the way!' said Jess. 'Tim told me about the name thing, it's so good.'

'Can you make the gig?' I prayed the answer would be no.

'Now I've seen what Tim can do with one wonky acoustic guitar,' she said, 'there is absolutely no way I'm missing seeing his band.'

His band? But I wasn't going to argue about that with her right now. 'That's brilliant!' My relentless cheerfulness was sounding deranged even to me. 'See you there!'

But still, I thought as I hurried across to the Arts Block, *but still, they were just hanging out with her family on Saturday.* And the hope remained.

The gig was on Thursday, the night before the last day of the college term. On Wednesday the band met up to go through the schedule. The gig was starting to seem very real now. And a huge deal. Would the magic we felt in Brian's garage vanish when we were playing in front of other people? Were we just fooling ourselves when we thought we were actually good?

When we left the Buttery, Tadhg and I found ourselves lagging behind the others and he said, 'How are you feeling?'

'What do you mean?' I said.

'About the gig.'

'Um, mostly excited,' I said, which was true. 'But also a bit nervous.'

'Don't be nervous. You'll be brilliant.' We were on the ramp that led to Front Square and he stopped and turned to me. 'We'll be brilliant.'

'Are you going to wear the dead man's suit?' I said.

'Course I am,' he said. 'Are you going to wear that dress?'

'I'm not sure,' I said.

'You should,' said Tadhg.

I didn't wear it, in the end. For a while after that night, I stupidly wondered if things might have been different if I had. But on the day I was too self-conscious about the low cut, and also genuinely worried about accidentally exposing myself while playing on stage. So I wore another charity-shop find instead, a black sixties sleeveless shift dress with a white lace collar, less sexy but still, I hoped, pretty cool, which I paired with bare legs and Converse low-tops. I had butterflies in my stomach as I descended the stairs that led to the venue for the sound check. Tadhg and Joanna were there already, chatting with Ruairí.

'The poster child herself!' said Ruairí. I gave him the finger. He ignored it and said, 'Shatner are about to soundcheck and then it'll be you.'

After our very brief soundcheck we barely had time to grab food and get back to the venue before the doors opened. People were coming in now, and one of the first was Jess, with some extremely glamorous friends. Jess was wearing perfectly fitting indigo jeans and a tight navy T-shirt with an asymmetric silver print. I was on my way to the loos to do my make-up when they passed me. I would have much preferred to meet them after doing my make-up. I would also have preferred to meet them while wearing the seventies maxi dress.

'Hi, Laura!' said Jess. 'Wow, I love the dress, it's so cute. Vintage?'

'Thanks,' I said. 'Yeah, it is.' And then, because I felt I had to say something friendly, 'Thanks for coming.'

'I wouldn't miss it. Is Tim here?'

'He's at the bar,' I said. 'Sorry, I have to dash.' I scuttled off to the bathroom, and by the time I came out, with an impressively clean cat-eye liner for someone whose hands were almost shaking with nerves, the venue was almost full. I looked around for the others and to my massive relief saw Katie and Sarah at a table at the back of the venue.

I slipped into a seat. 'God, I need a drink.'

Sarah shook her head. 'Turning to booze already. The rock-and-roll lifestyle is taking its toll.'

As if by magic, someone wearing a dark brown suit jacket reached over my shoulder and put a pint of cider on the table in front of me. I turned around in my seat.

'I thought you might want a pint,' said Tadhg. 'Hey, everyone.'

'Evening, Father Timothy,' said Katie, winking at him.

'Do you want to join us?' said Sarah. She was in college at UCD but she'd met Tadhg plenty of times on nights out.

'Thanks, but I've got a pint over there.' He pointed to a table where Jess and her friends were talking to Brian and his new girlfriend, the dreaded Caroline, then turned to me. 'You okay? No last-minute nerves?'

'I'm grand!' I lied. 'Thanks for the drink.'

And then, suddenly, it was time.

The venue looked a lot bigger and more full once I was up on the stage with my guitar slung around my neck. Tadhg gave me a reassuring nod.

'Come on, Lol,' he said. 'Let's show 'em how it's done.'

As soon as he walked up to the microphone stand, the entire room quietened down and heads started turning towards us. He'd had stage presence even when he was a teenage busker, and I don't know what he'd been doing in that band down in Cork for the previous three years, but now his onstage charisma was off the scale. It was like he'd turned a light on inside himself as soon as he got up there.

'I'm Tadhg Hennessy,' he said in that honey-and-gravel voice. 'That's Joanna Smyth, that's Brian O'Hara, *that* is Laura McDermott and we are, above all else' – he threw me a sidelong grin and I couldn't help grinning back – 'The Band Laura's In.'

Then Brian counted us in, and for fifteen minutes nothing else mattered.

This was the thing about our band: we only ever played four gigs, but every time we got on stage people who'd never seen us before were surprised by how good we were. They expected a shambolic student band and they got something else. Part of it was down to Tadhg and his undoubted star power, but I'm not being deluded when I say that it wasn't just that. Joanna was a brilliantly fierce bass player. Brian had become a genuinely good drummer. I won't indulge in false modesty and pretend I wasn't a good guitarist, because I was *very* good. And there were the songs, the ones Tadhg and I wrote. We started the set with 'Anyone But You', a garage-rock song with a ridiculously catchy, poppy chorus, and before we'd reached that chorus the previously empty space in front of the stage had entirely filled up. People were drifting across from the bar. By the time we finished the song the crowd was pressed right up to the edge of the stage. When I slammed down the final chord there was a tiny split second of silence and then the entire room went wild.

They stayed wild for the rest of our short set. The second song, 'Midnight Feast', was received with even more enthusiasm, and that enthusiasm was infectious – it made us play harder, play better. Years later I stumbled across a blog post looking back at what they called Tadhg Hennessy's first Dublin gig in 2002. They didn't mention the name of the band he was playing in, but it was that gig all right. They said everyone in that room knew they were looking at a star, that the two bands who played afterwards might as well have stayed at home. They wrote about the gig like it was Tadhg's solo show with some backing musicians, but that's not how it felt on stage that night. Playing with Tadhg never felt like that. When the four of us played together it felt like we were a team, we were a band, we were a *gang*. Joanna's bass and Brian's tight drumming kept us all in perfect sync, and Tadhg and I communicated without words, my lead and his rhythm guitar combining into one glorious noise.

And then, just as he said, 'Thank you, you've been amazing. This is our last song. It's called 'Tourniquet',' Jess and her friend moved to the front of the crowd. She was gazing up at Tadhg in just the way I'd have liked to gaze up at Tadhg if I were in the audience: cool, amused, impressed but not adoring. I remembered how nicely she had praised my dress. She said it was cute. It *was* a cute dress. Not sexy like the maxi dress, the one I should have worn.

And I thought, *Cute? I'll give you fucking cute.*

I launched into the ferociously choppy, poppy riff that opened the song, then Tadhg started singing and I threw myself into the music like I was going into battle. I turned and caught Tadhg's eye and for a moment it was just the two of us, playing together, facing each other, looking at each other as if we were the only two people on earth. We played the last notes, Brian gave a cymbal a final, thunderous smash, and the audience applauded and roared so loudly I felt dizzy. The four of us stared back at the crowd, a little shellshocked.

We'd done it. We'd played our first proper gig. And every second of it had been *magnificent*.

Then, as we were walking off the stage, still in a daze, Jess ran up and gave Tadhg a huge hug.

'Tim!' she cried. 'Oh my God, you were so good! That was incredible.' She turned to me and beamed. 'You were amazing, Laura. Tim never said you could play like that!'

Hours later, when I was in bed trying and failing to get to sleep, this was one of the sentences that kept replaying in my head. He'd never told her I was good in the band. Of course he hadn't. Why would he ever talk to her about me?

Then Katie was flinging her arms around me and Sarah was congratulating me and the two of them were dragging me off to the bar.

'Jesus,' Katie whispered in my ear, 'when you were playing that last song I thought he was going to start shifting you right there on stage, seriously.'

That sentence went round in my head later that night too.

The next two hours were a bit of a blur. People kept coming up to me and saying how amazing we'd been, how cool I'd been. People were buying me drinks, more drinks than I could consume. It was dizzying. Ruairí invited us all back to a party in his house. There was a febrile end-of-term mood in the air, as if anything might happen and any of us could do anything. I don't remember a single second of Shatner's and Sourpuss's sets. I just knew that I mostly lost sight of Tadhg, apart from glimpses across the crowded venue of him talking to various friends and classmates. Including Jess.

Then, when I was on my way back from the loo after Sourpuss left the stage, he was suddenly in front of me.

'There you are!' he said, smiling down at me. 'I've been looking for you.'

'Hey!' I said, beaming back at him. 'That was deadly, wasn't it? Playing up there?'

'That,' he said, 'was fucking brilliant.'

'We need to do it again.'

'We will,' he said.

'Ruairí's having a thing later back in his house,' I said. 'He's got a free gaff. What do you think?'

Tadhg hesitated and then said, 'Well actually, Jess asked me back to her flat in Fitzwilliam Square for a drink.'

'Oh, right!' I said. 'Okay. Cool.'

Back to her flat.

'But if there's, like, a big post-gig thing in Ruairí's I can see if she wants to go ...'

Don't beg him to go to the party. Don't show him how much you don't want him to go to Jess's flat.

'Tadhg!' I said, in a mock-scolding voice. 'You can't do that to Jess. If she's invited you back to her place she won't be up for Ruairí's house with a huge crowd instead.'

'Tim!' And here was Jess, right between us. 'Sorry, Laura, mind if I steal your bandmate for a minute?'

I plastered on a big smile. 'He's all yours!'

Back to her flat, back to her flat. He was going back to her flat. But maybe it was just a friendly thing. Maybe it was a party with all of their classmates. Maybe he wouldn't go.

'We've got to stop meeting like this,' said a voice behind me.

I turned round. '*Fiachra?*'

There he was, the library crush who'd chatted me up after my last gig, the man I lost my virginity to, the man responsible for my first orgasm, the first person I was truly, if briefly, in love with.

'You really were great on stage earlier,' he said.

'I think you might actually say that to all the girls,' I said.

'Only to you,' he said with a grin.

I noted, in an almost detached way, that he was still very, very cute. He was almost as tall as Tadhg, though his dark hair was shorter and his style was still more Mo' Wax DJ than shaggy retro indie boy.

'What are you doing here?' I said.

'Paul from Shatner is in my psychology class,' said Fiachra. 'You know, I hoped the Laura on the posters would be you.'

'Did you now?' I said. I glanced over to the back of the room and saw Jess and Tadhg standing very close together. She said something and he laughed.

I made myself turn back to Fiachra and moved a little closer to him.

'And why did you hope that?' I said, raising my eyebrows.

'Because you look really fucking hot when you're playing the guitar,' he said.

'Oh yeah?' I said. And despite myself, despite the fact that this was classic Fiachra – he was always incredibly flirty both while and after we were together, and whenever I flirted back even a little he pushed it with me as far as he could go – I felt a little thrill. *See, someone definitely finds me attractive!*

'You still look pretty hot now, if you don't mind me saying so,' he said. 'All … tousled.'

I looked towards the back of the room. Jess's hand was resting on Tadhg's arm now as she laughed up at him. And he was smiling down at her as if she was the best thing he'd ever seen.

Fuck it, I thought. Fuck them. *Mind if I steal your bandmate for a minute?*

I looked up at Fiachra. 'I don't mind you saying so.'

He held my gaze for a long moment that was suddenly, genuinely, full of tension. Then he kissed me. And I kissed him back. Hard.

Fiachra was always a *really* good kisser.

See? I thought. *See? I'm not just sitting around while Tadhg flirts with Jess.* I bit gently on Fiachra's bottom lip and he pulled me closer to him, letting out a low growl of a breath. His hands spanned my waist, something he always used to do when we were together, and it was very hot and familiar at the same time and I let myself go with it, I just kept kissing him and for a while I forgot about why I'd started doing it.

And then I remembered, and pulled back from him a little.

'Wow,' said Fiachra. 'I should come to your gigs more often.'

I looked over at Tadhg and Jess.

He was cupping her face in his hands and kissing her like she was the love of his life.

Even though I thought I knew it was coming, even though I had just kissed Fiachra because I knew it was coming, I felt like I'd been kicked in the stomach. I literally couldn't breathe.

'Laura?' said Fiachra. 'You okay?'

'I'll be right back,' I said. 'Sorry.'

I blindly pushed my way through the crowd and through the door to the tiny backstage dressing-room area. Then I stumbled into the loo, slammed the door behind me, sat on the toilet seat and let out a keening noise that I had never made before. An animal sound. I put my fists to my eyes as if that could stop the hot tears from coming. I thought I had braced myself for seeing him with Jess but I clearly hadn't done enough bracing because this felt worse than I could have imagined, this was terrible, this was *unbearable* …

'Lol?'

It was Katie.

'I saw them. I saw all of it. Fuck, Lol, I'm sorry. I'm *so* sorry.'

I dragged myself to my feet, wiped my eyes with the back of my hand, opened the toilet door and stepped into the dressing room.

'Are they still—?'

'Don't go out there,' said Katie quickly.

So they were.

'I need to go home,' I said. 'I can't … I can't be here.'

'Okay,' said Katie. 'What'll I say if he asks where you are?'

'He won't ask,' I said. I looked in the dressing-room mirror. My eyeliner was all smudged, but it had been a little smudged since I got off stage – it had been so hot and sweaty under the lights. My eyes and nose were red. My mouth looked swollen but that was partly from crying and partly from kissing Fiachra. 'I can't go out looking like this. He can't know I've been crying about him.'

'Just give it a minute,' said Katie. 'You can go soon.'

'I was with Fiachra,' I said.

'I saw that too,' said Katie. 'Don't worry about it. I know why you did it. Go on, splash a bit of cold water on your face and then powder your nose to take the shine off.'

I did all these things, feeling like a robot. Tadhg was with Jess. Tadhg was with Jess. I saw them together. I saw him kiss her like he loved her. Maybe he did love her.

He's all yours!

'There you go,' said Katie. 'You look grand now.' She handed me my coat and I put it on.

And then the door of the dressing room opened and Tadhg and Jess came in, laughing.

For a moment Tadhg and I stared at each other. I couldn't tell what he was thinking. I was terrified that he might be able to tell what I was thinking. I couldn't go home straight away now. It would look like I was running away. Which was exactly what I wanted to do.

'Hi!' I said. My voice was way too high. I sounded unhinged.

Jess was glowing. She was so *happy*. She was as happy as I'd have been if Tadhg had kissed me like that. 'Well!' she said. 'It looks like *you* met a fan tonight!'

It took me a moment to realise what she meant. And some supernatural strength I didn't know I possessed must have overtaken me because I somehow managed to laugh and say, 'Oh yeah, that was Fiachra. We, um, have a bit of history.'

'Ooh, really? Good for you!' said Jess. She was radiant. She was clearly just waiting to get Tadhg back to her posh flat so she could have sex with him. Oh God, that was actually going to happen tonight. He was going to have sex with her. The thought was so extravagantly, outrageously painful I almost laughed. This was ridiculous. How was this happening? How was I just standing there smiling at them like a normal human being? I wanted to run back into that manky toilet cubicle and howl like a dog. I looked at Jess. She didn't look at all uncomfortable to see me because, I realised, it had clearly never crossed her mind that I could be any sort of romantic competition.

I couldn't meet Tadhg's eye.

'We're actually going to head,' he said. 'I just came in here to get my guitar. Um, are you going to Ruairí's party?'

I said, 'I'll check with Fiachra.'

'Oh, right,' said Tadhg. He picked up his guitar from the corner where we'd all dumped our stuff earlier. 'Well, have a great night.'

'You too!' I chirped.

And then I watched Tadhg and Jess walk out of the room, hand in hand. Oh God, it hurt. It hurt, it hurt, it hurt.

Chapter Twenty-Three

2019

'Are you *sure* you're up for this dinner?'

Katie is standing at the kitchen counter stirring a large Le Creuset pot of ragu when I wander into the kitchen on Saturday afternoon.

'Jesus, how long do you have to cook that stuff?' I say. 'He's not coming till half seven.'

'Many, many hours. Come on, answer the question. Are you sure about this? We can postpone if you like. I'm sure Tadhg has a million showbiz parties he could go to instead, so he won't have to stay home alone.'

'Of course I'm sure!' I say. 'Why wouldn't I be?'

'Oh, I don't know,' says Katie, turning round to face me. 'Because of the whole Dave bombshell thing? Maybe you need a bit of peace and quiet this weekend to process it.'

'I've processed it as best I can,' I say honestly. 'Right now, I need distraction.'

And this dinner is certainly doing the job of distracting me from Dave's news. I am very, very nervous about it. This will be the first time Tadhg and I have seen each other outside our work together. What if it's all weird when we don't have the music to fall back on?

'Could you distract yourself by going to the off-licence with Jeanne to buy some booze?' says Katie.

'I know she's fussing over you,' says Jeanne when we're walking to the offie. 'She is being so dramatic. Because she cares about you. But I know you can deal with this Dave business.'

'Thanks, Jeanne,' I say.

'About Tadhg, though, I'm not so sure,' she says. 'Is Katie right? Do you have feelings for him again?'

'No!' I say. 'I mean, not really. Anyway, it doesn't matter if I do or don't – in ten days he'll be in Tennessee.' Not that I've been counting the days.

Somehow Jeanne can sigh in French. 'Why don't you just tell him how you feel, Laura?'

I look at her as if she's lost her mind. 'I won't dignify that with an answer.'

I push open the door of the off-licence.

'*Bordel*, I can't believe he's going to be in my house!' says Jeanne. 'I never told you this before because, well, you know, but I really love his first album.'

'Don't get too excited,' I warn her. 'I mean, I love him and everything but he's a pretty ordinary person.'

'You what?' says Jeanne.

'As a friend, obviously!' I say.

Jeanne looks at me suspiciously. 'As you say.'

When we get home with more beer, wine and fancy crisps than four people could possibly consume, Katie is hoovering the entire ground floor despite the fact Jeanne and I cleaned everything thoroughly last night. I realise she's feeling a bit nervy too.

'Okay,' I say. 'I think we all need to calm down a bit. Seriously, Kay, if you keep hoovering that rug you're going to wear it out.'

Katie sighs and turns off the hoover. 'I don't know what's come over me. It's just Tadhg, for God's sake! And I'm the one who wanted to invite him!'

'Well, exactly,' I say. 'Look, I will admit it's weird. After everything. But let's just … pretend it's not?'

'Fake it till we make it?' says Katie, putting down the hoover.

'Something like that,' I say.

Despite all my advice-giving, I continue to feel antsy as the day goes on. The ragu is still simmering on the stove when we all slip away to get ready, slightly earlier than we usually would when expecting a casual dinner guest. I spend way too long trying on outfits and end up wearing the dress I wore the day I met Tadhg for lunch in the posh restaurant, but I go for slightly bolder make-up, by which I mean I do a cat-eye liner. When I go down to the kitchen, Katie and Jeanne have already opened a bottle of wine.

'Don't worry,' says Jeanne. 'We won't get very drunk and disgrace you.'

'I know,' I say, joining them at the kitchen island. 'Pour me a glass.'

Jeanne, wearing incredible leather leggings, a vest top and an oversized cashmere cardigan, does so.

'Cheers,' says Katie, raising her glass. She's wearing an eighties vintage dress with a floral pattern and an elasticated waist. On me it might look like Rose from the *Golden Girls*, but Katie can pull it off.

'Christ,' she says. 'Jeanne looks like she's just stepped off a catwalk and the two of us look like we burgled an Oxfam shop.'

'We look chic!' I say. 'Don't we?'

Then the doorbell rings.

We all stare at each other.

'I'll get it,' I say. My mouth is suddenly dry. Why am I feeling like this? I was slagging off his headwear to his face yesterday.

But this is different. This is him coming to my home.

I open the door and there, leaning against the red-brick wall of the porch, holding a paper bag from a very posh food-and-drink shop and looking like a tall drink of water, is Tadhg.

'Hello, ma'am,' he says. 'Can I talk to you about the gospel of Our Lord Jesus Christ?'

'Did anyone ever tell you that you look like your man who sings 'Winter Without You'?' I say.

'Once or twice,' says Tadhg. 'Hey, Lol.'

'Hey yourself,' I say. 'Um, come on in.'

I stand back and he walks into the hall.

'Can I leave my coat here?' he says.

'Sure,' I say. 'How did you get here? Did you walk?'

'I wish.' Tadhg hangs his coat on the rack. 'No, I've got a regular driver called Paul. He's sound. He dropped me off.' He clears his throat and I realise, with a start, that he's nervous too. 'Where's Katie?'

'Through here,' I say.

Katie and Jeanne are still standing at the island when we enter the kitchen.

For a second no one says anything. Then Katie smiles, a little hesitantly, and says, 'Father Timothy.'

And suddenly, they're in each other's arms, hugging each other tightly.

'Shit, Katie,' says Tadhg into her shoulder. 'It's been *way* too long.'

'Oh well,' says Katie, 'it's not like anything big has happened in either of our lives since then,' and Tadhg laughs and they pull apart and smile at each other and suddenly I am very, very glad that I've been the means of bringing them together again. Especially as I was, inadvertently, the means of separating them in the first place.

'This,' says Katie, reaching her hand out to Jeanne's and drawing her to her side, 'is my brilliant wife Jeanne.'

'Hi, Tadhg,' says Jeanne. She leans in for the proper French *bisous*, which took me aback at first when I met her, and fair play to Tadhg, he reacts perfectly and *fait des bises* right back.

'Great to meet you,' he says. 'And thanks a million for having me over. Both of you.'

'You're very welcome,' says Jeanne.

Katie grins at him. 'You know we don't have a personal chef, right? Will that be okay for you?'

'I don't have a chef!' protests Tadhg. 'Back me up here, Lol!'

'Ah,' says Katie. 'But did you just tell Laura that because she's such a woman of the people?'

'Shut up, Katie!' I say, as Tadhg and Jeanne laugh.

And I know that the rest of the evening will be all right.

We sit around the table eating posh crisps and drinking wine as the ragu does its final simmer. Tadhg asks Katie and Jeanne questions about work and life and family and seems genuinely interested in the answers. He and Jeanne end up in a deep conversation about architecture – his sister Rosie does PR in Paris for a big French architect and it turns out Jeanne knows some of her colleagues. After a while, Katie ceremonially carries over the Le Creuset to the table and dishes up a feast so delicious that we all agree it was worth the hours of cooking.

'Who needs a chef?' says Katie.

'Not me,' says Tadhg. 'As I've said.'

'As you've *said*,' says Katie.

'Well,' says Tadhg, 'you'll all have to come over sometime and see for yourself.'

'Is that an actual invitation?' says Katie.

'Course it is,' says Tadhg.

'I'll hold you to that, Timothy,' says Katie.

I'm mopping up the last dregs of sauce with some delicious crusty bread from the bakery in Marino when Jeanne says, 'Laura, I almost forgot to tell you! You know my friend Steve? Yesterday I went for lunch with him and his brother Will who works in an ad agency.' She mentions the name; it's one of the most prestigious and cutting-edge agencies in town. 'Will told me they're looking for new senior copywriters, and your name's on the top of their list of potential hires. I know you've got that gig at Leafe lined up, but will I give him your phone number anyway? They might make you a better offer.'

'Oh! Um, wow, sure, that'd be great,' I say. 'Thanks a million.'

And a few weeks ago, this *would* have been great. More than great. This would be a dream job, even better than Leafe. So why is my heart sinking at the prospect?

I've been thinking of this time with Tadhg as a fortnight that I can get through and then move on and pay Katie and Jeanne a nice pile of money for their windows. But until now I haven't really been thinking of the reality of life after this fortnight. And the reality is writing ads. Which I love doing! It's just …

It's just that I've discovered that the old Laura, the rock-star Laura, might still exist after all. And writing ads might not be quite enough for her.

'Great,' says Jeanne. 'That agency's meant to be a good place to work, no? Will said they're taking the team to Moveable Feast this year, and those tickets are like gold dust.'

'Oh,' says Tadhg. 'You know, it hasn't been announced yet so keep it to yourself for now, but I'm playing there this year. I can get you tickets if you want.'

'Oh my God, really?' says Jeanne.

'Of course!' says Tadhg, glancing at me, and I realise I never told Katie and Jeanne about his offer. They were out when I came home that evening, and then Dave's call pushed it out of my mind.

Katie stands up and claps her hands. 'All right! You two' – she points at me and Tadhg – 'go into the sitting room while Jeanne and I prepare the next course.'

'Is she always such a bossy host?' says Tadhg, as we take our glasses and a fresh bottle of wine into the front room. Katie makes a shoo-ing motion at us.

'Pretty much,' I say. I do wonder why it takes both of them to put the posh cheese on a board and pop an apple crumble in the oven. Are they giving me and Tadhg alone time? Or do they just want to talk about him without me?

When we go into the sitting room, Tadhg closes the door behind us.

'I take it you didn't tell them about me asking you to play the festival?' he says. But not in an accusatory way.

I sit down at one end of the couch and he sits at the other end of it.

'No,' I say. 'They weren't in that night so I didn't get a chance. And then I got that news ...'

I do not want to think about stupid Dave right now.

'Shit, sorry, of course,' says Tadhg. 'Look, you know there's no hurry about deciding, don't you?'

'Yeah, I do.' I take a sip of wine. 'I appreciate you asking me, you know. And in theory it sounds amazing. A part of me would really love to do it. It's just ...' It's just that I'm scared. And not just about playing a big gig, though that's a huge part of it. I'm scared about taking a chance on music again. I'm scared of making Tadhg a regular part of my life again. 'I really don't want to go out and make a fool of myself in front of ... well, in front of the entire world, basically.'

'I don't think that would happen,' says Tadhg. 'Seriously, Lol, don't you remember how amazing you always were on stage? Everyone noticed it. And whatever magic you had back then, you've still got it. Sam sees it. I see it.'

The door opens and Jeanne sticks her head in. 'Do both of you want something sweet?'

'Definitely,' I say, and Tadhg says, 'Yes please.'

Just as he fit right into the band all those years ago, Tadhg fits right into this new little gang straight away. We're all talking and laughing so much I don't realise how late it is until Jeanne can't stifle a big yawn, which prompts Tadhg to look at his watch.

'It's nearly one,' he says. 'I'd better let you go to bed.'

We make protesting noises but I suddenly realise I'm exhausted. The strain of the day is catching up with me. Katie and Tadhg exchange phone numbers, and then Jeanne says, 'How are you going to get home?'

'You know what, I'll walk,' Tadhg says.

'What about your driver?' I say.

'Oh, I never leave him hanging around on-call this late,' says Tadhg. 'I'd normally call a car service but there's no point now. It's only down the road. And I'll walk through Marino so the roads will be even quieter.'

'Well, all right,' I say. 'If you're sure.' I hope he'll be okay. How likely is he to come across scary fans or lairy lads looking for a fight in a genteel 1920s housing development? Not very, I suppose. Still, you never know … 'But can you let me know you got home safe?'

He smiles and says, 'I'll be grand, but I will.' He stands up and turns to Jeanne and Katie. 'Thanks for a lovely evening.'

'*De rien*,' says Jeanne and Katie says, unusually sincerely, 'You know, it's been really, really good to see you.'

'You too, Cáit,' says Tadhg, and he hugs them both.

'I'll walk you out,' I say.

Out in the hall, Tadhg puts on his coat and says, 'So on Monday we'll try our song.'

'On Monday we'll try our song,' I say.

'We might even finish it this week,' he says.

'Steady on,' I say in mock horror.

'You're right, what was I thinking?' says Tadhg. 'That would be ridiculous.'

'Well, goodnight,' I say. 'Safe home.'

'Night, Lol,' he says. And then he says, 'Oh, c'mere.'

We haven't hugged each other for over a decade but now his face is in my hair and my face is pressed into the soft navy wool of his coat. He no longer smells of Radox shower gel and generic Sure deodorant, he's clearly using some posh slightly citrusy stuff these days, but underneath it is that familiar Tadhg smell, and for a second it sends me straight back in time and I almost feel like crying, remembering what it felt like to be twenty-one and hopeful, with a future full of musical and romantic possibility ahead of me. We hold each other tightly for a long moment and then I pull away.

'Don't get into any fights on the way home,' I say.

'I'll try not to,' says Tadhg. 'See you on Monday.'

I feel slightly dazed after I close the door and wander back into the kitchen, where Jeanne and Katie are finishing loading the dishwasher.

'So?' I say, a little hesitantly. 'How do you feel that went?'

'It was really, really good to see him,' says Katie. 'It was like old times. Except with better food and booze. And we're going to bed at a reasonable hour. Well, reasonable-ish.' She yawns.

'You go up to bed,' says Jeanne. 'Laura and I will finish this.'

Katie yawns again. 'If you insist. Night, Lol. We will fully debrief tomorrow.' She kisses Jeanne on the cheek and leaves.

'So … what did you think?' I ask Jeanne. I put some cutlery in the dishwasher and pick up a salad bowl.

'He's very *sympa*,' says Jeanne, and I wish, not for the first time, we had a word like *sympa* in English. It means nice, friendly, attractive, sympathetic, all of the above and more.

Then she says, 'And of course, he's in love with you.'

The bowl almost falls from my hands. 'What?'

'Give that to me,' says Jeanne, taking the bowl and putting it in the dishwasher. 'He loves you.'

'What … where is this coming from? Did he—' I swallow. 'Did he say anything to you?'

'No,' says Jeanne. 'But the way he talked to you, smiled at you, the way he looked at you, it wasn't like the way he was with me and even Katie. He was so … happy you were there.'

I let out a sigh. So that's all she meant. Ridiculous to get my hopes up, even for a second. 'Jeanne, you didn't see him in college. He was always like that with me. He treats me exactly the same way now as he did then. Seriously, it doesn't mean anything.'

'It looks like it means something,' says Jeanne.

'Well, yeah,' I said. 'That's why I thought he might like me back then. But believe me, I was wrong.'

As I go upstairs, I remind myself there's no real reason to think Tadhg's feelings for me have changed since 2003. But I break my no-phone-in-the-bedroom rule and take mine upstairs, just in case Tadhg takes me at my word and messages me to say he's got home. I'm just getting into bed when my phone pings and there it is.

Tadhg: As promised: proof of life. I survived my trek through the mean streets of Marino! Thanks for a really good night.

I'm still staring at it when my phone pings again. Jeanne has sent me a photo. She must have taken it earlier this evening from the doorway of the sitting room. It shows me sitting on one end of the sofa, doubled over laughing. Tadhg is sitting at the other end, leaning forward, elbows on knees, looking at me with such affection that it takes my breath away just for a second, knowing he looked at me like that when I wasn't looking at him.

And despite everything, despite the fact that I learned a long time ago that I definitely can't trust my instincts or my hope when it comes to Tadhg, I fall asleep hoping that Jeanne is right.

Then I wake up and see the texts.

Chapter Twenty-Four

2019

The first text arrives at around seven o'clock in the morning, but even though my phone is in my room it's on silent so it doesn't wake me. The second, the third and the fourth all arrive in quick succession around half-past eight, and the combined vibrating of my phone on the chest of drawers makes enough noise to rouse me.

The first is from Aisling.

> **Aisling**: Laura I'm so, so sorry. I shouldn't have said anything to Kev. He didn't realise what he was doing but he's a fucking idiot. He feels terrible. That's no excuse I know. Please please ring me when you get this.

My stomach lurches. What the hell is this about? And why have so many people been texting me first thing on a Sunday? I feel shaky and sick as I click on the next message. It's from Aoife, my old work pal.

Aoife: I'm so sorry, Laura, you have to believe me, I had no idea anything I said was going to appear anywhere. The woman said she worked for Tadhg Hennessy. I'm so so sorry, please ring me. I'm sorry.

The other two messages are from unknown numbers. I feel light-headed. What are Aoife and Aisling apologising for? And what has Tadhg got to do with it? I'm about to click on the next message to see if it can tell me any more when there's a gentle knock on the door.

'Lol?' It's Katie. 'Are you awake?'

'Come in,' I say. My mouth is dry.

Katie's expression is grave when she opens the door. She's holding her phone. 'So first of all, your family are fine, no one's sick, no one's had an accident or anything, but …'

'But what?' I say. 'What's going on? I've just got these weird texts and—'

'Sarah just rang me,' says Katie. 'There's a story in the paper. About you.'

'About *me*?' I say. 'What kind of story?' I remember her and Jeanne warning me I might end up in the tabloids. I know I said I didn't care if that happened but it turns out I might care after all. My blood runs cold. 'Oh Jesus, it's not something about me being Tadhg's mystery woman, is it?'

Katie swallows. 'Not exactly.'

And she hands me her phone.

Tadhg's 'Little Cinderella'
Rock Star's Charity Case

Pop superstar Tadhg Hennessy is known for his good works and charitable activities. Now Saint Tadhg has found his new cause: his homeless, unemployed former bandmate Laura McDermott. McDermott, 37, recently lost her home after the breakdown of a long-term relationship, and then her job as an advertising copywriter at Visions, the prestigious agency purchased by Zenith in 2017. But salvation has come in an unlikely form: her former friend Tadhg Hennessy.

'Laura and Tadhg Hennessy were close back in college,' says Kev Lacey, an old friend of McDermott. 'They weren't a couple or anything but they were in a band together. And then they had some sort of fight and stopped talking to each other. That was about fifteen years ago and they haven't seen each other since.' The reasons for the fight are unknown; what is known is that Hennessy and McDermott went from close collaborators to strangers seemingly overnight.

Until this month, when Hennessy reached out to McDermott and invited her to take part in a two-week songwriting workshop. 'Tadhg was really happy to do this for Laura,' said a source close to the star. 'She's been through a tough time and he's so glad he can cheer her up with some time in the studio. It's a Cinderella story – except instead of going to the ball for a night, this little Cinderella's getting to spend two weeks working in Tadhg's state-of-the-art studio. He's got an incredible collection of musical instruments so Laura will be able to play his guitars.'

Hennessy, 37, famously shot to stardom twelve years ago when his song 'Winter Without You' went viral. Since then he's released three critically acclaimed platinum-selling albums, headlined the Glastonbury Festival and Electric Picnic, and toured all over the world. With his rich vocals and innovative mixture of pop, rock and even trad folk, he's generally regarded as one of the most talented musicians and performers of his generation.

His old bandmate McDermott, meanwhile, did not go on to make a mark on the music world after her and Hennessy's band split. After graduating from Trinity College Dublin, McDermott studied communications in DCU and went on to work in marketing and advertising, eventually becoming a copywriter. There's no evidence that she ever played with another band.

'We've been friends for a good few years now but I had no idea Laura was ever in a band,' says McDermott's former colleague Aoife Keogh. 'Let alone that she knew Tadhg Hennessy. She's kept it very quiet.'

'Their band in college was really good,' says Ruairí Flynn, who organised gigs for Hennessy and McDermott's group several times when they were all students at Trinity. 'Tadhg? Well, I don't think anyone who saw him play back then was surprised when he ended up becoming really huge. He just had star quality. But Laura was brilliant too. Offstage she was this

*ordinary nice girl, but she was incredibly cool onstage. I think
everyone fancied her when she was playing the guitar.'*

*Sources close to Hennessy say that he has no expectations
of what will result from his time in the studio with McDermott.
'It's just two weeks,' said one source. 'Maybe they'll write
something, maybe they won't. The important thing is that
he's cheering up an old friend who's going through a tough
time.' While Hennessy was unavailable for comment, his
management confirmed that 'Tadhg is working on some songs
with his old friend Laura McDermott, who will, of course,
get full credit on anything they release as a result'. Could
Tadhg's Cinderella end up with a smash hit? That would be a
fairy-tale ending.*

When I finish reading the story I feel numb. It's like my head
is full of white noise. Katie gently takes the phone from my
hands. I don't say anything.

'Lol?' says Katie anxiously.

I feel like I'm watching myself from a distance. Did I really
just read those words about me? Did I really just see a photo
of me outside Tadhg's gate, looking like some sort of pitiful
orphan, clearly taken with a telephoto lens by someone lurking
in the park at the Crescent? I did, I did. But it doesn't feel real.
It *can't* be real.

'I think you should sit down.' Katie guides me gently over to
the bed and I drop down onto it.

'Give me back your phone,' I say.

'I don't know if that's a good—'

'Just give it to me!' I say.

Reluctantly, Katie hands me her phone and I read through the story again. It's almost worse the second time.

'His little Cinderella!' I say.

'It's total nonsense.'

'His little *Cinderella*!'

'I know. Look, come downstairs and I'll make you a cup of tea—'

'It says I'm homeless!' I say. 'And unemployed!'

'It does but—'

'There's nothing wrong with being homeless or unemployed!' I say. 'But I'm not either of those things!'

'No, you're not—'

'It's *lies*! If I wasn't doing this thing with Tadhg I'd just be freelance!' I say. 'Plus I've got a job lined up! And I'm living here and paying you rent!'

'You are,' says Katie.

'And Kev! Fucking *Kev*! What does he know about me and Tadhg? He didn't even know him! The band was like two years before we met Aisling!'

'I know,' says Katie.

'And saying I'll be able to play Tadhg's guitars. Like I don't have one of my own. I've got a guitar, thanks very much! I've got a *great* guitar! I've got two!'

'You do,' says Katie. 'Why don't we go downstairs—'

'And Ruairí! *Ruairí*! What's he doing popping up here? I

haven't seen him for ages. Calling me an "ordinary nice girl", like I was, I don't know, a plate of mashed potato!'

'But he says you were really good,' says Katie. 'And everyone fancied you.'

'Well, we know that's a lie,' I say. 'Because *some* people definitely didn't. Oh my God, look at the photo.' I zoom in on the picture, which must have been taken on a day when it was raining. The hood is up on my parka, but I'm facing the camera and looking up to the heavens like I'm checking the drizzle. It is both very recognisably me, and also not like me at all.

'I look like a teenager!' I say. 'A very haggard teenager who's had an incredibly hard life!'

'That's it.' Katie grabs the phone out of my hand and puts it in her dressing-gown pocket. 'Come on. Downstairs.'

Shock and anger mean I'm still in such a stunned state that it's not until I've followed Katie down the stairs and into the kitchen that the obvious question hits me.

'How did the journalist know about me working with Tadhg?' I say. 'She talked to Kev. And Aoife. And Ruairí. But I don't think any of them would have made the first move and contacted the press. And none of them knew about Tadhg and me working together again – I mean, Aisling might have told Kev, but I really don't think he'd have, like, approached a journalist about it. So how did the journalist know?'

Then an awful possibility hits me. And I feel physically sick. I sit down very quickly at the kitchen table.

'Oh my God,' I say. 'What if Tadhg and his team leaked it?'

'No!' says Katie. 'Absolutely no way. He wouldn't do that.'

But I'm remembering what he said when he first mentioned Hugo.

I think I've got Hugo off my back about working with those other producers, anyway. So don't worry, he's not going to make a fuss about us working together anymore.

I tell Katie about Hugo's plan.

'Maybe this was how he got Hugo off his back,' I say. 'Maybe he said there was another way to get loads of positive publicity and it was to leak a feel-good story about Saint Tadhg plucking some sad sack from obscurity and letting her write songs with him.'

'Surely not,' says Katie. 'I know it's been complicated but I'm a hundred per cent sure that man cares about you. He wouldn't throw you to the wolves like that.'

I take a deep breath. She's right. Of course she's right.

'Sorry, I'm being ridiculous,' I say. 'I know he wouldn't.'

Then a sleepy-eyed Jeanne comes into the kitchen, holding up my phone. 'Morning,' she says, putting it on the table. 'Your phone kept buzzing, Laura – I thought I should bring it down in case it's urgent.' She looks at my and Katie's faces. 'What has happened? Is everything okay?'

I check my phone. There are many, many messages. And several missed calls from one number.

Tadhg's.

I look at the earliest messages, the ones from the unknown numbers. They're all long.

Hi Laura, long time no see! This is Caroline White, though you might remember me as Caroline Moriarty. I got your number from a group mail for Brian's 30th. Anyway, I see you're working with our old friend Tadhg – how amazing! If you're doing any events with him, I'd love to talk to you about lending you a few pieces – I own a clothing and lifestyle brand called Moon. Anyway, give me a call! Xxx

Hi Laura, my name's Jenny Toolan and I'm a producer on the Chris Walsh show on RTÉ Radio 1. Might you be available on Monday to talk to Chris about your work with Tadhg Hennessy? I think our listeners would be really interested in your story. Please give me a call on this number. Thanks so much!

Laura this is Ruairí Flynn. I just saw the story, I'm SO sorry. I had no idea this woman was a journalist. She saw a photo of one of those college gigs on my Instagram and messaged me. She said Tim was doing some sort of official retrospective thing. I'm really sorry and I hope you're not offended by what I said. If there's anything I can do to help/make up for this, let me know.

I look at the other messages, some from good friends expressing concern, mostly from people I know but haven't seen for ages. Most are genuinely positive, expressing surprise or delight or congratulations. But it's a weird feeling knowing they're only contacting me because I'm connected to Tadhg.

And then a text from Tadhg appears.

Tadhg: I'm so sorry, Lol. Please ring me. I can explain everything.

He's apologising. He can explain it.

He's responsible for the story.

I feel like I might throw up.

I do not call Tadhg back.

Tadhg calls again. I let it ring out.

Then my phone starts vibrating again, and my parents' landline number comes up on the caller ID, and I groan aloud because I know I have to answer this one.

'Laurie!' I can hear the anxiety in my mother's voice. 'Are you all right? Your dad and I saw this article about you and Tadhg Hennessy …'

I try not to sigh. 'I'm fine, Mam. Don't worry about me.'

'That article said you were homeless!'

'I'm not! I'm still living with Katie and Jeanne. Seriously, this article is nonsense. I'm sorry you and Dad were worried.'

'So you're not working with Tadhg Hennessy?'

'No, I am, but—'

'Then it's not all nonsense!'

'The Cinderella stuff is nonsense! We're just working together. It's fine.'

Or it was. I don't think it's fine anymore.

'So you're not still unemployed then?'

I take a deep breath and remind myself my parents,

with their public sector jobs, have never quite understood freelancing.

'I was never unemployed, Mam. I was freelance. I *am* freelance. And I've got an agency contract lined up.'

'So this thing with Tadhg Hennessy is a freelance job?' says my dad. My mother's clearly put the phone on speaker.

'Um, yes, exactly,' I say. 'It's just a short-term thing, then I'll be back at an agency.'

'Oh, thank goodness. What should I say if anyone asks about you?' says my mother.

Oh Christ, I hadn't thought about this. 'Don't talk about it to anyone you don't know! If any strangers or anything get in touch, just tell them, um, no comment. And tell everyone else that it's just a job, and it's grand, and I'm grand.'

'You're sure you're okay, Laurie?' says my mother.

'I'm fine,' I lie. 'I'm really sorry you were upset.'

'We're just worried about you, pet,' says Dad and he really sounds it.

'There's no need!' I say. 'Look, I'd better go. Seriously, don't worry. I'll talk to you soon.'

I hang up and Katie hands me a cup of tea. Even though, God love her, Katie never puts in quite enough milk and always puts in too much sugar, I thank her and start drinking it.

'Your folks okay?' says Katie.

'Just worried I'm living on the streets.' I let out a groan. 'What am I going to do?'

'You need to talk to Tadhg,' says Jeanne.

'I really don't,' I say. 'I can't. Not right now. Fuck, I'm sorry about all this. I know you didn't sign up for all this drama when you let me stay here.'

'Oh, stop it,' says Katie. 'You don't need to apologise for anything.'

'You didn't cause this drama,' says Jeanne. 'It's this dreadful journalist woman.'

My phone vibrates with another call and this time it's Aisling. I have to answer it.

'Laura, I'm so sorry! And Kev's so sorry. Seriously, he didn't mean to cause any trouble. Are you okay?'

'Not really,' I say.

'I didn't think you'd mind me telling him about you and Tadhg.' Aisling sounds on the verge of tears. 'But I didn't think he'd tell anyone.'

It turns out Kev knew the journalist back in college. She found me on social media and discovered Kev was a mutual connection. She messaged him and asked him about me and Tadhg, and of course Kev was only delighted to share what he'd just discovered.

'He didn't know she was asking as, like, a journalist,' says Aisling. 'She said she knew Tadhg herself.'

I take a deep breath and try to convince myself it's not really Aisling's fault. I didn't tell her to keep me and Tadhg's history a secret. But I really can't bear to talk to her at the moment.

'I don't blame you,' I say. 'But I'd better go.'

I hang up just as my phone lights up with an alert. There's a new text from Tadhg. In fact it looks like there are quite a few texts from Tadhg, all more or less saying the same thing.

Tadhg: Please ring me, Lol. I can't apologise enough for this.

I can't ring him now. I have a feeling that if I do the shock and anger will turn into distress and I'll start crying instead. And I vowed a long time ago that I was never, ever going to cry in front of him.

'Come on, Lol,' says Katie. 'Have a shower and me and Jeanne will take you out for breakfast. How does that sound?'

Suddenly, the thought of getting out of the house is very appealing. I might even leave my phone behind.

'Okay,' I say.

Half an hour later, Katie, Jeanne and I are seated in our favourite local breakfast spot. We come here fairly regularly and the staff all know us to see. But today, after the server takes our orders, she looks at me oddly.

'This might be a weird question,' she says, pencil still posed over her order pad, 'but … is that you?' And she points at a newspaper left on the seat of the table behind ours.

My appetite vanishes. The story about me and Tadhg is not the lead headline. But over the masthead of the newspaper there's a text band saying 'Tadhg Hennessy helps desperate pal: full story page 4 and 5' and next to it is a photo of Tadhg looking extremely elegant and handsome next to the awful, awful photo of me staring into the heavens in my parka.

'Oh my God,' says Jeanne in a genuinely horrified voice.

'Um, yeah.' My voice sounds like it's coming from very far away. 'I suppose it is me.'

The server looks like she's going to ask something else but then Jeanne says, 'Could we get some tap water, please?' and the girl says, 'Oh yeah, of course,' and goes.

Katie reaches over, grabs the paper and then sits on it. 'Now no one else here will see it,' she says.

'It's on the front page,' I say numbly. 'People will see it in shops.'

It turns out it wasn't even the only copy in the café. More customers arrive for leisurely breakfasts over the Sunday papers, and I can see that appalling front page on a few tables. All the staff keep looking over at us, and at least one customer glances up from reading the story itself and does a double-take when she sees me. Who knew print media still had such power?

I haven't finished my eggs but I can't stay there a minute longer.

'Look, I'm going to go,' I say. 'You stay and finish your breakfast.'

Katie and Jeanne make protesting noises but I insist. I need to be on my own for a while. I pay for all our breakfasts on my way out, and a few heads turn as I make my way to the counter. The girl at the till, who's there most weekends, says, 'It's so cool about you and Tadhg Hennessy! You should bring him in here sometime!'

I smile weakly at her and think I would rather die.

Once outside, I cross the road to Fairview Park and wander along a path under the trees. My phone is on silent – I couldn't quite bring myself to leave it at home – but when I take it out of my bag there are more texts and messages. It feels like everyone I've ever known has heard about this story. Even if Tadhg somehow has an explanation for it coming out, it still won't change the fact that the whole world now thinks I'm his charity case. People will be talking about this, they'll be talking about me …

And somehow it's only now that it hits me they'll be doing all this on social media.

I'm not particularly active on Twitter, and my DMs are limited to mutuals only, but when I open it I see that I have 3,000 new followers. And hundreds and hundreds of people have tagged me in their tweets. Numbly, I click on the mentions feed.

If @tadhghennessymusic wants to rescue someone can he rescue me instead of some ugly hag like @lauramakesads?

OMG Tadhg can do so much better than you @lauramakesads

Leave Tadhg alone @lauramakesads!

So jealous of you and Tadhg @lauramakesads!!!!! Lucky girl

I close the app quickly. I feel hot and sick and my hands feel clammy. I stand there for a minute, letting the waves of sickness wash over me. But then, because I'm clearly a masochist, I open Instagram. Again, I've got thousands of new followers. There are many, many new comments. My hands are shaking so much I nearly drop my phone as I click on the comments under the most recent photo I posted on the grid, a nice one of me and Katie at a friend's birthday party a few months ago. A shallow part of me is glad that at least I don't look like a tragic waif in this one – I'm wearing my Paris vintage dress, the one I was wearing, fuck, how was it only last night? And Katie looks incredibly chic, with her bleached wavy bob and a batwing Cos top.

Then I look at the comments.

She doesn't exactly look destitute, does she? She must have spun Tadhg some sob story.

Tadhg has such a good soul. Can't believe he's been taken in by this grifter.

Amazing hair, amazing dress. And her friend is gorgeous!

OMG Tadhg can do so much better than this.

Jesus she looks good for her age, doesn't she? Isn't she practically 40?!

Aww you are so cute! Love the dress.

How much did you pay that guy to say everyone fancied you?!!!! 😂😂😂😂

I click on another photo. There are many, many more comments like this. There are comments analysing my face, my body, my hair, how old I look, how old I must be. There are comments calling me a whore, calling me a con artist, calling me a groupie. There are comments praising me, saying I must be so talented, that I look amazing. There are so, so, so many comments. I make my account private but it's too late, I've seen all the comments now. I've seen what people are saying about me. Hundreds, thousands of people, all over the world, all with an opinion of me. It's too much. It's just too much.

I sit down on a park bench and burst into tears.

Chapter Twenty-Five

2002–2003

It should have been me.

It should have been me who flirted with him after our gig. It should have been me he kissed that night. It should have been me who walked out of that venue holding his hand. It should have been me. It should all have been me.

But it wasn't me.

It was Jess.

Before our gig I'd been so convinced there was something between me and him. I'd been convinced he was going to kiss me that night we went for dinner, before Ruairí interrupted us. But because I wasn't a hundred per cent sure, because he had never actually declared his love for me, I hadn't done anything about it. Jess couldn't possibly have been totally sure either. But she still risked it. She asked him to that family party. She asked him back to her flat after the gig.

And it worked.

♪♪

I dragged myself into college reluctantly the day after the gig, my stomach churning at the prospect of seeing Tadhg and Jess together, but there was no sign of either of them. A few people came up to me and told me how great the gig had been, but I couldn't think about the band right now. I didn't see Fiachra either, though I did get a text from him that day.

You okay Laura? Hope I didn't do anything to upset you last night. xx

I told him he hadn't and wished him a happy Christmas. Over the weekend a part of me wished I'd sent Fiachra a very different reply to his text. A part of me wished I'd suggested finishing what we'd started. A part of me wished I'd spent the entire weekend in Fiachra's room in his shared house off Dorset Street, fucking him until he made me forget all about Tadhg. But I'd probably have started crying about Tadhg while Fiachra was going down on me or something. I wasn't in the right state to be with anyone else.

I didn't hear from Tadhg over the weekend, and I obviously wasn't going to contact him first. I tormented myself with thoughts of what he might be doing. In all of these miserable imaginings, he hadn't left Jess's flat. He hadn't left Jess's bed.

Katie was amazing throughout all this. She let me rage and she let me cry all over her. She told me Tadhg was an idiot, that he couldn't do better than me, that Jess was probably really high-maintenance and he'd get sick of her in no time, and I knew none of this was true but I let her say it anyway.

On Monday afternoon, the day before Christmas Eve, I finally got a text from Tadhg.

> Hey Lol, hope the rest of Thursday night was fun. We should do some music stuff over the holidays – let me know if you're free. Have a great Christmas!

I almost didn't reply, but then I thought that would look worse, so I just sent 'Sounds good, happy Christmas!'. Then I read his message again. And again. Over the next few days I spent more effort analysing that text message than I'd spent analysing any of my prescribed college texts all term.

'You don't even know if he's going out with Jess!' said Katie. She really did have the patience of a saint during all this. 'He just shifted her! You were with Fiachra and you're not going out with him.'

The day after St Stephen's Day, I was lying on my bed thinking about that stupid text yet again when my phone rang. I felt sick when I saw his name. For a split second I thought about not answering. As long as I didn't talk to him, there was still that uncertainty, that tiny possibility it might not be true.

But I knew it was true.

I sat up and answered the phone.

'Hey, Lol!' Did his voice sound nervous or was that my fevered imagination? 'Um, it's me.'

'Hey!' I said. 'How was Christmas?'

'Ah, you know, the usual. Lots of visiting relations, then eating loads of Roses and watching shit telly. Pretty good.'

'Same,' I said. 'I basically stayed in my pyjamas all day yesterday.' I didn't tell him I'd spent most of the day torturing myself with thoughts about him. 'Please tell me you're not secretly one of those awful hearty people who goes for a walk at, like, nine a.m. on Stephen's Day.'

'Ha! No, I'm not.' There was a pause. And that pause made my stomach drop. 'But I did go to Wicklow yesterday. So there were some walks.'

'Oh, right,' I said.

'Yeah,' he said. 'I went to Jess's folks' house.'

I squeezed my eyes shut tightly and prayed that I could keep my voice steady.

'Oh, right!' I said again. 'I bet they have a nice house.'

'They do,' said Tadhg. 'It's a big Georgian thing.'

'Wow,' I said. 'Fancy.'

'And actually,' he said, 'me and Jess.' He paused. 'We're together. Like, going out together. Since the night of the gig.'

Don't say 'oh, right' yet again, Laura. I took a deep breath.

'That's brilliant!' I said. 'She's so great.'

'She really is,' he said, and something in the tone of his voice made tears come to my eyes. 'So what's the story with you and ... was it Ferdia?'

I breathed out softly and tried to sound like someone who wasn't crying. 'Fiachra? He's that guy I went out with in first and second year. There's always been, you know, a spark between us.'

'He's not the one you wrote 'Midnight Feast' about, then?' said Tadhg.

'God, no! *Very* much not,' I added. 'That was Dan.'

'Ah yes,' said Tadhg. 'Anyway ... speaking of our songs, do you fancy playing some this weekend?'

'I do,' I said, though I wasn't sure this was the truth. 'But Jo's still in Galway and Brian's in Meath with his whole family. So we can't get into the garage. Unless Jess gave you some housebreaking tools for Christmas ...'

Look at me, saying her name as if it didn't cause me physical pain.

'I meant just me and you,' said Tadhg. 'You could call over to my place. But you know, if you want to wait for the others, that's grand ...'

I fell back on my bed and stared at the ceiling. I felt like Tadhg was trying to make a statement here, showing me that he and I were still friends and bandmates, even though he had a gorgeous new girlfriend who was probably going to take up all his free time from now on. And I felt I should make a statement too, and that statement was that I was totally cool with this.

So I said, 'No, let's do it.'

♪♪

The next afternoon I found myself walking up the drive of a nice 1930s semi-detached house in Clontarf, guitar case clutched in my hand. My mother had given me a lift, largely because she was worried about me, seeing as I had spent pretty much the entire Christmas holidays on the phone to the stalwart Katie or holed up in my room, crying quietly and writing heartbroken, angry songs on my guitar. She even refrained from reminding me I should be spending more of my final college year studying than messing around with a band.

Most of the songs were terrible, but that morning I had found myself strumming a chord sequence that had something special, nice and poppy but with a bittersweet edge. The more I played it the better it sounded, and I created a melody for it that worked perfectly. Then I wrote some intentionally bland lyrics for the chorus, trite and romantic words about wanting someone to be your summer girl, so silly and meaningless that it wouldn't hurt me hearing Tadhg sing them while knowing he was thinking about Jess.

As soon as I rang Tadhg's doorbell I wished I hadn't said yes to this. How could I be normal with him when my heart hurt so much? But it was too late to back out now because the door was opening and there he was.

'Hey!' he said. 'Thanks a million for coming over.'

'Hey yourself,' I said, and let him hug me.

I followed him into the kitchen, where a good-looking

middle-aged woman with dark wavy hair was emptying the dishwasher.

She looked up and smiled when we came in. 'Hello! You must be Jess.'

I think I physically flinched. Tadhg said, 'No, Mam, this is Laura from the band. Jess is calling over tomorrow.'

'Of course!' said Tadhg's mother. 'Sorry, Laura, I got the days mixed up. You know what it's like at Christmas. Lovely to meet you at last. I'm Marian.'

'Lovely to meet you too,' I said.

'Tim's told me what a brilliant musician you are,' she said, as Tadhg put the kettle on.

'I don't know about that,' I said.

'Don't listen to her,' said Tadhg. 'She *is* brilliant.'

It felt very strange seeing Tadhg's room for the first time. It was pretty much what I'd expected his former teenage bedroom to look like – indie film posters on the walls, some photos of friends, postcards and cuttings, packed bookshelves, piles of music magazines, a stereo and shelves of tapes, CDs and records. And a Casio keyboard and two amps.

'What's it like living back here again after being an independent gentleman in Cork for three years?' I said, sitting in a battered wicker chair.

'Not exactly ideal,' said Tadhg, sitting down on the single bed. 'But you know, my folks are grand. It could be worse.

And if I can get some teaching work next year I'll try to move out.'

And of course, I thought, Jess has her flat in Fitzwilliam Square. But I couldn't think about that now. And I really didn't want to hear him talk about her. So before Tadhg could potentially start telling me how wonderful she was and what a great time he'd had in her house, I said, 'I wrote a bit of a song this morning.'

And for the first time, I played Tadhg what we'd end up calling 'our song'.

I played the chords, and then I played the melody on the keyboard, and as usual he told me to just sing it and I refused. I handed him the lyrics, which I'd scrawled on a piece of paper.

He reached over to his desk and grabbed his minidisc player. 'Let's record it.'

We ran through the song, me playing guitar and him singing, and I realised I was definitely right – this song had something special, something potentially better than any other song we'd done. Tadhg's voice made the chorus – 'You're gonna be my summer girl, it's all that I dreamed of' – sound like an anthem. We played the two verses and choruses and then we stopped.

'Fuck, Lol,' he said. 'This is good.'

'It is, isn't it?' I said. 'I mean, I wasn't deluding myself.'

Not about the song, anyway.

'Definitely not,' he said. 'Let's play it again.'

It sounded just as good this time.

'The chorus feels a bit short,' I said. 'And we need to come up with a middle eight.'

'We will,' said Tadhg.

Of course, we didn't come up with a middle eight that day. But we did spend the afternoon playing music together, and it was almost normal. Almost but not quite. When there was a moment of quiet I found myself babbling random nonsense about guitar pedals or possible future gigs, anything to fill the silence in case he filled it by telling me how amazing his Stephen's Day visit to Wicklow was.

When we'd finished playing, Tadhg said, 'Do you want to go for a drink? There's a pub just around the corner.'

I knew that if we were just hanging out in the pub, without music to focus on, we couldn't avoid the subject of Jess all night. There was only so much babbling even I could do. So I said, 'Nah, I'd better head.'

'Do you want a lift home?' he said.

As the alternative was getting two buses or calling my parents like an actual child, I said, 'Yes, please.'

Neither of us said much during the short drive. He didn't suggest meeting up again before the end of the holidays, and neither did I.

It would have been easier if I could have told myself he didn't really like Jess. It would have been easier if she'd been horrible, if she'd been mean and unattractive and obnoxious and I could have told myself he clearly had terrible taste. But he did really like her. She was nice and friendly and incredibly smart. I mean, she was doing that master's – she was evidently smarter than I was. And she was taller and hotter than I was. More everything than I was, basically. I couldn't pretend otherwise. And I couldn't even indulge myself by hating her and bitching about her because she was so fucking nice.

The first time I saw them together was bad. A bunch of us were in the pub on Friday night, and I hadn't realised that Jess was joining us until Tadhg's face lit up and there she was.

'Hi, gorgeous,' she said with a grin, kissing him on the mouth. It was the grin that got to me more than the kiss. It stopped 'hi, gorgeous' sounding revoltingly cheesy and made it sound like their in-joke. Seeing them look at each other fondly, seeing her whisper in his ear, seeing his arm around her shoulders – it was as exquisitely painful as I had feared it would be. After about an hour I had to go to the loos and cry, just for a second. It was that or cry in front of him, which I vowed I would never, ever do.

And as I leaned against the door of the cubicle I kept thinking it wasn't fair, it wasn't fair, it wasn't fucking *fair*. I hadn't been totally deluded when I thought there was something between me and him. Katie had thought so too, and she had urged me to do something about it. There had been a reason I kept hoping, a reason I had been convinced we would have our moment. But whatever it was hadn't been enough, or I hadn't been enough, and now here I was, crying in a toilet, and Jess was out there wrapped in his arms.

When I was walking back to the table, I could see her say something that sent him into a fit of laughter. Somehow that bit was the worst of all.

As the months went by, Tadhg and I still met up regularly for lunch or a quick cup of tea, and we still had our bus journeys out to band practice, but most of the time we saw each other in groups. And increasingly, Jess was there too. One Saturday in February, as we were finishing up the practice, Tadhg said, 'Jess might drop into the Stag's later if that's okay?'

'Of course!' I said, and the others agreed, but for the first time I felt properly angry with him rather than with the universe or myself. I was well aware my annoyance was childish and unreasonable, but I couldn't help it. For fuck's sake, could we not even have our Saturday pub sessions? What next? Was he going to invite her to join the band? I tried to fight these bitter feelings as I sat next to him on the crowded bus into town, but I mustn't have been doing a great job because he said, 'Are you okay? You're a bit quiet.'

I turned to look at him, wide-eyed. 'Oh no, I'm fine! Just a bit tired. And I'm thinking about the gig.'

We were going to play our first headline gig in two weeks, in the same venue where we'd supported Sourpuss. This time they would be supporting us. Despite my feeble protests, we were still, at the insistence of the others, called The Band Laura's In.

'It's mad, isn't it? Our first headline gig already!' said Tadhg.

'I'm worried we don't have enough songs,' I said. 'We can't even finish that song I wrote at Christmas.'

'We have more than enough!' said Tadhg. 'Are you okay with playing 'On My Mind'? It's ready, right?'

I wasn't even vaguely okay with playing 'On My Mind'. 'On My Mind' was Tadhg's newest song and it was very clearly about Jess. Writing a guitar line for it that he said turned the song from ordinary to special, then playing that guitar line while he sang about Jess so tenderly, was absolute hell. But it was a good song. I couldn't lie and say it still needed a few more tweaks.

'Of course it's ready,' I said.

'Okay, great.' He was visibly relieved.

'Did you not think it was?' I asked.

Tadhg shrugged. 'I mean, I hoped it was. But it's hard to judge. And you know, playing music, writing songs … I know this sounds wanky but it's, like, everything to me. I mean, it really is all I want to do with my life. I just hope I'm good enough.'

Tadhg had never been cocky, but now there was a vulnerability in his voice I'd never really heard before. Despite my annoyance about Jess, my heart went out to him. I knew how he felt, after all.

'You're good enough,' I said.

Half an hour later we were in the snug, good-naturedly arguing over what song we should play at the upcoming college battle of the bands. The winners got to play the Trinity Ball, the massive end-of-year black-tie extravaganza. They played at the very beginning of the night, before half the attendees had even turned up, but still – you got to go to the Ball for free!

'We've got to play 'Midnight Feast',' said Tadhg.

'I think we should play a really loud one,' said Joanna. 'Oh, hi Jess!'

'Budge up there, Laura, let Jess in,' said Brian.

'Sorry, of course!' I said.

I budged and Jess slid into the banquette between me and Tadhg. He put his arm around her shoulders and the two of them exchanged a look of such mutual affection that, to my shame, I had to dig my nails into my palms to stop my eyes filling with tears. I had never felt anything like the jealousy I felt when she was around, a corrosive mixture of pain and anger and a resentment that I knew in my heart wasn't justified, which added guilt to the toxic mix. But I plastered on a smile and said, 'Okay! I'm going to the bar. What are you drinking, Jess?'

'Pint of Guinness, please!' she said, snuggling into Tadhg's side. 'Thanks a million.'

It wasn't the first time I'd seen them together, of course, but somehow seeing her here, in *our* place, in our little world, was just too much for me. Katie was going through one of her smoking phases, and when I got back from the bar with the drinks she took one look at my face and said, 'I'm going out for a fag. Come with me, Lol?'

I followed her outside. Once we were out in Dame Lane, she

handed me a cigarette, lit it and her own and said, 'You can't go on like this.'

'I don't have a choice,' I said.

'Yes,' she said. 'You do. You could put some distance between you and him. It's hurting you too much.'

'How can I put distance between us?' I said. 'We're in a band together!'

Katie took a drag of her cigarette and exhaled. 'You could leave the band.'

'*What?*'

'You could leave the band,' she said again.

'I can't leave the band!'

'Why not?' said Katie.

'Because it's … because it's *the band*!'

'You could start another band,' said Katie. 'You're so talented, Lol. If you wanted, you could get a whole new band together tomorrow.'

'But I don't want to!' I said. 'I want …'

What did I want? I wanted to make music with the band. I wanted to hang out with Tadhg. I wanted Tadhg to be in love with me.

Two out of three wasn't too bad, right?

'I want *this* band,' I said. 'And I want to stay friends with him.'

'But it's making you so unhappy,' she said.

'That'll wear off,' I said. 'It's just because him and Jess is still so new.'

'It's been nearly two months,' said Katie.

'I'm not leaving the band,' I said. 'I'm not letting fucking Jess push me out of my own band.' I stubbed out the cigarette I had barely inhaled. 'I'm serious, Katie. I'm not losing my band as well.'

Word of The Band Laura's In had clearly spread, because on the night of our headline gig there was a queue outside the venue before the doors opened. I sneaked in Annie and her best friend, Roo – they were barely seventeen and looked so young that if they'd tried to pay in they would definitely have been asked for ID they didn't have.

'Are all these people seriously here to see you?' said Annie in such disbelieving tones I'd have been offended if she weren't my little sister. Before I could answer she grabbed my arm and said, 'Oh my God, who's your man in the suit?'

I followed her gaze and saw Tadhg, talking to his sister Rosie at the bar.

'That's Tadhg,' I said.

'Your *bandmate* Tadhg?' She and Roo stared at me with something like awe.

'Yup,' I said. 'Okay, behave yourselves and don't get kicked out. I'm going to find Katie.'

I was on my way to her when Fiachra walked in. He looked even better than he had at the last gig.

'Back again?' I said. I was pretty sure he wouldn't hold the fact that I had kissed him and then basically run away from him against me. And I was right.

'I couldn't keep away,' he said. 'People are going to think I'm here as your groupie.'

'Are you?' I said. I was surprised by how glad I was to see him.

'That depends.' His grin was typically wicked. 'Do you want me to be?'

'Hmmm.' I returned his smile. 'Maybe. See me after the show.'

'Yes, ma'am,' he said, and saluted.

And the way he looked at me made me forget about Tadhg, just for a second.

This time the audience weren't surprised when we were good. This time they were anticipating it. And while this put us under a bit of pressure, their enthusiasm was infectious. There were huge cheers when Tadhg stepped up to the mic and introduced our first song, 'Midnight Feast', and it just got better from there. When he and I were on stage with Jo and Brian, it was like nothing had changed between us. When we were on stage, we had a bond that no one else could have. When we were on stage, nothing else mattered.

Until, towards the end of the set, we reached the one song I'd been dreading.

'This one is for Jess,' said Tadhg, looking down with a heart-melting smile at the front of the crowd, where Jess was standing with her glossy friends. 'I love you, you know. It's called 'On My Mind'.'

As I played the song's opening guitar line, I held my head high, looking towards the back of the room with a thousand-yard stare. I carefully avoided looking at Jess and her friends dancing in front of the stage. I avoided looking at Tadhg when I could help it. I was afraid he'd see how much this all hurt me. I was afraid Katie might have been right.

When we left the stage we were all besieged by friends and acquaintances but also total strangers. Tadhg made a beeline for Jess, who was waiting for him on the other side of the venue, her face aglow. Girls kept stopping him to, presumably, tell him how great he was, or give him their numbers, or simply proposition him, but he just smiled politely at them and kept going until he reached Jess and swung her around in his arms.

A few minutes later, just after the lights dimmed to announce last orders, I was on my way to the bar when I saw Fiachra on the other side of the room, talking to Ruairí. He glanced over, caught my eye and smiled. I didn't look away. Fiachra said something to Ruairí and made his way to me.

'Well, here I am,' he said. 'Reporting for duty.'

'How were we?' I said, gesturing towards the now-empty stage.

'You,' said Fiachra, 'were spectacular.'

I met his amused, appreciative gaze and I thought, *Yes*.

I was tired of having my heart broken by someone who didn't even know he was doing it. I was tired of passively standing there watching Jess and Tadhg have the romance of the new century. I was tired of letting stuff *happen* to me. I wanted to actively choose something. And now there was a hot, tall, flirty boy standing in front of me who made it clear that he wanted me and who would be completely happy with a no-strings-attached, mutually satisfying hook-up. Possibly multiple no-strings-attached, mutually satisfying hook-ups.

So I chose to kiss Fiachra in front of the stage that night. And then I chose to go home with him. And when he went down on me, I can honestly say I wasn't thinking about Tadhg at all.

I didn't see Tadhg until that Saturday, when we met as usual to get the bus to Stillorgan, and when we were walking to the bus stop he said, 'So are you and your ex back together, then?'

And I said, as airily as I could, 'Ah, you know, we're having fun. Neither of us is looking for anything really serious right now.'

'Oh,' said Tadhg. 'Cool. As long as you're happy.'

'I'm very happy,' I said.

I hoped seeing Tadhg and Jess together would get easier – it had to get easier, right? But it never did, not really. I just got used to it. I learned not to think about it too much when she wasn't around. I focused on making music with Joanna and Brian and Tadhg, which always made me feel better, and when Tadhg and I caught each other's eye at band practice and I felt that old spark, I reminded myself that we were just friends and nothing more. One Saturday I reluctantly had to miss band practice because my period cramps were so bad and I realised just how much I needed that weekly afternoon of music. The weekend felt utterly flat without it.

And so the months went by. I applied for a Communications MA in DCU, and Katie applied, to everyone's surprise, for the HDip in teaching. Jo and Brian applied for postgrads in the US and the UK, which made me worry about the future of the band, but they both insisted the odds of them being accepted were tiny so we didn't need to think about it. Tadhg landed a well-paid summer job, teaching at a teen rock camp in DCU. Fiachra and I sometimes met up and fooled around and it was always a good time. Katie and Sarah persuaded me to join them and book a J1-visa summer trip, working in New York. 'If the only thing stopping you going to America is Tadhg,' Katie said, 'think of being here all summer on your own while he works in that camp and then jets off to Jess's villa in the south of France. A break will do you good. It's only three months.'

I knew she was right. I needed to move on. I needed to look to the future. I needed to be far away from Tadhg and Jess, just for a while.

But then they broke up.

Chapter Twenty-Six

2019

I'm lying on my bed on Monday afternoon staring at the ceiling and making a list of the most surprising people who have contacted me since yesterday. A girl from my year in secondary school who I once hit with a folder because I saw her picking on a first year. My aunt who told me at my cousin's wedding last year that I should use some filler on that line between my eyebrows. A former colleague who I know used to bitch about me behind my back. And Brian's ex Caroline, of course. Who now has her own lifestyle brand. Of course she does. Not quite the little boutique I imagined during that lunch with Tadhg less than a fortnight ago, but almost. I have the urge to tell Tadhg about this, because he'd find it pretty funny, and then realise I can't. Or I won't.

I still haven't got back to him. He stopped trying to ring me yesterday afternoon. I suppose he thought all the calls might be getting a bit much. Or maybe he's just given up. I will talk to him eventually, of course I will, but at this moment all I can handle is lying in bed and staring at the ceiling. I haven't even cried since yesterday on the bench in Fairview Park. I've spent most of the time just lying and staring.

I barely got any sleep last night. I spent way, way too long looking at comments and messages yesterday, and they're all still scuttling around in my head like spiders. There were so many terrible, terrible comments. Even the compliments felt horrible and intrusive. So many people *saying* things about me. We're not meant to be exposed to so many opinions about ourselves. I don't think our brains can handle it. Mine certainly can't.

Eventually Katie took my phone away from me. I don't know where it is right now. She could have thrown it in the Tolka for all I care. Just thinking about it makes me feel sick. I don't want anyone to contact me ever again. Maybe I'll never leave this room. Maybe I'll become one of those modern-day hermits. Maybe—

There's a knock on my bedroom door and Katie says, 'Lol? You okay?'

'I'm fine,' I lie.

'Can I come in?'

I know she'd go away if I asked her to. But I've been in the house on my own all day while she and Jeanne were at work. Maybe I don't really want to be a hermit after all.

'Okay.'

She gently opens the door and walks in. 'So ... Tadhg just rang me.'

I sit up on the bed. 'What?'

'He's genuinely worried about you.'

'He shouldn't be using you to get to me,' I say.

'He's not,' says Katie. 'He just wanted to know how you are. He's not trying to pass on messages or anything.'

'And what did you tell him?'

'I said you were in shock,' she says. 'Which I think you are. And that this has all been very hard for you.'

'What did he say?'

'He says he knows it must be hard and he's sorry,' says Katie. She looks down at her hands. 'I think you should talk to him, Lol.'

I sigh. I know she's right. I can't keep putting it off forever.

'Okay,' I say. 'But I'll need my phone back.'

'I'll give it back,' she says. 'But first, you need some food.'

I barely ate anything yesterday and nothing but a small bowl of cornflakes this morning, so as soon as I smell toast I'm suddenly famished. I devour it before Katie hands me my phone. When I turn it on I see multiple missed calls, some from unknown numbers, and a ridiculous number of texts. I delete all the unknown numbers without reading them and text my parents and Annie to let them know I'm still basically okay. Annie was one of the few people I talked to yesterday before Katie took my phone away.

'I'm going to fly home and kill those pricks,' she said when she rang me from London.

'Which pricks?' I said.

'The journalist. Aisling's husband. Tadhg fucking Hennessy. All of them.'

I almost believed she'd do it too. It was weirdly comforting.

After I text Annie I make the stupid mistake of googling my name, which brings up a whole new rake of stories in other outlets from all over the English-speaking world and makes me realise that this story is not going to go away quickly.

Why we're so obsessed with 'Tadhg's Cinderella'

What we know about Tadhg Hennessy's protegée Laura McDermott

What the Tadhg Hennessy 'Cinderella' story tells us about women in music

Is Tadhg Hennessy dating his old bandmate Laura McDermott? What we know about the most mysterious woman in music

Ally or saviour complex? Tadhg Hennessy's Cinderella story

After looking at this I have to lie down on the bed and stare at the ceiling again for a while.

Then I text Tadhg.

The doorbell rings twenty minutes later, which was just enough time for me to shower, dress and put my contact lenses in, because I'm still stupidly vain and I couldn't bear the thought of him turning up and seeing me looking like the scruffy waif from that dreadful photograph. I can hear low voices coming up from the hall, and a few moments later there's a knock on my bedroom door. When I open it, Tadhg is standing there, looking like he hasn't slept in at least twenty-four hours. Well, that makes two of us.

'Shit, Laura,' he says. 'I am so sorry about this.'

'Me too.'

We just stand there for a moment, and I realise he's waiting to be invited into the room, so I say, 'I suppose you'd better come in.'

I sit on the bed and he takes the chair by the dressing table. He looks too tall for it.

'Are you okay?' he says. 'Sorry, that's a stupid question.'

'No, I'm not,' I say. 'Okay, I mean. And neither are my parents. I had to explain to them that I'm not actually destitute.'

'Oh Christ,' he says. 'I'm so sorry. I keep saying it, but I really am.' And he sounds it. But what do I know?

'Was it you?' I say. 'That story. Did it come from you?'

'What?' he says. 'No! No, of course it didn't!'

'Last week,' I say, 'you said Hugo wasn't going to object to us working together. Was this why? Did you say he could use me for publicity?'

'Jesus!' Tadhg looks genuinely horrified. 'Of course not! Oh my God, Lol, I would never … Is that what you've been thinking?'

My face must give him all the answer he needs.

'I swear I had nothing to do with this story,' he says. 'It's all fucking Hugo. Who is no longer my manager, by the way.'

'But did you know?' I say. 'Did you know he was going to do it?'

'No!' he says. 'Of course I didn't.'

'So he didn't mention it when he called over that day?'

'He just said he'd been thinking that me working with someone who wasn't a professional musician would be even better publicity than working with those producers,' says Tadhg. 'And I told him you and me were focusing on songwriting and we didn't need any publicity. I said maybe we could discuss making it public in the future, but right now it was a private arrangement. Working with you was my priority, and he could tell Ahlberg and Johns I'm otherwise engaged. He said he understood. He didn't mention leaking any story to the media – he didn't mention any publicity plan in particular. I realise now that he was asking for details about you but I swear, Laura, I didn't tell him anything apart from the fact we were in college together. I didn't even give him your full name.'

I remember Hugo asking for my surname that day. Asking where I worked. He must have been fishing for info because he knew Tadhg might shut down his scheme, and he wanted to be able to go behind his back and get someone to research me.

'I never thought he'd do anything like this,' says Tadhg. 'And

I know you don't owe me anything at the moment, but I really hope you believe me about this.'

I do. But still. But still. I think of my parents calling me yesterday, worried and upset. I think of Aisling. I think of all those articles. All those terrible comments. All those messages. All those thoughts about me. They've all been unleashed and I can't stop them and I can't unsee them. And they're going to keep coming, at least for a while. Why did I think I could ever be okay with any public scrutiny?

'I believe you.' I can see the relief on his face. 'I'm sorry for accusing you of something so awful.'

'That's okay,' says Tadhg. 'I understand. It would never have happened if you weren't working with me. I'm so sorry about that.'

Then I remember something.

'But … but last week you said you couldn't really trust Hugo,' I say slowly. 'At least not like you trusted his dad. So did you actually tell him not to leak the story about me? Like, explicitly tell him? Or did you just say it didn't need any publicity?'

'I don't— Maybe not explicitly but I thought it was obvious …'

'Well, clearly it wasn't!' I say. 'You just assumed it was. God, Tadhg, the world works so smoothly for you now and you don't even realise it! Everyone around you does what you want, so it doesn't seriously cross your mind that one day they won't. And now that day's arrived, and I'm the one paying for it!'

'I'm so sorry.' He looks it too. But that doesn't change anything. 'I really didn't think this would happen.'

'You should have *checked* that Hugo wasn't going to say anything!' I'm on the verge of angry tears now. 'You should have fucking checked!'

'You're right,' he says. 'I know you're right. Fuck. I've really messed up.'

'Yes!' I say. 'You have! All this attention …' I trail off.

'Yeah?' he says gently.

'It feels awful, Tadhg,' I say. 'I don't know how you deal with it. It feels really, *really* awful.'

He looks away for a second, and when he looks back at me his expression is so full of sympathy and guilt and something that looks a bit like love that I can't hold it in any longer. I dig my fingernails into my palms the way I always used to, but it doesn't work this time, and to my absolute horror I realise I am, at last, after all these years, doing what I vowed I'd never do and crying in front of Tadhg. Or rather, crying next to Tadhg, because now he's sitting beside me on the bed and his arm is around me and I'm sobbing into his shirt as he holds me tightly and strokes my hair and murmurs, 'It's okay, Lol. It's okay, sweetheart. It'll be okay.'

And somehow this doesn't feel tragic, or humiliating, or shameful.

It feels like comfort.

But once I've cried myself out a bit, I pull away from him and say, 'Shit, sorry. I didn't mean to cry all over you.'

I reach over, grab a tissue from the box on my bedside table and blow my nose loudly. I've basically given up on vanity now.

'You,' says Tadhg, 'have absolutely nothing to apologise for. I'm the one who has to keep apologising. If it weren't for me, you and your family wouldn't have to deal with all this shit. I wish I could … I wish I could stop it hurting you.'

'The stuff on social media,' I say. 'It's bad. I mean, it's *so* bad. And there's just so *much* of it.'

'It'll pass,' he says. 'I know that's not much consolation right now, but believe me, Lol, it will pass.'

'Have you seen what people are saying about me?' I say. 'Actually, no, I don't want to know if you've seen it. If you haven't, don't look at it.'

'It's all meaningless,' he says, 'whatever they're saying.'

'But it's relentless,' I say. 'And it's not just strangers. It's people I sort of know, all messaging me, asking questions … I even got a text from Caroline.'

Tadhg looks startled. 'Brian's ex Caroline?'

I nod. 'She runs a lifestyle brand. Called Moon. She wants to give me some 'pieces' if I do any events with you.'

We stare at each other for a second, and then his mouth twitches, and I let out a very undignified snort of laughter, and we both crack up until Tadhg is doubled over with mirth and I'm gasping for air.

When the laughter finally subsides, Tadhg says, 'Obviously you said yes to Caroline.'

'Well of course,' I say. 'I'll be wearing nothing but Moon from now on. Though actually she only offered to lend the pieces so I'll have to give them all back.' I flop back on the bed and stare at the ceiling again, but this time I'm almost smiling.

Tadhg looks down at me and suddenly I'm aware of the physical intimacy. Me lying, limp from laughing, him sitting next to me, the two of us on my bed.

'You know,' he says, 'if you want to stop working with me, I totally understand. If you never want to do it again, I don't blame you.'

I sit up and think of all those commenters calling me a grifter, calling me talentless ('If she's so great, why hasn't she done anything until now???'), feeling sorry for me, accusing me of sleeping with Tadhg (I fucking wish), accusing me of being after his money, after his studio, after his house. I have many, many complicated feelings about working with Tadhg, but one feeling isn't complicated at all: I am determined not to let those dickheads decide whether I do it or not.

'No,' I say. 'Let's keep going.'

I walk him downstairs and we stand in the hall where, just forty-eight hours earlier, I said goodbye to him after dinner, totally unaware of what I'd wake up to.

'I'm sorry to rush off, but my lawyer's coming over to the house in fifteen minutes,' he says. 'She's going to sort out legally firing Hugo.'

'Good.' When I think of Hugo, a sort of red mist descends over my eyes. Maybe I should get Annie on a plane to take care of him right now.

'So,' says Tadhg, 'do you want to come over to the studio tomorrow? We can wait a few days, if you'd rather.'

I do want to go to the studio. I've come to accept that I don't actually want to stay in my room forever. I'm about to say yes, but then I imagine making the short walk to Marino Crescent, past people who might recognise me from the pictures online. Past the fans in the Crescent park who definitely would. I'm suddenly flooded with panic.

'Are you okay?' he says.

I look up at his kind hazel eyes and shake my head.

'I really want to,' I say. 'But the thought of facing people outside your house ...'

My heart is beating faster just at the thought.

'I should have thought of that,' he says. 'How about ... how about if I come here?'

The panic subsides, just a bit.

'Yeah, okay,' I say. 'That sounds good.'

'Excellent,' he says. 'I'll see you tomorrow. Usual time?'

'Usual time.'

'And I know I keep saying it,' he says, 'but I'm really sorry for letting you down.'

I watch from the door as he gets in his car and drives away. Katie comes out of the kitchen.

'Were you listening in behind the door?'

'Not really,' she says. 'How did that go?'

'I cried all over him,' I say as I follow her into the kitchen. 'At my age. Proper snotty crying. After always swearing I'd never cry in front of him.'

'It doesn't count if you're not crying *about* him,' she says. 'Are you still angry with him?'

I sigh. I mean, if I weren't working with Tadhg, if he'd been more rigorous with Hugo, this wouldn't have happened. But no one forced me to work with him. Media attention was always a risk. Even without Hugo, someone could have noticed me going into his house every day for a week and taken a photo. Katie and Jeanne were warning me about that possibility just a few days ago.

'No,' I say. 'I'm not still angry with him.'

When I wake up the next morning there's a moment of blissful peace before all the events of the last week flood back into my mind.

'On the plus side,' I tell Jeanne when we're sitting in the kitchen, her drinking coffee and me drinking tea, 'at least the Cinderella stuff has stopped me thinking about Dave and his baby.'

'That's the spirit!' says Jeanne.

Tadhg arrives at ten and I've just handed him the first cup of tea of the session when he says, 'I had an idea I want to run by you.'

'If it's about Moveable Feast,' I say, 'I'm really not in the right headspace to think about that right now.'

'Don't worry about that,' he says. 'No, I was thinking I could post something online making it clear that this bullshit story and its sources were completely unauthorised by me, and that you and I had made a mutual decision to work together for a few weeks as songwriting partners. I know it won't make all this go away, but at least it'd make it clear that you're not …'

'Your charity case.' I think about it for a moment. He's right that a statement wouldn't change what's already out there. But my wounded dignity can't resist the opportunity to tell the world that I'm not Saint Tadhg's latest project.

'Okay,' I say. 'Let's do it.'

'Great,' says Tadhg. 'Um, I've actually written something already. I thought we could post a picture of the two of us with this as a caption. But only if you're happy with it, obviously.'

He shows me the note on his phone. He really has been thinking about this.

This is my old friend Laura McDermott, one of the very best guitarists I've ever known. ['Is that a bit much?' I say. 'No,' says Tadhg. 'It's just the truth.'] *For the last week we've been writing songs together again for the first time since we were in a band in college. I'm really happy to be working with Laura again and I'd like to take this opportunity to discuss the stories about our creative partnership that have appeared in the media this week.*

These stories wildly misrepresented both Laura's situation and our working relationship, and the statements by alleged sources from my team were absolutely not authorised by me. ['I'd love to publicly blame Hugo,' says Tadhg, 'but I legally can't because we're still in the process of firing him.'] *I'm asking you all to please respect Laura and her privacy and to understand how lucky I am to be working with her again. She's an incredible musician and songwriter.* ['You don't have to say that last bit,' I say. 'But it's the truth,' says Tadhg.] *Thanks everyone, and I hope I'll see some of you at my soon-to-be-announced live dates next year.*

'I hope,' says Tadhg, 'the news of the gigs will distract the more, um, unhinged fans from going after you.'

'What are the live dates next year?' I ask. 'Are you touring?'

I'm unsurprised but a little worried by how my stomach twists at the thought of him heading off on the road, far away from me.

'It's not finalised yet,' says Tadhg, 'but yeah, the plan is another big tour in 2020. For when the new album comes out next summer.'

I glance over at him. He's looking down at his feet, his face set.

'You don't look hugely excited,' I say.

He looks up and sighs. 'I'm not, to be honest. I love playing live, I really love it, but touring – it's not so fun anymore. It used to be fun, like a big working holiday, but I know that when I'm on the road next year I'll miss home, I'll miss my old friends, I'll miss … I'll miss everything. Fuck, I know I sound like an arsehole. Poor me, I don't want to play some gigs for the people who paid for my house!'

'You don't sound like an arsehole,' I say. 'I get it.' And I do.

'You don't think I'm an ungrateful shit?'

'Of course I don't,' I say. 'I totally understand. And, you know, you're not getting any younger …'

'I'm only a month older than you!'

'That's what I mean! At our age … well, you don't necessarily want to be out every night. You don't want to be away all the time. You want the odd night out and then some, I dunno, peace and security. A home life. Wow, that sounds quite boring when I say it out loud.'

'No,' says Tadhg. 'It sounds pretty good.'

Neither of us says anything for a moment, and then Tadhg claps his hands together and says, 'Right! Will we get a picture?'

'You'll have to take it,' I say. 'You've got longer arms.'

'Fine.' He sits down next to me on the couch. He get his phone ready, holds it out and looks down at me.

'You ready?' he says. And then, 'Oh bollocks, I think I took one by mistake.'

'Oh dear,' I say. 'Show me.'

I brace myself for a sobering experience as Tadhg hands over the phone. I'm sure we'll look like a study in contrasts: the devastatingly handsome rock star side by side with the sleep-deprived thirty-seven-year-old copywriter with a wonky fringe and considerably less Botox and filler than the gorgeous female celebs he's usually photographed beside. By which I mean none at all.

But actually, to my surprise, we don't look so wrong together. I'm looking up at Tadhg and he's looking down at me and we're each kind of smiling as if we're sharing a moment of complicity. I look positively fresh-faced. Even my hair looks okay. It is, I realise to my surprise, a really, really nice photo.

'I think we should use this one,' says Tadhg. 'I mean, as long as you're okay with it.'

'Sure,' I say. 'It's grand.' I'm aware this good photo might have been a fluke and the next one might live up to my worst expectations.

'We don't have to post anything, you know,' he says. 'Or we can wait and post it later.'

'Let's post it now,' I say. And he does.

I'm not sure why, but I feel slightly better once the post has gone up. At least we've *done* something. We plug our guitars in, keeping the volume sensibly low so as not to disturb the neighbours, and set to work. We run through all the songs we've written over the last week, and I'm struck again by how good they are. Better than the songs we wrote for the band back in the day. And then we start on our song. For the umpteenth time we run through that verse, chorus, verse and chorus. Over the next few hours we try lots of different things. But nothing is quite right. Our song is still incomplete.

'For fuck's sake!' I feel on the edge of tears of frustration. I throw myself back in my chair, clutching my guitar. 'What's wrong with us? Why can't we just figure something out?'

Then Tadhg says, 'Maybe we shouldn't.'

I sit up. 'Maybe we shouldn't what?'

'Maybe we shouldn't figure something out.'

'What do you mean?' Does he actually want to stop all this right now? Is this the end of it? My heart sinks at the thought.

'The song,' says Tadhg. 'Maybe we don't have to finish it after all.'

'But ... but that's the point of this whole fortnight.'

'Well, maybe it's not,' he says. 'Maybe it was just the, I don't know, trigger. Maybe the point was writing all these other songs. Because we've written some great songs over the last week, Lol. I mean, properly great songs.'

'They are pretty good,' I admit. 'Even if none of them have proper lyrics.'

'They will,' he says. 'Working with you ... I can't remember the last time I wrote so many songs in such a short space of time. Let alone good songs. They might even be better than *the* song.'

'I mean, maybe ...'

'Seriously,' he says. 'For the rest of the week, let's forget about our song. Let's, you know, just fool around with stuff and try things out and just *play*. Enjoy ourselves. Let's just be creative with no expectations. Just for the sake of it. If something happens with *our* song, then great. But clearly putting pressure on ourselves isn't the answer.'

'Maybe you're right,' I say.

'I'm pretty sure I'm right,' he says. 'It'll be fun. And with everything that's happened over the last few days, I think we could do with a bit of fun. And no pressure to perfect a sixteen-year-old song.'

He's definitely got a point there. Playing music for fun sounds pretty good right now.

'Okay,' I say. 'Let's fool around.'

And we do.

Liberated from the pressure to finish the song by Friday, I feel like some weight has been lifted from my shoulders. The rest of the day is great. We're so engrossed in what we're doing – and, it must be said, we're now playing so loudly – that I don't hear the front door open, and I get a shock when Katie sticks her head in the door.

'Is this a private concert or can anyone join in?' she says. 'Afternoon, Timothy.'

'Afternoon to you,' he says. 'Were we being obnoxiously loud?'

'A bit loud,' admits Katie. 'I think some of the neighbours might have figured out you're here.'

I hurry over to the window and peek out, grateful that Katie and Jeanne installed slatted shutters. Sure enough, I can see the woman who lives across the road standing in her small front garden, chatting with another neighbour and two teenagers who live at the end of the road. All of them are looking over at our house.

'Shit,' says Tadhg. 'Sorry. I think we've been getting gradually louder all day. I forgot we weren't in a sound-proof studio.' He turns to me. 'Would you be okay with coming back to my place tomorrow?'

It's clear we can't really keep playing here without attracting a crowd. 'Sure. That'll be fine.'

'I can send Paul to collect you,' he says. 'My regular driver.'

It's tempting. But I can't stop walking around my own neighbourhood. The longer I leave it, the more freaked I'm going to be.

'No,' I say. 'It'll be grand.'

After Tadhg goes home, I cautiously turn my phone back on and, because I'm afraid not knowing is actually worse than knowing, I google my name.

Tadhg speaks out: leave Laura alone!

The truth about Tadhg Hennessy's Cinderella

Why Tadhg Hennessy's collaborator deserves our respect

Why do we care so much about Tadhg Hennessy's 'Cinderella'?

There are more, of course. I don't read any of them. I'm not that stupid. People I know have clearly seen Tadhg's post because there's a flurry of new texts and messages. There's even one from Caroline, which I can't resist looking at.

> OMG Laura I just saw the pic of you and Tadhg – SO cute! You haven't aged a day! I know you must be up to your eyes right now, but let me know if you'd like to borrow some Moon pieces – and of course if you'd like to buy them, I can give you a friends discount. Let me know what you think!

I forward it to Tadhg, who instantly responds with 'That's it. She's won me over. I'm going to hire her as my new stylist', and I reply 'Do you actually have a stylist?' and he replies 'NO!'. But even though this makes me laugh, it's a reminder that all the unwanted attention isn't going to go away any time soon. And when the bubble bursts at the end of the week and he heads off to America, I'll be back in my old life, dealing with it on my own.

Chapter Twenty-Seven

2003

We played 'Anyone But You' at the Battle of the Bands, and the minute we finished it, I knew we were going to win. I wasn't being arrogant or anything, I just knew.

'Fuck,' said Brian, staggering out from behind the drum kit as the packed Buttery cheered wildly. 'I think we might have actually done it.'

We descended from the stage, sweaty and elated. The first person I saw was Jess, throwing her arms around Tadhg. And standing behind her was Fiachra.

Fiachra and I had been seeing each other regularly since that last gig, but we mostly saw each other in his bed. Or, on one memorable occasion, in the stairwell at the far end of the top floor of the Arts Block. And, once the weather improved, in an outdoor stairwell *behind* the Arts Block. I already knew he was at the Battle of the Bands – he'd led me out to the Atrium next door earlier that night for ten efficiently used minutes that had, I have to admit, given me a little extra glow on stage.

'How was that?' I said.

'Well, I'm pretty sure you've won,' said Fiachra.

'I think you might be right,' I said, beaming at him.

'I'm definitely right, you were the best band,' he said. 'Especially *you*. The way you were looking down at the audience when you were playing, like you didn't give a fuck if they liked what you were doing or not ...' He grinned. 'It was very ... imperious. I was kind of into it, I can't lie.'

I shook my head, laughing. 'Why does that not surprise me?'

'Seriously, though, Laura,' he said. 'You were brilliant. I'm really proud of you.'

'Oh,' I said, slightly taken aback by the affection in his voice. 'Um, thanks.'

'Oh God, don't look so worried,' said Fiachra. 'I'm not going to declare my love or anything.' Then it was his turn to look worried. 'We both still want this to be just a friends-with-benefits thing, don't we? No messing around, no one getting hurt?'

I let out a sigh of relief. 'Yeah, we do.'

'Good,' said Fiachra. 'Well, in that case, as your friend, with benefits or otherwise, I can say I'm very proud of you. Or can I? If it makes things weird, forget I said anything ...'

'It doesn't make things weird,' I said, smiling at him. 'And you can.'

He put his finger into the pull-loop of the zip at the neckline of my vintage dress. 'Can I unzip this later?'

I laughed. 'You can do that too.'

That was when a familiar female voice said, 'Hello!'

Fiachra let go of the zip and I turned to see Jess and Tadhg standing behind me, arms around each other's waists. Tadhg was wearing another well-cut charity-shop suit, grey this time. Jess extended her hand towards Fiachra. 'I don't think we've met before. I'm Jess.'

'Hi!' said Fiachra. 'Fiachra.'

'You must be so proud of Laura,' said Jess.

Fiachra and I exchanged an amused look. 'I was literally just telling her that.' He turned to Tadhg with a warm, genuine smile. 'You were great up there, man.'

That was when I realised that they had never actually met before.

'Sorry, where are my manners?' I said. 'Tadhg, this is Fiachra – Fiachra, this is Tadhg.' I glanced at Jess. 'Sorry, I mean Tim.'

'Good to meet you,' said Tadhg, offering his hand.

'Likewise,' said Fiachra. 'I've seen you play a few times now, you're deadly.' He turned to Jess. 'Are you a musician too? Or what are you into?'

'I'm a musician,' said Jess. 'I'm on the Music and Technology course with Tim.'

'Ah,' said Fiachra. 'Is it all Stockhausen and Schoenberg?'

'Sometimes,' said Jess. 'And Xenakis.'

'I mixed some Xenakis in with Aphex Twin when I was DJing last year,' said Fiachra. 'It worked pretty well!'

He asked about her work and she explained about the found objects and noise installations.

'I'm not sure I'm selling it very well,' she said. 'Back me up, Tim!'

'Well, I'm sold,' said Fiachra. 'I love an auld noise installation. Fuck, that sounded sarcastic. I genuinely do! I went to a great festival in Utrecht last year …'

And then somehow the four of us were chatting about festivals and the music course and our band. I had almost forgotten that Fiachra could be charming and engaging outside his flirting. I had forgotten how fun it was to talk to him about music. It didn't make me want to go out with him again, but it reminded me why I had gone out with him in the first place, before we both realised he wasn't ready for a committed relationship.

Then there was a crackle of static and one of the judges clambered onto the makeshift stage holding a microphone. Tadhg and I exchanged glances.

'Here we go,' he said.

Please, I thought, *please let my instincts be right*. I only had another few months left of college, or at least of Trinity, and a part of me wanted to go out with a bang, or at least out with the Ball.

Fiachra's hand took mine and gave it a reassuring squeeze.

'And the winner of the 2003 Trinity Battle of the Bands, and a coveted opening slot at this year's Trinity Ball, is …'

I squeezed Fiachra's hand back, hard.

'The Band Laura's In!'

The room, or at least the bit of it near me, erupted. I flung my arms around Fiachra, who swung me into the air and then kissed me. He put me down and I whirled around to face Tadhg. Our eyes met and then he hugged me tight and said, 'We did it, Lol.'

I hugged him back. 'We did it!' I turned to Brian and Jo and we wrapped our arms around each other in a big group hug.

Then Katie grabbed me and cried, 'Come here, rock star!' and the celebrations began.

The rest of the night was a blur of drinks and congratulations. We all laughed at how thrilled we were – it was just a college Battle of the Bands; we hadn't won the Mercury Prize. But it felt like a real triumph. We ended up in a late bar, the band and a gang of our friends. And Fiachra. When we were leaving the pub at the end of the night, he said, 'Do you fancy coming back to my place?'

'Yeah,' I said. 'I do.'

'Good,' he said, looking at the neckline of my dress. 'I've been dying to pull down that zipper all night.'

I put my arm around him. 'Never change, Fiachra.'

'As a psychologist,' he said, 'or at least as a future psychologist, I can't promise that.'

'Thanks for being my plus-one tonight,' I said.

'Any time,' he said.

The rest of the gang was still hanging around outside the pub, and we said our goodbyes to everyone, Tadhg and Jess last of all.

'We're off,' I said. It felt odd facing them as part of what, to others at least, looked like just another couple, announcing that 'we' were heading off. Jess and Fiachra bade each other farewell like old pals.

'Congratulations again,' said Fiachra to Tadhg.

'Thanks, man,' said Tadhg. He looked at me. 'See you on Saturday?'

'Of course!' I said. 'We've got a ball to practise for.'

Fiachra put his arm around my shoulders as we walked down the road. When we reached the corner I glanced back. Tadhg and Jess were still chatting with a group outside the pub, but as I looked at him he turned his head and our eyes met, just for a second. Then I turned back to Fiachra and kept walking.

On the bus out to practice on Saturday, Tadhg said, 'Fiachra seems sound.'

'Yeah,' I said. 'He is.'

'I'm really happy for you,' said Tadhg.

'Um, thanks?' I couldn't help feeling a little patronised by his tone.

'I mean it,' said Tadhg. 'You deserve someone great.'

'Yeah, I know.' Had he thought I wasn't already aware of that? That I'd take anyone? I did not particularly want to talk about me and Fiachra with Tadhg. 'So! We need to plan the Ball setlist.'

It was April now, the last term of my last year in college. Everything was happening very fast. The Ball would take place in the second week of May, just before our exams, so we didn't have a huge amount of time to practise. For me, Joanna and Brian, these were our final exams, and for Tadhg, they would determine whether he could go on to the second year of the master's. He had way more exams than I did and the pressure was getting to him. We saw each other even less than usual, and he always seemed slightly stressed when we had a rare cup of tea or grabbed a quick lunch.

One day an email arrived from Brian, sent to the entire band, asking if we could all meet in the Buttery that evening because he and Jo had some news. Jo and Brian were there already when I arrived, looking uncharacteristically nervous. *Jesus, they're not going to announce they're a couple, are they?* I thought. *So much for Joanna's desire to keep things simple!*

But once Tadhg arrived and we were all supplied with pints, Brian said, 'So … I heard back from Bristol on Monday.'

'And I heard from Stanford,' said Jo. She glanced at Brian. 'We've both been accepted for postgrads.'

'Wow!' I said. 'Congratulations, that's brilliant!'

And I was happy for them, of course I was. I knew getting those places was a big deal for both of them. But I couldn't help my stomach sinking at the prospect of my friends moving hundreds of miles away. And not just my friends. My bandmates. I'd be losing the band.

But I couldn't guilt-trip Joanna and Brian about that. So I said, honestly, 'I'm so proud of you both!'

'Me too,' said Tadhg. 'Well done. It's really great.'

'Thanks, lads,' said Jo.

'But listen,' said Brian. 'Jo and I, we want to make sure the two of you keep the band going.'

'We can't just replace you!' I said. And I meant it. I couldn't imagine playing with other people now.

'You can,' said Jo. She grinned. 'I mean, whoever you get won't be as good, of course ...'

'How could they be?' said Brian.

'But seriously,' said Joanna, 'academia is right for me and Brian. But you two ... you're meant to be making music. You're meant to be in a band together.'

I wished she and Brian weren't leaving. But their faith in me – and in Tadhg – made me feel hopeful about my musical future.

Tadhg turned to me. 'What do you say, Lol? I will if you will.'

'Come on, Laura,' said Jo. 'Promise me you won't stop.'

I smiled at her. 'I promise.'

And I meant that too.

Then, on one of those late April days where you can feel the first hint of real summer, I walked out of the Buttery and almost ran straight into Tadhg.

'Hey!' I said. 'I can't stop, I'm late to meet Fiachra.' Then I caught the look on his face. 'Tadhg, are you okay?'

His expression was grim, and his eyes looked like he might have been ... *Jesus, could he have been crying?*

'Eh, not really.' He paused and then he said, 'I broke up with Jess.'

I couldn't say anything for a moment. 'Shit, when?'

'Um, a few hours ago?' He took his glasses off and rubbed his eyes. 'I've just come from her flat. Fuck. Sorry. It was … It was rough. She didn't expect it. I feel like a total prick.'

'Oh, Tadhg, I'm sorry,' I said. And I really was. I mean, I couldn't pretend my first reaction to this news was total sadness. But he was clearly so upset. And Jess … shit. Poor Jess. She didn't deserve to be as unhappy as she probably was now.

'I know I had to do it,' he said. 'It just wasn't right anymore. She was talking about me going to her parents' house in France when my job finishes in the summer, and I couldn't let her start making plans, it wasn't fair, I didn't want to … shit, I don't know.'

He looked so shaken I was genuinely worried. 'Where are you going now?'

'I'm meeting Ruairí in the Long Hall. Sorry to dump all of this on you. You're going to be even more late for Fiachra.'

'He won't mind,' I said. 'Will you— Are you okay?'

'I will be,' he said. He let out a long breath. 'I know I did the right thing. It just doesn't feel all that right at the moment.'

'Okay,' I said. 'Well, take care of yourself.'

Then I hugged him. He rested his head on my shoulder for a moment and said, 'I will. Thanks, Lol. I'll see you tomorrow.'

Fifteen minutes later, I arrived at Fiachra's house. 'There you are!' he said when he opened the door.

'Come here,' I said.

And as I kissed him, a shameful little part of my brain was thinking just one thing.

Tadhg was single again.

Chapter Twenty-Eight

2019

I'm leaning on the kitchen counter, waiting for my toast to pop up and listening to a ridiculous but entertaining podcast about Sweet Valley High books when I glance at the calendar on the wall and realise what date it is. And despite myself, I feel a little pang.

Today would have been my and Dave's eight-year anniversary. Eight whole years since we went for a drink and ended up kissing on the corner of Aungier Street on the way home. It feels like a lifetime ago.

We're both in very different places now.

I walk to Tadhg's through Marino, avoiding the busier main road at Fairview, and it's all so normal that I wonder why I was so nervous about walking over to his place. But then I reach Marino Crescent, and things are very different. It's scarier than I thought it might be. There are more people than ever in the park, including some who are clearly members of the paparazzi rather than Tadhg fans. And – oh God! – now they know my name.

'Laura! Over here! Laura!'

'Laura, is it true you're homeless?'

'We love you, Laura!'

'Leave Tadhg alone!'

'Laura!'

'Laura!'

They crowd around me as I get closer to Tadhg's house. I pull my parka hood as far forward as it'll go and hurry up to the gate, where I realise a burly security man is standing. When I approach, he gets between me and the photographers.

'In you go, Ms McDermott.'

The gate buzzes before I can even hit the bell, and I all but run through it and slam it behind me. That was horrible. Maybe this was a mistake. Maybe we should just have called it a day. Maybe this is impossible.

The front door is open when I get there, and Tadhg is in the hall, his face grim.

'Shit, Laura, I'm so, so sorry about this.'

I put down my guitar case and pull off my parka. 'Stop apologising, it's getting annoying. I told you, I know it's not your fault.'

'Well, if it wasn't for me, you wouldn't be in this situation.'

'Hugo's the one who leaked the story,' I say.

We head out to the studio, but I just can't concentrate on the song we're trying to write. I'm too aware of the hordes outside the house. I've turned my phone off, but I know there'll be loads of messages waiting for me when I turn it back on, so it almost feels like an unexploded bomb. I keep looking over at it and Tadhg clearly notices because after an hour and a half he says, 'Look, if it's all too much being back here today, I totally get it. We can take a break.'

The thought of going home (See, world! I'm not homeless!) and staring at the walls makes my heart sink even further. 'No, I'm grand. I need the distraction. If I go home I'll go mad.'

'I don't mean you going home,' says Tadhg. 'Sorry, I should have said.'

'What do you mean, then?' I say.

'Well, we could just hang out here,' he says. 'Watch a film or something. You haven't seen the screening room yet.'

'You have a *screening room*?'

'Um, yeah, it's in the basement, where the original kitchen used to be.' He catches my expression and says, 'I mean, it's just a big screen and some comfy chairs – it's not, like, my own multiplex or anything.'

'Of course,' I say. 'Just an average private screening room.'

'Hey, don't mock it till you've watched *Casablanca* on that big screen. Well, medium-sized screen. I don't want to raise your expectations too high.'

I would *love* to watch *Casablanca* with him in a private screening room. But I think I might be too emotionally fragile for it. 'We'll always have Paris'? I suppose Tadhg and I will always have the bus stop on Westmoreland Street. My mixed feelings must show on my face because Tadhg says, 'Or – and I hope you say yes to this one, because I would love an excuse to get out of the house – we could get lunch at—' And he names another restaurant where dinner costs more than my week's rent.

'We won't get a table,' I say. This is the sort of place where a table usually has to be booked a year in advance. Dave tried to book one for my birthday two years ago and they basically laughed at him over the phone.

'I know this sounds really wanky,' says Tadhg, 'but they usually keep a table free for, um, VIPs who might need it at the last minute. So I'm sure we'll be fine.'

'Jaysus.' I raise my eyebrows. 'First special sandwich deliveries and now this.'

Tadhg bows his head. 'Sorry. But what do you think?'

I have to admit, the thought of a fancy meal does appeal. But the thought of being seen in public does not. I say this to Tadhg.

'Oh, you don't need to worry about that,' he assures me. 'The table's in a little alcove. It's really private – we won't have people gawping at us. It'll be grand. Paul can drive us in.'

Fuck it, if I'm going to be Tadhg's little Cinderella, I might as well go to the ball. Or the posh restaurant, as the case may be.

'I'm in,' I say. 'As long as we can stop off at my place so I can change my clothes. I don't think they'll let me in wearing a band T-shirt and trousers with an elasticated waist.'

'Deal,' says Tadhg.

♪♪

Tadhg calls the restaurant and confirms that the alcove table is indeed free.

'Do you want to come in while I'm getting ready?' I say, when we pull up outside my house ten minutes later. As we head inside, I hope any potentially curtain-twitching neighbours are at work.

'Um, make yourself at home.' I am suddenly weirdly conscious that he knows I'm about to go upstairs and take my clothes off. Not that he'll be giving that matter a second thought. Or even a first one, probably.

'I will,' says Tadhg. 'Do you have any biscuits?'

I point him in the direction of the custard creams and run upstairs.

Fifteen minutes later, having put my glasses into my bag just in case we somehow stay out so late I have to take my contact lenses out, I descend the stairs in a 1980s Laura Ashley frock and find Tadhg sitting on the couch in the sitting room reading *Devil's Cub*, one of Katie's beloved Georgette Heyer novels.

'Can I borrow this?' he says without looking up. 'I'm learning a lot of surprising things about the eighteenth century.'

'I'm sure Katie won't mind as long as you look after it,' I say. 'Her Georgette Heyer collection is sacred.'

'I'll treat it with kid—' He looks up. '*Oh*. You look really nice.'

'Thanks,' I say. 'Charity shop.'

'You always did find the best things in those shops,' says Tadhg.

'There's slim pickings in them these days,' I say. 'Mostly tat from the nineties. This was a miracle find.'

'I miss going to charity shops,' says Tadhg, unfolding himself from the couch. 'I found some amazing things in George's Street back in the day.'

'The dead men's suits!' I say.

'I think it could have been just one dead man with a really sharp wardrobe,' says Tadhg. 'Who was exactly my size.'

'His family must have dumped a different suit at each shop,' I say. 'Do you still have them?'

'They're probably still in my parents' house,' he says. 'I should dig them out. Though I doubt they'd still fit me.'

'You could get them altered,' I say.

'I'd have to get them fumigated,' says Tadhg. 'I played so many gigs in those suits they could probably stand up by themselves.'

He's not talking about shows he played with me. We only ever played four gigs together that year. I feel a pang at the thought of all those shows he must have played in those suits later, after we went our separate ways. I saw his name on posters around town and outside music shops quite a few times in those early post-Trinity years, when I was doing my postgrad and starting my first agency jobs. It never failed to give me a moment of genuine pain, and a jealous rage, one that I couldn't justify even to myself, that he was still making music without me.

Well. I suppose he's making music with me again now.

♪♪

Half an hour later, Tadhg and I are sitting in the alcove at the back of a beautiful room in a Georgian townhouse, with a bottle of Fleurie in front of us. The room is lit by low, soft lamps and decorated in warm cream and gold. It's like being inside a pearl. A few heads turned as Tadhg walked through, but the fanciness of the clientele means that no one actually gawked. And once we're tucked into the cosy little alcove, only the people on the nearest table – a couple who look like they're in their seventies – can see us.

'Wow,' I say. 'This really is perfect.'

'Here, have some of this.' Tadhg pours me a glass of wine and I take a large sip.

'If ever there was a time for day drinking,' I say, 'it's today. But not, like, in a getting hammered way,' I add hastily, lest Tadhg think I'm going to start dancing on the table.

He laughs. 'I fully agree.'

We clink glasses. I let out a sigh that sounds more despairing than I meant it to.

'I know it's very easy for me to say,' says Tadhg, 'but this will pass.'

'Will it, though?' I take a sip of wine. 'I mean, it's not just all the attention I'm getting now. What'll happen when I'm looking for work in the future? Even if they don't remember the story, this Cinderella stuff will be the first thing that appears when people google me.'

I think of Amanda Sorohan. Despite the fact that she won a huge international art prize last year, the first thing that comes up when you search for her online is the fact that she used to go out with Tadhg. It *is* easy for Tadhg to say comforting things, because he doesn't have to worry about stuff like that. Me supposedly being his little protégée will be just one more feel-good Saint Tadhg story in a long list.

'I know,' says Tadhg. 'But I talked to Tara, and she said we can hire experts who specialise in cleaning up search results for people's names.' He looks at my miserable face. This is one situation when I really don't care if my feelings are obvious. 'I know that's not ideal, though. And I keep saying it, but I'm so sorry, Lol.'

'I know,' I say. I make myself sit up straighter. I'm having lunch in a beautiful restaurant with someone I genuinely enjoy spending time with, despite my very complicated feelings about him (they're not that complicated, Laura, they're just inconvenient). 'D'you know what, I'm going to forget about all this for a while and just have a nice lunch.'

'That sounds,' says Tadhg, 'like an excellent idea.'

Still, it's impossible to totally ignore what's happened. While we're eating our starters I say, 'I know we're not in the same boat, but how do you get used to it? Being written about as if you're a character in a soap opera rather than a real person?'

'I don't know if you ever do,' says Tadhg. 'The first time there was anything in the news about my personal life I totally freaked out.'

'Seriously?' One thing about Tadhg, he's not one of nature's freak-outers. He's always been pretty chill.

'Oh, yeah. I had just started going out with Charlotte Fitzpatrick – you know her?'

I do. Everyone does. She won a BAFTA last year. And I certainly remember their relationship. 'Charlotte and Tadhg' (the media tried to form a decent portmanteau word for their union but had to admit defeat – Tadhlotte sounded way too like 'toilet' in a strong Dublin accent and Chadhg was far too close to either 'shite' or 'shag', depending on how you pronounced it) were presented as a gorgeous Irish showbiz power couple. The story broke four years after Tadhg and I went our separate ways, and I remember being taken aback by the strength of my visceral reaction to paparazzi photos of him and Charlotte kissing in the Jardin des Tuileries in Paris.

'Photos of us appeared in the tabloids,' Tadhg continues. 'And basically, I freaked. I know it sounds naïve – I mean, I was what, twenty-six? I wasn't a naïve kid. I thought I knew what tabloids were like. But somehow I couldn't believe they could just do that to *me*, to us. I couldn't believe they'd spied on us when we were having what was meant to be a romantic weekend away. I don't think I understood that I was, you know, famous enough for anyone to bother with me, so it was a huge, huge shock. For a few months I didn't want to go out anywhere. I was paranoid there'd be paparazzi snapping me everywhere I went. I really liked Charlotte, and she liked me, but my reaction to all that bullshit basically destroyed our relationship.'

'What a very cheering story,' I say.

'I know it doesn't sound very positive,' says Tadhg. 'But I did get through it. I found ways to adapt. And, no, it's not fun, but I mean, my job is hardly going down the salt mines. I know plenty of people who have proper jobs that are much harder than anything I have to do.'

This is very sensible. For him. But he gets the good parts of fame to balance out the negative stuff. He gets his dream career and his gorgeous house. I still have to live in the real world. He must guess something of what I'm thinking because he says, 'Sorry, I know that's not hugely helpful for you right now.'

'Well, I did ask how *you* dealt with it.'

'I suppose the most useful thing I did was ... disassociation,' says Tadhg. 'Consciously telling myself all those stories and photos had nothing to do with me. They were about some imaginary Tadhg. But the real me ... I could tell myself that was still Tim Hennessy. A different person.' He pauses. 'It's actually useful, going by two names. It can create a sort of distance between the person who plays big shows and gets photographed in the street and the person who, like, goes for Sunday dinner with his mam and dad in Clontarf.'

On one hand, disassociation is helpful advice. On the other ...

'Do you mind me calling you Tadhg?' I say.

'What? Of course not!'

'I mean ...' What do I mean? That I'm suddenly feeling *really* sad that I might not know the real him? That I never did? That he was creating a distance between me and him the whole time? I think of Jess calling him Tim and how odd that made me feel. Like maybe she knew his real name, his real self, and I didn't.

'Me and Katie and Jo and Brian, us calling you Tadhg ... did that make you feel like we didn't know you? Like we just knew, I dunno, a persona, but you were always Tim to your real friends?'

'God, no! *No.*' Tadhg is literally shaking his head. 'It wasn't like that. You were my real friends too. You calling me Tadhg wasn't about a persona. It wasn't a stage name. It felt ... it was affectionate.' He looks away for a moment and then turns back to me, with that old awkward smile. 'Shit, at least I hope it was!'

I laugh, at least partly in relief. 'Yeah, it was.'

'You know,' says Tadhg, 'a few months after we ... after the band split up, when I started playing solo gigs, I was initially going to bill myself as Tim Hennessy. But I stuck with Tadhg.'

'Because Tim wasn't rock-and-roll enough?' I say.

'Ha! Well, partly,' he says. 'But also ... I wasn't ready to stop being Tadhg just yet.'

'Oh,' I say.

'Yeah,' he says. 'And here we are.'

'You're stuck with it now,' I say. 'Even though no one outside Ireland can spell it. Or say it.'

'Yep,' he says.

But he doesn't sound like he minds.

This entire conversation makes me feel better. We talk about his early gigs and my brief periods in other bands after college. I don't tell him none of them worked out because nothing was as good as playing with him. We talk about the new songs and how good it'll be to try them with Sam when he's back in the studio tomorrow. We imagine suitable punishments for Hugo. We finish the bottle of Fleurie and look at each other and Tadhg says, 'Fuck it, will we get another?' and I say 'Yes!' and we do. It's fun. It's good. And most importantly, it's distracting.

'This was such a great idea,' I say. 'Thanks a million.'

'Absolutely no need to thank me,' says Tadhg. 'It is very much the least I could do.'

'And I really don't think anyone's noticed you,' I say. I cautiously stick my head out of the alcove as if I'm looking for a sniper. 'All clear!'

And then I see them in a booth on the other side of the room, getting their bill from a waiter.

He's changed his hair. That's the first, stupid thing that comes into my head when I see Dave putting his card in the machine to pay the bill. The last time I saw him his sandy hair was short, but not exactly styled. Now it looks carefully groomed. He's been using product. He never used hair products. Maybe his fiancée got him some hair wax. Her back is to me, but I can see her glowing honey-blonde hair. Sleek, well-behaved hair. Very unlike mine.

Why are they even here on a random weekday? How the hell did he get a table? I was just thinking earlier that you have to book this place a year in advance. And a year ago he was engaged to me. A year ago today was our seven-year anniversary.

Oh. *Oh*.

He must have booked it for our eight-year anniversary. And now he's here with his new pregnant fiancée and I'm – well, I'm here with a hot rock star. In other circumstances that would look pretty good. But given what the papers have been writing about me, if anyone recognises me they'll think it's like a Make-A-Wish foundation outing.

I look out again to make sure it's definitely him. It is.

'Laura, what's wrong?'

'Nothing,' I say. 'Sorry, seriously, I'm fine.'

'You keep poking your head out of the alcove. Are you sure nothing's wrong? Maybe it was a bad idea coming here after all ...'

I sigh. 'My ex Dave is over there with his new fiancée.'

'His new what?'

'His fiancée,' I say. 'His betrothed. The woman he's going to marry.'

'He's engaged again already?'

'Well, I suppose he's more traditional than I thought,' I say. 'She *is* pregnant, after all.'

'Sorry, she's *what*?'

The over-the-top awfulness of it all hits me and I let out a laugh despite myself. 'It's so cartoonishly terrible it's kind of funny.'

'Ah, Lol,' says Tadhg. 'I'm sorry.'

'It's okay,' I say. 'No, seriously, it is. It will be. I don't want to be with him anymore. It's just … we were going to get married. And now it's like I never existed for him. He's got a whole new life.'

'Yeah, well,' says Tadhg, 'so do you.'

I roll my eyes. '"Tadhg's little Cinderella: rock star's charity case"?' Those words are still burned into my head. Along with all the other headlines.

'The people who matter know that bollocks isn't true,' says Tadhg.

I lean out and gesture over at the booth, where Dave and my replacement (Liz, I tell myself, her name is Liz) are getting up to go. '*They* don't know that.' And without thinking, I say, 'God, I genuinely wish the tabloids had said I was your new girlfriend. At least then Dave would think I'd moved on as fast as him.'

That's when Dave's eyes meet mine and widen in shock. Unthinkingly, I grab Tadhg's arm and lean back into the alcove so Dave can't see us. But it's too late.

'Oh shit, he's spotted me! No, no, no, no, no, I think he's coming over!'

'Lol,' says Tadhg. 'Did you seriously mean what you just said? Do you really want him to think you've moved on?'

'Oh God, yes!'

'Do you mind if I put my arm around you?'

'Um, no?'

'Then,' Tadhg is whispering in my ear now, 'let's give him something to think about.'

I turn my head to look at him as he slips his arm around my shoulder. Our faces haven't been so close in a long, long time.

'Laura?'

I turn around to find Dave awkwardly standing beside the table. The girl from Instagram – Liz, I remind myself – is next to him, holding his hand. Could there possibly be a hint of a bump underneath her elegant floral dress?

'Oh, hi!' I flash the most brilliant smile I can muster. 'I thought I spotted you over there!'

I turn my beaming smile (don't overdo it, Laura) on Liz. 'Hi, I'm Laura!'

'This is Liz,' says Dave. We haven't seen each other since I moved out last year, but I can still read him like a book. I know he thinks he's doing the brave, honourable thing coming over to say hello. He probably wants to make sure I haven't, like, slit my wrists or something. For someone who avoids serious emotion, he must be very proud of himself. Whether this is all fair to Liz or not is another point.

Or maybe he just wants to have a close-up gawp at the famous Tadhg Hennessy.

'Lovely to meet you!' I say. 'This is Tadhg. Tadhg, this is Dave.'

Tadhg's left arm is still casually, affectionately slung over my shoulder. I take his left hand in my own and his thumb gently strokes the calluses on my fingertips. It is *very* distracting. In a good way. I can see Dave's gaze focus on our hands in confusion.

'Hi,' says Tadhg.

'Tadhg and I have been working together,' I say.

'Well,' says Tadhg, dropping a tender little kiss on my cheek and pulling me closer to him, 'not *just* working.'

Liz's eyes are wide as saucers, and Dave looks frankly stunned.

I turn and smile up at Tadhg with real affection. His eyes are sparkling. He looks back to Dave. 'Though of course, as you probably know, Lol's basically a musical genius, so the work is going pretty well too.'

I let out a perfectly genuine laugh. 'Is it now?'

Tadhg bumps the end of my nose with his and despite, or maybe because of, the ridiculous cheesiness of the gesture, I feel myself beam back at him.

'You know it is,' he says.

I turn back to Dave and his fiancée and take in their dazed expressions. I don't have to force my smile now. 'Well, it was good to see you. Oh, and congratulations!'

'Um, thanks,' says Dave. 'I suppose we'd better go.'

'Nice to meet you,' mutters Liz. I feel a bit bad for her – she hasn't done anything wrong, and she's been put in a weird situation.

But I can't feel that bad. I'm not a saint.

'Bye!' says Tadhg.

I lean against him as Dave and Liz turn to go. Before they disappear from our view, Dave looks back for a second as if to confirm that Tadhg's arm really is around me, and that we really are holding hands. I give him a little wave with my free hand.

'Was that okay?' says Tadhg when they're totally out of sight.

'That was *perfect*,' I say. 'Thanks.'

'My pleasure,' says Tadhg, and that's when I realise our fingers are still entwined. Even though it would be worryingly easy to imagine it meaning something, I gently extract my hand from his and slip out from under his arm. Then he says, 'Are *you* okay?'

'Yeah, I'm fine.' I sigh and lean back in my seat. 'It's just … this is the first time I've seen him since we broke up.'

'Ah,' says Tadhg. 'And you haven't been in contact since?'

'Nope,' I say. 'Not until last week when he rang me and told me Liz was pregnant.'

'Last Friday when you said you'd got some weird news,' he says, 'was that what you meant?'

I nod. 'Yeah. It was … it was a shock. I mean, I'm glad we're not together anymore. I didn't care when he told me they were engaged. But her being pregnant … it brought up a lot of stuff.' I sigh. 'What Dave said when he left me made me— It made me feel bad about myself.'

Why did I admit that? It must be the shock of seeing Dave and his new woman. That, and the more than half a bottle of wine I've just drunk. I've always wanted Tadhg to think I'm confident and that I don't give a shit what anyone else thinks of me. Even though that isn't even vaguely true. I could never, ever bear the idea of him feeling sorry for me.

But fuck it, maybe it's time we were more honest with each other.

'Well,' says Tadhg, 'then he's an arsehole.'

I laugh despite myself. 'No arguments there.'

319

'I don't know what he said to you,' says Tadhg, 'but if it made you feel bad about yourself, it was bollocks.'

'Well, some of it was just factual,' I say. 'He wanted something and I couldn't give it to him.'

'Like what?' says Tadhg and then catches himself. 'Sorry. Ignore that. It's none of my business.'

And I find myself saying, 'He dumped me because I can't have kids.'

Wow. I'm really being honest now.

There's a moment of silence and then Tadhg says, 'If I say you're better off without him, will you believe me?'

'Oh, I know I am,' I say. 'But the whole thing … It was a lot.'

'Do you … Do you want to talk about it?'

And to my surprise, I actually do.

So I take a deep breath, and I tell him.

'I always had really bad period pains, and it turned out to be endometriosis. You know what that is?'

'Not exactly,' admits Tadhg.

'This is massively oversimplifying, but it's when the tissue that's meant to be on the inside of your womb grows outside it. Which isn't a good thing, obviously. Anyway, it can lead to fertility problems and that's what happened to me. We'd stopped using contraception and nothing had happened after a year, so I went to get everything checked out – I was in my midthirties after all – and that's when they diagnosed it.'

I remember the day in 2017 when the consultant broke the news after the laparoscopy. It turned out that I was an extreme case. The tissue had grown around my fallopian tubes, scarring them badly, blocking them beyond any treatment. There was extensive scarring in my womb too. There was so much ... damage.

'Could they treat it?' says Tadhg.

'I had surgery,' I say, 'which removed some of the tissue, and afterwards the doctor made it clear that there was absolutely no way I could get pregnant naturally, and even with fertility treatment the odds were essentially non-existent.'

'And ... how did you feel about it?' says Tadhg. I meet his eyes. He doesn't look sorry for me. He looks as if he cares about me.

I look down at the table. 'I mean, I'd always assumed I'd have children. It wasn't like being a mother was my greatest dream, but I like kids and I wanted to have my own and I always thought it would happen. And suddenly I was told it wouldn't. Because I was ... broken.'

When I look up again, Tadhg's still looking at me with that kind, steady gaze. 'You're many things, Lol. But broken is not one of them.'

'Well, that's what Dave thought.' I close my eyes as the memory floods back. 'I thought infertility was something we were both dealing with. But it turned out he thought it was *my* problem.'

And I tell Tadhg what happened after Dave told me he didn't want to marry me.

At first I simply couldn't believe he was serious about leaving me. It was ludicrous. Impossible. This was *Dave*. Dave, the man who had gone down on one knee eighteen months earlier and proposed to me on the corner of Aungier Street where we first kissed. My Dave. Dave who loved me. How could he have stopped loving me? He couldn't. He just *couldn't*. I felt like I was going mad.

'I still care about you,' said Dave. 'Of course I do. But I think … I think we want different things.'

'How do you know what I want?' I cried. 'You never talk to me properly these days! You've been weird and distant for the last few months and—'

The last few months. Ever since I had the surgery.

In the immediate aftermath, when we were both in shock and trying to accept the diagnosis, we had proper conversations about what we would and would not do in the future. I thought we were on the same page. I thought we were going to make a new, different life for ourselves. But quite quickly Dave seemed to … withdraw.

A thought struck me, so horrible I could barely bring myself to say it aloud.

'Is this … is this about the fertility stuff?'

He didn't look at me.

'I thought we both decided we didn't want to try fertility treatment.' My voice was shaking. 'Or adoption or anything. You said you didn't want to do that.'

'I don't,' said Dave. 'That's all … It's too much.' He still couldn't look at me. He was such a fucking coward. 'But I still—' He swallowed. 'I still want to have a family.'

'But you and me,' I said. 'Aren't we a family? Just the two of us? Aren't we enough?'

I only said it because I thought it would make him realise the utter madness of what he'd been saying. I only said it because I thought it would make him come to his senses. I only said it because I was sure he'd say 'Yes, of course we're enough'.

But he said, 'I'm sorry. I'm so sorry. But we're not. Not for me.'

'And so,' I tell Tadhg, 'he left me and found someone who could give him a baby with no trouble at all.'

'Well,' says Tadhg, 'he's a dickhead who didn't know how lucky he was.'

We sit for a moment in surprisingly easy silence, and then Tadhg notices the maître d' is looking nervously over at our table. He clearly doesn't want to bother a superstar, and we've got three-quarters of a bottle of wine left, but they must need the table for the next customers. We've been here for over two hours.

'I think we'd better go,' says Tadhg, and then he says, 'Do you want to go home just yet?'

'Not really.'

'Do you fancy going back to my place and playing the guitar very, very loudly?'

'Yes,' I say. 'Yes, *please.*'

Chapter Twenty-Nine

2003

The day after his break-up with Jess, I met Tadhg as usual at Front Arch to get the bus out to Brian's garage. He looked like he hadn't slept much. Or shaved.

'You okay?' I said.

He nodded. 'More or less.'

We started walking towards the bus stop.

'Have you talked to Jess?' I said. 'Since yesterday, I mean?'

'I rang her this morning,' he said. 'She's ... not great.'

We walked in silence for a moment.

'You know,' I said, 'if you're not up for playing the Ball, we don't have to do it.'

But to my relief he said, 'God, no, of course I want to do it.' He smiled down at me. 'I want to end this college year with something good.'

I smiled back at him. Inside my heart, the hope started to rise. And something else. Determination.

'So do I,' I said.

Tadhg and I were still determined to follow Jo and Brian's wishes and keep the band going somehow when I got back from my New York summer, even though we weren't going to be in the same college anymore.

'We can't stop now, Lol,' he said. 'We're only getting started.'

'We should record something,' I said. My mind raced with possibilities. 'We could release an EP.'

'We could do *everything*,' said Tadhg.

Now he wasn't with Jess I was starting to regret my plan to go to America for three months. What if he met someone new while I was away? A fellow teacher on that summer camp, someone even hotter and cooler than Jess?

If I wanted something to happen with him, I was going to have to make sure it happened soon.

I had just left the library in the Arts Block one sunny afternoon a week later when I got the bad news. Joanna was coming through the door from Fellows' Square, a miserable expression on her face.

'Hey,' I said, hurrying down the steps to join her. 'What's happened?'

She took a deep breath. 'The Ball's been cancelled.'

'The Trinity Ball?' I said ridiculously, as if there were some other ball going on around here. 'But it's on Friday!'

'The security guards are going on strike,' she said. 'The whole thing's been called off.'

'But that means …' The full devastating extent of Jo's words was dawning on me. 'We won't get to play.'

Joanna nodded miserably.

'But … *fuck*!' I said. 'That's our last gig!'

An hour later, we were sitting on the grass outside the college's Pavilion Bar with Tadhg and Brian, the four of us drowning our sorrows with cheap cans. Everyone was too miserable to talk much.

'Maybe we can organise another gig,' I said, without conviction. But I knew we wouldn't. We were all under exam pressure. None of us had the time or mental energy to start ringing around venues, trying to put on a gig at the last minute. This was it. We'd never play on stage together again.

Then Ruairí was standing in front of us.

'I suppose you've heard the shit news?' he said. 'Well, I might have something that'll cheer you up.'

'The strike's off?' Joanna's face lit up.

'What? Oh no, that's still happening. And rightly so. Up the workers! No, the official ball is off. But …' He paused for dramatic effect.

'Spit it out, Ru,' I said. I wasn't in the mood.

'The Alternative Ball is on.' He was grinning from ear to ear. 'This Friday. BYOB and black tie. And at this ball, you won't be the opening act. You'll be the headliner.'

We gawped at him.

'So, you know Paul from Shatner?' We all nodded. 'He and his mates live in this massive old ruin of a house on the North

Circular Road. Seriously, it's huge. We can have bands and DJs in there. His housemate knows somewhere we can rent a sound system for fuck all.'

'Can they sort that out by this Friday?' said Tadhg.

'They've already booked the sound system,' said Ruairí. 'It's happening, lads. Ah, look at your happy little faces!'

And so the Alternative Ball was born.

I wore the seventies maxi dress. If there was ever a time to wear it, it was that night: the last hurrah before the exams and New York and, after that, a whole new life. I'd got a conditional offer from DCU, so unless I really messed up my finals, I'd be starting my master's there in October. This night was going to be my goodbye to Trinity, to my full college experience. And it was, we all knew, goodbye to The Band Laura's In. Our last gig was going to be special. It *had* to be special.

I spent longer doing my hair and make-up than I ever had before, and I must have done something right because when I was leaving, wearing a fake fur jacket over the maxi dress, Annie stuck her head out of her room and said, 'Wow. You don't look that bad.'

Praise indeed.

College was closed early because of the security-guard strike, but Tadhg and I arranged to meet at the locked Front Gate. I didn't know it would be the last time he'd ever wait for me there. It was a sunny evening with a hint of chill, and I was glad of the fake fur jacket as I walked along the curve of the college railings towards the gate. And there he was, in the golden early-evening light. Carrying his guitar case and wearing a perfectly fitting tux.

Fucking hell.

'Hey!' he said.

'Hey yourself,' I said. 'What charity shop did you get that in?'

'Shit, does it look too ridiculous?' he said.

'Not at all,' I said.

'It's actually my dad's,' said Tadhg. 'He needed it for my cousin's wedding years ago. Her family have notions. Hence the black tie.'

'It's great,' I said truthfully.

'What are you wearing?' he said. 'Is that the dress you bought with me?'

'I figured our last gig was worth wearing it for,' I said.

'Definitely.' He looked down at me and grinned. 'Right, Ms McDermott. Shall we go to the ball?'

We got the number 10 bus out to the North Circular. It was just the two of us; Brian and Joanna were getting lifts from the southside. People stared at us when we got on the bus and went upstairs, Tadhg in his tux and me in my floor-length floral frock and fur jacket, both of us carrying guitar cases.

'Do you think this is how REM are getting to their Glastonbury headline slot next month?' said Tadhg, as we sat down in the upstairs front seats.

'Definitely,' I said. 'They're getting paid in cans of Dutch Gold and Scrumpy Jack too.'

'Who else is playing tonight, by the way?' said Tadhg. 'Sorry, I've been kind of distracted all week.'

'Sourpuss and Shatner, obviously,' I said. 'And a hip-hop band called Astroturf. And then Fiachra and some other people are DJing.' I hadn't seen Fiachra since that last encounter in his house ten days earlier, but we'd been texting each other.

'Oh, right,' said Tadhg. 'Cool.'

'Fiachra said Ruairí's going to be on the door checking people's names off the list,' I said.

In case the house got swamped, Ruairí had come up with a scheme: anyone who wanted to attend the Alternative Ball had to email him and get added to a list, and if your name wasn't on it on the night, you weren't coming in. 'But I don't know how long that's going to last.'

Tadhg laughed. 'I can't imagine anyone involved in this ball being a very effective bouncer. Myself included.'

'Oh well,' I said. 'We just have to worry about playing the set. Our last-ever set,' I added morosely.

'Come on,' said Tadhg. 'You and me will still be a band next year, remember? We're going to record an EP! And I know it won't be the same, but we'll find people to fill in for Brian and Jo.'

'We won't have the garage,' I said.

'We'll find somewhere,' said Tadhg. 'I believe in us.'

I smiled at him, his beautiful face golden in the evening sunlight that was streaming into the bus. 'I do too.'

We knew we had the right house as soon as we saw it.

'Wow,' I said. 'Ruairí's actually put some work into this.'

An extension lead was coming out of the open fanlight above the front door, and into it were plugged multiple strings of fairy lights, which were strung up over the porch of the large three-storey house. We were walking up the steps when the door opened and Fiachra appeared, looking extremely handsome in black tie. I had never seen him in a suit before.

'Hey!' he cried. He gave me a big hug and raised a hand in greeting to Tadhg. 'The stars of the show! *Very* cool dress, Laura.'

'Thanks very much,' I said.

'I'm just going to the shop to get some Rizlas while every-thing's being set up,' said Fiachra. 'Do you want anything?'

'I'm good,' I said.

'How about you, Tim?'

'I'm fine,' said Tadhg. 'Thanks.'

'Then I'll see you later!' Fiachra kissed me on the cheek and bounced down the steps, and Tadhg and I went inside.

'What do you think?' said Ruairí, when we found him in what was officially the dining room at the back of the enormous house. He hadn't been exaggerating about the size. It was in rag order – plaster peeling from the walls, damp stains on ceilings –

but it was huge. 'We all raided our folks' Christmas decorations. My mum's going to kill me in December.'

Every room on the ground floor was strewn with fairy lights and the effect, while definitely a fire hazard, was also totally magical.

'It's amazing,' I said, and I meant it.

By nine o'clock the house was rammed. Brian and Jo had arrived just in time for us to do a quick soundcheck, and then Katie turned up with a gang of our mates.

'Oh my God,' she said when she saw me. 'That dress is fantastic.'

I had taken off the fake fur jacket by now and put it in the scullery that was serving as a dressing room.

'It's not too …' I gestured at my chest.

'It's just the right amount of …' She gestured back.

'Oh,' I said. There were butterflies in my stomach. I just knew something big was going to happen tonight. I was going to make sure of it. 'Good.'

By the time the first band started playing, the crowd was spilling out of the house and into the front and back gardens. There were people on the stairs, people in the bedrooms, a couple shifting in the bath (thankfully the toilet was in a separate room). Ruairí's careful list-checking had been abandoned by about eleven. It felt like everyone I'd ever known over the last four years was there. I lost track of Tadhg for a while, and then, when I was out in the fairy-light-covered back garden, he appeared in front of me, reached out his hand and said, 'There you are! We're on!'

He led me through the crowded garden, through the happy, hot, sweaty throng that packed the house, and to the stage area, where Brian was getting in place behind the drums. Tadhg had already brought our instruments from the scullery, where we'd left them at the start of the night, and when Joanna hurried onto the stage wearing an amazing slinky pink dress, he handed her her bass. Then he stepped up to the mic and casually said, 'Good evening!'

The crowd cheered. And, miraculously, the chatter died down. That stage presence again.

'We're The Band Laura's In,' said Tadhg. 'And this is our very last gig.'

There were noises of outrage from the crowd.

'The amazing Joanna Smyth and Brian O'Hara are leaving the country for academic glory,' Tadhg went on. 'But before we say goodbye to them we're playing one last show. And our first song is called 'Anyone But You'.'

I wish I remembered every second of that gig. I wish I remembered exactly what songs we played in what order. I wish I remembered what Tadhg said between songs. But while I might not remember the details of that gig, I do remember how I felt. I felt like I had magic in my hands, and I was making magic stream from my guitar. I felt that the four of us were a gang and that, whatever happened, we always would be. I felt such a strong connection with Tadhg it seemed impossible he didn't feel it too. I felt like the audience loved us. I felt like I had felt the first time I played a gig with Tadhg.

I felt like a goddess.

Then I smashed down the last chord of 'Midnight Feast', and it was over.

The crowd lost their shit. The entire building felt like it was shaking (worryingly, it possibly was). Brian looked like he was about to cry as he wrapped Tadhg in a big bear hug. Joanna was definitely crying as I hugged her.

'We'll do it again some day,' I said. 'It's not over forever.'

'Right,' said Tadhg, 'I need a drink. Do you want anything, Lol? Jo?'

'I'm good,' I said, holding up a half-full can of Bulmers.

'Can you get me a beer?' said Joanna.

'I may be some time,' said Tadhg. 'I think Ruairí locked our rider of Dutch Gold out in the shed.'

Tadhg headed off through the crowd. Several girls stopped him on his way out of the room, including a tall girl with glossy black hair who'd been standing right in front of him during the set, but he just smiled politely and kept going.

'Getting ready for my DJ set?' said Fiachra, emerging from the crowd and looking immaculate for a man I had seen sitting up a tree in the back garden sharing a spliff with some fellow future psychologists an hour ago. 'You were great, by the way.'

'Thanks very much,' I said.

'And you look incredible,' he said.

'So do you,' I said.

Oh, he really did look good in that suit. And Tadhg wouldn't be back for a while. And I was on a post-gig high, a mixture of adrenalin and endorphins and music and God knows what else.

The next thing I knew Fiachra and I were kissing under the fairy lights on the edge of the makeshift dancefloor. Until a loud voice said, 'Oh come on, you two, get a room.'

We pulled apart to see Ruairí shaking his head. 'Actually, don't get a room.' He pointed at Fiachra. 'You're on in two minutes.'

He disappeared into the crowd and Fiachra said, 'Sorry. Duty calls.'

'Break a leg,' I said.

'God, I hope I don't,' he said. 'I want to dance with you later.' He kissed me on the cheek and disappeared into the crowd.

Then Katie was grabbing my hand and pulling me onto the dance floor, Tadhg came back with a beer in each hand, Fiachra put on 'Burning Down the House' by Talking Heads and the real party began.

Despite how it ended, that was still one of the best dancing nights of my life. It was one of those nights where everything the DJ plays is exactly what you want to hear at that moment, where every bassline, every beat, is danceable and filled with joy. The dance floor was hot and sweaty and magnificent and I wanted to dance all night, I wanted to dance forever. About fifty minutes into his set, Fiachra put on the new Beyoncé song 'Crazy in Love' and it was like an explosion of happiness. Tadhg was a few feet away from me on the dance floor. He held out his hand to me and I took it and he twirled me around, just for a moment, and then we both kept dancing. And smiling. We couldn't stop smiling.

I'm going to kiss him tonight, I thought. *I know it.*

There wasn't a single dud song in Fiachra's set and none of us wanted to stop dancing. Every so often someone would get a bottle of water from the kitchen and we'd pass it around. But eventually all the water drinking had the inevitable result.

'I'm going to the loo!' I yelled in Katie's ear. There were only two in the whole giant house, and I figured the upstairs one might have a smaller queue. It might have been smaller, but it was still pretty long. I stood there next to a girl wearing a tattered turquoise fifties dress, a tiara and a prom-queen sash who was quietly puking into a pint glass. The music was almost as loud up there as it was in the main room. After I finally made it to the loo, I looked at myself in the toothpaste-splattered mirror above the sink. My eyes looked huge beneath my fringe, which was behaving itself for once. My curls looked bouncy. My skin was glowing. The dress was as ridiculously flattering as it was the first time I'd tried it on.

If he doesn't fancy me tonight, I thought, *he'll never fancy me.*

This was it. I was going to go downstairs and finally take action.

I took a deep breath and went back to the dining room. Ruairí was behind the decks now. The dance floor was a mass of people, boys in suits, girls in everything from 1970s nighties to big 1980s prom dresses. I scanned the room, looking for Tadhg, and then I saw him at the far side of the room, standing close to the girl from earlier, the one with the glossy black hair. I saw her wrap her arms around Tadhg's neck and kiss him.

I saw Tadhg put his hands around her waist and kiss her back.

Everything froze, just for a second.

Even when he's single again, I thought, *even when I'm looking the hottest I've ever looked, the hottest I could possibly look in my life, he chooses someone else. I didn't even get a chance to try.*

This is it. There's no hope.

I turned on my heel and ran.

I couldn't face anyone I knew right then, so I hurried up the stairs, past couples getting off with each other, past some of the newspaper gang having an argument, past a drunk boy who had fallen asleep on the first-floor landing. I kept climbing until I reached the top of the house, three floors up. Then I sat down. When I first saw him kissing Jess I had felt nothing but pain. Now the pain was overlaid with exhaustion. I didn't want to feel like this anymore. I didn't want to care so much about him anymore.

After a while I heard footsteps coming up the stairs and tried to pull myself together. But when I saw who it was, my shoulders sagged with relief.

'There you are!' said Fiachra. 'Bloody hell, those stairs are steep. I've been looking for you. Are you okay?'

'No,' I said. 'I'm really not.'

I was so tired of pretending to be okay. Why did I keep pretending?

'Is it Tim?' said Fiachra. He sat down next to me and put an arm around me. 'Or Tadhg? Or whatever his name is?'

I pulled back from his embrace and stared at him. 'How do you know?' A wave of horror washed over me. 'Does *everyone* know?'

Ah yes. *This* was why I kept pretending to be okay. This feeling of appalled humiliation.

'No, everyone doesn't know,' said Fiachra gently. 'I didn't know until, like, two minutes ago. I saw your face when you spotted him with that girl. You looked … well, you looked kind of devastated. Just for a second. And then you literally ran out of the room.'

'Do you think other people noticed?'

'I really doubt many people down there were capable of noticing anything,' he said. 'Most of them have taken a bunch of yokes by this stage.'

'You can still notice stuff when you're on yokes,' I said with feeling.

'Words to live by,' said Fiachra. 'But seriously, Laura. Don't worry. I just noticed you because I was … Fuck, it feels weird and wrong to say it now.'

'I'm beyond weird and wrong now,' I said. 'Say whatever you want, I won't mind.'

'Okay. Well, I was looking over at you and thinking how sensational your tits look in that dress,' he said.

'They do, don't they?' I said sadly.

'They look amazing,' he said. 'It's a great dress.'

'Tadhg doesn't care what they look like,' I said. 'He doesn't care what any part of me looks like.'

'Are you sure about that?'

'Fiachra,' I said, 'he just got off with some random girl in front of me.'

Fiachra didn't say anything for a moment. He just put his arm around me again and I laid my head on his shoulder. It felt nice. It felt comforting.

Then he said, 'Laura?'

'Uh-huh?'

'Are you in love with him?'

'In love with Tadhg?'

'Yeah.'

'I think I've been in love with him,' I said, 'since the moment I met him.'

'So me and you,' he said slowly. 'Has that all been a … distraction? From him?'

I put my head in my hands. 'Oh shit, I'm sorry.'

He kissed the top of my head. 'Absolutely no need to

apologise. Glad to be of service. It's been, and I can say this with my hand on my heart, an absolute pleasure.'

'You and me,' I said, 'it's been really fun. And so good for me. But I love Tadhg. It's so stupid, but I really do.'

'And you're *sure* he doesn't feel the same way?' said Fiachra. 'Because every time I've seen you on stage there's definitely a vibe between you.'

'There is no vibe,' I said, my voice breaking on the last word. I let out a shaky breath. 'Seriously, Fiachra. There's no vibe.'

'Okay,' said Fiachra. 'Well, if you really feel like that ...'

'I don't just feel like that,' I said. 'I know that.'

'Fine,' said Fiachra. 'If you know that, then I think it's a good idea for you to keep your distance from him for a while. When are you off to New York?'

'The tenth of June,' I said. 'Just after my last exam.'

'So in a month, basically. Okay. Well, just tell him you've got to focus on your exams until then. No band practice, no hanging out. Nothing.'

'I can't—'

'Yes, you can,' said Fiachra firmly. 'You can.' There was something about his voice that made me believe him. It hit me for the first time that he could make a very good psychologist some day. 'It's just for a few weeks. Then you'll go to New York, you'll have an amazing time, you'll meet cool American boys, and you'll forget about Tadhg for a while. You're not saying goodbye to him forever – you'll see him and start your band again when you get back in September. But until then you can … get him out of your system. Have fun without him. You can do it. I *know* you can do it. For yourself. I don't like seeing you so unhappy, Laura. He's been making you unhappy, hasn't he?'

I sighed, slowly.

'Yeah,' I said. 'Not on purpose. But he has.'

'Well,' said Fiachra. 'There you go.' He looked at me, his brown eyes full of kindness. 'Do you want to stay up here? Or go back to the party? Or do you want to go home? I'll get your stuff and find you a taxi if you do. Your home, I mean, ' he added. 'I don't think you want to go to my place tonight.'

I put my arms around him and he hugged me tightly.

'Home, please,' I said. 'And thanks, Fee.'

'Any time, Laura,' he said. 'Any time.'

Chapter Thirty

2019

Two hours after we leave the restaurant, I'm standing in the middle of Tadhg's studio bringing a plectrum down on the Danelectro's strings to play a massive power chord. Tadhg is behind the drum kit and we're playing what's by far the loudest, hardest song we've written over the last week. I gather all my misery, all my frustration, all my rage at Dave and Hugo and the internet and all the vultures who started texting me, and I throw it into the guitar, getting louder and sharper and more ferocious. We end with one final chord and one last mighty roll across the drum kit and look at each other, dishevelled with the sheer physical effort of playing – you forget how physical it is, properly rocking out – and grinning.

'That,' I say, 'was exactly what I needed.'

'Want to take a break?' says Tadhg.

'What I really want,' I say, 'is some of that wine we abandoned in the restaurant.'

'How about the next best thing?' says Tadhg.

The next best thing, it turns out, is a fruity red wine that, to my unsophisticated palate, tastes even better than the fancy Fleurie in the restaurant. I should have known Tadhg would have a wine cellar. ('It's not a cellar, Lol!' he protested. 'More like a wine cupboard.')

'I hope you know,' I say, as we sit on the floor of the studio some time later, him leaning against the sofa, me leaning against one of the armchairs, the half-empty bottle between us, 'that I don't make a habit of drowning my sorrows. If I did, I'd have been permanently pissed since last Thursday night.'

'I think the odd bender is allowed,' says Tadhg. 'This has been some week.'

'It sure has.' I take a sip of wine and look over at him. 'Today has helped, though.'

He raises his eyebrows. 'Seriously? I feel I just threw money at the problem. I know a fancy lunch and some wine can't cure everything.'

'It wasn't just the lunch,' I say. 'Katie and Jeanne and my other friends … they're sympathetic and lovely, of course, but they don't get what it's like. And you do. The being written about in the tabloids bit,' I add, 'not the finding out your ex is having a baby with someone else bit.'

'Well,' he says, 'I'm glad I helped.'

'You did,' I say. 'And this' – I gesture in the vague direction of the instruments – 'this helps too. And this.' I point at the wine. 'Just hanging out, having a drink. All this stuff is fun.'

'Yeah,' says Tadhg. 'It is.'

We sit in contented silence for a moment. Then Tadhg says, 'Would it bother you if I rolled a joint?'

'It a hundred per cent would not,' I say.

He scrambles to his feet, goes over to the drawers under the mixing desk and takes out a small wooden box. Inside is a packet of Rizlas, a packet of filters and a little plastic bag full of weed.

'I hope those drugs are ethically sourced,' I say.

'They are, actually,' says Tadhg, rejoining me on the floor. 'A friend of mine in Carlow grows it. And it's nice and mellow. Not too strong.'

'Good,' I say. 'Last thing I need is some skunk-fuelled paranoia.'

Tadhg laughs. 'Seriously, don't worry, it's nothing like that.' He sets to work.

I watch him expertly roll a neat little joint. 'You're pretty good at this.'

'Well, I don't do it every day.' He runs his tongue along the edge of the paper to seal it. 'I've seen enough people fuck themselves up and become extremely boring by self-medicating with weed. But sometimes it's just a nice way to chill out.'

'Sounds like just what I need.' I look around the studio.

'We're not going to smoke in here, though, are we? I should get my coat.'

He looks up from his task and grins. 'Don't worry, Lol. We won't freeze.'

A few minutes later, we're stretched out on a pair of astonishingly comfortable sun loungers in front of the studio, wrapped in cosy swimming robes.

'I got these when Aideen and I had deluded ideas of going out swimming in the sea at the crack of dawn,' says Tadhg. He lights the joint and inhales deeply.

'Did the two of you live together?' I ask.

Tadhg exhales a plume of smoke. 'Nope. We didn't really have time to plan big stuff like moving in together.' He passes me the joint and I reach out and take it. The sun loungers are just a couple of feet apart. 'Or maybe that's just what we each told ourselves. Maybe both of us knew it wasn't the right thing to do.'

I take a very small drag on the joint and hold it in my lungs for a moment before letting it out. He wasn't joking about it being gentle and mellow. I feel some of the week's tension start to ease.

'You were right,' I say. 'This is really nice weed.'

I snuggle down into my robe and take another, slightly longer drag.

'I told you so,' he says. Our fingers briefly touch as I pass him back the joint. Maybe it's the weed, but I am suddenly very conscious of the physical contact.

'You're a very accurate drug pusher,' I say.

Tadhg groans. 'I'm like something out of a nineties teen drama. "Hey, kids, just have a toke of this joint! It'll chill you out!"'

'Saint Tadhg's drug shame,' I say in a dramatic headline-announcing voice.

Tadhg lets out a hoot of mirth that turns into a proper fit of laughter, and I crack up too. It's a clear night despite the freezing cold, and as I look up at the stars – surprisingly visible even though we're not far from the city centre – a feeling that seemed impossible for much of the last week bubbles up inside me.

Happiness.

We lie there on our loungers, passing the joint back and forth. I feel cosy, and happy, and safe. Maybe that's why, after a while, I say, 'What about you and kids? Do you want to have them?'

If it weren't for the fact that I'm slightly stoned, I would have been too nervous to ask him. I would have dreaded hearing 'Yes, being a father is my dream and nothing is more important than passing on my genetic material'. Obviously Tadhg and I are not together – I'm not so high that I've lost my grip on reality – but it would have broken my heart, just a little bit, to know that I wouldn't have been enough for him if we were. And yet somehow, right now, I feel like I can handle whatever he says.

'I think I've always felt that if it happened, great,' says Tadhg. 'And if it didn't happen, also great.'

'Did you ever come close to planning it?' I say. 'Sorry, that's way too personal.'

'No, no, it's fine.' Tadhg takes another drag on the joint, which is almost finished now, and hands it over to me. 'My ex Amanda knew she didn't want kids. And I thought about it a lot and realised I was fine with that. After her, I didn't have another serious relationship for a few years – just short-lived things. Then I got together with Aideen and, like I said, we never got round to doing any serious relationship-changing stuff. I mean, I've thought about having kids. I suppose most people do, when they hit their mid-thirties. But it's not something I feel I really have to do.'

I didn't think it was possible for me to relax even more, but it turns out it is. I take a last drag on the joint and stub it out in the 1970s standing ashtray that's positioned between the loungers.

'Feel free to tell me this is none of my business,' says Tadhg, 'but how do you feel about it now? The whole kids thing.'

I exhale softly. 'Weirdly enough, I kind of feel … good? Maybe that's not the right word.' I look up at the stars. It's so clear I can make out all the constellations. 'Actually, I think it is, but it took a while. It was a huge deal when I realised I would never have a baby. It was … it felt like proper grief.'

'But now?' says Tadhg.

'I still feel sad about it every so often,' I admit. 'Maybe I always will. Or maybe I won't. Pregnancy announcements are still, I don't know, triggering. I don't exactly feel jealous – it's more like … excluded. Like, I'm happy for people, of course I am. It's just every time someone tells me she's pregnant, there's one less woman like me in my life. I'm the outsider. Because I failed.'

'You didn't fail anything, Lol,' says Tadhg gently.

'I know,' I say. 'In my heart I know that. And it's not like there's some huge gaping hole in my life. Day to day I'm genuinely okay with it all. Much more than okay, actually.'

'Good,' says Tadhg.

'Yeah, it *is* good,' I say. 'And the whole thing made me confront how much I might really want to have children. Like, would I be prepared to go through fertility treatments that almost certainly wouldn't work for me? Or try adoption? And I realised I don't want to do any of that. Which I guess means there are limits to how much I actually want kids, even if I do feel sad about it sometimes.' I keep my eyes fixed on the stars. 'If it had happened, it would probably have been wonderful. But maybe it wouldn't. The thing is, I'll never know. What I do know now is that there are a lot of other things that can make me happy. And I can have a happy life without having kids.'

Tadhg sits up on his lounger and looks at me. 'But didn't you believe that already?'

'Well, yeah, in theory,' I say. 'But it's hard to feel it's true when the entire world is always telling you that you're a tragic failure. That's really what makes me feel bad these days, not my actual life. I mean, every story where a couple doesn't have kids or can't have kids seems to end with a fucking miracle baby at the last minute. Like you can't be a proper grown-up or live happily ever after unless you have children.'

Tadhg ponders this for a moment and then says, 'Shit, yeah, you're right.'

I take a sip of wine. I'm pretty sure I wouldn't be saying all this if I weren't slightly high and slightly drunk but I can't stop now. 'It feels like the only women without kids I ever see in the media are the ones who never wanted to have them anyway, or the ones who did want to and couldn't and never got over it. Why don't I see women who wanted to, but it didn't happen, and they were sad but eventually they were fine? I know I'm not the only one!'

'Well, maybe you can be that woman,' says Tadhg, 'for other people.'

I laugh. 'Is this your new way of trying to persuade me to perform in public? Telling me I can be a role model for guitar-playing women with no kids who can't sing?'

'No!' Tadhg protests. 'Though I still think you can sing. And you should sing.'

'No,' I say. 'No way.'

'Do you want to go back in and play the guitar and *not* sing?'

I do.

We play some of our new songs. We play some old songs. We play some of Tadhg's songs. And then we start playing cover songs. We drink lots of water to counterbalance the wine. We drink more wine. We laugh a lot. I even sing, albeit very, very quietly, and not into a microphone so Tadhg can't actually hear it.

Eventually Tadhg says, 'I didn't think I'd ever be hungry again after that giant lunch, but I am. Do you want a snack?'

We make toasted sandwiches and eat them at his kitchen table. We drink tea. We talk nonsense. It's like one of those magical college days when we hung out together for hours on end. And like those days, I both don't want to go home and don't want to overstay my welcome.

But then he says, 'Are you too tired to watch a film in the screening room?'

And I realise I'm not.

The screening room is gorgeous – like a miniature version of one of those posh indie cinemas, with leather armchairs and side tables. Tadhg opens a big cupboard at the back of the room and reveals shelves of DVDs.

'What film do you fancy?' he says.

'Oh, I can't decide,' I say, scanning the shelves. 'Pick one at random and I'll say yes or no.'

Tadhg closes his eyes, reaches out and pulls out a case. '*Jaws*?'

Two hours, lots of snacks, a tiny bit of wine and lots of fizzy water later, Roy Scheider and Richard Dreyfuss are splashing in to shore and Tadhg and I are stretching in our too-comfortable seats.

'You know, Mrs Brody in *Jaws* dresses like you,' says Tadhg.

My laugh turns into a yawn. 'It's the other way around.' I glance at my watch and get a shock. 'Bloody hell, it's nearly one!'

'It can't be.' Tadhg leans over and looks at my watch. 'Shit, it is.'

Suddenly I'm exhausted. 'I'd better call a taxi.' I pull my phone out and try the usual app, but no drivers are available.

'Sorry,' I say, stifling another yawn. 'It's usually faster than this.'

'I'll try my car service,' says Tadhg, but there's nothing there either.

The long day, the wine and the weed are all catching up on me now. Tadhg looks as exhausted as I feel.

'Look,' he says, 'why don't you just stay over?'

'Ah no,' I say. 'I'm only down the road.'

'You can use the room Rosie uses when she comes over from Paris. The bed's made up, there's toiletries in the en suite, there'll even be clean pyjamas.'

I try the app again. Still no drivers. I'm so, so tired. The thought of going to bed right now is irresistible.

'Okay,' I say. 'Thanks a million. If you're sure.'

'I'm sure,' he says.

As I follow him up the stairs I realise I've never seen most of Tadhg's house before. I've never even gone up to the first floor. There are framed posters on the wall for Tadhg's gigs, from his

Glastonbury headliner to his early solo shows. We're almost at the top of the stairs when I freeze at the sight of one that's all too familiar.

'Wow,' I say.

Tadhg turns around and looks down at me, and then at the poster.

'You kept it,' I say.

There it is, in black and white. That first poster. *Sourpuss. Shatner. The Band Laura's In.* My name on his wall.

'Well, yeah,' he says.

'I think I've got a copy of that poster too,' I say. 'But not framed. Rolled up in a tube somewhere in my parents' house.'

We stand on the stairs for a moment looking at the poster and then Tadhg says, 'Right! Your room.'

The room is large and beautiful, with high ceilings and huge windows. A corner of the room has been sliced off to create a small en suite bathroom. Tadhg stands by the door as I walk in.

'Whoa,' I say. 'This is gorgeous.'

'The pyjamas should be in the drawers over there. And there'll be a new toothbrush in the bathroom. I'll set my alarm for nine and we can be in the studio by ten.'

I try and fail to stifle another yawn. 'Thanks for this. And for today. It all … It really helped.'

'I told you, it's the very least I could do.'

'Well, thanks for doing it,' I say. 'It was a really good day, despite everything.'

'I had a great day too,' he said. 'So, you know, thanks for that.'

'Don't mention it,' I say.

For a moment I think he's going to hug me. For a moment I think I'm going to hug him. But it's been a long, weird, wonderful day. I'm not going to risk making it awkward at the last minute.

'Well, goodnight,' I say.

''Night, Lol,' says Tadhg. He turns to go, his hand on the doorknob. Then he pauses and says, 'Did I already tell you your ex-fiancé is a dickhead who didn't know how lucky he was?'

'Um, yeah, you did,' I say.

'Good,' he says. 'Just checking.'

And he closes the door.

Chapter Thirty-One

2019

I wake up laughing.

I'd been having a lovely dream, a dream that's now fading from my consciousness, leaving nothing but a vague feeling of happiness and something to do with Tadhg. I float right out of it into happy wakefulness and it takes a moment before I realise where I am. I try to fall back asleep again, but after a while I accept my wakeful state.

I wait for the post-big-night psychic hangover to hit me. I'm expecting all yesterday's conversations with Tadhg to start replaying in my mind. I'm expecting to cringe at all the stupid, embarrassing or overly revealing things I said. But the hit never comes. Yesterday really was a good day. I mean, seeing Dave wasn't great, but how we dealt with it was good. Spending all that time with Tadhg was good. I don't even regret my little rant about not having kids. I feel I can be myself with him. Apart from, of course, the inconvenient unrequited-love aspect.

I left my phone charging overnight after texting Katie to say I wasn't coming home. Just as I lean out of bed and pick it up, she sends a reply that's essentially all emojis.

I smile and ring her.

'You dirty stop-out!' says Katie gleefully.

'I'm in the spare room!' I say.

'Still, this is all very cosy,' she says. 'You really are okay with being friends with him again, aren't you? And seeing him when this fortnight is over? Because I want to hold him to that dinner invitation. I need to see his fancy house.'

'Of course we're friends. And actually,' I say, 'I didn't tell you before because I got distracted with Dave and, well, everything but ...' And I tell her about the Moveable Feast offer.

I expect her to sympathise with my dilemma, but instead there's a moment of silence and then she says, 'Oh, for fuck's sake, Lol, don't tell me you're not going to do it. Are you seriously dithering about this?'

I'm taken aback. 'It's not that simple!'

'Lol, he's not asking you to go on tour with him for a year.' Katie's tone is pure exasperation. 'It's just a few months of weekly band practices and then one gig! One amazing gig! You can totally handle that. You've made it clear you've been fine working with him for the last two weeks.'

When she puts it like that, it does sound reasonable. But still ...

'It's a gig in front of thousands of people!' I say. 'Possibly millions if you count the live stream!'

'So what?' says Katie. 'You won't be able to see most of them. You have to do this, Lol. You can't keep drifting away from music.'

'What are you talking about?'

'You let music just drift out of your life after college,' says Katie. 'You can't do that again. I'm not letting you.'

I'm getting annoyed now. 'You're talking like I had loads of options back then. It's not that easy to find another band. I never found another Tadhg!'

'Yes, and he never found another *you*!' says Katie. 'Didn't he say you're the only person he could write with? But he kept going anyway. And you didn't!'

Her words hit me like a blow.

I sit up in the bed. 'He could play solo gigs!' I protest. 'I couldn't. I can't sing.'

'You keep telling yourself that because you don't sing like the star of a school choir,' says Katie. 'But loads of your favourite singers don't sound like that either! You could have *tried* singing. You could have delivered your songs in your own way.'

It's almost exactly what Tadhg said to me last week.

'I'm not saying all this to make you feel bad.' Katie's tone is more gentle now. 'I'm saying it because I remember how good you were on stage. How much you loved it. And I think you owe it to yourself to at least, at the very least, just play one more gig.'

Just one gig. How I can turn down the opportunity to play

just one gig? The opportunity to keep music in my life for a few hours a week? Of course I can handle it.

'Fuck, you're right.' I take a deep breath. 'You're right. Okay. I'm going to tell him I'll do it.'

It's only half seven when I hang up and Tadhg said he was setting his alarm for nine, so he won't be up yet. I'll just pop down and make a cup of tea and take it back here. Then I can have a shower and face the day properly. I head down the stairs, past that poster with my name on it and down the hall. I open the kitchen door.

And there, sitting at the kitchen table, a mug of tea and a book in front of him, his hair sticking up in tufts, looking more bleary than I've seen him since 2003, is Tadhg. He sits up straight and runs his hand through his hair when I come in. There's something so familiar, so *Tadhg* about that gesture that it pulls at my heart.

'Morning.' He's wearing pyjama bottoms and a navy T-shirt with a clean but tatty hoodie over it. It might even be the hoodie he lent me back in 2002.

'Hey,' I say. I am suddenly very conscious of my own bedhead, which I suspect is considerably less flattering than his. And the fact that I'm wearing pyjamas that don't really fit me. 'Sorry, I didn't think you'd be up yet.'

'I woke up half an hour ago and couldn't get back to sleep.' He yawns. 'Fancy some breakfast?'

'I'd love some tea first,' I say. 'No, you stay there and finish your own. I'll make it.'

I fill the kettle and get out a mug – I already have a favourite mug in his house, one of the ochre seventies-style ones I used on the first day.

'Sleep okay?' says Tadhg. He's put down his book – *Commonwealth* by Ann Patchett, I notice – and turned around to face me.

'Really well, thanks,' I say. 'It's a very comfy bed.'

This is the first time Tadhg and I have been together first thing in the morning and I'm struck by the weird intimacy of it all. Our messy hair. Our nightwear. The fact that I'm wearing my glasses. The fact that he hasn't shaved for a few days now. This is not the polished Tadhg that I met in the restaurant with Tara – wow, two weeks ago. It's all weird, but not in a bad way. At least, not as far as I'm concerned.

'If you want to have your tea in peace, I'll take this back to bed.' I point at my mug. 'That's what I was planning on doing.'

'No, stay here!' he says. 'I mean, unless you want to go back to bed.'

I suddenly imagine hearing those last words in a very different context. 'Um. Cool! I mean, I will. Stay, I mean. It's closer to the toaster down here, after all,' I add, because once I start babbling it's hard to stop.

'So,' says Tadhg, 'are you still up for playing with Sam today? Because if you don't fancy seeing anyone, we can cancel. He'll understand.'

'No,' I say. 'It's grand. And after all … well, we've only got two days left in the studio.'

I'm about to tell him that I've decided to do the festival when Tadhg says, 'Yeah. About that …'

I brace myself. I'm not sure what I want him to say.

'How would you feel,' says Tadhg, 'about keeping this going for a bit longer?'

'Keeping what going, exactly?' I say carefully.

'You and me,' he says. 'Writing together. Playing together.'

'You mean do another week later this year? To make up for the time we lost over the last few days?'

'No,' he says. 'I mean we could … keep going. Open-ended.'

'But what about Nashville? Aren't you going there on, like, Monday?'

'Fuck Nashville!' he says. 'I can reschedule.'

'But I've got a job lined up!'

'Fuck the job!' says Tadhg. 'Seriously, Lol, I meant it the other day when I said I couldn't remember the last time I wrote so many good songs in such a short space of time. We shouldn't stop now!'

'So you mean you want to work on songs for your next album?' I say.

'No,' he says. 'I mean we should write songs for *our* next album.'

I stare at him. 'What?'

'We should start a new band, Lol,' says Tadhg. 'That's what I mean.'

And there it is. He wants to keep making music with me.

He doesn't want this to end. He doesn't want the bubble to burst.

Yes, says my heart. *Yes, yes, yes. Yes to all of it!*

And I almost say pretty much that, when something stops me. A part of me, a self-protective, sensible part of me, is aware that it's really, *really* not as simple as that.

What would it mean, in reality, to keep working with Tadhg? I've just about been able to handle this songwriting situation when I thought that it was finite. This has stopped me, to some extent, overindulging in wild, stupid fantasies. This was just two intensive weeks with Tadhg, then he'd go to America and I'd start a new job and life would go back to normal. Even the festival would just be a band practice a week and then a one-off show. But what if there were no back to normal? What if I could have the life I used to dream of? What if I could be a full-time musician? What if me and Tadhg could really be bandmates again? How would I deal with that?

Because I'm in love with him. It's not just a chemical response to his undeniable hotness or whatever I told myself at the start of this fortnight. I'm in love with him, even more in love with him than I ever was when we were both young and stupid. His life has been so different to mine over the last sixteen years, and sometimes it shows, but it still feels so *right* being with him. I want to see him every day, for always, forever, but not if it's just as friends. I did that before, when I was much younger and much more willing to suffer. Never again.

He's looking at me now, all scruffy and happy, and my heart aches. I can barely manage my feelings for him now, when he and I are only seeing each other in this songwriting bubble. But what about when he's out touring again? What about the next time he's invited to some swanky celebrity party? What if he starts seeing someone? It was agony sitting there watching him and Jess when I was twenty-one, pretending I didn't care, going off to the loo to cry when it all got too much. I'm never, *ever* going to put myself through anything like that again.

If I accept his offer, could I handle working with him every single day, going on tour with him, helping him write songs about other women? Could I handle being financially dependent on him, at least for a while? I don't think so. And what's more important, do I *want* to handle it? When I was twenty-one, I'd have said yes to this offer straight away. I'd have given up any job to play music with him full-time. I wouldn't have had to think about it, even though it could have caused me huge pain in the long run. It doesn't matter how old you are, feelings of misery and jealousy are the same. But what changes with age is what you choose to do with them. I'm thirty-seven now. I'm too old to be an emotional masochist. Back in 2003 I stayed in the band even though my heart was breaking. But that was then. And this is now.

And besides, it's not just about my feelings for him. It's about my whole life. It's about changing everything I thought I knew about my future. My advertising career could be seriously taking off. My interesting, challenging career that I care about. Could I really just abandon it? And for a man who broke my heart over a decade ago, and might well break it again without even realising it?

I know I want to keep playing music. And I know I want to keep playing it with Tadhg. But it's anything but straightforward. I thought I'd rediscovered the old Laura over the last few weeks, but now I see I haven't. I've discovered a new Laura. A new Laura who wants music in her life, who needs music in her life, but not at any price.

I need to weigh it all up. I need to figure out what I will put up with and what I won't.

I have a lot to think about, and none of it will be easy.

'Laura?' says Tadhg. 'Lol?'

I realise I haven't said anything for a weirdly long time. I pull myself together. 'Sorry! Sorry.'

'So what do you say?' he says. 'About keeping this going? You can play at the gig in August and we'll take it from there.'

And I say, 'I need to think about it a bit.'

Tadhg laughs. 'What's there to think about?'

His laugh needles me, just a little. He's taking it for granted I'll jump at this.

'Lots of things!' I say. 'I'm sorry, I just need to be totally sure it's a good idea.'

'Seriously?' Tadhg looks genuinely surprised. 'I don't get it. This has been going so well.'

'Well, yes, apart from my very public humiliation …'

'I just don't understand why you want to stop.'

'I didn't say I wanted to stop! I just said I had to think about it.'

'Okay, okay, I get it, I just thought …' He trails off.

'You just thought what?' I say.

'I thought you'd be more enthusiastic,' he says.

'It's not that simple,' I say.

'Seriously?' he says. 'Because I thought it would be a no-brainer!'

I keep my voice light. 'Oh you did, did you?'

'Well, yeah,' he says. 'I mean, what have you got to lose?'

I put down my cup. 'What have I got to *lose*?'

'You know what I mean. What else would you be doing right now? After you lost your job and everything?'

'Tadhg,' I say, trying to keep the irritation out of my voice and failing. 'You do know I wasn't actually fired, don't you? I'm good at writing ads. I actually like writing ads. I'm literally being headhunted by top agencies. You were there last week when Jeanne told me someone wanted to hire me!'

'Sorry, I know, I know.' Tadhg is all contrition. 'But wouldn't you ... Wouldn't you rather do this?'

And the truth is that of course I would, despite how much I've loved my advertising career. Rediscovering this part of me has been like letting sunlight into a room I didn't even realise was dark. But his *assumption* that I'd drop everything in my life for it, the way he assumed Hugo would listen to him, that the café would deliver to him, the restaurant would have a table for him, the assumption that it was a 'no-brainer'...

I take a deep breath. 'Look, working with you has been brilliant, despite all the media bollocks. And it's great that we're … that we're friends again. But you know, I don't think it's unreasonable to suggest I spend a few minutes considering whether I should turn down an amazing career opportunity and change my whole life for you.'

'Of course it's not,' says Tadhg. 'I'm sorry. I'm being a dick.'

'It's okay,' I say.

And then he says, 'It's just, well, being able to do this for you really means a lot to me. And I'd like to keep doing it.'

I freeze.

'Do this *for me*?' I look at him and his smile dims a little bit when he takes in the expression on my face.

'Ah, you know what I mean,' he says.

'Is that how you see the last two weeks?' I'm trying to hide how hurt I feel. And how angry. 'You doing something for me? Like, out of the goodness of your heart?'

'No, that's not what I meant! I'm just glad I can, you know, give you the opportunity to work on music instead of ads.'

'I thought you contacted me because you wanted *me* to do something for *you*. Or at least *with* you.'

'I did. I do!'

'Okay,' I say. 'So why are you talking like you're … you're saving me from my perfectly good life? And why are you taking it for granted that I'll drop everything and let you?'

And then I realise why this whole conversation is upsetting me so much.

'Oh shit,' I say. 'You really *do* think I'm your little Cinderella.'

He's not even the romantic handsome prince in this fairy-tale scenario. He's the fairy godfather.

'Of course I don't!' he says. 'Lol, come on, that's not what's been happening. We're a team.'

I'd thought we were. But maybe I was wrong.

'Okay,' I say. 'Look me in the eyes and tell me that since you decided to contact me you've never felt, not for one *second*, like you were doing me a big favour.'

He meets my gaze, his eyes troubled. There's just a moment of silence. But it's enough.

'I knew it,' I say. Although I hadn't really known it until now. I really had thought we were a team again. I thought we were equals. But maybe we never can be. Maybe we never were, as far as he was concerned. Maybe that's what this is all about.

Saint Tadhg. Fuck it, I should have known. I should have known.

'Laura, I'm sorry, I didn't mean … I just wanted to work with you again.'

I can't believe I'm having this conversation in Tadhg's sister's pyjamas. I think I need to leave. I don't want to talk to him any more right now because I have no idea what I might say. I might tell him everything, including how I feel about him. And that would really wreck everything. Forever.

I take a deep breath.

'You know what,' I say. 'This is a lot for this hour of the morning. I think I should go home for a while. I need a change of clothes anyway.'

'Don't go, Lol. Please.'

He follows me out into the hall and stands there as I climb the stairs, nearly tripping over the stupid too-long pyjamas.

'Can we just talk about this?'

'We will. But not right now,' I say. 'Seriously, Tadhg. Not right now.'

I throw my clothes on, grab my charger and my bag and go down the stairs. Tadhg is still in the hall. He moves aside to let me pass.

'Lol, I just want you to know …' He looks really upset. 'I don't take you for granted. I never did.'

I wish I could believe him.

'I'll talk to you later,' I say, and walk out the door.

As I fumble with the lock of the gate and finally, swearing, manage to get it open, I thank God it's barely eight o'clock and there's no one in the park to see me stumble out in this state. I haven't even been able to brush my hair.

And as I walk down the road in the vintage dress he told me looked nice less than twenty-four hours ago, my hair still faintly smelling of last night's smoke, I think of another time, another conversation, many years ago, when I realised I'd got things very wrong about us and ended up walking down a street alone.

Maybe this is how me and Tadhg always ends.

Chapter Thirty-Two

2003

For years I wondered what would have happened if I hadn't rung Tadhg the day before I went to New York. Would I have kept in touch with him over that summer, with emails and postcards and maybe even letters? Would we have been friends again in the autumn? Would we have been in a band together again? Would Fiachra have been right about me getting over him? Would everything have turned out very differently?

But I did ring him.

And that changed everything.

I followed Fiachra's advice after the Alternative Ball. Tadhg rang me twice the next day but I let it go to voicemail both times. He left a message asking if I'd left early because he hadn't been able to find me. He asked if I was okay. I texted back to say I was fine – I'd just crashed and wanted to slip away without big goodbyes. I said I was going to have to focus on studying for the next few weeks. I wished him luck with his first exams. And then I stayed out of his way. I bumped into him once or twice around college, but fourth-year exams were, of course, a pretty good excuse for not hanging around to chat. As far as Tadhg was concerned, I was spending every minute of every day with my nose buried in books of literary theory. We sent each other a few cursory texts but that was it.

The weeks went by. Katie nobly avoided Tadhg as well ('What sort of example will I be to my future pupils if I can't devote myself to studying?' she told him when he suggested a meet-up). She agreed that it was better for me to stay away from Tadhg until I was back from America, by which time my heart would hopefully have moved on and we could be normal friends and bandmates. I knew she was right, I knew Fiachra's plan was a good one in the long-term. But in the short-term, I missed Tadhg very, very much. I missed hanging out with him. I missed making him laugh. I missed him smiling at me. I missed everything apart from the moments of aching misery and the time between those moments when I feared they were coming.

And then …

And then it was my last few days in Dublin, and the thought of going thousands of miles away and not seeing Tadhg before I went suddenly became unbearable. What if the plane crashed and I died without seeing him again? What if he was hit by a bus over the summer and I never saw him again? I knew it was ridiculous. And I knew I had to see him. Just once. How bad could it be?

So on the morning of the day before my flight, I rang him.

'Hey,' I said. 'It's me.'

'It's you!' He sounded tired, but also happy to hear from me. At least, I hoped he sounded happy.

'Shit, did I wake you up?' It was around eleven o'clock.

'No, no, I was up.' There was a pause. 'Well, just about.'

'Were you out late?'

'Yeah. Ow. Sorry, I'm very hungover. Simon from my class had a party last night.'

'Ah,' I said. 'I was going to see if you were free to meet up later today, but if you're not able for it—'

'No!' he said. 'I'm able. Or I will be after I have a fry and a can of Coke. When exactly are you off to America?'

'Tomorrow,' I said.

'I thought so,' he said. 'Well, then I'll definitely be able to meet later.' There was a pause. 'You know I'm staying in Rosie's flat while she and her boyfriend are away? You could come over here this evening. We could get a takeaway and play some music. Have one more go at our song. I mean, if you're free tonight.'

'I'm free,' I said. At least, I'd make sure I was free. The packing I'd been planning on leaving until as late as possible would now be done in the afternoon.

♪♪

For someone who had been audibly hungover that morning, Tadhg looked pretty good when he opened the door of Rosie's flat on Heytesbury Street that evening.

'How's the head?' I said, as I walked in.

He grimaced. 'It's okay now. Though I should probably go easy on the booze this evening.'

'Good,' I say, holding up a tote bag. 'Because I could only afford to get us two cans each. And I've got to be up early to catch a plane tomorrow.'

'Shit, Lol,' he said. 'I can't believe you're going to be thousands of miles away for three whole months.'

'You won't notice,' I said. 'You'll be teaching at rock camp for most of it.'

'I'll notice,' he said, taking the cans out of the tote bag and putting them in the fridge in Rosie's kitchenette. 'Do you fancy getting falafel from the Hot Chilli? It's just round the corner.'

Half an hour later we were sitting at the tiny square table of Rosie's kitchenette, eating a truly delicious, if very messy, takeaway. The table was wedged into a corner with only two free sides so we sat at an angle to each other. *It's a good thing I'm leaving the country to forget about him*, I thought, wiping tahini off my cheeks, *because I hope he forgets me looking like this*. He had paid for the falafels ('You brought the cans!') and for a stupid treacherous moment I found myself imagining what it would be like if this was our life, the two of us living in an apartment like this, me buying the drinks and him buying the takeaway, me not worrying about being covered in falafel because I knew he loved me anyway.

I pushed the thoughts out of my head and said, 'So. One last mini band practice?'

'One last mini band practice,' said Tadhg.

He sat on the couch and I sat in an armchair. Then he handed me his guitar and I played the opening chords of 'Anyone But You'.

We ran through all our songs that night. It was almost as if some part of us knew it was the last time we'd play together for a long, long time. We drank our first cans, then Tadhg made some tea and we kept playing. We did some covers. We did songs that didn't have full lyrics yet. We opened the second cans. We even played our song, though we didn't make a serious stab at figuring out any new bits of it.

'We'll give it another go in September,' said Tadhg.

God, after tonight I wasn't going to see him again until the end of September. It was ridiculous. But that reminded me I had to wake up early tomorrow and get on a plane. I looked at my watch and realised it was ten o'clock.

'Shit,' I said. 'I should go soon.'

'Let's do one more song,' said Tadhg.

We did 'Midnight Feast'. Even then I knew the lyrics were bad, but I also knew it was a good song. Maybe we could write new lyrics in the autumn. And as I played the last chord

I thought, *I'll miss this over the summer. I'll miss him. I'll miss him so much.*

I played the last chord as loudly as I could. Then we looked at each other and smiled.

'I'll help you clean up the dinner stuff,' I said.

When the table was cleared and the dishes washed, Tadhg picked up his beer can.

'Huh, there's more left of this than I thought,' he said.

I picked up my cider. 'Same here.'

'We might as well finish them,' he said.

And because I was literally leaving the country the next morning so he couldn't possibly think I was after anything, I didn't insist on leaving straight away. I said, 'Sure.'

We sat down at the kitchen table and clinked our cans off each other.

'Cheers,' I said, taking a swig of cider.

'We've written some good songs this year,' said Tadhg. 'And almost written one great one.'

'It really is good, isn't it? As a song. It's properly good. At least,' I acknowledge, 'it will be when we finally finish it. If we finally finish it.'

'We'll finish it,' said Tadhg. 'We'll still be in a band together.'

I sipped the cider. I wondered if you could get cider in America. 'It won't be the same without Brian and Jo. And without us both being in Trinity.'

'No, it won't.' Tadhg drank some beer. 'But we'll still be in Dublin. The others are okay with us playing the old songs.

And we'll write new ones. And record them. We can record *our* song!'

'Steady on,' I said. 'That would be a miracle.'

'Nah, we'll do it,' said Tadhg. 'I have faith in us. You'll come back from New York full of inspiration.'

'I hope so,' I said. 'I mean, I can't wait to go to New York. Obviously.'

'Obviously,' said Tadhg.

'But I'll really, really miss playing music for the whole summer.'

Then I thought, surely I could risk a little bit of honesty, seeing as we weren't going to see each other for over three months.

I said, 'And I'll miss you, I suppose.'

'I'll miss you too,' said Tadhg. 'No supposing about it.'

'Yeah?' I laughed.

'Yeah,' he said. We drew a little closer to each other, across the corner of the table. 'You know I love playing music with you.'

'I love playing music with you too,' I said.

It was still okay to be honest, wasn't it?

'And hanging out with you too, of course,' he said.

'Well, of course,' I said. 'Same here. Hanging out with you, I mean.'

Still okay. We both laughed. Now we were even closer.

'I'm going to miss you so much,' he said. And closer. 'Because you're brilliant, Lol.' Closer. 'You're so fucking brilliant.'

And then we weren't laughing anymore.

We were kissing.

Afterwards, I agonised over who had kissed who first, but in my heart of hearts I was always sure that we both kissed each other at the same time, months and months of tension finally breaking. Tentative for just a second, and then anything but. We stood up, still kissing; I heard Tadhg's chair fall backwards to the floor.

This is what Tadhg tastes like, I thought, this is what it feels like when those arms are wrapped around you, pulling you closer as if he can't get enough of you. This is what it feels like to hear his breath catch as he pulls away from you, his teeth grazing your lower lip just for a second, before his lips meet yours again and his tongue is in your mouth, his stubble scratching your chin. This is what it feels like to slide your hands under his T-shirt, this is what it feels like when your arms are wrapped around his bare back. This is what it's like when his hands are on you, under your clothes, at your heart. This is what it's like. At last, I thought, at *last*, this is what it's like ...

And for a while I didn't think of anything at all.

I had never had a first kiss like this before. I had never had a first *anything* like this before.

I pulled him closer to me, kissing him harder, and in one movement he scooped me up under my thighs so that I clung to him, my legs wrapping around his waist, and then, still kissing me, he set me down on the edge of kitchen table. He was pressed between my legs and I could feel his erection through his jeans.

Oh my God, Tadhg is hard because of me. The idea turned me on so much I felt faint.

He pushed my skirt up, and now his hands were on my thighs, now his right hand was between my legs.

'Is this okay?' he said, his voice low.

I nodded. And then we were kissing again, and his hand, God I should have known he'd be good with his hands, was sliding below the waistband of my knickers and I didn't even care that they were a very unsexy pair of Dunnes mini-shorts because now Tadhg's fingers were moving against me in a circle and doing something extraordinary. My face was buried in his neck and I could smell him, so familiar and now so utterly not, and I could smell me, and it was almost too much, it was all almost too much but it was glorious too.

Then he stopped, and I was about to tell him to keep going when he said, 'I've got a condom in my wallet?'

He met my eyes, questioning, his gaze heavy with desire.

'Okay,' I said. 'Yes. *Yes.*'

My breathing was ragged and so was his as he took out his wallet from his back pocket and looked for the condom. I started to undo the straining buttons on his jeans, my fingers trembling. *I'm going to have sex with Tadhg*, I thought. *Oh my God oh my God oh my God I'm going to have sex with Tadhg …*

Tadhg ripped open the condom wrapper.

But then he pulled away from me a tiny bit.

My hands fell away from the buttons.

'You okay?' I said.

The pause lasted way too long.

'Laura,' he said. 'Um … Maybe this isn't a good idea.'

'What?' A cold feeling went down my spine.

'I mean, we've been drinking,' he said. 'I … I don't want you to do anything you'll regret.'

I was flooded with relief. It was very good he was checking. But I wasn't drunk and neither was he. I just wanted us to keep going.

'Oh no, don't worry. We've only had two drinks, I know what I'm doing. And we don't have to actually, you know …' I pointed at the condom. 'Obviously.' I would have been more than happy if he'd kept doing what he was doing to me moments earlier. 'But of course if you want to stop, we'll stop …'

'I don't want to stop! *Fuck*, I don't. But …'

How had this all gone weird so quickly? If he really wanted to do it and I definitely wanted to do it, why weren't we still kissing? I was suddenly very conscious that my bra was unfastened under my top. I wrapped my arms around myself.

'Look,' said Tadhg. He took another step back. Now he was buttoning up his jeans. 'It's just … I think I know how you feel about me and I don't want to mess you around.'

It was if a bucket of ice water had been poured over my head.

'You know *what*?' I pulled my skirt down over my thighs.

'I know you have … feelings for me. For a while now.'

I felt sick, physically sick, with horror.

I'd thought I was being so careful. The last year with Tadhg was flashing before my eyes. I thought of those unbearable evenings when he was going out with Jess, when I tried so hard to act as if I didn't give a shit, when I made myself not flinch when he had his arm around her in the pub. I thought of him seeing through my act the whole time. I thought of him feeling *sorry* for me. His sad little friend with the embarrassing crush. After all this, I was just one of the string of lovestruck girls I'd imagined at the start of the year. The realisation was unbearable. It would have been unbearable under any circumstances but *now* ...

Now we'd had what I'd *thought* was about to be the most intense sexual encounter of my life but was clearly just a tipsy ill-judged fumble as far as Tadhg was concerned, the grown-up equivalent of that post-gig kiss in 1999. And because he was a fundamentally decent person, he didn't want me to think it might actually mean something.

So he was stopping before we could go even further, even though it had already gone far enough to leave me feeling utterly humiliated. How could he let things go this far if he knew how much I liked him? How could he have kissed me like that, how could he have – oh *God*. I thought of the times over that last year when I'd been convinced that we'd shared a moment, moments that were clearly all in my head. The times I'd thought he might actually kiss me because he fancied me as much as I fancied him. I thought of the noises I was making a few minutes ago when his hand was between my legs, before he stopped to get a condom that we were definitely not going to use now.

I wanted to die, I literally wanted to die of shame.

But I couldn't show him how I felt. That would make me even more pathetic. And so I forced out a laugh and went on the offensive.

'Wow, Tadhg. I knew you had a bit of an ego but I didn't think it was that big.'

'I didn't mean it like that, I just mean—'

'Do you honestly think I've been tragically pining for you all year?' I snapped.

'What? No! Of course not!'

'Fucking hell, you're unbelievable, do you know that? You get a bit of attention after a few gigs and what, suddenly every girl you know is madly in love with you?'

'That's not what I'm saying!'

'Well, you're right, this is a very bad idea,' I said. I jumped down from the table with as much dignity as someone can muster when her bra is still undone.

'Oh my God, Lol, would you calm down,' said Tadhg, which enraged me even further. 'I'm just trying to be, I don't know, a gentleman!'

'Oh yeah, you're such a gentleman,' I said. 'If you don't want to sleep with me, Tadhg, that's fine! Just don't tell me it's for my own good. Christ, you're so fucking patronising.' There were tears in my eyes now but they were tears of anger.

'I'm not being patronising! I think you're amazing, it's

just …' He looked away from me. 'It's me and Jess. She was at the party last night. And …'

'And what?'

'And something happened.'

Oh, wow. I didn't think this could get any worse but it turned out it could.

'Good for you,' I said. Where the fuck was my jacket? And my bag? I spotted them on the couch and grabbed them. 'Maybe she can write some new songs with you. God knows you need help.'

'Okay, come on, Lol—'

'That's why you don't want to "mess me around", isn't it?' I snarled, pulling on my denim jacket and buttoning it up to my chin. 'Because you need me here to make your stupid boring songs sound halfway decent.'

'Is that really what you think?' Tadhg looked like I'd just slapped him in the face.

And I thought, *Good*.

Because just in that moment, at the height of my humiliated pain, I wanted to hurt him. I wanted to make him feel as small and stupid and awful as I felt now. I wanted to wound him at his very core.

And that meant attacking the thing he cared about the most. Even if what I said wasn't true.

'Oh my God, of *course* it is.' My voice was full of contempt. 'Jesus, Tadhg, have you actually listened to those shitty little songs before I made them sound interesting?'

The stunned, horrified look on his face showed my arrow had hit home, and I instantly wanted to take it back. But it was too late, I couldn't unsay it. I couldn't undo anything.

Everything was wrecked now anyway.

'Have a good summer.' I marched out of the room, slamming the door after me with such force it rattled in its frame. I didn't burst into tears until I was halfway down Camden Street.

The next day I flew to New York.

And that was that. For sixteen years.

Chapter Thirty-Three

2019

Katie and Jeanne have both left for work when I get home, and I'm glad because I don't think I can face anyone right now. Maybe I do want to be one of those hermits after all. I'll just sit in my room forever, writing music just for me. I won't be reliant on Tadhg. I won't be reliant on anyone.

I'm on autopilot as I go into the kitchen and put the kettle on. While I wait for it to boil, I check my email. Maybe there'll be an amazing job offer that will change everything. Maybe Leafe wants me to be their creative director. Maybe …

There's an email from Tara Kelleher entitled 'Minidisc Recordings'.

I stare at it for a minute before I open it. With everything that's happened over the past few days, I had forgotten all about those files being digitised. But here they are. A WeTransfer link to my past. To my and Tadhg's past.

I make the tea. I sit at the table and drink it. And I think.

Then I go upstairs, get my laptop and download the files.

They're not dated and of course there's no way to know what's on each file, so I click on one at random.

The first thing I hear is laughter. My and Tadhg's laughter. Then his voice, sounding just a little bit lighter, or younger, than it does now, saying, 'Come on, Lol! Be serious!'

And there's me, still laughing, saying, 'Sorry! Sorry. I'll behave myself now.'

Then I hear the opening guitar line of 'Anyone But You'.

Except it's not. At least, not the final version. In this version, the end of the guitar line goes down instead of up. I hear my twenty-one-year-old self play the line twice, then stop and say, 'I think it might be better this way,' before playing the version I would go on to play countless times over the next nine months. The version I've played a few times over the last week.

'That's better,' says Joanna, and I feel a pang at the sound of her voice. I haven't talked to her in so long. How did I let her drift out of my life too? How did I let so many things drift out of my life?

'Definitely,' says twenty-one-year-old Tadhg. 'And then this for the chorus?'

He plays a chord sequence and sings a familiar melody.

'Oh yeah,' says younger me. 'That's really good.'

I realise this was the moment we wrote it. The actual moment we wrote one of our best songs. Together. As a team.

We really were a team.

I stop the recording and close my eyes, just for a moment. Then I click on another file.

This time it starts with me playing a keyboard line, one that I recognise as the melody of the chorus of 'Midnight Feast'. I hear Tadhg saying, 'Come on, Laura! This is ridiculous! Just sing it!'

And there's me calling back, 'Never!'

When that recording finishes I click on another file.

A sequence of crunchy guitar chords. Then me saying, 'What if you play A minor at the end instead of D minor?', followed by Tadhg doing just that and saying, 'That's it!'

Another file.

A shimmer of jangling guitar, a bouncing bassline, syncopated drums, Tadhg improvising a melody over it all, no words, just *da-da-da* sounds, and then me going, 'You genius! That's perfect.'

Another file.

The opening chords of *the* song. Our song.

My heart is in my mouth. Sixteen years ago, our younger selves play through the song. There are no drums, no bass. It's just me and Tadhg. Which means I know when and where we recorded this.

I hear us finish the second chorus and twenty-one-year-old Tadhg says, 'Fuck, Lol, this is good.'

'It is, isn't it?' says twenty-one-year-old me. 'I mean, I wasn't deluding myself.'

'Definitely not,' he says. 'Let's play it again.'

Sixteen years ago, the two of us play it again.

'The chorus feels a bit short,' says younger me. 'And we need to come up with a middle eight.'

'We will,' says Tadhg. 'What about adding this to the chorus to make it longer?' He sings a lilting wordless vocal.

I freeze. I wrote that bit. Didn't I?

But there he is, in 2002, singing it for the first time.

And there I am saying, 'Oh yeah, that works.'

The recording ends. I don't move. That was the first time I played the song for him, in his childhood bedroom. The day after he told me about him and Jess. I sound totally normal in the recording. You'd never know how I was feeling that day. I really was a good actor.

I have such a strong memory of that day. At least I thought I had. But I had totally forgotten Tadhg coming up with that bit of the song. Over the years I told myself that song was all me. And it was mostly me.

But it was also, just a little bit, us.

I get up from my bed, walk across the room and pick up the guitar. I sit on the wicker chair, the one Tadhg sat on just a few days ago, and play the opening chords of our song. I start singing the melody.

Then, for the first time, I write a song about Tadhg.

I write lyrics from the perspective of my younger self, about how crushed I was by how things turned out. I write about how I tried to forget him and stop loving him. I keep some of the words of the old chorus, to remind myself why I wrote it, but I twist them a little. Then I reach the point where a middle eight should be, and after all these years and all these attempts, I finally find myself coming up with a new chord sequence that flows perfectly after the chorus, and singing a melody that fits perfectly on top of that.

That's when I stop writing about my younger self. I start writing for me. I start writing about what I want now, what I yearn for, what I dream of, even if I know I can't have it. I write about how I wish we were meant to be together. I write about how I can't help hoping it's not too late for us. I write about getting a second chance. Back in the day, Tadhg's lyrics were always better than mine because he wasn't restraining himself. Now I owe it to my younger self, who started writing a song this good when her heart was breaking, to finally, at long last, make something honest. Even if the words are stupid. Even if no one else ever hears it. Even if it's just for me.

So that's what I do.

I finish our song.

And then the doorbell rings.

I know it's him even before I see that tall silhouette through the stained-glass panel in the front door.

I seriously consider not opening the door. I might be ready to be honest about him in a song that no one else has heard, but I'm not ready to be honest *with* him. To his face. And I still need to think about his offer.

Then I remember how I totally erased the songwriting he did in the past from my mind, and maybe I feel a pang of guilt about that because I open the door.

He's still wearing the navy T-shirt and old hoodie from this morning, though he's wearing jeans instead of the pyjama bottoms.

'I'm sorry for turning up here,' he says. 'If you want me to go, just say. I'll leave.'

'No,' I say. 'Come in.'

He follows me into the kitchen.

'I want to apologise,' he says. 'For making you feel like that. For making assumptions. For being a spoiled brat. For all of it.'

'Okay,' I say.

'You were right, I've got too used to things going my way,' he says. 'Which is shitty of me. I suppose that's why I was surprised when you didn't say yes straight away. And that's *really* shitty of me. So I'm sorry, Lol. I'm really sorry.'

I believe him. But what he just said is the crux of the problem. The imbalance between us. I'm in love with him. I don't think he's in love with me. He is the gorgeous rock star with the studio. I'm the hired help.

'I do want to work with you,' I say. 'But I need more time to think about it. Because I don't know if it'll work.'

'Okay,' says Tadhg. 'Um, why not?'

'Because you're you!' I say. 'And I'm me!'

'Well, yeah.' Tadhg runs a hand through his hair, pushing the waves into tufts. 'What does that mean?'

'Tadhg,' I say. 'You've won two Grammys and the Mercury Prize and you live in a Georgian townhouse. I'm living in my friend's spare room and I write ads about pension plans.'

'So?' says Tadhg.

'Come on, Tadhg, don't be obtuse,' I say. 'You must see the difference!'

'I'm not being obtuse!' he says. 'I just don't see what this has to do with us actually writing songs together.'

'I just … I don't think working together can work if there's this imbalance between us,' I say. 'If we're not proper equals. I can't bear it if you expect me to be, I don't know, grateful to you.'

'Grateful to *me*?' says Tadhg. 'Laura, I'm incredibly grateful to *you*! I always have been!' He takes a deep breath. 'You asked if I thought I was doing you a favour, and yeah, I did want to do you a favour. I wanted to give you the chance to work on music full-time, and I shouldn't have assumed you'd want it, but as far as I'm concerned, I was just repaying all the favours you've done for me. Jesus, if there's an imbalance between us it goes the other way!'

I look at him, so tall, so handsome, so successful. 'What on earth are you talking about?'

'You're ridiculously talented, that's what I'm talking about,' says Tadhg. 'You always have been. Much more talented than I am.'

'Our careers beg to differ,' I say. 'You're an incredible songwriter, Tadhg. You must know you are.'

'If I'm any good,' says Tadhg, 'it's because I've kept working at it. And that's because of you. I owe you so much, Lol. *So* much. You always made my songs better. You knew just what they needed. You taught me to be a better songwriter. You're *still* teaching me. You're the single biggest influence on my music, you know that? To this day I've never written a song without thinking *What would Lol add to this?* I always knew I could never be as good as you, but I kept trying. I *keep* trying.' He runs both hands through his hair, which is a total mess by now. 'And besides all that, I owe you my career! If it wasn't for you I'd never have written 'Winter Without You'.'

'I had nothing to do with 'Winter Without You'!' I say. 'You wrote it after we'd stopped speaking to each other.'

'But it's *about* you!' says Tadhg.

The world spins around me for a moment. Did I just hear him correctly? I can't have. This makes no sense.

'*What?*'

'It was my apology to you,' he says. 'For making a mess of things that night in Rosie's flat. It was me saying how much I missed you.' I think I must appear worryingly shellshocked because he looks concerned as he says, 'Hang on, did you never realise?'

It's like finding out his real name is Tim all over again. But this is bigger – much, much bigger.

'But it's a love song,' I say stupidly. 'Like, a romantic love song. Isn't it?'

'Yes!' says Tadhg.

'But you weren't in love with me,' I say.

'Of course I was!' he says. 'And then I got over you. And now I've fallen in love with you again.'

'You have?' I say.

'Yes!' says Tadhg.

'Oh,' I say. 'Same here.'

We look at each other for a second that feels like an eternity, our eyes full of stars.

But this can't be right. It just can't. None of it makes sense. I need to bring myself back to earth. I need him to explain.

'I don't understand,' I say. 'That night in Rosie's flat, you stopped because you knew I liked you and you didn't want to mess me around. And you and Jess were back together—'

'But we weren't!' he says. 'Oh God, it was a mess. Me and Jess were both pissed at Simon's party the night before, and when I was leaving we were with each other – which was obviously really, really stupid of me but, you know, it happened. It was a drunken kiss. That was all. And then the next day, just before you came over to Rosie's place, Jess texted me and ... well, she obviously thought the kiss meant more than it did. I felt totally shit about it, and I told myself I'd have that awkward conversation with her later. But before I could have it, you arrived and then you and me happened. Or started happening.'

'Until you stopped it,' I say.

'I know I handled it really badly,' he says. 'I just didn't think being with you was fair to Jess if she thought we were a couple again. And I didn't think it was fair to you to go any further before I talked to Jess and cleared things up. If you and me were going to be together, I wanted it to be *perfect*. I didn't want any baggage hanging over it. And I thought you wouldn't want anything with me if you knew I had, I dunno, unfinished business with Jess.'

'With all due respect to Jess,' I say, 'I would not have given a shit.'

But now I see what he meant that night when he said he was trying to be a gentleman. The words that have been burned into my brain for sixteen years now take on a new meaning. He wanted a clean conscience about Jess. He wanted to be with me without making me an accessory to cheating. Which wasn't even real cheating, because he and Jess weren't actually together. *Oh, Tadhg. Why didn't you explain yourself properly?* But then I remember I didn't exactly let him.

'What I said about your music that night,' I say, 'I felt awful the minute I said it. I'm so sorry. I was embarrassed and angry and I turned on you. But I didn't mean it. And it wasn't true. It was never true.'

'It was kind of true,' says Tadhg. 'That's why it got to me.'

'No it wasn't,' I say, and I mean it. 'Your music's always been great.'

'But you always made it better,' he says.

It's all too much to take in. He loved me then. It wasn't in my head. It still isn't.

'That night when you said you knew I had feelings for you,' I say. 'How long had you known? Did you always know?'

'No!' says Tadhg. 'I mean, I always hoped you liked me. I kept thinking there was something between us. But I was never sure. Every time I tried to change the mood, you'd say something that made me think we were just friends. Whenever I suggested we stay out late somewhere, you made an excuse to go home. Or you'd, like, tell me to go out with Jess. Do you remember?'

'I remember,' I say. 'But I …' And then I think about it. All the times I insisted on calling it a night. All the times I made such an effort to assure him I didn't have any designs on him. It never, ever crossed my mind I could have been *too* successful. 'Why didn't you ever say anything?'

'Why didn't *you*?' he says. 'I didn't want to make a move unless I knew you felt the same way. It would have messed up our friendship – it would have destroyed the band …'

I can't believe it. I had always thought that if Tadhg liked me, he would just assume, correctly, that I would like him back. I thought that was how really hot people operated. I had taken for granted that he'd take me for granted.

'Anyway,' he says, 'I couldn't risk it. I couldn't risk fucking things up between us. I couldn't risk losing you altogether. And I liked Jess, that was real, but fuck, Laura, I always liked you more. I just didn't think you liked me the same way. And then you got back together with Fiachra and that seemed to prove it.'

'But I didn't get back with him!' I say. 'Not really. It was a friends-with-benefits thing. To distract me from you and Jess.'

'*Seriously?*' says Tadhg. I nod. He shakes his head in disbelief. 'Well, it distracted *me*. Or at least it really got to me. The first time I saw the two of you hanging out as a couple I was so jealous of him. It made me realise me how strongly I still felt about you. And once I acknowledged that, I couldn't keep going out with Jess. It wasn't fair to her.'

'So … so that's why you broke up?'

'Yeah,' says Tadhg. 'But as far as I knew you were with Fiachra. And I didn't think you were into me anyway.'

'In Rosie's flat you said you knew I liked you!'

'Only since the Ball,' says Tadhg. 'I was with that girl and then I looked up and saw your face, and then you ran out and suddenly I knew. At least I was pretty sure I knew. I *hoped* I knew.'

'You told me you'd known for a while!' I say. 'The Ball was, like, a month earlier at most.'

'That's a long time when you're twenty-one!' says Tadhg. 'And then you basically disappeared off the face of the earth. You wouldn't even return my calls!'

'I was avoiding you because seeing you with other girls hurt too much,' I say. 'And then that night in Rosie's I thought you realised crossing the sex line was a huge mistake because you didn't actually fancy me.'

'Didn't *fancy* you?' says Tadhg, his voice incredulous. He's looking straight at me now, his eyes blazing. 'That night when you were on that table I remember thinking, *Jesus, I'm going to make Laura come*, and it's still one of the hottest moments of my entire fucking life. I'm just sorry I stopped before I actually did it.'

I meet his burning gaze.

'Well,' I say. 'You can always try again.'

He reaches out and pulls me to him.

I didn't realise I remembered the taste of his mouth until now, because he tastes the same, and he tastes so right. I bring my hands to the sandpaper roughness of his jaw just as his arms go round my waist, drawing me to him, pressing me against him. I *want* him, I want him so fucking much, it seems impossible he could want me as much as I want him, but it's not impossible, it's definitely not impossible, because his want is gloriously evident in the intensity of his kisses, in the urgency of his hands. Eventually we pull away from each other and meet each other's eyes, our breathing heavy. But I can't stop smiling and neither can he.

'Do you want to go upstairs?' he says. 'We haven't had the best luck in kitchens.'

'Oh my God, yes,' I say. '*Yes.*'

He takes my hand and we're almost running as he leads me out of the kitchen and up the stairs and into my room where, laughing with happiness, we tumble onto the bed.

'Now,' he says, 'I'm finally going to finish what I started.'

And he does.

I should have known he'd be good with his tongue as well.

♪♪

Later, we lie in my bed, his arm around me, my head on his chest.

'That,' says Tadhg, 'was worth waiting for.'

'It really, really was,' I say. I'm so blissfully exhausted I feel dizzy. I might not be able to walk for a while.

'You're worth waiting for,' says Tadhg.

I look up at him, his beautiful profile, and he turns his head to look down at me with such tenderness that I draw in a quick breath. It could feel weird, being in bed with him like this. I could feel very self-conscious. No one but Dave has seen me naked for a decade. It could feel weird seeing Tadhg like this, resting on his bare chest (pretty hairy, unsurprisingly). But somehow it doesn't feel awkward at all. There's a radiant clarity to all of it, a lack of mess, a lack of complication. The way he looked at me when he took my clothes off was such a pure combination of desire and love and awe, my own feelings reflected back to me in his eyes. I want him to look at me like that every day for the rest of my life.

'You're worth waiting for too,' I say.

'This is serious,' he says. 'Isn't it? You and me?'

'It's serious,' I say. 'But it's fun, too.'

He laughs and pulls me closer to him. 'Very, very fun.'

'I love you, you know,' I say. A part of me, the part of me that used to tell myself to leave early, the part of me that couldn't bear to be vulnerable in front of Tadhg, can't believe I'm saying this. But I'm not going to listen to that part of me anymore. 'I tried not to fall in love with you again, but I couldn't help it.'

'And for that,' says Tadhg, rolling to his side and kissing me, 'I am very, very grateful. I love you so much, Lol. I think I've loved you since the moment I met you. I'm just glad I can finally tell you.'

'I'm glad,' I say, 'that I can finally show you.'

And I do.

It seems miraculous to both of us that we're actually doing this, that we *can* actually do this, that finally, after all these years, after all that yearning, all that longing, it's finally this easy. It's almost too good to be true. As I wrap my legs around his waist I say, 'This is real, isn't it?'

He laughs and kisses me, a slow, deep kiss, and says, 'God, I hope so.'

'Good,' I say. 'Because I— oh! *Oh.*'

We stay in my bed for hours, sometimes just talking, sometimes laughing. And always, at last, being honest.

'We've wasted so much time,' I say, nestling into his embrace and closing my eyes. 'We could have been doing this for the last sixteen years.'

'We can't look at it that way,' says Tadhg. 'We were so young.

We might have messed everything up in another way. Maybe it's right that we're finally together when we're old enough to make it work.'

'So we should be grateful to Fiachra, then? For accidentally keeping us apart?'

'Bloody Fiachra,' says Tadhg. 'I still turn the radio off whenever he comes on.'

'Ha! You're not a fan of the nation's favourite psychologist?'

'Someone gave me his book for Christmas a few years ago,' says Tadhg. 'They said he changed their life. I didn't tell them he'd changed mine too.'

'He meant well,' I say. 'He was a good guy. And seeing as I'd convinced him you didn't fancy me, he gave me pretty sensible advice.'

'True,' says Tadhg. 'I'll leave the radio on next time.'

'The last time I heard him on *Liveline*,' I say, 'he was talking about the importance of radical honesty.'

Neither of us says anything for a second, and then we both start laughing. When my mirth subsides I say, 'Speaking of radical honesty, if we hadn't had that discussion this morning, were you planning to tell me how you felt?'

'And risk losing you all over again?' says Tadhg, kissing the top of my head. 'No, not yet anyway. It would have felt wrong telling you so soon. And also unethical. I mean, I'd just asked you to work with me. I could hardly say "Oh, by the way, I'm falling in love with you' a week after you started."'

'Fair,' I say.

'And speaking of the work thing ...' he says. 'If doing these songwriting sessions feels weird, if you feel it fucks up the power dynamic between us, then we'll stop right now. Don't feel obliged to keep working with me. You're meant to make music. You know it and I know it. But you should do it however and with whoever you want. On your terms.'

'I know,' I say. 'And I will. I want to write songs for lots of people. But I want to make music with you too.' I kiss him. 'Always.'

And then we stop talking for a while.

Later, when I'm lying on my side, Tadhg spooning me, his arm around my waist, his forearm pressed against my breasts, I realise there's one thing we haven't discussed. One thing I need to make sure he understands. One thing I need to know for sure. I take his hand in mine and gently kiss his knuckles. Then I say, 'Tadhg?'

'Hmmm?'

'I have to tell you something,' I say.

'Okay,' says Tadhg.

I turn around to face him.

'You must know,' I say, 'that there is never going to be a miracle baby. I'm not going to put myself through any sort of fertility treatment, or an adoption process. That's just not the right thing for me. This is it. If you want me, that's all you get. Just me.'

'Lol.' Tadhg looks genuinely baffled. 'Why on earth would I want anything else when I have you?'

I once vowed I'd never cry in front of him. But I don't care about that anymore.

And these are happy tears, so they wouldn't count anyway.

Eventually hunger drives us out of bed. We reluctantly get dressed and go down to the kitchen, where I make toast and Tadhg puts the kettle on.

'You know,' he says, taking the mugs out of the press above the counter, 'if we can force ourselves to stay out of bed long enough to actually play some music today, we could always give our song another try.'

'Ah,' I say. 'Well, it's funny you should mention that ...'

Chapter Thirty-Four

The Stars

(Hennessy/McDermott)

Our first kiss
Wasn't meant to end this way
What a twist
In a game I just couldn't play
Oh what bliss
Thought I had it in my sights
But I missed
When you turned on the lights

But I could have been your summer girl
It's all that I dreamed of
I could have been your summer girl
It's all that I dreamed of

Side by side
In a room without a view

Our Song

I can't hide
The way I feel about you
Oh my pride
Was never hurt this way before
So I tried
Not to love you anymore

But I could have been your summer girl
It's all that I dreamed of
I could have been your summer girl
It's all that I dreamed of

And maybe it is not too late
And maybe I believe in fate
If fate's what brought you back to me
To write a whole new history
We are the ones that got away
But maybe this time we should stay
No more running on our own
This time we are coming home

Here we are
We've been talking through the night
And the stars
Say this time we'll get it right
Because this time
We're wiser than we were before
And we'll find
That we're worth waiting for

And I'm gonna be your summer girl
It's what we both dreamed of
I'm gonna be your summer girl
It's what we both dreamed of

Winter Without You

(Tadhg Hennessy)

The earth is cold and the world is still
The sun's not come back and it never will
I can't remember when the sky was new
But I remember that I love you
And I can't do
Winter without you
I can't do winter without you

One day the north star was gone
Now I've nothing left to wish upon
I cannot set my ships to roam
Without you there to guide them home
And I can't do
Winter without you
I can't do winter without you

Our Song

And though my heart is worn
There's still a home
There for you
And as an icy cold
Grips my soul
My heart is true
And in a far off state
I'll always wait
For a sign
You'll write a melody
That's just for me
I'll know it's mine

I hurt you, love, but I wish you knew
That I was in awe of you
You were my cosmology
My north star, my moon and sea
And I can't do
Winter without you
I can't do winter without you

Chapter Thirty-Five

August 2019

'How are you feeling?' he says.

'Um, mostly excited,' I say. 'And a bit nervous.'

'Don't be nervous. You'll be brilliant,' he says. We're standing at the side of the main stage at Moveable Feast, ready to go on and play the headline slot on Sunday night in front of a massive field of very excited festivalgoers. 'We'll be brilliant.'

A tech guy appears and says, 'Right, everyone, you're on.'

Sam strolls up and winks at me. 'Good luck! Not that you'll need it.'

He walks past me and on to the stage followed by Tony, the bass player. As soon as they step out the crowd goes wild. And suddenly I think, *Fuck, I can't do this. I can't go out and play in front of literally thousands of people.* It'd be a lot to go out and play in front of fifty people. But this is the population of a small town. I can feel panic rising. My hands start to shake.

'Oh shit,' I say.

But Tadhg takes my hand and gives it a comforting squeeze, and when I look up at his face, the face I've woken up next to almost every morning for the past six months, I know he has total faith in me. And it reminds me that, deep down, I have total faith in myself.

'Come on, Lol,' he says. 'Let's show 'em how it's done.'

He doesn't let go of my hand until I'm on the stage, when a guitar tech hands me my Danelectro and I slip its hot-pink vinyl strap over my head. As I reach my mark, I look out at a sea of cheering, screaming people and beyond them to the trees that mark the main-stage boundaries in this eighteenth-century country estate. The sun is setting to our right, sending golden light over the crowd. I spot my parents and Annie standing near the front. Annie looks like she finds the whole thing hilarious, but she's clapping as enthusiastically as Mam and Dad. Katie, Jeanne, Aisling, Kev, Sarah and Rob are nearby, with Ellie on Rob's shoulders. Ellie waves wildly at me, and I wave back. I can see people whispering at each other and pointing at me as they realise who I am. Some look amused. Some look suspicious. I feel the panic rising again. Then I look over at Tadhg, who's taking his position behind the mic stand in the centre of the stage, and he looks back at me and grins and I feel safe.

He always makes me feel safe.

'Hey, Moveable Feast,' says Tadhg. 'It's good to see you all again.'

Then Sam plays a drum intro and we're off.

And for the first time in a long, long time, I feel that surge of power.

This is what I want. Playing music. Being on stage. Being here with Tadhg. This is it.

I can pinpoint the moment when the initially sceptical audience mood changes towards me. It's four songs into the set, I'm playing the solo in 'Another City', and when I finish there's a massive cheer, a huge supportive wave of sound that hits me with the force of a bear hug. I look over at Tadhg and catch his eye, and then we both start laughing with pure, giddy joy. I don't realise it at the time, but in the pit at the front of the stage a photographer is taking a photo of this moment. It's that photo, not the more dramatic one she takes later of me and Tadhg kissing at the side of the stage at the end of the gig as the final fireworks go off, that will end up on front pages and culture and gossip websites the day after the festival, and that will accompany pretty much every story about me and Tadhg that appears in the media from now on.

I don't mind. It's a really, really nice photo.

Three-quarters of the way through the set, Tadhg says, 'And now, we'd like to play you a song that Laura McDermott wrote with me a long time ago. It's called 'The Stars'.'

There's another big roar of approval from the crowd.

He turns to me, and I can feel the love from all the way across the giant stage.

'Ready, Lol?'

I nod and start playing the chord sequence that I wrote in my bedroom more than sixteen years ago, on a day I thought I'd lost Tadhg forever.

Then I open my mouth.

And I sing.

A Note from the Author

As Laura says, her endometriosis is an extreme case.

While some people with endometriosis experience infertility, the majority do not. To find out more facts about endometriosis, go to www.endometriosis.ie.

Acknowledgements

Many thanks to my agent Louise Lamont, without whom I couldn't have written this book. Thanks for the encouragement, the advice, the reassurance (so much reassurance) and for being such a brilliant champion of Tadhg and Laura, and of me. You deserve a lot more than just having a fictional summer Irish college named after you. Go raibh míle maith agat, a Laoise!

Many thanks to Ciara Doorley at Hachette Ireland for giving me the opportunity to write *Our Song*, for which I will be eternally grateful, and for thoughtfully guiding it through its first round of edits, which helped me see exactly what the story needed. Thank you Joanna Smyth for taking up the baton with such insight and enthusiasm (and for letting me name a bass player after you!). Both the book and I owe both of you so much. Thanks to Emma Rogers and Lauren Mortimer for creating the perfect cover.

A huge thank you to Marian Keyes, Sarra Manning and Louise O'Neill for saying such lovely things about this book. I appreciate it more than I can say.

Ever since my last novel came out in 2020, my dad kept asking, 'When are you going to write another book?' He died a few months before I started writing this one and I'm very, very sad that I never got to tell him about it. I miss you, Aged Sage. Thanks and love to all the extended Carey and Freyne families, especially my sister Rachel Carey for sharing her advertising-industry wisdom and tolerating my creative angst, and my nephew Eli 'Da Puntle' McGurk, the best drummer I've ever worked with, for drumming so brilliantly on 'The Stars'.

Thanks to Daragh Keogh for designing the original poster for a gig by Sourpuss, Shatner and The Band Anna's In back in 1996, thus immortalising the first time I shared a stage not just with you and my future husband, your Sourpuss bandmate Patrick, but also two friends with whom I would do a lot of singing over the subsequent decades: my future bandmate Pól Ó Conghaile (the original Paul from Shatner) and the shining genius Angeline Morrison.

Thanks to Helen Carr for the support and reading the first draft; Simone George, the ultimate musical hostess, whose singing journey inspired aspects of Laura's own; my patient pen pal Erin Leafe, whose entertaining and insightful letters and postcards from New York over the last four and a half years made me feel understood and encouraged; Emilie Pine for the walks and inspiring, affirming chats, and the realisation that relief equals happiness; my podcast partner Karyn Moynihan and all our *Double Love* listeners – I hope you enjoyed the Sweet Valley references! Thanks to my writer friends for their encouragement, cheering and pep talks, especially Aoife Barry, Jane Casey, Edel Coffey, Harriet Evans, Elaine Feeney, Sinéad Gleeson, Sarah Griffin and Jeanne Sutton. Thanks to everyone on Instagram who cheered on my word-count updates – it really did help. Thanks and love to the women who DMed me about your own infertility stories, and to let me know you shared my feelings about the miracle baby narrative. You made me cry and you reminded me why I wanted to write about this. I hope you all live happily ever after, however things turn out.

Thanks to Sarah Bannan and the Arts Council of Ireland, who awarded me a bursary in 2020 that changed my life.

While the Trinity chapters of this book are set in 2002–2003, I must admit I was basically writing about the Trinity I knew when I was a student there from 1993 to 1997, right down to the Ball being cancelled because of a security-guard strike (as it was in 1996). But I did want to be vaguely accurate, and I knew the Buttery was renovated some time in the early 2000s, changing its layout, so thanks to Emer McLysaght and Kiva Brennan, who provided me with a drawn map of the Buttery as they remembered it *circa* 2002, proving that during Laura and Tadhg's era it looked very similar to my nineties memories.

A very special thanks to Miriam McCaul, the Katie to my Lol during my own youthful dramas. Thanks for diving into the unhinged archive of the timeline with me and for making me laugh a *lot* when I was writing this book. May our lives always be interesting.

And most of all, thanks to my husband Patrick Freyne for supporting me so patiently during the highs and lows of working on this book, for reading the drafts and tolerating my constant subsequent questions about them, for sharing your own memories of doing Tadhg's Music and Technology MPhil, for co-writing 'Winter Without You' with me (and writing almost all the lyrics) and for being my favourite person in the world. It's thirty years since we met in the Trinity Arts Block, twenty-six years since we first wrote a song together and twenty-four years since we ended up kissing for the first time after one of our gigs, and there's still no one I'd rather make music with than you. Starting a band with you is the best thing I ever did.